Shepherd's Quest

THE MORCYTH SAGA

THE BROKEN KEY

Shepherd's Quest

The Broken Key #1

A Novel

Brian S. Pratt

iUniverse, Inc.
New York Lincoln Shanghai

Shepherd's Quest
The Broken Key #1

iUniverse books may be ordered through booksellers or by contacting:

iUniverse
2021 Pine Lake Road, Suite 100
Lincoln, NE 68512
www.iuniverse.com
1-800-Authors (1-800-288-4677)

This is a work of fiction. All of the characters, names, incidents, organizations, and dialogue in this novel are either the products of the author's imagination or are used fictitiously.

ISBN-13: 978-0-595-42825-0 (pbk)
ISBN-13: 978-0-595-87163-6 (ebk)
ISBN-10: 0-595-42825-8 (pbk)
ISBN-10: 0-595-87163-1 (ebk)

Printed in the United States of America

For Joseph, my son.

Chapter 1

Riyan looked out over the landscape, his position on the ridge afforded him a commanding view of the valley. The moonlight overhead painted the world in shadows, among which who knew what sorts of beasts may lie. Undaunted, he turned to his companion and directed his attention to the castle nestled in against the backdrop of the far side of the valley. "Look," he said, "there across the valley."

His companion, a man like himself who had seen many a battle, nodded. "We'll find her in there for sure."

The lady in question had been snatched from her home by person's unknown. Her family contracted Riyan and Chadric to track down those responsible, rescue their daughter, and slay her captors. After several days of following their trail, it has led them here.

"Let's go," Riyan said and then headed out. Chadric followed close behind.

They worked their way down from the ridge and soon found themselves in the shadowy darkness of the valley floor. Heavily forested, this area gave off a less than comforting feel as they made their way closer to the castle.

Howrrrrrrrr!

Not very far off a wolf's howl split the night. Riyan and Chadric came to an abrupt stop as they turned their attention toward the direction from which the sound had originated. The moon's light did little to dispel the shadows as it was unable to effectively reach this far below the forest's canopy.

"What ...?" began Chadric when Riyan held up his hand to silence him. Becoming silent once more, Chadric focused his attention on the shadowy boles of the trees before them.

Then all of a sudden, one of the mountain wolves that infested these parts launched itself out of the shadows. Moving straight for Chadric, it snarled and its teeth became pale shadows in the darkness.

Riyan pulled his sword from its scabbard just as his companion was bowled over by the beast. "Chadric!" he hollered.

On the ground, the wolf had one of Chadric's gauntleted forearms in its mouth and was shaking it furiously. "Ahhh!" he cried out. With his other fist, Chadric began hitting the beast alongside the head but the blows did little in persuading it to release his arm.

Then Riyan came to his aid. Striking out at the back of the wolf with his sword, he cleaved the beast almost in two by his thunderous blow. Kicking out with his foot, he knocked the wolf from off his friend.

"You okay?" he asked. Offering a hand, he helped his friend to his feet.

Chadric nodded. Then he took a look at the gauntlet covering his forearm and saw where the wolf's teeth had indented the metal. "Yeah," he replied.

"We better hurry and reach the castle," Riyan said. "Wolves never hunt alone." No sooner did he say that than another howl split the night not very far away. Wiping his sword off on the wolf's hide, he gave Chadric a hand up and then they were back on their way to the castle.

They passed among the trees much more quickly now, the howling of the wolves driving them onward. Despite the frequency and close proximity of the howls, no other wolf made an appearance.

At last they reached the far side of the valley. Here the forest became less dense and it wasn't long before the outer wall of the castle appeared through the trees. High on the upward slope of the valley where the mountains began, its dark edifice loomed hauntingly. The wall ringing the castle rose high from the valley's floor, beyond which climbed a spire even higher into the sky. A single light broke the darkness as it escaped from a window high in its upper reaches.

When they reached the edge of the forest across from the wall, they paused for a moment. "Something's not right," observed Chadric.

"I know," agreed Riyan. No guards were present upon the battlements and the gate stood open. "It can't be this easy."

"Could be they didn't expect anyone to have trailed them back here," suggested Chadric.

"You may be right." But deep down inside, Riyan didn't think so. "Come on," he said. Moving quickly and quietly, he raced towards the open gate. Other than the normal sounds one would expect while in the forest, nothing else could be heard.

Upon reaching the gate, they pressed themselves against the wall and peered through its gaping maw. The inner courtyard looked clear. A courtyard stretched forty yards from where they stood to the door leading into the castle. The tower they saw with the light was but one of three that extended upwards from the main body of the castle. Two shorter ones extended upward at either end while the one with the lighted window towered to twice their height out of the castle's central keep.

Riyan raised his hand which bore the Ring of Evil Detection. Calling upon its power, it took but a moment before a glow began surrounding a three foot statue that stood on a short column situated between them and the door leading into the castle. Exactly what the statue was couldn't be readily determined in the moonlight from this distance. "I thought so," stated Riyan. He glanced back to see if Chadric had seen the glow.

"Now what?" Chadric asked, he too had seen the glow.

"I'm all out of protection scrolls," he replied. "The ring will afford me some protection against whatever it is." He glanced back to the statue and drew his sword. "Stay here." When he heard Chadric say, 'Alright', he moved into the courtyard.

Working his way around the statue, he kept one eye on it and another on the rest of the courtyard. As he came closer, he could tell the statue was of some demonic beast. There were wings on its back and a single spiraling horn protruded from out of its forehead. The head had a cruel visage with what looked like two dagger-sharp fangs extending upward from out of its lower jaw.

Then all of a sudden he felt a vibration in the ring, one he always felt when evil was near. The eyes of the statue flashed a dark red and the head slowly turned towards him. As the statue came to life, he now understood why there were no guards on the walls or in the courtyard. This was the castle's guardian.

Coming out of its sitting position, the demonic creature stretched upright and raised its head. Then it gave out with an ear-piercing screech. Growing silent, the creature launched itself off the column and towards Riyan.

With a war cry of his own, Riyan raised his shield to ward off the creature's attack. Bringing his sword into position, he waited.

Beating its wings, the creature flew through the air and struck out at Riyan with the claws of its feet. Riyan raised his shield and felt the creature strike it with jarring impact. Then he retaliated with his sword, striking out at the creature with a resounding blow.

The blade of his sword rebounded off the creature, doing little more than chipping away a small piece of the marble it was constructed of. The jarring impact of the sword on the marble left Riyan's arm tingling.

With wings flapping, it rose into the air only to turn and strike once more.

By this time, Chadric had reached his friend's side and used his mace. He smashed the creature as its attack was thwarted again by Riyan's shield. The mace did more damage, being a bashing weapon such as it was. But it still did not do enough to stop the creature.

As the creature made ready for another attack, Chadric came up with an idea. He reached into his pouch and pulled out a small crystal vial. Then as the creature again moved to attack Riyan, he threw it. When the vial struck, it shattered upon the hard marble surface and the fluid it had contained began burning the creature.

Shrieking, the creature fell to the ground and started thrashing about as dark smoke wafted from where the liquid had touched it. Chadric and Riyan move forward quickly and begin laying into it with sword and mace. They soon had it reduced to a pile of broken marble. When at last its movements stopped completely, Riyan stepped back and looked to his friend.

"What was in that?" he asked.

"Holy water," Chadric replied. "Got it before we left Rynwall."

Riyan nodded his head and grinned at his friend. "That was fortunate," he said.

"Turned out that way," agreed Chad.

Leaving the shattered remains of the creature behind, they ran toward the door leading into the castle. Upon reaching the door, Riyan flung it wide and strode fearlessly into the castle. Dark and ominous, the interior was full of shadows as the moonlight made its way in through the many windows.

The hall they now found themselves in had the appearance of having been left unattended for some time. Cloth covered many of the pieces of furniture, spider webs hung in the corners of the room, all in all the place gave the feeling that no one's been here for some time. If that was the case, then why did the trail of the woman's captors lead them here? And what can it mean that a light shone from the window at the top of the tower?

Riyan glanced around the hall for a brief moment before crossing over to the stairway leading up. Taking the steps quickly, he and Chadric ascended up to the landing on the second floor. "We have to find the entrance to the tower," Riyan said.

Chadric moved down to the entrance of a hallway that headed in the general direction of the tower. "Could be down here," he suggested. He saw that it extended further into the castle.

Riyan nodded and then moved to join him at the hallway. Taking the lead, he left the landing and headed quickly down the hallway with Chadric right behind.

The hallway itself was rather wide with several doors lining both sides. Moving past them, Riyan walked quickly towards the end of the hallway where he hoped to find the entrance to the tower. When he reached a little over halfway to the door at the end, his ring all of a sudden began vibrating to tell him evil was close. He no sooner paused and was about to tell Chadric to be on his guard than the doors lining the hallway opened. From out of the opened doors, skeletons bearing swords and shields rushed forward to attack.

Immediately, Riyan and Chadric formed up back to back to face the onslaught. Easily a dozen skeletons boiled from the adjacent rooms. Striking out, Riyan's sword removed the head from one only to see its body continue the attack. "We have to go for the arms!" he hollered to Chadric. His next swing severed the sword arm from the headless skeleton. Kicking out with his boot, he knocked the one armed headless stack of bones backwards. It broke apart when it struck the wall.

"Yeah!" Chadric yelled as his mace smashed through the ribcage of another.

Laying about them, they quickly destroyed the skeletons. Having only received a few minor cuts, they left the pile of bones behind and hurried to the door at the end of the hallway. So far, what they have faced hasn't been all that challenging.

Upon reaching the door, Riyan grabbed the handle and pushed it open. On the other side they found a room where the staircase leading up into the tower began. A roar filled the room as a fur covered creature leaped from the stairs. Taller than either of them, it must have stood over six and a half feet. Naked other than the covering of fur, it's only weapons appeared to be a pair of nasty looking claws and the razor sharp teeth filling its mouth.

Shouting his war cry, Riyan raced forward with sword drawn to meet the attack. He raised his shield as one of the creature's massive paws struck out at him. The force of the blow upon his shield knocked him backwards several steps. As he saw Chadric moving past him to engage, he yelled, "It's stronger than it looks."

Chadric nodded that he heard then attacked with his mace. Impacting the creature's side, the hit elicited a roar of pain. Then another of the creature's paws swung forward. Chadric raised his shield to block the blow and sailed backwards through the air when the blow connected. Slamming into the wall, he slid down and settled to the floor.

"Yaaaaa!" screamed Riyan as he thrust his sword toward the creature. The sword's point struck the creature's side and sank in several inches.

The creature tilted its head back and howled at the pain Riyan's sword inflicted. Then the creature struck the sword with one of its paws and knocked it from Riyan's grasp. As the sword flew across the room, the creature struck Riyan with its other paw and sent him sailing. He hit the wall with an 'oof' and settled to the floor.

From across the room, Chadric was getting back to his feet. He saw the creature moving toward where Riyan was lying on the ground and hollered, "Hey you!" When the creature turned, he threw his mace and smashed the creature right between the eyes. The force of the blow was such that it caved in the creature's skull, smashing the brain within. Falling backwards, it hit the floor and twitched for a few seconds before becoming still.

Chadric rushed to his friend's side and asked, "Are you okay?"

Riyan opened his eyes and nodded. "I think so." Glancing over to where the creature lay he said, "Hope there aren't many more like that one."

Offering his friend a hand up, Chadric helped him to his feet. Then he went over to the dead creature and recovered his mace.

"Hey, would you look at this?"

Turning around, he saw Riyan standing before a closed chest sitting against the wall. "Wonder what's in it?" he asked.

Riyan shrugged then turned back to face the chest. "Only one way to find out," he said. Grabbing hold of the lid, he lifted it up.

Chadric crossed the room and stood beside him as he swung the lid all the way up. Inside, the gleam of coins and gems could be seen. "Must be a fortune!" he exclaimed excitedly.

They both reached in and started removing the coins and gems. A few gold coins mixed in with a handful of silver, the majority of the coins the chest held were that of copper. They filled their pouches with the treasure and in so doing, discovered a secret compartment hidden in the bottom of the chest.

Riyan took out his knife and pried it open. Within they found a plain, brass key. He held it up and said, "This could be useful."

"Better take it with us," agreed Chadric.

Putting it within his belt pouch, Riyan then turned and headed towards the stairs leading up. The steps rose as they wound their way around the outer wall of the tower in a spiraling fashion until finally disappearing through the ceiling. With Chadric following closely, Riyan moved onto the stairs and quickly began moving to the next level.

"Wait a second," Chadric said as he pulled one of his torches out of his pack. Once he had it lit, he indicated for Riyan to continue.

For a brief moment the stairs passed through a narrow section as it went from the first level to the second. Then it opened up again as it reached the second floor landing. Here they found boxes and crates stacked neatly in various spots across the second floor.

As it turned out, the tower itself wasn't very wide and the light from Chadric's torch was able to reveal it in its entirety. With nothing here other than boxes and crates, they continued following the stair as it wound its way along the outside wall up to the third floor.

Just as it had between the first and second floor, the stair entered a narrow area when it passed from the second floor to the third. When Riyan entered the narrow area between floors, his ring once more began to vibrate. He paused a moment as he informed Chadric that something was ahead, then took the torch from him as he resumed his forward progress.

Now with the torch held before him, Riyan stepped cautiously as he neared where the stairs opened up onto the third floor. First the torch, then his head cleared the opening as he slowly crept his way forward. The light from the torch cast shadows in the room as he completely emerged from the opening.

The room as it turned out looked to be someone's bedroom. A bed, dresser, and table all gave this room a rather homey appearance. Another chest similar in nature to the one they found below sat at the foot of the bed. Riyan moved forward into the room toward it as Chadric began to emerge from the opening leading from the second floor.

"Be careful," he warned when he saw what Riyan was moving toward.

Riyan came to a stop before the chest and placed his hand upon the latch. Gripping it tightly, he pulled the lid open. Inside, he found another pile of coins. Nestled in among the coins were two bottles that were normally used in conjunction with potions. He moved his torch closer and saw that both bottles contained liquid.

He reached in and took one of the potion bottles out. "Hey, look what I found!" Always excited when finding potions, Riyan tuned back to Chadric. "Wonder what they do?"

Chadric moved closer to the chest and reached inside to pull out the other one. Looking closely at it, he saw a feather inscribed upon a wax seal. "Maybe this is a flying potion?" he guessed.

"Possibly," stated Riyan. "Mine has the sign of the healer."

"A healing potion," nodded Chadric happily. "Can always use one of those."

"You got that right," replied Riyan.

They then removed their packs and set them on the floor. Once the potions were secured within their packs along with the coins from the chest, they slung them again across their backs.

"There can't be too many more floors remaining to this tower," observed Chadric.

"I know," replied Riyan. "Need to be extra careful from this point on. My ring indicated evil was present but there's nothing here."

"If what it sensed is on the next floor," said Chad, "it must be powerful indeed."

Riyan just nodded his head.

The two friends then went to the stair and began climbing up to the fourth floor. Before they reached the narrow area between floors, they saw light coming from above. "Better put that out," Chadric told Riyan as he indicated the torch.

"Good thinking," he replied. Then putting the burning end against a step, he rolled it until the flame went out. Leaving it smoking on the step, Riyan looked up at the light coming from the fourth floor. Removing his sword from its scabbard, he resumed moving into the narrow area between the third and fourth floor. His ring began vibrating once more.

When he came to the end of the narrow area, he slowed down and continued until he was just able to gaze into the fourth floor.

"Come in gentlemen," said a voice.

On the far side of the room sat a man hunched over a desk with his back to them. Over the desk were two shelves lined with books. Sitting at the right end of the lower shelf was a gilded cage containing a small creature. Upon closer examination, it was revealed that the creature within the cage was almost an exact duplicate to that of the statue creature they destroyed down in the courtyard below.

Riyan exited the narrow passage and entered the room. "We've come for the girl," he said.

"I know," the man replied. Turning around, the man looked to where Riyan stood with sword drawn. "But she's mine." He then glanced towards Chadric as he emerged from the narrow passage behind Riyan. Grinning he said "And now so are you."

"I think we'll be a bit more difficult to deal with than a girl," countered Riyan.

The man scooted his chair back and stood up. Turning to face the pair, they saw that he was dressed in a robe of some sort. Could possibly be a magic user of some kind.

Moving his hands in arcane gestures, the man began speaking words neither of them could understand.

Realizing he was casting a spell, Chadric threw his mace in an attempt to disrupt the magic user's concentration. Unfortunately the man finished his spell in time and bolts of reddish energy lanced from his fingertips, striking both Riyan and Chadric. The man then easily dodged aside to avoid the mace.

When the bolts struck them, it felt like fire. Indeed, where one bolt had struck Riyan's ring mail armor, the rings in that area were slightly melted. Giving out with a cry, Riyan charged the man as another round of fiery bolts left his fingers. This time, the bolts were directed solely at Riyan. His shield bore the brunt of the attack though two made it through and knocked him back a step.

Then the magic user began chanting another series of magical words and a shadow formed before him. Roughly man-shaped, it began moving towards them.

"Get the magic user!" yelled Riyan as his sword lashed out at the oncoming shadow. His sword seemed to have minimal effect as it passed right through.

As the magic user began another chant, Chadric drew his knife and rushed him. He made it to within a couple feet before the man finished his spell and a green glob formed before him. Unable to stop, Chadric ran right into the acidic green glob. Pain flared as the green substance began eating his flesh away. "Riyan!" he cried out as his momentum carried him forward into the magic user.

Then the magic user began crying out in pain too as Chadric gripped him in a death grip. The green substance that covered Chadric was now beginning to eat away at the magic user.

With his concentration now broken from the pain of the green goo, the shadow that was moving on Riyan disappeared. Riyan ran forward to where Chadric gripped the magic user only to find both men were beyond his help.

Most of the exposed skin of Chadric's body had melted away to expose the bones underneath. The screams of the magic user continued to ring out as the green goo ate his flesh away.

Riyan knelt down by the side of his lifelong friend. He could see that his friend was still alive and in great pain. Chadric's eyes looked up at him beseechingly and he knew what he was asking.

With tears in his eyes, he took his sword and plunged it into the chest of his best friend to end his suffering. The magic user's suffering, he allowed to continue until the end came.

When he pulled his sword free from Chadric's body, he found the blade pitted by its brief contact with the goo covering Chadric. No longer serviceable, he cast it aside. He collapsed on the floor for some time, grief over his friend's death heavy upon him. But then he remembered why they had come. The woman.

"Bye Chad," he said then moved to the stairs and hurried up to the top. The stairs ended at a locked door with a small window set into it. Going to the window, he put his mouth near it and said, "Hello?"

"Go away!" a woman's voice yelled at him from the other side.

"Lady," replied Riyan, "I've come to rescue you. Your father sent me."

Then he saw the face of a most beautiful woman appear in the window. "My father?" she asked.

"That's right," he said. He tried to open the door only to find it to be locked. Remembering the key he had found in the chest on the ground floor, he took it out of his pouch and placed it in the keyhole. Turning it, he nodded satisfactorily when the lock turned. Then he opened the door wide and stepped within the room.

Barely dressed in anything, and looking all the more sexy because of it, the woman rushed forward and clasped her arms around him. "Thank you gallant knight," she said. Then reaching her lips up to his, she gave him a most passionate kiss. Her breasts were rubbing into his chest and …

"Wait a second right now," Chad demanded.

"What?" asked Riyan.

"Here you have me dead on the floor below," he stated with dissatisfaction, "my skin eaten away by acid, and you're about to get it on with the woman?"

"So?" his friend said with a grin. "It's just a story."

"I know it's just a story," Chad remarked. "But I always seem to be the one to die."

The two friends were sitting upon a hillock under a bright sunny summer day. Down the hill a ways grazed the flock of sheep that Riyan was supposed to be keeping an eye on.

"You're one to talk," replied Riyan. "Don't you remember the time before last when you were telling the tale?" When he saw his friend get a grin on his face, he knew that he did. "You had me lying on a torture rack with an arm and a leg missing, hot lead being poured into my eye socket and where were you? Off having a little fling with the daughter of the man who was torturing me!"

"Okay, okay," he said. Then they both broke into laughter.

This was one of their favorite pastimes. On the days Chad could get away from his father's mill, he was usually to be found out here with Riyan as he minded the flock. They would spend hours telling each other stories of adventures they wished they could have. Being stuck in a small town such as Quillim all their lives has allowed them little chance for such experiences.

For Riyan whose family was poor shepherds that barely made a living from their sheep, and Chad who detested being a miller's son, life in this border town was dull and uneventful. The only time adventure came their way was when one of Riyan's sheep managed to wander away and they had to go track it down, which was more often than not.

Baaaaaaa!

"Not again," Chad moaned as Riyan got up and began scanning the area.

"Looks like Black Face got stuck in the thicket again," Riyan told his friend.

"Isn't that the third time this week?" asked Chad.

Nodding, Riyan began making his way down the hill as he replied, "Something like that. Give me a hand."

Shaking his head, Chad pushed himself off the ground and went to help his friend. "Can't wait until shearing time," he said.

"You got that right," agreed Riyan. "It's his wool, it keeps getting snared by the thorns." Sure enough, they found Black Face trapped within the thicket. Sometimes he wished that he could just leave him there for a day or two to teach him a lesson, but his mother would skin him alive if he did. So working very carefully, he and Chad spent the next half hour working the thorns from out of Black Face's coat.

Chapter 2

Later that day when the sun began its trek to the horizon, Riyan and Chad gathered the flock and started the return journey to Riyan's home. It wasn't safe for the herd to be left out in the hills at night. Aside from wild animals, there's always the chance that the goblins might be in the area and will help themselves.

The village of Quillim, which both lads call home, sits on the border where the lands of Duke Yoric abuts that of the mountains whose other side marks the beginning of the goblin territories. Peace between the two races has lasted for over a century, ever since the goblins were pushed back across the mountains during the War of the Three Clans. Now, it's only the occasional raid here and there by goblins that has the people in Quillim worried. Those living in the area have found that if you keep your flock in close to your home at night, there's less of a chance one will turn up missing in the morning.

"My father has me helping with the mill tomorrow," Chad informed his friend. "Seems my brother is down in Wardean on business."

"Oh?" asked Riyan. "What takes him down there?"

"A friend of father has a mill there and may be interested in apprenticing Tye," he explained. "He wants Tye to stay a week so he may see what kind of person he is."

"If he gets apprenticed, won't that mean you'll have to help your father more?" Riyan asked.

Chad sighed. "Unfortunately, yes. As long as Tye was helping with the mill, he didn't need me. My whole family knows of my dissatisfaction with the life of a miller, and they are okay with me pursuing another trade. But if Tye gets apprenticed, there'll be no one to help out. At least not for a few years until Eryl gets a little older."

"Tough break," said Riyan with a pat on his friend's back.

"If I had settled on a trade by now," Chad told his friend, "I wouldn't be in this mess."

Just then from up ahead, four young men who were a little bit older than Riyan and Chad appeared over the crest of the hill. "Great," complained Riyan.

When Chad spied who was coming towards them, he too gave out with a groan.

"Well, well, well," one of the approaching young men began to say as the two groups came together. "I thought I smelled the foul odor of sheep dung."

Only two years older than Riyan and Chad, the one who spoke has been a thorn in their sides all their lives. Being the son of Quillim's magistrate, not to mention the fact that his family holds title to most of the lands the local shepherds use to graze their flock, has given him the idea he's better than everyone else. His father was a nice enough person, but the son is a right nasty piece of work.

"Good evening Rupert," Riyan said.

"Didn't I tell you not to use this area for your stinking sheep?" Rupert asked.

"We pay your father for the use of this land," argued Riyan. "He's the only one who can tell us not to use it."

"Sounds pretty uppity for a sheep dung boy," one of Rupert's cronies said.

"I don't care what you think you can and can't do, sheep dung boy," Rupert asserted with a scowl. "You aren't to use this area." He moved to stand in front of Riyan and poked him hard in the chest with his finger. "Do you understand me?"

When Riyan failed to respond quickly, Rupert slaps him across the face. "I asked you a question!"

"I understand you all too well," replied Riyan. Face beginning to turn red, he stared at Rupert with undisguised hatred.

"Scatter 'em boys," he said to his cronies. As the three young men with him began scaring off the sheep, he added, "Maybe this will help you to remember." Then he too started yelling and waving his arms to scatter Riyan's flock.

Riyan and Chad stood there in the road and did nothing. They had long ago learned that if they tried to stop Rupert and his friends, that things would only get worse. So they stood there and waited for them to stop. When at last Rupert and his cronies ceased chasing Riyan's sheep, they laughed and continued along their way.

"I hate him," Riyan said with great feeling.

"I know," replied Chad. "Everyone does. I don't know how a nice man such as his father, could spawn such a person."

From the surrounding area, the sound of bleating sheep rang out. "We better go find them before the sun goes down," Riyan said.

So while the sun sank further to the horizon, Riyan and Chad combed the neighboring hills until all the sheep were accounted for. Then they resumed their way to Riyan's home.

It was a small house with only three rooms; one for his mother, one for himself, and the outer living area. His father had died several years ago while out watching the flock. One of the mountain spiders had attacked and bit him. The venom quickly worked through his system and before he could return, had passed into unconsciousness. He was dead when they found him the next day.

Riyan still blamed himself for his father's death. Had he been with his father that day, he could have gone to Old Glia for one of her potions which would have cured the poison coursing through his father's veins. Instead, he and Chad had gone fishing.

Mountain spiders such as what attacked his father were rare in these parts. At most they were sighted once or twice a year. In the last five years, his father had been the only one to have encountered one.

"We better hurry, or my mother will be getting worried," said Riyan. Then with Chad's help, they herded the flock along the trail leading to Riyan's house. By the time Riyan's home came into view, the stars were already beginning to appear.

Chad helped him get the flock into the fenced area where they spend the night. Then he said, "I better hurry along too, or my father will get on me again about not being home on time."

Riyan patted him on the back and said, "Thanks for the help."

"You're welcome," he replied. "Don't know when I'll be able to join you in the hills again. With Tye gone for a week, I'll be stuck at the mill."

Riyan shrugged. "What is, must be," he waxed poetically. "Next time it'll be your turn to tell the tale."

"Already figured out how I'm going to kill you off," he replied with a grin.

Laughing, Riyan gave him another good natured slap on the back. "Can't wait." Then Chad hurried home.

Riyan turned toward the door just as it opened to reveal his mother. "Everything okay?" she asked, worried.

"Rupert again," he explained.

"I'm going to talk to his father in the morning," she said as she stepped aside to let him enter. "He has no right to do such things. We pay them good money to graze our flock on their land. We should not be treated in such a manner."

Riyan went to the table and sat down. "It'll do no good," he said. "The last time you went to his father after something like this, all that happened was that I got a beating the next day." He reached out for the ladle in the stew pot and began filling his bowl.

His mother sat across the table from him and looked at her son with sad eyes. She wanted something better for him than a life as a shepherd, especially one around here. It wasn't so bad before Rupert grew to adulthood, but now things for her son were not so good. But there was little hope of improving their lot in life.

"He can't do anything serious," he said to his mother between bites. "If he does, then his father would be forced to intervene. He'll not risk that."

Throughout the rest of the meal, they talked about more inconsequential things in an attempt to put Rupert out of their minds. Afterwards, Riyan headed off to bed as he must be up with the dawn to once again shepherd the flock.

The following morning he was up well before the sun crested the eastern horizon. The place where he planned to take the flock to graze was a bit further into the hills than where he took them yesterday. But as his father taught him, if the sheep were allowed to graze too long in one place, it would eventually ruin the area for grazing. His father once related an experience he had while a young man. He was just learning the art of shepherding and had allowed his flock to graze one area for several weeks in succession. Such constant grazing had left the area unusable for many weeks. So now Riyan always made sure that he rotated the flock between the various pastures among the hills.

It took him well over an hour to bring the flock to the desired pasture. Nestled in among the hills such as it was, it had always been one of Riyan's favorite places to take them. The quiet and tranquility of this area of the hills was accentuated by a stream that worked its way from one end to the other.

Once the flock was situated where he wanted them, he made himself comfortable under a tree while he kept an eye on them. Off to the west rose the mountains that separate these lands from that of the goblins. He often wondered what they looked like. Oh sure, he heard tales of them all his life. Supposedly they were about half to two-thirds the size of the average human with a slight greenish hue to their skin. But he's never seen one and always wanted to. Though from a distance, as they're reputed to be rather antisocial creatures and prone to attacking anything that came near.

The day went by as every other day of his life has, boring and dull. Most of his time was spent simply doing nothing but sitting and watching his flock. Other times he took out his sling and pretended that he was a fighter in one of the stories he and Chad tell one another. He would run around the hill and 'kill' enemies with stones slung from his sling. Of course the plethora of enemies he killed was in actuality small plants, trees and the occasional rock. His aim has improved greatly over the years. Even at a run he could hit his target more often than not.

He always carried a staff with him as well as his sling while out watching his flock. There had been times over the years when between his staff and sling, he was able to fight off predators that tried to make off with one of his sheep. When not spending time 'killing monsters' with his sling, he worked on his staff. He's become pretty decent at twirling it, but not so good that it hummed when he spun it. In the stories the bards always tell, the great staffers could cause their staves to hum. There were times when he believed some of the tales the bards told were a bit overexaggerated.

Baaaaaaa!

"Now what?" he asked himself. He had been dozing under the tree, basking in the warmth of the morning sun. Looking over the flock, he tried to ascertain which one of them was bleating. Black Face, the trouble maker, was nowhere to be seen. "Of course." Leaving his staff leaning against the tree, he got to his feet and followed the sound of the bleating.

The sound was coming from over the far side of a nearby hill. He walked quickly towards it, dreaming of the time when they would sell off some of the flock. He's going to make sure Black Face is one of the ones to go.

He hurried up the side of the hill and when he crested it, looked down the other side. "Black Face!" he cried out as he took his sling from his belt.

Baaaaaaa!

Black Face again cried out in fear as one of the predators of the mountains circled it. A small animal barely half Black Face's size, yet with a strong jaw and sharp teeth they were a constant threat in these parts.

Riyan placed a stone within the cup of the sling and quickly got it up to speed. Then he launched it at the animal just as it readied to attack. The stone flew straight and true towards the small dog like creature and struck it in the side of the head. The blow sent it reeling to the side before collapsing to the ground.

He raced down the hill and when he reached Black Face, shooed the sheep back up the hill towards the rest of the flock. Then he turned his attention back to the predator and saw that it was still breathing. Riyan stepped closer and pulled out his knife. With a quick strike, he killed it.

Quillim's city council has posted a two silver piece bounty on the animal due to the menace it posed to the community. Many sheep have been lost to them over the years. Riyan picked the animal up by the scruff of the neck and carried it back to where he's been keeping watch over the flock.

The rest of the day passed uneventfully and when he returned home with the flock later that night, showed the dead animal to his mother. "I'm going to go in early tomorrow and collect the bounty," he said. "Then I'll take the flock out in the afternoon."

His mother took the carcass and cut the animal's head off. That's all that was required by the Council in order to receive the bounty. The rest of it she dressed and began to prepare it for the next evening's dinner.

The following morning an hour or so after they finished their morning meal, Riyan walked into town with the sack containing the animal's head. Quillim's not much of a town. It has the essentials required of every town; a chandler's shop, baker, butcher, etc. All the places the neighboring townsfolk needed in order to survive.

The building housing the Magistrate's Office and the Council's meeting hall sat prominently in the center of town. It was to this building that Riyan took the animal's head. He slowed down when he saw the three young men who were Rupert's cronies talking with one another near the town hall's front entrance. When they noticed Riyan approaching, they grew quiet and turned toward him. Just then, Freya and her father exited the building through the front door.

"Freya!" he exclaimed quite happily. He and Freya have been friends for as long as either one could remember. In his heart he has always cared deeply for her and even had thoughts that they may one day be married.

His mood quickly sobered when she failed to meet his eyes. Her father nodded his head in greeting and gave him a curt, "Riyan." Then they brushed past him without speaking. He turned to look at them as they left and Freya glanced over her shoulder back to him. Their eyes locked for a brief second before she broke the contact and turned her head forward once more.

He came to a stop as he watched her leave, puzzled by her reaction. Usually she was quite excited to see him. After all, with him out in the fields with the sheep most of the time, there was little opportunity for them to spend any time together.

"What's the matter?" one of Rupert's friends asked as the three of them came and surrounded him.

"Maybe she doesn't like him anymore?" another one quipped.

"Could be she found a better man, one that doesn't smell like sheep dung," the third one said. At that he and the others started laughing derisively.

Riyan ignored their taunts as he knew that to respond in any way would only egg them on. He tried to continue on to the town hall's entrance but was blocked when the first one stepped in front of him and put his hand on Riyan's chest.

His eyes went down to look at the sack Riyan held in his hand. "What do you have there?" he asked.

"Nothing you'd be interested in," replied Riyan.

"Oh yeah?" asked another of them. Then he snatched it out of his hand.

"Give it back!" demanded Riyan.

Holding the sack before him, the young man asked, "Or what?"

Before Riyan had the chance to reply, Rupert and his father the Magistrate exited the building. The Magistrate quickly grasped what was going on by the way the three young men had Riyan surrounded and how the one young man was holding the sack out before him.

"What's going on here?" he asked.

The three young men turned toward him quickly, startled by his sudden appearance. "Uh, nothing."

Riyan turned to face the Magistrate and said, "I killed a kidog. I was bringing it to collect the bounty when they took the sack containing its head from me."

The Magistrate's face darkened as he turned to face the one holding the sack.

"Was nothing like that your honor," the young man explained. "Just having a little fun is all."

"Give it back Girg," the Magistrate ordered.

"Sure thing," Girg replied. Then he handed the sack back to Riyan. "Here you go."

Riyan snatched the sack out of his hand and then said to the Magistrate, "Thank you."

"You're welcomed my boy," he replied to Riyan. "Go inside and Ceci will take care of it for you."

Riyan nodded and as the young man stepped out of his way, he walked towards the door. Behind him he heard the Magistrate begin to berate his son about the conduct of his friends. Riyan doubted it would do any good, more than likely would cause him to get a beating the next time he and Rupert met.

He walked through the entrance and then entered the first door on his right. Within he found Ceci, the lady who looked after the town hall as well as paid for the bounties and various other duties. She looked up from her desk and saw him standing there just within her doorway. From the blood stains on the sack, she knew what he was here for.

He held up the sack and said, "Bagged a kidog yesterday."

She motioned for him to come forward and then took the sack from him when he offered it to her. Opening it up, she saw the severed kidog head and then nodded. She set the sack on the floor behind her and then opened a strong box that was resting on the floor next to her desk. After removing two silver pieces, she handed them over to him. "Good work Riyan," she praised.

"Thank you," he replied as he took the coins.

"Did you hear?" she asked with a smile.

"I haven't been in town lately," he explained. "Something going on?"

"Oh yes," she replied. "Rupert and Freya are to be married."

"What?" he exclaimed loudly.

"Sometime last night Rupert asked her father for her hand and he said yes," she explained. Then she saw the look in his eyes and realized something was amiss. "Are you okay?"

Dazed, his mind numb and heart breaking, Riyan paid her question no heed. Instead, he turned around and rushed from the building. Once outside, he searched for Freya and her father but they were no longer in sight. He then began running towards their home that set on the edge of town.

How could she be marrying Rupert? All his life he had thought that one day they would get together and be married. He just hadn't worked up the courage to ask her father as yet. Now there was no longer any time, he had to state his intentions and get him to change his mind.

Several people hailed him as he ran through town, but so intent on his own inner turmoil was he, that he didn't even know they were there. Finally, their house appeared down the street before him. He could see the front door was just closing. Running up to the door, he gave it three firm knocks.

When it opened, Freya's father stood there before him. "I thought you might show up," he said.

"You can't let Freya marry Rupert," he said. "He's a terrible person."

"I know you care for her," her father replied. "But I have to think of what's best for Freya. This marriage will assure her of never having to worry about what tomorrow will bring. His family is wealthy and well connected."

"But ..." Riyan stammered. When Freya's father looked questioningly at him, he blurted out, "But I love her and want to marry her!"

Her father's eyes turned sad at that. "I know son," he said. "I've known for awhile now that you've felt this way."

Then behind her father Riyan saw Freya appear from the back room. "Freya!" he hollered to her. "You can't marry Rupert!"

Her father turned around and said, "Get back in your room Freya. Riyan and I need to have a little talk."

She looked with deep sadness to Riyan and then replied, "Yes father." Then turning around, she went back into her room.

Freya's father stepped outside and joined Riyan before shutting the door. "I like you boy," he said. "I always have. But I can't let that get in the way of making the best match I can for my daughter."

When Riyan tried to break in, he held up his hand and stopped him. "You are a poor shepherd," he continued. "You don't even own the land on which your sheep graze. What life could you give her?"

"But I love her," he asserted.

"Son, in life, love simply isn't enough." He laid his hand on Riyan's shoulder. "My daughter cares for you, I would hate for her to lose your friendship because of this."

Riyan snapped his eyes to his and replied, "She'll never lose it. I just ..."

"Go home Riyan," her father said. "Go home and work to get over it." He then turned and opened the door. He paused there a moment before saying, "It might be best for all concerned if you don't have any contact with my daughter until after the marriage." Without waiting for Riyan's response, he went back into the house and shut the door.

In the instant it took for her father to enter the house and shut the door, Riyan saw Freya there in the hallway. Their eyes locked for a moment before the door shut.

With the shutting of the door, his heart fell. Sadness overtook him and it was all he could do to simply keep his emotions under control. Then as he turned, he saw Rupert standing there across the street. Anger and hate burned in his heart when he saw the smug smile of satisfaction appear on Rupert's face.

Riyan almost crossed the street to wipe it off with a well place blow, but then he realized that would solve nothing. So he turned his back on him and walked home.

Chapter 3

Once back home he told his mom what had happened. "How could her father agree to this union?" he asked with great emotion. Then he flopped down in a chair.

"I'm sure he's doing what he thinks is best for her," his mother replied.

He looked at his mother with hurt filled eyes. "Don't tell me that you agree with this?"

She shook her head negatively then walked over to him. "Sometimes parents do the wrong thing for the right reason," she explained as she wrapped her arms about him to offer comfort.

"Rupert is a swine," he said. "Someone needs to do something about him."

"But not you," she insisted. "Respect her father's wishes and do nothing."

Riyan abruptly came to his feet and started pacing. "I can't stay here," he said as he came to a stop. "I need to get away for awhile."

"That's a good idea," agreed his mother.

"I'll take the flock out for a few days to the edge of the mountains," he told her. "Chad will be working at the mill for the next week so this would be a good time for me to be alone."

"Are you sure you want to go that far?" she asked. "There have been rumors of goblins."

He turned his face towards hers and smiled. "There are always rumors of goblins," he replied. "So far I have yet to come across one and we live as close as anyone."

"Still, be careful," she cautioned.

"I will," he promised.

She insisted on cooking him a good lunch before he started off. Outside, the sheep have already begun their bleating. According to their schedule, they should have been heading out to greener pastures long before now.

They shared a meal of cooked mutton, potatoes, and bread. Then she packed enough food for him to last several days, even though he planned on using his sling to hunt for food while he was gone.

As he slung his pack over his shoulder and prepared to head out, she placed her arm on his. "Just think on this while you're out there," she began. "Freya has no choice in this, such is the fate of all girls. She'll need friends like you to lean on." When he turned his head to look at her, she added, "Lord knows being married to Rupert will not be an easy life."

He nodded and hung his head. "I will mother," he replied. "Why can't her father see that?" He then gave her a peck on the cheek.

His mother handed him his staff before he stepped out the door. She went with him to the sheep pen and gave a hand with removing the flock. As he herded the sheep away from the house, she waved goodbye to her son.

"See you in a few days," he hollered to her as he left.

"Be careful," she cautioned with another wave.

He then continued herding the flock away from the pen and towards the distant mountains. This wasn't the first time he had taken the flock towards the mountains on an overnight excursion, usually he would return a day or two later. But this time he planned to go further than he ever had before and didn't plan on being back for at least four days, maybe longer. He needed time to get over the hurt in his heart.

For the rest of the afternoon, he continued pushing deeper into the hills. When nightfall came, he stopped the flock near a small stream and settled in for the night. He made sure the flock was accounted for before darkness came. Then he spread out his bedroll and fixed himself a quick bite to eat.

Later that night as he laid there under the stars, he sobbed.

"Riyan!"

Early the following morning, Chad came running down the lane towards the home where Riyan and his mother lived. "Riyan!" he hollered again and then saw that the sheep were not in the pen.

The front door opened before he reached the house and Riyan's mother stepped out. "Good morning Chad," she said.

"Have you heard?" he asked as he came closer.

"About Freya and Rupert?" she asked in reply. When he nodded his head, she said, "Yes. Riyan told me about it yesterday."

"Was he upset?" he asked.

"You could say that," she replied sadly. "He's taken the flock up near the mountains for a few days. Said you were working at your father's mill."

"I am," he said. "When I heard about Freya getting married to that piece of trash, I got angry. So my father gave me an hour to come here and talk to him about it."

"Sorry you missed him," she said.

"So am I." He turned his gaze towards the mountains. "Tell him to come see me as soon as he gets back will you please?"

"The minute he gets back," she assured him.

"Thank you," he said then turned and headed back to the mill. Worry for his friend weighed heavily on his mind. So heavy in fact, that once he was back in town and moving down the main street, he failed to notice the individual coming towards him. He almost walked into him.

He looked up at the last minute and saw his and Riyan's friend Bart a scant foot in front of him. Bart was a recent arrival to their little town of Quillim. He showed up about a year and a half ago and has worked odd jobs at various farms in the area since. Currently he's out at old Rebecca's place helping with tilling her fields. Ever since her sons married and moved away, she's had a hard time making it.

At first when Bart had tried using that horse drawn plow of hers, it was a disaster. He couldn't get the horses to go in a straight line to save his life. But now that he's been doing it for about a week, he's started to gain a modicum of proficiency. From what he's told them, he could do a little bit of everything, the result of having no trade and forced to live on what work he could get here and there.

The one thing Bart could do that really impressed Chad was how well he threw darts. Now we're not talking about the darts people used for sport, no. These were the deadly darts that could do some serious damage if they hit you. A few inches longer than the regular darts, these had barbs at the end that became embedded in whatever they hit. If you were to pull it out of your flesh, it would take a chunk of it with it.

Once when the three of them were out on an overnight camping excursion earlier this summer, he took down a rabbit with one. From that point on Chad's been calling him Bart the Dart off and on which has annoyed him to no end. Recently though, Rupert and his friends have begun to use the term and not in a friendly manner. Ever since they took to calling him 'Bart the Dart', it lost the friendly nuance it once held so he stopped using it.

Coming to an abrupt halt, he noticed the smile playing across Bart's face.

"Was wondering if you were going to see me," Bart said.

"Sorry," he apologized. "Just thinking about Riyan."

"You heard?" Bart asked.

Nodding, Chad said, "Yeah. His mother said he took it rather rough."

"I can imagine," replied Bart.

"He's taking the flock up into the hills at the base of the mountains for a few days," he told him. "I think he needed time to come to grips with it."

"Will do him good," stated Bart.

Chad looked up the street and groaned, "Oh no."

"What?" Bart asked as he turned to look. Coming toward them down the street was Rupert, alone this time. Dressed in his fine clothes, he appeared to be strutting down the street as if he owned it. Which, truth be told, isn't too far from the truth as his family owned quite a bit of the town.

He came directly to them and stopped a few feet away. "Either of you seen Riyan this morning?" he asked.

They both shook their heads and Chad said, "No."

"Well if you do, tell him I'm looking for him," he said.

"We'll do that," Bart assured him.

"Did you hear I'm getting married?" he asked. When he saw their faces turn into scowls, he grinned. "Guess so. Lovely girl Freya."

"You've never been interested in her before," said Chad. "This seems rather sudden."

He shrugged. "My father pestered me to pick a bride," he explained. "So I chose her. One's as good as another if you know what I mean." Then he laughed and moved past them as he continued on his way.

"He doesn't even care for her," Bart said with barely controlled anger.

"Six will get you ten that he's doing it more to anger Riyan than anything else," Chad said.

Bart turned and gave him a mischievous grin. "What say we do Riyan a favor then?" he suggested.

"What do you have in mind?" Chad asked hesitantly. He saw the twinkle in Bart's eye that always foretold that what he had on his mind would usually land them in trouble. Once when just such a twinkle came to him, the three of them had wound up spending a whole week working in Bocker's shop. The details leading up to it were far too embarrassing for him to dwell on.

Bart simply turned and gazed at Rupert's departing back and smiled. "Can you meet me back here after sundown?" he asked.

"I think so," Chad replied. "Need to finish my chores, but I shouldn't be too long after sundown."

"Good," he nodded. "Riyan's going to be gone the better part of a week." Turning back to Chad he continued. "That should give us plenty of time."

"Plenty of time for what?" Chad asked.

"To make life for Rupert a merry hell," he replied with finality.

That night after the mill closed, Chad had raced home and flew through his chores. Then after a quick meal with his family, he was out the door on his way into town. He found Bart already at the town square waiting for him. "Sorry I'm late," he said as he approached his friend.

"You're not that late," he replied. "Didn't really expect you for another half hour."

Chad noticed the bag Bart had slung over his shoulder and asked, "So what are we going to do?"

Bart directed his gaze to the Sterling Sheep, the only inn and eatery Quillim has. "Rupert and his father are in there having dinner with Freya and her father," he explained. "They just sat down, so with any luck will remain in there for some time." Patting the bag slung over his shoulder he added, "Now let's get to it."

"What's in there?" asked Chad.

"Just some things I borrowed from a friend of mine," he replied.

Chad had thought they were going to the Sterling Sheep, but instead Bart headed off in another direction. It didn't take him long to realize where he was headed when the estate Rupert called home came into view. "Are you crazy?" he asked.

"Don't worry," Bart assured him. "This will only take a minute or two."

The estate was one the largest in the area, three stories tall and the envy of the entire community. It had been in Rupert's family for years, each generation adding their own touch. The grounds that surrounded it were meticulously kept by a score of servants whose combined wage was more than some families earn in a year or more.

Upon reaching the lane leading up to the manor house, Bart stopped for a brief moment while he made sure there was no one about. When he saw the coast was clear, he gestured for Chad to follow.

They ran across the lawn as two shadows in the moonlight. Bart angled towards a vine covered lattice that extended from the ground all the way to the roof's edge on one end of the house. Once they reached the base he paused and scanned the area one more time. Not seeing anyone, he whispered to Chad as he pointed to the window near the top of the lattice. "That's Rupert's room," he explained.

Chad nodded and then Bart stepped to the lattice and began to climb. "Be careful," he warned, "this isn't very strong." After he had climbed up several feet, Chad followed.

He worked his way up to the window and when he came abreast of it, pulled out his knife. Then while gripping the lattice with his left hand, he leaned over and slid the knife blade between the two halves of the window before gently sliding it up. The blade moved up along the crack between the two sections until it met resistance. Pushing harder, he felt the latch that was locking the window from the inside come free.

He then used his knife to pry the window open. When it swung open, he replaced his knife in its sheath and used his hand to swing the two sections of the window wide. "Come on," he said as he climbed in through the window. Once inside, he turned and helped Chad through.

Just as Bart had said, Chad found himself in Rupert's bedroom. "Now what?" he asked.

Bart set his bag down on a chair and opened it. "Now we make it look like he's got a girlfriend," he replied. From within the bag, he pulled out two pieces of clothing no betrothed man should have in his possession. Rather intimate articles that women wear beneath their clothes.

"Rumple the bed a little," he told Chad. "Make it look like he and a girl had a tumble before he left for dinner."

Chad grinned and nodded. While he was doing that, Bart laid one of the pieces of clothing on the floor just under the bed. He situated it in such a place that a casual look wouldn't immediately reveal it. But when the servants came in to clean the room, they would most assuredly discover it. The other he put at the very foot of his bed under the sheets.

"Toss me his pillow," he said to Chad.

Chad took it off the bed and tossed it over to him. "What do you want that for?" he asked.

Bart grinned and went back over to his bag. He pulled out a small vial with a stopper. Setting the pillow on the table, he opened the vial and rubbed the stopper across the pillowcase.

From where Chad was standing, he could smell the unmistakable odor of perfume. "That smells like what Mirriam wears," he observed. Mirriam of course was a very beautiful girl here in Quillim who's had her sights on Rupert for some time. It's well known that she's been after him for years.

"I know," he replied with a chuckle. "Let him explain this." After putting the vial of perfume back in the bag, he pulled out a small jar of rouge, the type girls put on their lips to make them look rosy. Unscrewing the top, he set it on the table next to the pillow.

Chad came to stand next to him as Bart flipped the pillow over and ever so carefully dipped his finger into the rouge. He watched as Bart used great care in drawing what looks like two lips on Rupert's pillowcase with the rouge. Once he was done, it looked just like a woman with rouge on her lips had made the mark.

"What do you think?" Bart asked as he wiped his finger off on a cloth that he had in his bag.

"He could find all this and get rid of it before someone else discovered it," Chad said.

"We're not done yet," he replied. After replacing the pillow back on Rupert's bed with the imprinted lips' side down, he walked over to a chest of drawers sitting against the wall. There he pulled open the top drawer and began rummaging through it.

Chad came over with him and saw him take something out of the drawer and place it in the bag. "We're not thieves!" he insisted quietly.

"Relax," Bart replied as he put another item in his bag. "I'm not taking anything of any great value, and I'm sure not going to keep it."

"What do you plan to do then?" Chad asked.

He took one more item then closed the drawer. "Mirriam is going to receive a present from a secret admirer," he explained with a grin.

Suddenly, footsteps from the hall beyond the bedroom door came to them. They both froze as they listened to the footsteps draw closer. Only after the footsteps passed by the door and continued down the hallway did they relax.

"Let's get out of here," urged Chad.

"Alright," agreed Bart. He took but a moment to make sure everything inside the drawer was exactly like he found it before pushing it closed. When he turned for the window he found Chad already climbing out to the lattice. Moving to join him, Bart swung the bag across his back and reached within his tunic. He pulled forth a thick piece of rolled leather and untied the leather thong that bound it closed.

He unrolled the piece of leather and then removed one of the small tools secured within the leather. The tool in question was three inches long with a curved hook at the end. Placing the tool between his teeth, he rolled the leather back up and tied it closed once more with the leather thong. He then replaced the rolled leather within his tunic and begun making his way through the window.

Once out on the lattice, he looked down and found that Chad had already made it to the bottom and was standing there waiting for him. Turning his attention back to the window, he closed it almost all the way. But before it completely shut, he took the tool he held in his mouth and hooked the end around the arm of the latch used in locking the window.

He moved the latch upward until it was above the eye ring it latched into. Then he carefully closed the window the rest of the way. Once closed, he lowered the arm of the latch until he felt the end touch the eye ring. With just a quick yank, he sank the latch into the eye ring, thus securing the window from the inside.

Placing the tool once more between his teeth, he started climbing down the lattice. At the bottom he removed the tool from between his teeth and set it once more within the rolled piece of leather.

"What's that?" Chad asked when he saw the tool as Bart was putting it back with the others.

"Just something my father gave me some time ago," he replied. "I've found they come in useful every now and then."

"I've never seen anything like them before," he said.

Bart nodded at that. "Not too surprising. Now, let's head back to the Sterling Sheep."

"You mean we're not through yet?" asked Chad.

"Good heavens no," replied Bart with a grin.

Chad followed Bart as he again ran across the lawn to the lane leading back to town. He wondered about his friend. Bart had never gone into very much detail about his life before coming to Quillim, though of course he and Riyan hadn't been all that curious in the first place. But now he wondered who this Bart could be and what had driven him to choose this area to live in. He was pretty sure he knew what those tools in the piece of leather meant. Though he had never seen their like before, he would bet anything that they were lockpicks.

Back at the lane leading into town, Bart picked up speed. "Have to get there before they leave," he said.

Not understanding the hurry, Chad didn't really care. This was the most adventure he had ever been a part of. They made their way through the darkened streets until the inn appeared ahead of them.

When they drew close, Bart had Chad stay back as he went to the window and looked in to the dining area of the Sterling Sheep. He stood there a moment peering inside before turning around and rejoining Chad. "They're still in there," he said. "Wait here." Then without an explanation, Bart returned to the window. While he stood there, Chad saw him remove the jar of rouge and do something with it. In the dark he couldn't see just what he did. After a few minutes Bart closed the jar and replaced it within the bag.

Another five minutes passed as he stood there looking in through the window. Then he abruptly turned towards the back of the inn and signaled for Chad to join him. "Whatever you do, don't make a sound," he said in a hushed whisper when Chad joined him. "Understand?"

Chad nodded and then followed him to the rear of the inn. They reached the rear courtyard just as a figure exited from the back door. Even in the shadows of the courtyard, Chad recognized Rupert's silhouette. He was walking across the courtyard to the jakes along the rear wall.

Bart motioned for Chad to stop while he continued toward Rupert. Chad was amazed at how silently Bart was able to move. Other than Rupert's footsteps and the music coming from the inn, no other sound disturbed the quiet of the courtyard. Then just as Rupert opened the door to the jakes, Bart grabbed him. Putting one hand alongside his throat and the other on his back, Bart pushed him into the jakes and shut the door.

Chad saw Bart motioning for him to hurry and join him. He hurried over and Bart indicated for him to keep the door closed.

Bang!

Rupert struck the door from the inside and Chad almost failed to keep it closed. "Let me out!" he hollered.

Chad looked to Bart who was now on his knees before the door and looked to be sliding something between the door jamb and the door about a third of the way up from the ground.

Bang!

Again Rupert hit the door and the force of the blow knocked out whatever Bart had been sliding into place. Picking it up off the ground, he again worked to get it into place.

"Help!" yelled Rupert. "I'm being attacked!"

Then all of a sudden, Bart stood up. In the moonlight Chad could see he was holding a string that was attached to whatever it was he placed within the crack between the door and the door jamb.

"Come on," Bart whispered as he began moving away from the jakes.

Bang!

As they hurried to the side of the courtyard that was deep in shadows, Rupert again hit the door in an attempt to get out. And to Chad's amazement, the door held.

Bart brought them to a stop as soon as the string he held had reached its end. They stood there in the darkness as Rupert continued hollering for help and trying to break his way out. Fortunately the music within the dining area of the inn was loud enough to drown out his cries.

They waited for at least five minutes before another person left the inn on their way to the jakes. When Bart saw the man leaving the inn, he pulled the string. The wedge he had keeping the door to the jakes' closed came free and the door swung open.

Chad about laughed when Rupert came stumbling out and crashed down into the dirt before the jakes. The man who was leaving the inn rushed over to help him but Rupert knocked away his hand and got to his feet. What he said to the man couldn't be heard, but they saw the way he stalked back to the inn.

The following morning when Chad was at the mill working the giant grinding stones that turned grain into flour, his younger brother Eryl came running in all excited. "Did you hear?" he asked his brother.

"Hear what?" replied Chad.

"Last night at the Sterling Sheep ..." his brother began but was forced to stop and catch his breath. Obviously he felt that what he had to say was so good that he ran the whole way to tell him. By this time their father had moved closer to hear.

"The magistrate and his son Rupert were dining with Freya and her father," he continued. "Apparently Rupert had gone out back and dallied with some girl." He turned to his father. "And with his betrothed there waiting for his return." His eyes gleamed, every kid in Quillim hated Rupert and any story that showed him in a bad light was like gold.

"He claimed someone locked him in the jakes," Eryl said in a tone that said he didn't believe it. "But when he returned to the inn, there was rouge on his neck that people say looked just like a woman kissed him." He laughed. "As it turned out, Freya wasn't wearing any that night."

Their father smiled as he too didn't care much for Rupert. He did feel sorry for Freya though, it must have been a humiliation.

"Rupert is still saying he didn't do anything and is sticking to his story," Eryl explained. "But really papa, who is going to believe such a story?"

Chad grinned to himself as the grinding wheel continued to turn grain into flour. *Who indeed?* Bart had explained to him last night after they left the vicinity of the Sterling Sheep how he had put rouge on his hand in the shape of a girl's lips. So that when he grabbed Rupert by the neck and threw him in the jakes, it would come off and leave the tell-tale mark.

"Are they still betrothed?" asked Chad.

"I hadn't heard," his brother replied. "But her father took it hard."

"I can imagine," their father said. Then to Eryl he added, "Don't you have chores at home you should be doing?"

"Yes papa," he replied and turned to head out the door.

"Another hour or two and the flour will be ready," Chad's father said before he too left.

Chad nodded in reply. The rest of the afternoon was spent in grinding flour. How he hated doing this. Last night when he and Bart were, as Bart said 'making Rupert's life a merry hell', he had felt more alive than ever before. But all in all, he'd rather be doing this than be in Rupert's shoes right about now.

Chapter 4

The evening of the second day found Riyan deeper into the hills than he had ever been before. Ahead to the west the mountains raised high into the sky. With the crystal blue sky above and the rolling green foothills below, the mountains were a breathtaking sight. A cool breeze blew across the hills to help alleviate the heat of the day. If only he could get Freya off his mind, he would be able to enjoy it all so much more.

The first day out, he railed, shouted, and screamed at the injustice in the world. That actually had helped to rid his soul of the worst of the feelings the situation in Quillim had instilled in him. Now it was more a sense of loss that continued to plague him more than anything else.

If he couldn't change the situation he must make the best of it. His mother was right in that Freya was going to need a friend in the coming years. And he decided that if that was all he's going to be able to be to her, he would at least be that.

Near the end of the day he and his flock crested another of the many hills in this area. On the far side was a small lake that stretched outward from the base of the hill for quite some distance. A truly scenic place with the mountains as a backdrop, he decided to stop here for the night. While the flock grazed nearby, Riyan began collecting sufficient firewood to last him through the night.

Baaaaaaa!

The sheep cried out to him whenever he disappeared out of sight in his hunt for decent fuel for the fire. They continued to cry out until he reappeared again. Now that they were in unfamiliar territory, they didn't want to be very far from him. Even Black Face hasn't strayed off since they left behind the lands they usually grazed upon.

He built his fire and then hunted for a small animal to roast for dinner. Though he had plenty of food from home to last him, there was nothing like the taste of a fresh kill roasted over an open fire. Moving off from the campsite, he held his sling ready with a stone in hand. He worked his way through the trees until he came across a rabbit out for a last bite before returning to its burrow for the night.

With a quick twirl, he launched a stone at the rabbit and struck it in the head. The force of the blow knocked it backward over a foot. As the rabbit laid there twitching its last, he walked over and picked it up. It didn't take him long before the rabbit was skinned and roasting over the fire. The smell of roasting meat made his all but empty stomach growl.

The flock remained close for the rest of the evening and was still nearby when he stoked the fire before turning in.

Baaaaaaa! Baaaaaaa!

The panicked cries of many sheep woke him in the middle of the night. He tried to get to his feet to see what was going on but was thrown back to the ground. The earth was shaking violently.

An earthquake! He'd been in a couple during his life, but none with the force of what he was experiencing right now. The ground itself seemed to roar as it shook. Off in the distance came the sound of a tree crashing to the ground as it no longer could withstand the forces assaulting it.

The best Riyan could do while the shaking continued was to get to his hands and knees. All around him the sheep bleated in fear, he could tell they were no longer together. In their fear they had ran off across the hills.

When the ground finally stopped its shaking and calmed down, he stood up and looked around. The light from his fire didn't extend all that far, and only three of his sheep were in sight.

Putting two fingers in his mouth, he whistled loudly. Three long, loud bursts then he stopped to listen. From all around he could hear the sound of his sheep change from that of fear and panic to a more normal baaing.

One more time he put his fingers in his mouth and whistled another three long, loud bursts. When he listened for the sheep's response, he could hear them crashing through the underbrush back towards the camp. One by one they made their appearance and Riyan was sure they were relieved to once more be back with him.

He counted the flock after the night grew quiet again and as the last one making its way through the bushes arrived. When he finished, he realized he was still two sheep short. He whistled again and then listened for the tell-tale sound of them making their way through the underbrush. But the night remained silent.

"Damn!" he cursed. *Two sheep gone!* There was no way he was about to go searching for them in the dark. Aside from it being way too dangerous to move around in unfamiliar territory at night, he would also risk the chance that more of his sheep would become lost.

Mad and upset, he counted the flock one more time in the hopes that he miscounted the first time. But the count remained the same, two sheep missing. That's when he noticed one of the sheep who was missing was Black Face. "Of course," he said to himself.

Unable to do anything until the sun came up, he placed several more logs on the fire and laid back down. In the morning he was going to have to find the wayward sheep.

The first rays of the sun upon his face woke him. First thing he did was to recount the sheep on the off chance that the others had made their way back during the night. To his surprise one of them had returned. Of course it wasn't Black Face. At least he has only one to find now which should make his job that much easier.

He left the flock where they were grazing and went to the top of a nearby hill. There he whistled loudly and scanned the forest for any movement. When he failed to see or hear any indication which direction Black Face lay, he returned to his camp. He had half a mind to simply forget about it, his life would be a whole lot easier if Black Face were to be lost forever. But he and his mother needed every copper that Black Face's wool, and ultimately meat, would bring them.

So after having a quick breakfast of food his mother had packed for him, he left the flock in the small area between the hills and set out in search of Black Face. He didn't feel there was much of a threat to the flock where they were, and he wouldn't be going very far from them. He mainly was planning to do a circuit around the immediate area as he didn't think Black Face would have wandered that far. Of course, if after that time there was still no trace of him, he would give up. He had to at least make the attempt.

For the next several hours, he worked his way in and around the hills. Once he reached as far as he dared to go from the flock, he would pause and whistle. Then he would listen for a moment. When he didn't hear Black

Face's bleat, he continued. Every once in awhile he would return to the flock, only to find them still grazing contentedly.

He was searching the area closest to the mountains, and had almost completely blanketed the area where he felt Black Face could have wandered to, when he heard a very faint, frightened bleating. Relieved to have found him, he rushed forward toward his wayward sheep.

Following the sound of Black Face's cries, he headed further west towards the slopes of the mountains. After fording a stream, the trees opened up on a clearing wherein a large expanse of berry bushes lay. He nodded to himself when he saw them for they were just the type Black Face always seemed to gravitate towards back home.

Pausing just within the clearing, he looked around but couldn't see Black Face. Raising his fingers to his lips, he whistled loudly for a second then stopped. He stood still as he waited for the bleating to come and after a moment, it did.

Baaaaaaa!

The cry was coming from the right side of the berry patch but the sheep was nowhere to be seen. "Black Face!" he hollered. "Where are you, you stupid sheep?"

Baaaaaaa!

Again the cry came. Shaking his head, Riyan moved towards the sound. As he drew closer to the edge of the berry bushes he saw a snatch of sheep's wool dangling from one of the vines. He walked quickly to it and plucked it from the vine just as the cry came again. This time, it sounded close, and was coming from just before him. Yet there was no sign of Black Face.

Baaaaaaa!

When it came again, he looked more closely and saw a fair sized hole in the ground hidden beneath the berry vines about four feet in. It was from out of that hole Black Face was calling from.

"You really got yourself in a fix this time didn't you?" he asked.

Baaaaaaa!

"No use complaining at me," he said to the sheep. "You've got no sense whatsoever." He then took a moment to figure out how on earth he was going to get him out of there. The hole in which Black Face had fallen was covered in a thick layer of thorn laden vines. He was sure that he could get him out of there, but it wasn't going to be easy.

Turning his attention to the vines, he contemplated his best course of action. Pulling his knife from his belt, he sighed and began cutting away segments of the vines. Almost a quarter hour later, his hands were covered in dozens of pin-prick sized holes, some of which were still welling blood. He had managed to clear a good portion of the vines away and reached the edge of the hole. His attitude towards Black Face continued to deteriorate every time another of the thorns pricked his skin.

Baaaaaaa!

"Oh shut up," he yelled down to the hole. When he at last reached the edge of the hole and had cleared the vines back enough to look down, he saw Black Face moving down below. The side of the hole sloped down a steep embankment until reaching where Black Face stood.

He gauged the angle of the slope and determined that it was inclined sufficiently that he could possibly make it back up if he went down to get the sheep. Though with Black Face in his arms, it would be a little trickier. So after another few minutes of pruning the branches back a little bit further, he went to the edge of the hole and began climbing down.

Baaaaaaa!

When Black Face saw him coming down towards him, he started baaing excitedly. "Yeah, just wait until I get you out of here," threatened Riyan, "then we'll see how happy you are."

Baaaaaaa!

The threat of possible repercussions for being down here didn't seem to worry Black Face any. He was just happy to be with someone familiar again.

Sliding down into the hole was relatively easy. Once he hit the bottom, Black Face immediately came to him and practically jumped into his lap. "Calm down," he said as he got to his feet.

He glanced around and was quick to realize that this was not just some hole in the ground. The light filtering down from above revealed that he was in what looked to be some kind of passage. It was roughly ten feet high, half that wide, and extended into darkness to his left and right.

Excitement filled him as he saw the unmistakable signs of human construction. Though the sides of the passage were worn with time, they still showed where stone blocks were used in its construction.

"What did you find?" he asked Black Face. Visions of treasure and adventure raced across his mind as he wondered what wealth may be hidden down here. Then, from down the passage to his right, something caught the light from above and glittered. Turning his head towards it, he tried to see it but had lost it in the dark.

Unwilling to give up on it, he moved slowly down the passage until the glitter came again. Then he rushed forward and discovered that the glitter came from a tarnished coin almost completely buried in the dirt covering the floor. "Treasure!" he exclaimed excitedly. Never in his wildest imagination did he ever think he, a shepherd boy, would find something like this.

Dropping to his knees, he reached down and picked up the coin. He couldn't see it too clearly and got back to his feet. Returning to just beneath the hole, he held the coin in the light from above and saw that it was made of copper. It was roughly the size of the coins he's used to using, but the impressions on both sides were nothing like he had ever seen before.

On the one side was a bust of what could have been a man, but it wasn't easy to make out as the coin was quite worn. The other side bore a symbol the likes of which he's never seen before. "This has to be old," he said to himself. Looking down the passage that extended into darkness in both directions, he wondered just how many more such coins could be down here.

Then he turned his gaze to Black Face. "I guess I can forgive you," he said. Rolling the coin through his fingers, his mind began churning with possibilities. He slipped the coin into his pouch before removing two short lengths of rope. "Sorry about this old boy," he said.

Taking one of the pieces of rope, he tied Black Face's rear legs together and then the front. "Baaaaaaa!" complained Black Face. The sheep didn't care for being treated like this, but Riyan couldn't have his legs loose and thrashing about as he tried to return him back to the surface.

Once the legs were tied, he picked up Black Face. He placed him over his shoulders and around his neck. He held onto the legs with one hand as best he could while using the other to maintain his balance as he maneuvered up the slope.

Black Face wiggled, baaed and kicked the whole way up. Riyan lost his grip a couple times due to the sheep's thrashing and was thankful that he had the forethought to bind the legs or it would have been much worse. When he at last reached the top, he braced his feet securely before launching Black Face up and out of the hole with a mighty shove. After

Black Face hit the ground and began baaing pitifully, Riyan climbed the rest of the way to the surface.

Once out, he untied Black Face and then turned back one more time to look at the hole. If it wasn't for the fact that the flock was some distance away and unattended, he would have tried to explore the passage further. But without a source of light such as a torch or a lantern, he wouldn't have been able to go very far anyway.

As he returned with Black Face back to where the rest of the flock was grazing, he made sure to set the landmarks and the lay of the land in his mind. He wanted to be sure he could find this place again. For when he returned home, he planned to get some supplies together and come back.

He immediately got the flock moving once again back towards Quillim. As they set out, he removed the coin from his pouch and looked at it. A grin spread across his face at the adventure it promised.

The day after the debacle at the Sterling Sheep, the town was simply abuzz with rumors and gossip. Of course a couple of the more juicy ones were started by Bart. He's simply enjoying himself to no end.

Still though, the betrothal between Rupert and Freya had yet to be called off. Bart really had no expectations for it to be called off for Freya's family, even with the humiliation the events were giving them, could ill afford to not go through with it. He felt bad for her, but he despised Rupert more.

To up the ante, he dropped off the necklace he took from Rupert's drawer the night before at Mirriam's door. He didn't leave a note with it, instead he twined it around several beautiful flowers and laid it upon a finely embroidered kerchief. That by itself wouldn't have led people to believe that it was from Rupert. So right afterwards, he went into town and stood near the window of the biggest gossip in town.

He could hear her inside talking with a couple other ladies as they worked on their needlework. Every year she and her circle work on a quilt which they give to one of the more underprivileged families in the area. This year they planned to give it to Clara Jenis and her family. Clara has been ill. for the past few months and her husband was having a hard time keeping things together. Between working, their three children, and her illness, he was about worn to a frazzle.

From his position by the window, he heard them talking about somebody or another. Then he said sort of loud, but not too conspicuously so, "I tell you I saw him!"

Then in another voice like he was another person he replied, "Rupert?" From within the house, all talking ceased.

Bart grinned to himself as he said, "Yes Rupert. You would think he'd leave well enough alone after his problems of the night before."

In his second voice he asked himself, "What happened?" The inside of the house was as quiet as a tomb, he knew every ear within was straining to hear what he had to say next.

"I saw him placing something at the door of Mirriam's home," he said in voice one.

"Mirriam?" voice two asked. "Isn't she the one who's been trying to get her hooks in him for years?"

"That's the one," voice one replied. "Looks like she finally hooked him."

"What did he leave?" voice two asked.

"I'm not exactly sure," voice one explained. "Some flowers for sure though I thought I saw something glittering among the stems."

Then as he started to say, "We'll have to see what ..." he began moving away from the window and let his voice trail off. After he became quiet, he snuck back to the window and listened. Inside it remained silent for only a few seconds before the women all started talking at once. Now, if Mirriam would just find the necklace and put it on, it would lend credibility to the seed he just sowed.

He hung around town for a couple hours and sure enough, Mirriam appeared wearing the necklace. Her eyes were aglow and she walked briskly through town. By this time the rumor he planted had circulated widely. Two people already had approached him and told him about it, each telling seeming to add some new detail. As she passed through the people on the streets, they would grow quiet. Then after she went by, their eyes would follow her as they talked in hushed whispers.

Bart watched as she continued along the street, her hand would at times go to the necklace and rub it as if she didn't really believe it was there. She paused at the corner for a second before her eyes lit up. Across the street, Rupert and his three cronies had just appeared.

She waved and hurried across the street to meet him. Bart followed her at a discreet distance to see what would happen. He wasn't alone, many of those on the street saw where she was heading and followed too.

Rupert came to a stop and his eyes turned dark when he saw the necklace around her neck. He recognized it as one that had been in his drawer. Bart was too far away to hear what was said, but after just a couple exchanges between Rupert and Mirriam, Rupert ripped the necklace from around her neck. Then Mirriam turned and fled, tears in her eyes.

Bart stood there a moment too long, for Rupert noticed him. His face turned darker and he began moving quickly towards him. Bart remained where he was until the four young men came to him.

Rupert held out the necklace and demanded, "Do you know anything about this?"

"Why no Rupert," Bart replied innocently. "It looks to be a necklace of some sort."

"Someone's been messing with me," he stated, "trying to get my betrothal with Freya annulled." Rupert glared at him and added, "I can only think of one person who would want that."

"Freya?" guessed Bart.

Rupert's eyes narrowed and his face turned red in anger. "Don't play with me, Bart!" he warned. "I know Riyan is behind this and you two, along with Chad, are tight as thieves."

"Riyan has been out with his sheep since just after your betrothal," he replied. "I don't see how he could be behind anything."

Rupert glared at him. "This betrothal is going to continue," he said. "If there are any further 'occurrences' like this," he continued as he held up the necklace again, "Riyan will pay the consequences."

It was Bart's turn to get a dark look. "Be sure you know with whom you're messing with before you act," he warned.

"Is that a threat?" Rupert asked. "Are you daring to threaten me?"

"Merely offering a piece of advice," he answered.

Then Rupert became aware of the people who had gathered to watch the drama unfold between himself and Bart. To Bart he said, "This isn't over."

Bart merely remained silent as Rupert and his three cronies quickly left the street. Once they've gone down the street a ways, Bart turned and left in the opposite direction.

Moving through town, his mind churned over the encounter. What had started out as a prank has developed into something a bit more serious. He feared that Rupert was planning on taking out his anger over what's been happening on his friend Riyan. Thankfully Riyan isn't due back for several more days. Hopefully by then all this will have blown over.

He hurried back across town to old Rebecca's place to finish the work she wanted done. Along the way, he came to the decision to lay low for awhile and leave Rupert alone. At least until Riyan returned, then he would see how things turned out.

Chapter 5

The night of the earthquake rocked the town badly. Several businesses were damaged in one way or another, but the worst was Chad's father's mill. The quake had cracked one of the two grinding stones.

"Can't we continue with it like it is?" Chad asked his father the following morning.

Shaking his head, Chad's father turned to him, "No. Once they get a crack in them, it's only a matter of time before they break altogether. Not only that, but pieces of the stone will find their way into the flour." His father sat down with a worried expression.

"What can we do then?" Chad asked.

"If we wish to continue to operate, we have to obtain another grinding stone," he told his son.

Chad looked to his father and saw the worry in his eyes. He knew that his father didn't have all that much gold stashed away and grinding stones didn't come cheap. "Are we going to be able to purchase another one?" he asked.

His father turned to him and smiled a sad smile. "Things will work out," he replied. "But it will be a week or more before a new stone can be brought here and put into place."

Just then, the Magistrate stepped through the door. "Heard about your grinding stone," he said. "Too bad."

"Chad, could you go see if your mother needs anything?" his father asked.

Chad knew that he wished him to leave for some reason, then it dawned on him why. His father was going to ask the Magistrate for a loan. The Magistrate was the only person in town who could possibly help. "But ..." he began.

"Please son," his father insisted, "go help your mother."

Nodding, Chad got up and said, "Yes sir." Then he headed for the door. He gave the Magistrate a respectful nod of the head before he passed from the mill and to the lane outside.

He thought of what his father was about to do. There was no way they would ever be able to repay the Magistrate for the grinding stone. Most years they barely made enough to pay the taxes, feed their family, and buy other essentials they required. His father must know that, and so will the magistrate.

As scenarios played out in his mind, he came to realize that it wasn't so much a loan his father would be getting from the magistrate, but more like selling the mill. All his life, his father's one pride was that he owned that mill outright. Now, it's likely he was going to have to work for the magistrate for the rest of his life. The thought angered Chad.

He wasn't exactly sure where it was he was heading, he just put one foot in front of the other while his mind was preoccupied. Then Bart came into view as he rounded a corner up ahead. When he saw Chad, he hurried towards him.

"Hey, did you feel that quake last night?" Bart asked.

Chad came to a stop and nodded his head. "I think everyone felt it," he replied.

Bart noticed something was wrong so asked, "You okay?"

Shaking his head, Chad said, "The quake cracked the upper grinding wheel. We're going to have to buy a new one before we can turn any more grain into flour."

"That's tough, man," he said condolingly.

Then Chad noticed one of Rupert's cronies appear behind Bart. The young man stopped when he saw Bart and Chad talking before ducking quickly behind a building. A second later, he peered around the corner at them.

Chad nodded to Rupert's crony. "Are they keeping an eye on you?"

"You could say that," replied Bart. "Yesterday when Mirriam appeared, I was there when he accosted her and took back the necklace."

A worried looked came to Chad as he lowered his voice and asked, "Do you think he suspects?"

"I think so," Bart told him in a quiet whisper of his own. "As long as all he can do is suspect, we'll be fine. He thinks Riyan is behind it."

"But he wasn't even in town," said Chad.

"I know." Bart glanced behind him and saw the crony peering around the corner again. "We'll have to let Riyan know what's going on as soon as he gets back. But right now, I need to return to the farm. She's got me removing an old tree stump near the house. She wants to plant flowers there." Rolling his eyes heavenward, he sighed.

"I feel for you man," Chad said.

"If she was rich I would tell her to get a scroll from Phyndyr's," he said.

"Phyndyr's?" Chad asked.

"Yeah," nodded Bart. "He sells scrolls down in Wardean. One of the better scroll merchants if you ask me."

"Like what?" Chad asked, a glimmer of hope coming to him.

"Oh, all sorts of stuff," he explained. "Take this stump I'm going to be spending the next several days digging out. One scroll from him and it would be gone."

"You mean vanish?" Chad looked at his friend in disbelief.

Bart shrugged, "Maybe if I wanted to pay that much for it. But a simple burn spell would probably do the trick. Or maybe one that would dissolve it."

"Do you think he would have one that could fix the crack in the grinding wheel?" he asked with newborn hope.

"I would think so," he replied. "But some of the scrolls get pretty pricy."

"Thanks," he said, not really hearing him. If he could get a scroll cheap that would fix the crack, then his father wouldn't have to sell. "How much do the scrolls go for?"

"I've heard that some can go as cheap as two silvers," he explained. "Others, though, could go for over a hundred golds, or more."

"I hardly think a scroll to fix a crack would cost very much," he said. "I have almost a gold of my own saved."

"Maybe," Bart agreed.

"We could be there and back by nightfall," he said.

"I think it's a bit further than ..." Then realization hit. "What do you mean 'we'?" he asked.

"Yes," he nodded. "You and I could ride down and be back after dark."

"I ... I don't know if I could get away," he said a bit nervously. "I, um, really have to get that stump out."

Chad looked to his friend and saw something in his friend's face he hadn't seen before. "I'm sure she wouldn't mind," he assured him. "You go ask her and I'll tell my father what's going on."

"But …"

"This is great!" Chad exclaimed. "Meet me at the mill after you talk to her." Then he turned around and hurried back to the mill.

Bart stood there for a minute watching the excited steps of his friend. Not nearly sharing his friend's enthusiasm for going to Wardean, he swallowed hard. *Only be there a short time*, he said to himself. Then he began walking down the lane to tell old lady Rebecca that he would have to start on the stump tomorrow.

"No!"

"But father," argued Chad, "this could save us."

"No!" his father repeated. When Chad had gone to tell his father that he and Bart were going to Wardean and why, he found his father emphatically against it.

"Why?" he asked.

"I will not take the chance on magic to save us," he explained. "Nothing ever good came from such things."

"But Bart said this Phyndyr was a master scroller," insisted Chad. "He guaranteed that we could get this fixed without having to borrow from the Magistrate."

His father gave him a look he's seen many times over the course of his seventeen years. "I wouldn't trust anything that friend of yours says," he told his son. "What do you know about him anyway? Just up and rolled into town a year ago. Where did he come from? What drove him to come here?"

Chad could only stand there as his father railed at him. He didn't know the answer to these questions. Bart had never been one to talk about his past. He and Riyan had always respected that and never pried into it.

"I think it's a good solution," Chad insisted.

His father turned to him and said, "No! You are not to think about this any more. The new grinding wheel will be here by the end of the week. All the arrangements have been made."

"So you've already sold the mill to the magistrate?" he asked.

"I'm not selling the mill," his father replied. "Merely getting a loan to cover the cost of the new wheel."

"You'll never be able to pay him back," Chad said. "It amounts to the same thing."

His father's face turned red in anger. "I'm through talking about this," he said with finality. "The subject is closed." He glared at his son until Chad finally left the mill.

When Bart finally arrived, he found his friend still in the vicinity of the mill. Chad didn't see him right away, so engrossed was he with his thoughts. "You ready?" Bart asked him.

Chad's eyes turned to his friend. "He won't even consider it!" he exclaimed.

"Your father?" guessed Bart.

Chad nodded. "He said, *'Nothing ever good came from magic'.*"

"So what do you intend to do now?" he asked. He could see the hard set of Chad's jaw. "You aren't planning on going against the wishes of your father are you?"

Nodding, Chad replied, "Yes I am. If this can save our mill, we would be fools not to do it." He saw the look in Bart's eyes. "What?"

"Maybe you should respect your father's wishes," he said. "It's his mill after all."

"It's our *family's* mill," Chad corrected him. "I'm not about to stand by and do nothing when there's a way to save it." When Bart failed to comment, he asked, "Are you still coming with me?"

"Yes," he replied. "I doubt if you would be able to find Phyndyr's place otherwise."

"Good." Leading Bart to where he and his family live, they bypassed the house and headed directly to the barn out back. They quickly got a couple horses saddled and Chad left Bart in the barn while he went up to the house. Secreted in his room was his stash of money that he intended to use in purchasing the scroll.

The sound of his mother in the kitchen reached him as he entered the front door. He closed it carefully so as not to alert her to his presence. He moved through the front room towards the hallway leading further into the house. The first doorway he came to led into the kitchen area and he paused there a moment. Peering around the corner, he saw that his mother's back was to him as she worked on dinner.

Hurrying past the doorway, he moved down the hallway and entered his room, closing the door behind him. His secret stash was hidden under a loose floorboard that one of the legs of his bed rested upon. He pushed his bed over a few inches until the leg was off the board, then bent over and pried it up.

In his secret hiding place was a sack containing his life savings. Nestled in the compartment with the sack were several other items that held value for him. Chad took the sack out and placed it in his shirt before replacing the floorboard. Once it was set in flush with the floor, he pulled his bed back to its original position with the leg once again on top of the floorboard covering his stash. He got back to his feet, crossed the room, and opened the door.

"What are you doing?" His brother Eryl stood there in the hallway looking very curiously at him.

"Nothing," he replied. "Doesn't mother need help with dinner or something?" He stepped out of his room and closed the door behind him.

"No," he said, "and father's busy at the mill getting it ready for the arrival of the new stone."

"Go bother someone else, Eryl," Chad said as they stood there in the hallway. He turned to retrace his steps back down the hallway when he realized Eryl was following him.

"You're up to something," Eryl said with a grin.

Coming to a stop, Chad turned to his brother and said quietly so his mother wouldn't hear, "No I'm not. Now go away."

"Can I come?" he asked.

"What?" Chad replied. "Of course not."

"Aha!" exclaimed Eryl in victory. "I knew it!"

"I'm not doing anything," he insisted in a quiet voice.

"Then why are you talking so quietly," countered Eryl. "Why don't you want mother to hear you?" Then raising his voice loudly, he asked, "Because you'll get into trouble?"

"Shhh!" urged Chad as he glanced down the hallway towards the kitchen. When their mother failed to make an appearance, Chad sighed.

"I'm coming too," Eryl said. "Or I'll tell mother."

Chad gazed into his eyes and could see the mischievous look that always foreshadowed him doing something that Chad would hate. Little brothers, sisters too for that matter, always have a way to annoy their older siblings. Giving in, Chad said, "Alright. But you have to do what I say."

"You bet," agreed Eryl. Happy and excited now that he wrangled his brother into taking him along on whatever adventure he was planning, Eryl practically danced in anticipation.

"Just be quiet until we get out of the house," Chad told him. When he received Eryl's nod, he began heading back down the hallway. At the entrance to the kitchen, he paused momentarily to make sure his mother was still busy, then he and Eryl hurried past.

Bart looked questioningly at him when he and Eryl showed up at the barn together. "He's coming with us," Chad explained.

"I don't think it's wise to take him all the way to Wardean," Bart said.

"Wardean?" Eyes alight with the prospect of going to such a large town, he turned to his brother. "Is that where we're going?"

"With just you missing," Bart said, "your parents would only be a little worried. But him?" Indicating Eryl he added, "They'll be positively frantic."

"If we don't take him, he'll tell my mother and then the whole thing would be off," Chad countered.

Bart rolled his eyes heavenward. "Sibling blackmail." Then he turned his attention back to Chad and said, "At least leave them a note or something so they won't worry."

"Alright," agreed Chad. Getting a fairly smooth board from the scrap pile, he wrote in charcoal:

Went for a ride with Bart, took Eryl. Back after dark.

When he showed it to Bart he asked, "Will this do?"

Nodding, Bart replied. "Yes. But there will still be hell to pay when you get back."

"Not if the stone is fixed I won't," he said.

"What's going on?" asked Eryl.

Chad turned to his younger brother and said, "I'll fill you in on the way." Then he and Bart mounted the horses then Chad gives his brother a hand in swinging up behind him. They rode quickly from the house and entered the hills surrounding Quillim until they intersected the road.

Once on the road heading out of town they were soon up to a canter and Quillim disappeared behind them. Eryl was having the time of his life riding behind his brother. In all his seven years, the times he had been more than a couple miles from home could be counted on one hand. And to top it off, his parent's were not with them. All he had to deal with was his brother. Chad, even with all his older brother bossiness, was still a whole lot better to deal with than his mother and father would be. They rarely let him have any fun.

Chad filled him in on what they planned to do soon after they were on the main road that traveled north and south along the foothills of the Western Mountains. This road was very well maintained and they were able to make good time.

As the sun arced overhead, Bart knew they were never going to make it to Wardean and back by sundown. Or even remotely close to sundown. But that wasn't what was on his mind as they drew ever closer to the city of Wardean. His past was a tangled skein, and some of the worst of it had to do with the city they were heading toward.

Before he came to live in Quillim, he had vowed to himself never to set foot within the walls of Wardean again. Yet here he is, on his way. With any luck, they'll be able to get in and out without anyone the wiser.

It was an hour away from sundown when the walls of Wardean came into view. They had pushed their horses hard to try and reach the city before the sun went down. For that's when Bart said Phyndyr closed his shop.

"There she is," Bart said as they rode closer.

"Wow," said Eryl in wonder. He had never been to a city this large. Whenever his father had business here, he always took either Chad or his other brother Tye. "Isn't this where Tye is seeing about his apprenticeship?"

"That's right," Chad replied. "I wish we had time to visit."

"Why don't we?" his brother asked.

"Need to return home before mother and father worry too much," he explained. "We're already away longer than I had anticipated."

"Too bad," he said.

Beyond the wall they saw the Keep of the Border Lord where it sat like an indomitable fortress. Wardean is the Seat of Duke Yoric, the Border Lord given the task of keeping the goblins on their side of the mountains.

Bart took the lead when they reached the gates leading into the city. "Unless there is trouble nearby they keep the gates open throughout the night," he explained.

"What kind of trouble could there be?" asked Eryl.

"Oh, goblins for the most part," he replied. "Though ever since Duke Yoric became the Border Lord hereabouts, they've been fairly quiet. Haven't been seen on this side of the mountains for years."

Once through the gates, Bart led them quickly through the streets. The light was fading fast and if they didn't get there in time, they risked the unpleasant choice of either staying the night or returning home empty handed. "It isn't far," Bart said as they turned off the main thoroughfare and down a side street.

Half a block down, Bart indicated a two story building coming up on their left. It looked rather formidable, with only slits for windows that were far too narrow for even a small child to squeeze through. The face of the building had but a lone door that stood open. Thick and strong, it would take a lot of punishment before it failed.

Bart noticed the way they were looking at the building. He cracked a smile and said, "It's protected by magic too," he replied. "Only one thief has ever tried to sneak in since it was built."

"And what happened to him?" Chad asked.

"The exact details no one talks about," he told them. Dismounting, he turned to glance at them and said, "But there's a skull over the door on the inside that is rumored to belong to the thief."

"Really?" asked Eryl.

"So the story goes," Bart replied. He wrapped his horse's reins to the post out front and then waited for the two brothers to dismount and do the same. Then he turned and led them up to the open door.

Just as they reached the door, a middle aged man appeared from the other side. "Oh I'm sorry," the man said when he saw them approaching, "but I am closing now. You'll have to come back in the morning."

"Couldn't you stay open for just a few more minutes?" asked Bart with a grin.

Phyndyr turned his head towards Bart and was just about to tell him 'no' when he stopped. "Well, Bartholomew Agreani, as I live and breathe," he said in astonishment as a smile came to his face. "I haven't seen you for over a year."

"Good to see you too Phyndyr," replied Bart. He then indicated Chad and said, "My friend here is in dire need of a scroll to fix a cracked grinding wheel for his father's mill up in Quillim."

"Quillim?" he asked. "Is that where you've been?"

"Sort of," he replied. "Now, can you help him?"

"Oh, very well," he said. Stepping back into the building he allowed Bart, Chad and Eryl to enter. Then he closed the door and locked it. With a single word he caused a dozen candles set about the room to burst into light.

"Wow," exclaimed Eryl. "Are you a magic user?"

Phyndyr smiled at the boy. "Not really, no. I just know a few simple cantrips."

They found themselves in an average sized room with three wooden tables, each surrounded by six chairs, spaced evenly around the room. Another door leads from the room across from the one they had just passed through. Eryl turned to look above the front door and saw a human skull mounted there. His eyes widened then he glanced to Bart who just grinned.

Phyndyr indicated the closest table and said, "Have a seat." He sat down on one side of the table while the three boys sat on the other. Turning his attention to Chad, he asked, "What exactly do you require?"

"Last night there was an earthquake," he explained. "It was pretty bad and when we went to the mill in the morning, we found a crack in the upper grinding wheel. Bart told me you might have a scroll that would repair the crack?"

Phyndyr nodded. "I have several such scrolls that could possibly help you young man." He then began asking questions about the size of the wheel, the length of the crack, and so forth. When he finished the questioning, he grew silent for a moment.

"Can you help him?" Bart asked.

"I think so," he replied. "You three stay here," he told them as he got to his feet.

They watched him cross the room and pass through the door leading further into the building. "Phyndyr's pretty nice," Bart said as they waited.

"He seems to know you fairly well," Chad replied questioningly.

"I've known him since I was no older than Eryl," he explained. "He and my father go way back."

Chad looked to him to expand further on the details, but he remained silent.

Just then, Phyndyr exited from the back with a scroll in his hand. "You're in luck," he told them as he came and sat back down at the table. "Usually it takes a day or two to have a specific scroll ready. But seeing as how I am training a new apprentice, I have a few scrolls lying around. He's been practicing on various different Peasant Scrolls." He placed the scroll on the table between them.

"Peasant Scrolls?" asked Eryl.

Phyndyr smiled and turned to the young boy. "There are three types of scrolls young man, Peasant, Noble, and King," he explained. "Don't ask me why they are named that, they just are. Been that way for as long as there has been a Scriber's Guild."

Bart turned to Eryl and said, "Peasant Scrolls are the simplest types of scrolls there are."

Phyndyr nodded. "That's right."

"So what does it do?" Chad asked as he looked at the scroll lying on the table before him.

"It's quite simple really," Phyndyr said. He taps the top of the scroll gently. "This scroll is designed to repair cracks in masonry, such as bridges, walls, or anything else made of stone."

"How do you use it?" Eryl asked. His eyes were wide and full of wonder at the magic scroll sitting before him.

Phyndyr turned his attention to Chad and said, "First you place it on top of the cracked grinding wheel then say the word to activate it."

"What's the word?" asked Chad.

Phyndyr looked at him and smiled. "I can't tell you the word or it will activate the scroll."

"Then how am I to learn what the word is?" he asked.

"I will tell it to you in two parts," he explained. "First I will tell you the last half of the word, then I will tell you the first half of the word. When you are ready to activate the scroll, you simply put the two parts together in the correct order and say the word." He glanced to Chad and asked, "Understand?"

Chad nodded. "Yes."

"Good. The last half of the activation word is,—nyx," he said.

"-nyx?" replied Chad, trying to pronounce it just like Phyndyr did.

"That's right," Phyndyr said. "The first half is crit-."

"Crit-," pronounced Chad.

"Critnyx?" asked Eryl aloud. Suddenly, the scroll before them flared with a yellow glow, it lasted for half a second then went out. As the glow disappeared, the scroll crumbled into dust.

"Eryl!" cried Chad. "You wasted our scroll!"

"There, there," interjected Phyndyr in a calming manner. "I do have another."

Eryl turned towards the others with eyes aglow with excitement. He had activated the scroll. He had done magic! "That was so cool!"

"Do it again and I'll leave you here in Wardean," threatened Chad. Then he looked to the table and noticed that it appeared the same as it had before the scroll was activated. "Nothing happened to the table," he observed.

"Of course not," replied Phyndyr. "The scroll was for stone, not wood."

"Oh, right" said Chad. "How much is this going to cost me?"

Phyndyr put his finger into the dust that once was the scroll as he said, "A gold and three silvers."

"For one scroll?" asked Bart. "I didn't think it would be that much."

"The price is for two," Phyndyr clarified for them as he picked up a pinch of the dust on the table.

"Very well," Chad sighed. After giving his brother a stern glare for making him pay for an additional scroll, he pulled out his coin pouch and removed the required coins. Once they were on the table, Phyndyr collected them and then returned to the back for the other scroll.

Chad turned to his brother while they were waiting for Phyndyr and asked, "I trust we won't lose another scroll? I don't have enough for a third."

"I promise I won't say Critnyx," Eryl assured him.

"Don't say that!" exclaimed Bart and Chad at the same time.

Another minute went by before Phyndyr returned with the scroll. "This is my last one," he told them. "Be a bit more careful with it than the first one."

"Thank you," Chad said. "We will." He took the scroll and put it in his tunic for safe keeping. Standing up, he said, "I appreciate you staying and helping us."

"Not at all," Phyndyr replied. "Always glad to help out a friend." Then to Bart he said, "Don't be such a stranger. Stop by from time to time."

"I will," Bart assured him. "But we need to be going. It's a long road home."

"Surely you're not going to ride back to Quillim tonight are you?" he asked.

"We have no choice," replied Bart. "They need to get the grinding wheel fixed as soon as possible."

"Good luck to you then and safe journey." Standing up, he walked with them to the door.

"Thank you again Phyndyr," Bart said and then they left him at the door. Once out at their horses, they were soon in the saddle and headed down the street towards the gate.

Phyndyr watched them ride off before he turned and locked the door. When he turned back to the street to head home, he saw a figure detach from the shadows of the building across the street. Once the figure left the shadows, he readily recognized the man. He also understood why the man was crossing the street towards him.

"Good evening to you," Phyndyr said as the figure approached.

"And to you, Master Scriber," the man replied.

"My shop is closed," Phyndyr said. "I am on my way home."

"I'm not interested in your scrolls as well you know," the man told him. "I saw Bartholomew leave your shop?" It was less a question than a statement of fact.

Phyndyr sighed and nodded.

"Did he tell you where he was going?" the man asked.

He gazed at the man and decided whether he should tell him or not. To cross the man before him, or rather the people he represented, wasn't conducive to a long and happy life. If it were but himself on the line, he wouldn't have cared. But with a wife and three children at home, he couldn't afford the trouble such defiance would bring them, even if it meant betraying a friend.

Then slowly, he nodded.

"Where did he go?" asked the man.

It was almost more than he could do to say the word, "Quillim."

Chapter 6

By the time they made it back to Quillim, the night was almost gone. Off to the east, dawn's first light had begun to creep back into the world and the town lay quiet in the burgeoning morning. As they made their way through the streets to the mill, the only sound to disturb the silence was the clip-clop of their horses' hooves and the occasional cry of a dog.

Chad reached around and shook his brother awake, he had fallen asleep behind him some time ago. "We're back," he told him. He felt his brother pull himself up from where he had been lying against his back for the last few hours.

"Hope it works," Eryl said sleepily.

"It will," he replied.

As they continued to work their way through town, Chad thought about how worried his parents had to have been. His note only said they would be back a little after dark, not the next morning. But once the stone has been fixed, all would be forgiven.

Out of the dark ahead, the giant arms of the mill came into view. They turned slowly in an early morning breeze. "Want me to come in with you?" Bart asked.

"Yeah," replied Chad, "I'd like that."

Bart nodded and together the three of them rode to the mill and dismounted before the front door. "Eryl," Chad said, "watch the horses."

"But I want to come in too," he pleaded.

"Just stay out here," his brother told him. Eryl didn't look too happy but nodded and did as his brother wished.

Then with Bart, he entered the mill. Chad lit a candle that was sitting on a small table just within the doorway to dispel the darkness. When the light filled the mill, he saw where his father had already begun to dismantle the frame that held the upper grinding stone in place. Wooden sections of the frame were stacked in a neat pile against the side of the mill.

He took out the scroll and walked to the grinding wheels. "Place it over the cracked area," suggested Bart.

"Yeah, I was going to do that," he replied. Moving around the stones, he located the area with the crack and placed the scroll on top of it. Stepping back, he glanced to Bart with a grin. Then he turned his attention back to the scroll and said the activating word, "Critnyx".

The scroll flared with a yellow glow just as the other one had back in Phyndyr's. Only this time, the stone began to glow with the same yellow hue. Chad and Bart moved closer to better observe as the crack in the stone began to fuse together. The glow continued for a few more seconds after the crack was completely mended, then it went out.

"It worked!" he hollered in jubilation.

"Of course it worked," Bart said. "Phyndyr's scrolls always work."

Chad caught movement out of the corner of his eye and turned to see Eryl standing in the doorway. "The stone is mended little brother," he said triumphantly.

Eryl stood there staring at the grinding stone without responding. The look on his face was not one of happiness or jubilation, rather it was a look of trepidation. "Chad ..." he said then grew silent again.

"What?" his brother asked, his own good mood beginning to be dampened by that of his brother.

"The stones," he said and pointed to the grinding wheel.

Chad looked at the stone but couldn't see anything wrong. "It all looks okay to me," he said.

Bart stepped back and that's when his face fell too. His eyes flicked to Chad. Grabbing his tunic, Bart pulled Chad back away from the stone so he could see it in its entirety.

"Oh my lord," he breathed when realization finally came. The scroll had worked alright, but it had worked too well. When he had activated the scroll, its magic had worked to seek out and repair any cracks in the stone. Somehow the magic must have considered the gap between the bottom stone and the top as a crack as well, for the crack had been 'fixed'. The two stones were now fused together.

"What are we going to do?" Chad asked. Crestfallen and in fear of what his father will do to him, he stood there and began to tremble.

"He's going to kill you," Eryl said. Not in the literal meaning, but Chad's life won't be worth spit when his father learned about this. Not only had he gone against his father's wishes, but he made the situation worse.

Chad collapsed into a nearby chair and stared at the single massive wheel. An errant breeze blew through the mill and some of the dust that once had been the scroll was picked up and carried away. Visions of his family destitute and impoverished because of this played through his mind. He had only wanted to help.

Then from outside, footsteps could be heard approaching. Eryl stuck his head out the door to see who it was and brought it back in quickly. Turning to look at Chad with a frightened expression on his face he said, "It's father."

"Man you've got to get out of here," encouraged Bart.

"Come on Chad," Eryl said as he raced across to the door in the back.

Shaking his head, Chad said, "No. I can't run from this." He then turned to Bart and his brother. "You two shouldn't be here though." As the footsteps drew ever nearer, he pantomimed them leaving and said in a hushed whisper, "Now!"

Bart nodded and with Eryl leading the way, they left a split second before Chad's father entered the mill.

His father's face upon seeing him was one of elation as he had been worried about him all night long. Bags under his eyes showed that he hadn't had any sleep. Chad stood up and turned to face his father. Bracing himself for what was to come he said, "Father ..."

Riyan had pushed the flock relentlessly all the way home. The coin he had found was a constant companion as he continued staring at it, rubbing his fingers over it, and dreamt of the untold wealth that lay buried in a passage no man had trod in for ages.

At some point he came to the realization that if there were enough down there, he might be able to change the mind of Freya's father. If he were rich enough, he was sure that the betrothal between Rupert and Freya would be annulled in favor of him.

He knew that he had some time before they would get married, as custom dictated that the betrothal must last a minimum of three months. That was to give the prospective couple a chance to get to know each other, and for their families to ensure this was in fact a good match. Though a broken betrothal was an extreme humiliation to the one being left and should only be undertaken under the direst of circumstances.

Quillim came into sight around midafternoon. The sheep had been voicing all morning their desire to stop and graze. He allowed them two brief stops to assuage their hunger, then it was back to the trail.

He angled the flock to skirt the town until he came to his home. When the sheep saw that they were to be put into the pen, they complained most heartily. Black Face was the worst. After all the others had gone into the pen, he bolted for freedom. Riyan had to chase him down and carry him back. Once Black Face was in the pen with the others, he shut and locked the gate.

"You're back early," his mother said as she came up behind him.

He turned to find her with a basket full of roots and leaves that have been a staple of their diet for as long as he could remember. Smiling, he replied, "I got over it and realized I didn't really want to be alone."

All the way back he had debated about whether to tell his mother of his discovery or not. He finally decided that she would only worry and that it would be best to come home with the treasure in hand before informing her.

When he saw her arc her eyebrows in question, he added, "Thought about going for a campout with Chad and Bart. Don't worry," he said before she could start objecting, "I can get Davin to watch the flock while I'm gone. He owes me."

Just then Chad's brother Eryl appeared running towards him. "You're back!" he exclaimed.

"Figured that out did you?" joked Riyan. Then he noticed how Eryl's eyes were red rimmed and bloodshot. His mood sobering quickly, he asked, "What's wrong?"

"Father's kicked Chad out!" he said.

"What?" Riyan asked in disbelief. "Why?"

Then Eryl went into the story of how the earthquake damaged the grinding wheel and of Chad's idea in fixing it. Finally, he wound it up with the two grinding wheels becoming fused together and his father kicking Chad out. "He's staying with Bart right now," he explained.

Riyan turned to his mother and said, "I better go see him." He gave her a quick kiss and then rushed off towards where Bart stayed with old lady Rebecca.

Eryl accompanied him for a short time until he saw Rupert and his cronies standing against the side of a building talking up ahead. When he saw them, he mumbled some excuse to Riyan then bolted the other way.

Riyan saw them too and altered his course to put more distance between them.

"Hey!" he heard on the cronies yell. "Look who's back!" Then Rupert moved away from the wall and hurried to meet him.

Riyan could see the set of his face and knew the meeting was going to be bad. So he altered his course even further and ran as fast as he could in an attempt to flee.

"Stop, Riyan!" Rupert yelled at him but he ignored the command. Instead, he tried to move even faster.

Then all of a sudden, something struck the back of his legs. Losing his balance, he fell to the ground and hit hard. In a second, they were on him. Fists struck and feet kicked as he curled himself up into a ball in an attempt to keep the blows from doing any serious damage.

"You keep your nose out from between me and Freya!" Rupert yelled as he kicked him even harder.

Several more blows landed before they stopped. Riyan looked up at his tormentors and saw Rupert standing there, staring down at him. "You meddle in this again and I'll kill you," Rupert threatened. "Do I make myself clear?"

Riyan wasn't sure what he was talking about and was trying to make sense of it in his mind. Then another kick struck his back as a crony said, "He asked you a question."

"Yes!" he cried. "I understand."

"Good," Rupert said. "Let's go boys." Then he and the others left him lying there in the street as they walked off.

Riyan felt something trickling out of his nose and wiped it with his hand only to discover it was blood. Looking around, he saw several townsfolk standing there watching. When his eyes met theirs, they lowered theirs to the ground and moved off. Not one of them came and offered him any aid.

He pushed himself off the ground and back to his feet. Checking his nose again, he found the blood had stopped flowing. He did a quick self examine and found nothing broken, but he's sure that he'll feel it tomorrow. Moving off, he resumed his trek to Bart's place, albeit this time at a much more moderate pace.

When he arrived at old lady Rebecca's, he found Chad and Bart working to dig out an old stump. They stopped when they saw him coming. Throwing down their shovels, they ran over to him.

"What happened to you?" Bart asked when he saw the state he was in. Hair disheveled, a bruise beginning to form on his arm, and dried blood around his nose all said something bad had happened.

"Ran into Rupert," he explained.

"Man I'm sorry about that," he replied.

"It's not your fault," Riyan assured him.

"Well, actually it is," Bart said. Then he went into a brief explanation of the escapade he and Chad had undergone to mess with Rupert. "If I would have known this was going to happen, I never would have done it."

Riyan grinned and said, "If you caused him any anxious moments, it was worth it." Then he turned to Chad. "Ran into Eryl."

"Oh, you heard then?" he asked.

Riyan nodded. "What exactly happened?"

His tale and the one Riyan had heard from Eryl were pretty much the same until he came to the part when his father entered the mill. "When he saw the two fused slabs, I thought I was dead," he admitted. "He even went so far as to ball his fist like he was going to strike me, which is something he's never done."

He went silent a moment and Riyan could see the emotions running through him as he gathered the words to continue. When he turned sad eyes that were welling tears towards him, he said, "Then my father looked like he just deflated. I don't know how else to describe it. It almost seemed like the life went out of him."

"I was expecting an argument, even a beating, but not that." His voice grew very quiet as he said, "He didn't even look at me. Just turned his back and walked out." Tears began to well in earnest as he internally relived the experience. "I tried to follow but he just shook his head. 'Leave, Chad,' he said. 'Just go.'"

Emotions took over and he couldn't continue. Neither Riyan nor Bart knew what to do other than stand there and wait until it was over. "I was waiting outside when he came out," Bart told him. "Later, I took him back to his home so he could reconcile things, but his father wouldn't even talk to him. His mother came out and told him that his father didn't want him around anymore. Frankly I couldn't understand his father's reaction." He glanced to Riyan and added, "It seemed a bit too extreme."

"I can't go home!" Chad cried out. Grabbing onto Riyan he asked, "What am I to do?"

Bart looked at Riyan over Chad's shoulder and said, "I offered to let him stay here. Rebecca won't mind."

Riyan placed his hand on his friend's shoulder and said, "Don't worry. I'm sure that once your father has had a chance to cool down, he'll reconsider."

"So do I," agreed Bart. "Maybe you need to get out of town for awhile, give him some time to get over it. The heat of the moment is never a good time to settle anything. My father always said, 'Hot heads lead to anger, cool minds lead to reason'."

Riyan nodded. "True words." He then glanced to Chad then to Bart, "Why don't we go on a camping trip? Give your father the time he'll need to cool down."

"That might not be a bad idea," agreed Bart. Patting Chad on the back, he asked, "How about it?"

Shrugging, Chad said, "Sure. It's not like I have anything else to do anymore."

"Great!" said Riyan. "Just get your things and we'll head out right away."

Chad's face fell again when he realized he'll have to go to his home to get his camping equipment. Turning to Bart, he asked, "Can you go find Eryl and have him get my stuff? I don't think it would be wise for me to return."

"No problem," he agreed.

Riyan then said, "Chad, why don't you return with me to my home and we'll wait for Bart there?"

"Okay, sure," he replied.

"Meet you there," Bart told them. "Need to tell Rebecca she'll have to wait another couple of days before I can work on the stump again. I'll be at your place as quickly as I can."

It took Bart the better part of an hour before he arrived at Riyan's home, Eryl was with him. Eryl had managed to sneak out all the things Chad would need for a campout; bedroll, cooking pots, bowls, etc. He even managed to bring along a lantern.

"Thanks Eryl," he said. "Is father any better?"

Shaking his head, he replied, "No. I've never seen him like this before."

Sighing, Chad grabbed his brother and held him a moment. Eryl looked stunned, maybe even on the verge of panic at this display of affection. Quickly disengaging himself, he said, "I wish I could go with you, but I think it would be better for me to stay around. That way I can remind father what a loss not having you around is going to be."

"I appreciate that," his brother said. "Just don't go overboard on it."

"I won't," he assured him. "I best be getting back, it's almost lunch."

"See ya," Chad said then watched as Eryl raced down the lane.

Riyan's mother had packed plenty of food for them and they distributed it among their three packs. Between them, they were taking two lanterns and two small bladders of lantern oil. The other two looked questioningly at Riyan but he just grinned and shrugged. "Never know what may happen," he explained. "One could break."

"You boys be careful now," Riyan's mother said. "And Chad, I'm sure your father will come to see reason before your return."

"I hope so," he replied.

Riyan shouldered his pack and announced, "Let's go. Found this new area while out with the sheep that I think you both are going to like."

As they headed out, Riyan gave his mother a peck on the cheek. Riyan brought his shepherd's staff for a walking stick, the other two didn't feel the need for one. They walked in silence until they entered the hills and Riyan's home disappeared behind them.

"I think this is just what I need," Chad said. Already his mood seemed to be improving.

"To tell you both the truth, I had planned on asking you two on a campout even before discovering what happened between you and your father Chad," Riyan said. He glanced around to make sure they were alone and pulled the coin he found out of his pouch. "What do you two make of this?"

He handed it first to Bart who looked it over then gave it to Chad. "Looks old," commented Bart. "I don't think I've ever seen similar markings on any other coin before."

Chad nodded. "Me either." After carefully looking at it, he handed it back to Riyan. "So where did you find it?"

"In a hole in the ground," he explained. He then went on to relate how he came to find it, the fact that there was a passage that led somewhere, and his hopes that it might yield treasure.

"There's no guarantee that there is anything of value there," argued Bart.

"No, that's true," admitted Riyan. "But, the coin was there. Where there is one, there could be more." Then he turned to Chad, "If there's enough, maybe you could give some to your father to help with the grinding stones."

"That would be great," agreed Chad. "He would have to forgive me then."

For the rest of the day they worked their way deeper into the mountains. Riyan continuously scanned for the landmarks he noted on his way out. One by one, they came into view to tell him that they were on the right course.

That night when the sun dipped towards the horizon, they stopped and made camp. "I think we'll be there sometime tomorrow morning," he announced while they were setting up camp. "Noon by the latest."

Once the fire was going, Riyan went in search of dinner and returned shortly with a rabbit and a wild fowl. The three friends spent the rest of the evening enjoying each other's company and trying to figure out what kind of treasure they would find tomorrow.

As the shadows grew long and the people began returning to their homes, a stranger entered the quiet town of Quillim. Strangers as a rule were not too uncommon here in Quillim, it being but a short ride from the main road running north and south. Quite often travelers would cross the river running between the town and the main road to seek lodging for the night.

This stranger was no different. The first place he went was to the Sterling Sheep where he acquired a room. When asked how long he would be staying, the stranger replied that he wasn't sure and paid for three nights up front. This of course made the innkeeper quite happy.

Later that night when the common room filled with diners and others who just came to hear the bard play, the stranger was found among them. A quiet individual who sat with his back against the wall, his eyes seemed to take in and examine everyone who entered. At one point, he waved over the serving woman. When she arrived at his table, he asked her, "I was wondering if you could help me?"

She gave him a smile and replied, "Sure, that's what I'm here for."

Returning her smile, he said, "I was wondering if you might know of a friend of mine. Last I had heard, he was moving to this area but have since forgotten the town to which he was moving."

"What was your friend's name?" she asked.

"Bartholomew Agreani," he told her. "Ever heard of him?"

"I know of a Bart," she replied. "Never heard what his last name was though. I think he came here about a year ago."

"He's a young man, brown hair and just under six feet tall," he said.

She nodded. "That sounds like him."

"Do you know where I could find him?" he asked.

"I think he works out at old Rebecca's farm," she replied.

"Could you tell me where I could find it?"

"Oh sure," she replied then gave him the directions to the farm. Just then, another customer hollered for her assistance and she said, "Hope I've been of help."

"Yes you have my dear," the stranger assured her. "Thank you very much."

As she walked over to see what the other customer needed, the stranger sat back in his chair, took his mug in hand, and smiled.

Chapter 7

It took the entire morning and the better part of the afternoon before Riyan found the clearing he was looking for. It was surprising how many different areas in these hills looked exactly the same. And after finding the 'area' three times, the others were beginning to wonder if he would ever be able to locate it.

He knew he finally found it when he crossed a stream and saw a mass of berry vines with an area of the outer fringe cut back. "There it is," he said as he led them towards the opening. Coming to a stop before the hole in the ground, he turned back to the others and grinned.

"That's it?" Bart asked. Staring down into the black hole, he said, "Doesn't look like much."

"Maybe not from up here," Riyan replied. "But at the bottom of the hole is a passage that moves off to the right and left.

"What are we waiting for?" asked Chad. He unslung his backpack and laid it on the ground a little bit away from the opening.

"Shouldn't leave our equipment out here," Bart said. "We wouldn't want a wild animal taking off with something." When the other two turned toward him he added, "Our packs are full of food after all."

Seeing the wisdom in what he was saying, Chad picked up his pack.

Riyan moved to the edge of the opening. He then sat on the edge with his legs extended within. While visions of chests, crypts, and hordes of gold ran wild through his mind, he scooted into the opening.

The other two watched as he disappeared into the hole. A couple seconds later they heard him holler from where he came to land down below, "Come on down!"

Chad glanced to Bart who grinned. "You first," he offered.

"Alright," agreed Bart who cautiously approached, then entered the hole. Once he slid to the bottom, he found Riyan there already working on getting the lantern lit. By the time the wick was burning and illuminating the passage, Chad had joined them.

With the lantern in one hand, Riyan moved down the passage to the right until he reached the spot where he had found the coin. Turning back to the others he pointed to the floor. "That's where I found the coin," he said. The lantern's light revealed his footprints from his earlier time down here.

Bart nodded and then looked closely at the walls. He saw how they showed the unmistakable signs of human construction. "This place is old," he observed.

"How old do you think?" Chad asked.

"I don't know," he replied. "But giving that none of us are familiar with the markings on the coin, I doubt if anyone's been down here for several hundred years." Then he glanced at Chad. "Maybe longer."

"There could be anything down here!" exclaimed Riyan.

"True," Bart agreed. "But I would advise caution. There's no telling what safeguards the previous occupants could have put into place."

"You mean traps?" Chad asked.

Bart nodded. "Exactly."

A worried look came over Chad as he glanced towards the floor of the passage leading away.

"Don't worry," said Bart. "I doubt if there would be anything in the middle of the passage."

"But let's be careful anyway," Riyan added. Taking the lead, he moved down the passage to the right. They didn't get very far before coming to where another narrower passage branched off to their left. When they reached it, they found that it curved back around further to the left.

Riyan brought them to a halt and glanced back at the others. "Which way?" he asked. The excitement of the moment making him almost giddy.

"Take the smaller passage to the left," suggested Chad. "It's narrower so may not be a main passage."

Nodding, Riyan entered the new passage. Barely wide enough for a grown man to pass through without scraping his shoulders, it continued to curve back around to the left until it was running parallel to the passage they had just left. As the passage finished the curve and straightened out, they saw where it ended at an open entryway leading into what had to be a room.

In his excitement, Riyan hurried to the entryway and passed through to the other side. The room he found himself in was only about fifteen feet by ten. A stone sarcophagus sat in the center of the room indicating they were in a burial chamber. The walls were plain, unadorned stone similar to that which was used in lining the passages.

"Wow," Riyan breathed under his breath as he came to stand next to the sarcophagus. He ran his hand across the top as he took in the ancient inscriptions engraved within the stone.

"We must be in an ancient catacomb," Chad observed, eyes lighting up. "They often bury gold and jewels with the dead."

Bart nodded. "Let's get it open," he said indicating the sarcophagus.

"Do you think that's wise?" asked Riyan. "I mean, stealing from the dead is supposed to be bad luck."

Shrugging, Bart replied, "It's up to you. We could always come back if there's nothing else down here."

"Yeah," agreed Riyan, "that might be a better idea. If there was a chest or something in the room with it, that's one thing, but to take something from the dead itself?" A shiver coursed through him at the very thought.

"Then let's go find something else," urged Chad.

"Wait a second," Bart said as something caught his eye from the other side of the sarcophagus. He moved around the sarcophagus and reached down to pick up another of the coins. He grinned as he held it up for the others to see.

"It's exactly like the other one I found," Riyan exclaimed.

"Yes it is," nodded Bart. He put it in his pouch and then indicated for Riyan to lead the way from the room.

Once they passed through the narrow passage and were back in the main one, he turned and continued down they way they had previously been heading. It wasn't long before the passage they were following ended at a 'T' junction. Riyan paused momentarily to shine the light from the lantern down the left, then to the right. Both directions extended further than the light could reach. Riyan decided to take the right.

The new passage was exactly like the one they had just left, and it too ended in a 'T' junction not too far down. This time however, the passages to the right and left were narrower, just as the curving passage leading to the room with the sarcophagus had been.

Again he chose the right and hurried along. The narrow passage extended straight ahead for a short span then turned abruptly to the right. As Riyan turned the corner, he saw an entryway to another burial chamber. Moving forward, he passed through into the room and gasped.

No sarcophagus within this room. Rather, within the walls on the right and left sides of the room, were stone biers. Laid out upon each of the stone biers was a corpse. Both of them had been dressed in armor, yet time had reduced the armor to nothing more than rust. Skeletal faces looked out from within the helms they wore.

But it wasn't the sight of the dead that made Riyan gasp. Rather it was the chests that sat on the floor beneath each of them. "Oh man," he said with renewed excitement. Moving forward to the chest on the right, he set the lantern down as he gripped the lid. But try as he might, he couldn't get it open. The chest was locked. Behind him, Chad was trying the other chest only to find that it too was locked.

Riyan stood up disappointed and said, "It's locked."

"So is this one," Chad said.

Bart took off his pack and set it on the floor. He opened it and pulled out a rolled piece of leather. Holding it up, he glanced to Riyan and grinned. "I may be able to do something about that." Leaving his pack on the ground, he carried the rolled piece of leather and moved to the chest where he knelt down before it. He then untied the thong securing the piece of leather and set it on the ground next to the chest.

Riyan watched as he unrolled it. Within were small tools ranging in size from two to four inches in length. "What are you going to do with those?" he asked.

"You've never seen lockpicks before?" Bart asked.

"No," replied Riyan.

"Can't you be arrested for just having them in your possession?" asked Chad.

"So I've heard," he replied. Taking out two of the tools, he inserted their tips within the lock and began working the tumblers inside. After a few moments, he felt the 'click' that always accompanied the unlocking of the lock. He then replaced his tools in the rolled leather before taking hold of the lid and opening it.

Inside was what had to have once been several weapons but were now nothing more than piles of rust. Riyan held the lantern close to better see the interior in the hopes of there being treasure. After sifting through the rusty remains, they came up with nothing.

"Try the other one," suggested Chad.

Bart nodded and picked up his lockpicks and crossed the room to work on the other chest. Then just as before with the first one, he felt the 'click' and lifted open the lid.

Inside this chest were the rusted remains of weapons, similar to the ones that had been in the first chest. But this time, there were several stacks of the coins they found earlier. "There must be twenty or so of them!" Riyan exclaimed excitedly. After pulling them out and counting them, they discovered there were twenty four. Riyan divided them among himself and the others. Each put eight coins in their packs.

"Wonder how much they're worth?" Chad asked as they were leaving the tomb.

"If you consider just the copper used in making them, not much," explained Bart. "But due to their age, certain people would be willing to pay more for them."

"Excellent." Riyan gave them all a grin as they returned to the 'T' junction. He then crossed over to the other narrow passage and began making his way through. After going straight for a short span, the passage turned back to the left and they came to another tomb with two biers, one on each side of the room.

Just as in the previous room, the dead were arrayed in rusted armor and a chest sat on the floor beneath them. Again, the chests were locked and Bart used his lockpicks to get them open. This time they found thirty of the coins and two small gems among the rusted remains of ancient weapons. They got quite excited about the gems until Bart explained they were rather common and wouldn't bring much gold. Riyan didn't care, he was having the time of his life.

They left the room and returned to the 'T' junction where they turned and followed the wider passage back the way they came. Once they returned to the first 'T' junction of the two main passages, they continued on past the passage leading back to the hole out to the surface.

They came to another 'T' junction with two narrow passages leading right and left to two more crypts. These also each held two stone biers upon which the dead were laid out, with matching chests below.

The first room of the new pair yielded eighteen of the coins. Riyan was slightly disappointed at not finding more. "You can't expect more treasure with each room we come to," Bart said. "Frankly, I'm surprised to have found what we already have."

"I know," replied Riyan.

They left the room behind and went to check out the room on the other side of the 'T'. When Bart went to pick the lock of the first chest, he paused.

"What?" asked Chad.

Bart tapped an area near the lock. It had a marking on it that didn't blend in perfectly with the overall design of the chest. "I didn't see this on the other ones," he explained.

Riyan moved the lantern closer and saw what looked to him little more than scratches. "So?" he asked.

"This may indicate a trap of some kind," he said as he turned to glance up at them.

"Why would you think that?" asked Chad.

"Just something my father told me one time," he replied. "You see, chests such as these that are trapped, often have some marking on them telling the owner what kind of trap it holds."

"That's stupid," scorned Chad. "I mean, wouldn't that give a thief an idea that something is not right?"

"Yes," agreed Bart. "But most chest makers who specialize in traps always put an unobtrusive mark on it so they'll know what it is and how to disarm it. Just because I know it's there, doesn't mean I can disarm it."

"But why would they do that?" Riyan asked.

Sighing, Bart stood up and turned towards them. "Suppose you commissioned a chest for a specific purpose and with a specific type of trap. And suppose further that once you got it home you accidentally closed the lid and locked it before whatever you wanted to put in it was inside. How are you going to get it back open?"

"I would think the chest maker would have given the owner instructions on how to open it," said Chad.

"Oh they do," agreed Bart, "but there are stupid people out there who forget, lose the instructions, etc. So chest makers put markings on each chest that holds a trap so if they are called out to open a trapped chest, they will be able to do so."

"I guess that makes sense," said Riyan.

"How do you know so much about this?" Chad asked.

Bart gave him a look, shook his head as he rolled his eyes, and then knelt back down in front of the chest.

"He's got lockpicks," Riyan informed his friend. "Who has lockpicks?"

"Thieves?" replied Chad.

"Or sons of thieves," added Bart. "Now be quiet and let me work on this. You two may wish to wait out in the passage, just in case something goes wrong."

Riyan nodded for Chad to join him as he moved out of the room and waited at the entryway. They watched as Bart first examined the outside of the chest very closely before scrutinizing the area around the lock. After a few tense moments, Bart placed the tips of his thumbs on either side of the keyhole and pressed. Then he turned to them and grinned, "I got it."

The other two hurried back into the room and saw a needle protruding from the keyhole. "It was a 'Prick of Poison' as my father would call it," he explained. "It's designed to prick the finger of the thief and deliver a poison of some kind. Some poisons become ineffective over time, while others grow more potent."

"Is it unlocked?" Chad asked.

Bart shook his head. "Not yet." Turning back to the chest, he removed the same two tools he used on the previous chests from his lockpicks and very carefully began working around the needle. Once he had the lock picked, he opened the lid.

Riyan moved closer to see what treasure may be inside. "You've got to be kidding!" he exclaimed when he saw the usual fare of rusted weapons and a scattering of the coins. "What's the point of putting a trap on this garbage?"

"Vanity maybe" replied Bart. "Or it could have been for some other reason. Who knows?"

"Seems a waste of time to trap this sort of stuff," Chad agreed with Riyan.

Riyan knelt down in front of the chest and said, "Maybe there's a secret compartment lining the bottom or top." Bart moved aside and then collected his lockpicks as he went to work on the other chest. Running his fingers along the inside, Riyan hunted for anything that might indicate something was hidden.

Remembering a tale told by a bard about treasure hunters, he tapped the bottom of the chest and the top. After several minutes of fruitless searching, he was unable to find anything. "Ten coins!" he exclaimed as he collected them. "Ten lousy coins!"

"It's better than nothing," offered Chad.

Riyan glared at him then came to his senses. "You're right," he said. "It's just that I was expecting something a bit more ..."

"Expensive?" his friend finished for him.

"Something like that, yeah" Riyan nodded.

Just then, Bart raised the lid of the other chest. "More coins," he told them. He did a quick count and said, "Twenty three."

"Every little bit helps," Chad said when he saw the disappointment in his friend's eyes.

Bart collected the coins then stood up. "You may have unrealistic expectations about this place," he said as he turned back towards Riyan. "Judging by the construction and the state of the dead, I would guess that finding something worth real gold is unlikely."

"Exactly," agreed Chad. "Let's hope we find at least enough so I can help my father with the new grinding wheels."

Riyan gave him a grin and laid his hand on his shoulder. "You got it," he said. "At the very least, we're living the dream of being treasure hunters."

"Just like the sagas," agreed Chad with a grin of his own.

"Onward fearless treasure hunters!" Riyan exclaimed then the three friends broke into laughter. They left the crypt and returned back the way they came until they reached the 'T' with the main passage leading down to where they entered this place.

"Pack's getting heavy," Chad said.

"You've only got about thirty coins in there," Bart told him. "If it gets too heavy, you can give me some of yours."

"That's okay," Chad assured him, "I'm sure I'll manage." Riyan laughed.

They left the 'T' behind them and headed down the passage back towards the hole in the ceiling through which they entered. When they passed the curving narrow passage that led to the sarcophagus, they knew they were almost there.

Then Bart all of a sudden came to an abrupt halt. The other two who were walking behind him stopped as well. "What?" asked Chad.

He pointed down the passage ahead of them and in a quiet whisper said, "Look." When the other two looked down the passage to where he was indicating, two red dots could be seen. They looked for all the world like a pair of eyes and they were staring right at them. Light filtering down from outside showed them the hole in the ceiling and the way out, unfortunately it was closer to the red eyes than it was to them.

"Back up slowly," Bart said as he began walking backwards. Riyan and Chad both started moving backwards as well when a god awful roar reverberated through the passage.

"Run!" yelled Bart as he turned around to flee. Behind them, they could hear the grunting of a large animal as it thundered towards them.

When the lantern's light revealed the curving passage coming up on their left, Chad got an idea and said, "Into the passage." Leading the others, he raced into the passage and followed it quickly to the room with the sarcophagus. "Help me with the lid!" he replied. Moving to the sarcophagus, he gripped the side of the lid and waited for the others to come and help.

"I can't do it by myself," he told them. "We can block the entryway with it!"

Getting the idea, Riyan and Bart each came and took hold of an edge. Then giving out with groans of strain, they lifted the heavy stone lid up and off the sarcophagus. "Man this is heavy," gasped Riyan.

From the narrow passage outside the room, they heard the growls of the beast as it worked its way towards them. "Hurry!" Chad exclaimed.

Once the end of the lid that was nearest the entryway was past the edge of the sarcophagus, they rested the lid on the edge and slid it the rest of the way to the floor. Out in the passage, the red eyes of the beast were now visible as it rounded the curve. The sheer size of the creature hampered it as it tried to navigate through the narrow way. It was wedged in on both sides and had to push its bulk through to get to them.

They worked the lid closer to the entryway. When it was within inches, they lifted the other end and set it against the top of the opening. "Now what?" asked Bart.

"I don't know," replied Chad. "My plan only went as far as blocking off the room."

Riyan glanced to the body that was lying within the sarcophagus. A sword lay along the top of the body, its hilt clasped in the corpse's skeletal hands. Perhaps it was the fact that it had been within a sealed sarcophagus, but the metal looked to have withstood the passage of time.

Bam!

The creature struck the other side of the lid where it blocked the entryway and almost knocked the lid back into the room. Chad and Bart put their shoulders against it to keep it upright.

Bam!

Again the creature struck the lid, this time a small piece of it broke off. "It's not going to withstand blows like that for much longer," Chad said.

"Oh yeah, this was a good idea," said Bart rather sarcastically.

"There was no other place to go," insisted Chad. Then he glanced back at where Riyan was bent over the sarcophagus. "Riyan, we could use your help right about now!"

"Just a second," replied Riyan. He gripped the hands of the corpse and was in the midst of trying to remove them from the hilt of the sword. Once he had the hilt free, he grabbed it and tried to lift it out with one hand. When he could barely move it, he used both hands and struggled to get it out.

The sword was massive, what you would call a two-handed sword. It took all of his strength simply to raise it and carry it towards the entryway. "Careful with that!" Bart exclaimed when the edge of the sword came close and almost struck him.

Riyan took the sword and moved to face the gap between the lid and the entryway. He saw the forepaw of the creature poke through for a moment before it withdrew. "I think it's a mountain bear," he told the others.

"Great," replied Bart. "Now kill it!"

Riyan lifted the sword until it was parallel with the ground. Then he aimed it at the gap between the lid and the entryway. He gave out with a cry and ran forward, at the same time he thrust the sword through the gap. His forward momentum was abruptly halted as the point of the sword struck flesh.

The beast roared in pain as the sword sank into its flesh. Whatever part of the body that was struck suddenly jerked and Riyan almost lost his grip on the hilt. But he yanked back quickly and retained the sword. The blade was stained red six inches from the tip. From the other side of the lid, the beast had grown quiet.

"I got it!" replied Riyan as he showed the others the sword.

"But whether you killed it or not remains to be seen," Bart stated.

They listened for a few seconds and could only hear muted breathing from the other side. Riyan propped the sword against the wall a foot down from the entryway as it was growing more difficult to hold.

"It isn't dead," Chad finally said as the sound the beast's breathing from the other side continued.

"Riyan," Bart whispered, "take a look." He then indicated the gap between the lid and the entryway through which he had struck the creature with the sword.

"Alright," he agreed. Leaving the sword where it was, he grabbed the lantern and moved towards the crack. The crack itself wasn't all that big as the base of the lid was only six inches from the base of the entryway. Now that he took a good look at it, he's surprised that he was even able to hit the creature through it.

He moved closer, and even got down on his knees to peer through to the other side better. Chad and Bart maintained their position against the sarcophagus' lid should the creature again try to bull its way in.

At the base of the entryway was a small pool of blood. "It's lost some blood," he told the others. Peering through with the lantern next to him, he tried to locate the creature. After a minute off looking, he backed away and said, "I can't really see anything."

"Try striking with the sword again," Bart said. "If it's close, you might hit it."

"But that might make it mad," Chad said.

Bart glanced to Chad. "Do you want to stay down here forever?" He waited for him to shake his head no then added, "It's that or we move the lid aside."

Chad turned to Riyan and said, "You better try the sword."

Riyan nodded, he didn't relish the idea of removing the protection the stone lid was affording them. So, taking up the sword again, he did just as he did the first time. He aimed the point of the sword for the crack and with a cry, thrust hard. The blade slid through the crack and failed to hit anything.

"I guess we're going to have to move the lid aside to see," he said after the failed attempt.

Bart nodded. "Stand ready," he told Riyan. Then to Chad he said, "We'll pull it back a little ways. But be ready should the beast move to attack again." When Chad acknowledged the plan, Bart glanced to Riyan. "Ready?"

Riyan raised the sword and nodded.

"Easy now," Bart told Chad. With great care, they began pulling the sarcophagus lid away from the entryway.

Sweat beaded his forehead as Riyan watched the lid begin to move away from the entryway. He expected at any minute for the beast to launch another assault, and as the lid inched its way further back, his apprehension grew.

They finally had moved the lid back far enough for Riyan to see the creature lying just on the other side of the entryway. The rise and fall of its back told him that it was still alive. "It's right on the other side," he whispered to the other two.

"Can you get at it?" asked Chad.

"I think so," Riyan replied. Raising the sword, he drove it forward and the point struck the creature in the side. The creature gave out with a grunt.

"Well?" asked Chad.

"I hit it but it didn't move," he replied.

"It's not doing anything?" Bart asked.

Riyan left the sword in the creature's body. He turned to his friends and shook his head.

Bart indicated to Chad that they should move the lid to the side. Once it was out of the way, they looked to the creature and found that it was indeed one of the large mountain bears common to this region. The sword stuck out of its side and blood continued to pump with every beat of its heart.

"Why doesn't it attack?" asked Chad.

Bart moved closer and saw blood welling from just behind its head. "I think your first blow took it in the spine," he said. Then he saw the eyes of the beast upon him and he took a quick step backwards. When the bear made no move to attack, he knew that the bear's spinal column had been severed.

He turned to the others. "We need to put it out of its misery."

"You two do it," Riyan said. His arms and legs are shaking from the earlier attacks. The weight of the sword plus the adrenalin rush that was wearing off, had sapped his strength.

Bart nodded and grasped the hilt of the sword in both hands. Pulling it out of the bear's side, he raised it high over his head. Using every ounce of strength he had, he thrust it into the bear. He was rather surprised that he managed to sink half of the blade into it before the tip hit bone and stopped.

"That had to do it," said Chad.

They watched the sides of the bear continue to go in and out as it breathed. Then, the frequency of its breaths went down until they stopped altogether.

"Maybe we should get out of here and make camp for the night," suggested Riyan. "I for one could use some rest."

"Might not be a bad idea," agreed Chad. "I'm getting hungry."

Bart pulled out his knife and began carving off a hunk of the bear for their dinner.

Riyan stopped him before he could cut very deep. "Wait to do that until we're on the other side," he said. "It's going to be bad enough as it is."

He stopped carving when he realized what he was talking about. The bear's body completely blocked the lower half of the entryway and most of it was already covered in blood. Then he laughed. He's not sure why, but he started laughing and it wasn't long before Riyan and Chad joined him.

They worked their way over the bear's carcass and once on the other side, Bart carved out a chunk of meat. He carried it as he followed the other two down the narrow curving passage and back to the main passage. Then it was just down a little ways until they reached the opening leading to the surface.

"Look," Riyan when came to the slope leading up. They could see the tracks the bear made as it came down the slope. "Wonder what it was doing in here?"

"Maybe looking for a den," suggested Bart.

"Or dinner," added Chad.

"I just hope there's not another one out there," Riyan said as he headed up the slope first.

The sun had already dipped past the tops of the mountains to the west. They got a fire going and once Riyan had a spit put together to roast the meat, they went down to the stream and washed the blood off.

That night as they sat around the fire, they talked about what they found down below, the bear attack, and what they may possibly find in the morning.

Chapter 8

The clinking of coins woke Chad the following morning. He turned over and saw Riyan stacking his share of the coins on the ground before him. Chad sat up and groaned, "Not again."

Riyan glanced over to his friend and grinned. "I can't help it," he replied.

"You must have counted them ten times last night before we went to sleep," he stated.

"Sorry," his friend said. "I just like to look at them."

The morning dawned a beautiful day with just a hint of clouds forming a wreath that circled the mountain peaks. Chad looked around and didn't see Bart anywhere. "Where did Bart go?" he asked.

Riyan nodded toward the stream. "He went that way," he explained. "Said would be back shortly." Now that Chad's up, Riyan put his coins away and they got breakfast going. Soon the odor of bacon and eggs was wafting through the hills.

Down by the stream Bart was walking along, simply enjoying the quiet of the hills. When he first came to Quillim, it was more out of need than desire. Having lived all his life in the city, it was hard for him to adjust to the openness of the country. But it didn't take long before he grew to cherish it.

Oh sure, he still longed for the city; the hustle, bustle, and constant noise, even late at night there was always something dispelling the quiet. It was home. When he accompanied Chad to Phyndyr's, it had reawakened his longing for the streets. He just wished that he could go back.

Stepping along the edge of the gently flowing water, his thoughts drifted back to his days in Wardean. His life on her streets had never been dull. Then he smelled the odor of bacon wafting from camp and realized he'd better return before the other two ate it all.

Their camp wasn't situated near the opening to the underground area. Instead, they had crossed the stream and camped a hundred yards away. Not having their camp near the entrance was Riyan's idea. He didn't want someone to stumble upon their camp and then discover the entrance, at least not until they were through exploring it for themselves.

When they were finished with breakfast, they carried all their equipment with them to the underground area. "Wish we could block this off somehow," Chad said as he worked his way down to the passage below.

"I know what you mean," replied Riyan. None of them wished for a repeat of the incident with the bear.

"Don't know how we could," added Bart as he entered the hole in the ground and slid down.

Riyan already had one of the lanterns lit and was looking down to the left hand passage where they had yet to explore. "Hope we find something interesting today," he said.

"Me too," agreed Chad. He then took off all his equipment and bedroll and laid them on the passage floor. "I'm not going to haul this around again today."

The others removed their equipment as well. All each of them took with them were their packs which they slung across their shoulders. Bart also brought the other lantern just in case. None of them wished to be down here without a light in the event something happened to their other one.

"All ready?" Riyan asked with renewed excitement.

"You bet," Chad replied. Bart nodded.

Setting out, Riyan took the lead and moved down the passage. He didn't go far before another curving narrow passage branched off to their right. Without hesitation, he entered the passage. It continued to curve back to the right until it was running parallel to the main passage. The narrow passage went straight for a few more feet before ending at an entryway to another crypt holding a sarcophagus.

"Just like the other one," observed Chad.

Riyan nodded and entered the crypt. A quick search turned up nothing so they left the room and returned through the curving passage back to the main passage. Then they turned to the right and continued down for a ways before coming to another 'T' junction.

He glanced down to the left and right but couldn't see any difference between them. Riyan decided to take the left passage and moved into it. It didn't go very far before they came to yet another 'T' junction. To their left and right, narrow passages branched off just like the ones they discovered the previous day.

They explored them and turned up two more of the rooms with the stone biers within the walls on either end. The chests below the biers contained a sum total of fifteen of the coins and another small gem. Once finished with searching the two rooms, they returned to the main passage, and this time took the right at the 'T'.

"This place seems to be laid out according to a pattern," observed Bart. "The bier rooms are in pairs, while the rooms with the sarcophagi are by themselves with a curved passage connecting them to the main passage."

"That's been true so far," agreed Chad.

Continuing down the passage, they came to where another main passage connected to theirs on the left. When Riyan shined the lantern's light down it, the light revealed the ceiling of the passage had caved in.

"That didn't happen too long ago," Riyan told the others. "The dirt's still fresh."

"Could've happened during the earthquake," suggested Chad.

Nodding, Riyan glanced to him. "I was thinking the same thing."

"Wonder what was down there?" Bart asked. "We should have thought to bring a shovel."

"If we come back here another time, let's remember to bring one," said Chad.

Riyan nodded then turned back to the main passage and continued on. Twenty feet or so after they left the blocked passage behind, they came to a flight of steps descending into darkness on their right.

"Alright!" exclaimed Riyan when the lantern's light revealed the steps.

He started moving into them when Bart said, "Let's finish up here first."

Riyan turned to him and was about ready to argue the point. For in all the sagas he's ever heard that tell of treasure hunters, the deeper one goes, the better the treasure gets. But then he realized there's no point in hurrying it along and nodded. "Okay."

They spent the better part of a half hour finishing the exploration of this level. Two crypts holding sarcophagi and six bier rooms later, they returned to the stairs leading down. Two of the chests in the bier rooms had the Pricks of Poison trap which Bart readily disarmed. He told them that once you know what's there, it's pretty simple to take care of it. Riyan had his doubts about that, but trusted in Bart's skill.

Their packs were now fifty three coins and three gems heavier when they finished searching this level. At least one of the gems was slightly larger than the others that they found and should bring more coins.

Riyan took the lead again as they descended to the next level. They descended twenty steps before the stairs ended at a passageway moving to their right and left. Here the stonework was of much better quality. The walls of the passage looked as if more care had been put into their construction than what they saw up above. Also, sconces that once must have held torches are spaced along the walls at ten foot intervals.

"Looks like we've entered a better area," Riyan said.

"Or it was built later than the one above," added Chad.

When Riyan glanced back at them, they could see the grin that's spread across his face. They also noticed how his eyes were practically dancing in anticipation.

"Relax," Bart told him. "The last thing we need to do is get in a hurry in a place like this."

"I'll try," he said but the tone of his voice belied the statement.

Moving down to the right, they followed the passage until it turned abruptly to the left. Not far past the corner, another passage, slightly smaller than the main one they were in branched off to their right.

Riyan shined the light down the new passage and saw at the edge of the light how it opened up onto another room. "May have something here," he said and moved forward.

The room at the end of the short passage was rectangular in shape, stretching to the right and left. Two large tapestries that hadn't survive the passing of time well, hung upon the walls. The fabric had deteriorated so badly, that whatever they at one time depicted was no longer discernable.

In the center of the room, two stone biers sat six feet apart. Lying upon each were the skeletal remains of warriors. The skulls were encased in helms and armor covered the rest of the body. Their hands gripped the hilt of the swords that lay upon their breasts.

Bart entered the room and moved to the skeleton on the right and briefly examined its sword. The blade showed extensive damage by rust as did the armor.

"No chests here," said Riyan unhappily.

"That's true," said Bart. Then he had Riyan follow him with the lantern as he closely examined the biers upon which the dead lay. "However, there are other means by which people store their valuables than simple wooden chests." The biers were more than just simple blocks of stone. They were carved with figures locked in battle.

As Bart ran his fingers across one of the figures, he felt it shift under his touch. "Aha!" he exclaimed.

"What?" asked Riyan as he moved in closer to see.

"May have found something," he told him. "Back off a little and give me some room."

"Sorry," he said and then backed up a foot. Chad came over and stood beside him as they watched Bart feel around the figure.

Bart was sure that if he pressed the figure it would release a catch holding open a secret compartment. But he also remembered his father telling him how in situations such as he now found himself, devices like this invariable were trapped. The problem was that he didn't know how to disarm it.

He stood up and turned around to Riyan. "I wish you would have brought your staff down here with you." It's currently sitting up on the upper level with all their other equipment.

"Why?" he asked.

"I think I found how to open the compartment," he explained, "but it may be trapped. If I had your staff, I could do it from a distance."

"No problem there," Riyan told him, "I'll just run up and get it."

"Alright," Bart nodded.

As he turned to leave, Chad grabbed his arm and said, "Hurry."

He grinned at his friend and said, "I will." Then he hurried from the room and took the lantern with him. In short order, Bart and Chad were left in the dark.

They waited there for what seemed like hours, and when Chad began to express worry about what may have happened to him, the passage leading to the crypt began to lighten. Soon, Riyan rejoined them with staff in hand. "I'll be sure to keep this with me from now on," he told the others as he handed it to Bart.

Bart took the staff and said, "It might be safer if you two waited out in the passage. Leave the lantern on the ground first though."

Riyan set the lantern on the ground near Bart then he and Chad left the room. They came to a stop several feet from the entryway, just far enough out of the room to still be able to see what happened.

Once Bart saw that they were safely out of the room, he too stepped back as far as he could and still be able to place the end of the staff on the figure. Then he lifted the staff and held it at arm's reach. He positioned himself a little to one side as he moved the end of the staff to lie against the figure. Holding his breath, he depressed the figure with the end of the staff.

No sooner had the figure been depressed then a liquid squirted out from two different places on either side. The liquid shot out and landed a good two feet from the bier. When the liquid hit the stone floor, it began to eat away at it.

Bart turned back to the others and said, "Acid."

"If you had pressed that with you finger, it would have hit you," Riyan said as he moved back into the room.

Handing him back his staff, Bart replied, "That was the whole idea of the trap I'm sure." He glanced to the stone where the liquid hit and saw that the corrosiveness of the acid ate away almost a quarter inch of the stone's surface before it began to fizzle out. He thought to himself, *That would have hurt.*

Turning his attention back to the bier, he noticed that over a foot long section of its side had popped out a little bit. Moving closer, he took hold of the edge and pulled the piece of stone. As it turned out, it was a long drawer filled with the deceased's belongings.

"That is cool," Chad said as Bart pulled the drawer out. It finally came to a stop when it was two feet out and no amount of pulling would budge it further. Making sure not to step in the acid on the floor, Chad and Riyan moved closer to see what was inside.

Within the drawer lay a weapon wrapped in cloth. The cloth lay in tatters, and when they unwrapped the dagger that was inside, found the blade to be brittle.

Another sack lay alongside the dagger. Within they found twenty of the coins, plus five coins of another type. These were slightly larger and silver in color. "Are those silver coins?" asked Chad.

Riyan picked one up. "Looks like it," he replied. "But they're heavier than what we use now."

Bart took one of the silver coins and nodded. "I'd say it's about one and a half times the weight of the coins in use today." The design on the two sides of the silver coins matched what was on the copper coins.

They removed the coins and left the dagger. Then Bart moved on to the other bier in the room. A quick search located another movable figure. Using the same strategy he employed on the first one, he pressed the figure with the staff. Again, a spurt of acid and a similar drawer popped open.

Within they found a set of daggers and what may have been a book, but time had destroyed them beyond use. When Riyan touched the book, its pages cracked and disintegrated under his touch. The drawer wasn't without treasure as they found another ten silvers and thirty coppers. There was also a gold necklace nestled in among the coins.

Riyan held up the necklace and showed it to Bart. "Think this is worth anything?" he asked.

"If it's real gold, yes," he replied.

"Don't know why it wouldn't be," Riyan said as he put it in his pack.

Once their booty was stowed in their packs, they left the room and continued down the passage to the right. Fifty feet further down, they came to a larger entryway on their left. When they reached it, the light revealed a much larger room than any they've come across so far.

The room was quite large. Three columns were spaced evenly down the center of the room, moving from the entryway where Riyan and the others stood, to another entryway in the wall directly across the room from them on the other side. To the left and right of the columns sat three stone biers, six altogether. They were identical to those that had been in the previous room they found on this level, except that the armor the dead were wearing was slightly different. These too were ravaged by rust.

"This must be someplace special," said Chad.

"It would seem so," agreed Bart.

The walls of the room bore carvings of men in battle from one end to the other. Riyan took a closer look and saw that what the men were fighting wasn't entirely human. "Look at this," he said to the other two.

Bart and Chad came to stand by him as he pointed out the creatures the men were fighting. They were roughly the same size and shape as the fighters. Bipedal humanoids, but that's where the similarity ended. Their faces were bestial, small horns sprouted from their foreheads, and a long scaly tail touched the ground behind them.

"Ever seen anything like this before?" asked Riyan.

"No," admitted Bart. "But burial chambers such as these often have murals and such depicting the dead in a heroic and favorable light."

Chad nodded.

Bart then set about trying to find the hidden catch that would open each of the drawers in the six biers. The first one he came across, he did the staff trick again to open it. Only this time when he depressed the figure with the staff, nothing happened other than the drawer popped open a little bit. No liquid this time.

Riyan moved forward and said, "Guess it was broken." He reached the drawer and gripped the part that was protruding. Just as he began to pull it open, Bart yelled "Stop!" But his warning came too late.

No sooner had the cavity within the drawer cleared the side of the bier than a dart flew out and struck Riyan in the arm. "Damn!" he cursed as his other hand quickly moved to remove the dart. He cried out as the dart came free for its head had two nasty barbs that ripped his flesh as he pulled it out.

"Flush it with water quick!" Bart yelled.

Chad removed his water flask and upended it over the wound. He emptied its entire contents as he washed the blood away. A tearing sound drew his attention and he turned to see Bart tearing off a piece of cloth to use as a bandage.

"It's not that bad," Riyan said through gritted teeth. "I'll live."

Bart wrapped the cloth around the wound and tied it off. "It's not the wound itself that concerns me," he said. "It's what may have been on the dart that has me worried."

"You mean poison?" asked Chad.

Bart nodded. "That's usually what you'll find on a dart in circumstances like this."

Riyan turned fearful eyes to him and asked, "Am I going to die?"

"I don't know," he replied. "How do you feel?"

He took a moment to see if he felt the poison taking affect then said, "I don't feel any different."

"You could be lucky in that the potency of the poison has deteriorated over the years," he said. "If you start feeling nauseous or dizzy, let us know right away."

"You got it," he said.

Then Bart glanced at both of them and said, "From now on, no one opens anything until I say it's okay."

Both Chad and Riyan nodded affirmatively.

Then Bart set about searching the remaining five biers while the other two examined the contents of the drawer they just opened. More rusted weapons and a few coins, three of the silver and ten of the copper.

"You know," commented Chad, "it just seems odd to me that soldiers for whom someone took such care to build this place for and were laid out so respectfully, would have so little in the way of valuables." When Riyan glanced at him he gestured to the skeletal remains of the man in armor atop the bier and said, "I mean, wouldn't you think this guy here would have more than a couple weapons and a modest amount of coins?"

Riyan shrugged. "Maybe it was their custom. Or perhaps their family only gave them what they had too and saved the rest for themselves."

Chad grinned and nodded. "I'd probably do the same."

Ahhhh!

Bart's cry drew their attention and they looked over at the next bier just in time to see him jump back out of the way of an acid spray. "What happened?" Riyan said as he and Chad hurried over to him.

"I got sloppy," he said. "I forgot that when there are many of the same type of traps in the same place, they are often set to go off differently to foil thieves." He pointed to the bier he was working on. "That one had the spray come out at a little different angle and almost got me."

"You're okay though?" asked Chad.

Bart nodded. "Yes," he replied. "That one's safe, you can go through it while I finish the rest of them."

So that's what they did. While Bart would work on one, Chad and Riyan would go through the ones he already opened. When they were at last done with this room, Bart had managed to again narrowly avoid another acid spray as well as two more Pricks of Poison. The drawers of the remaining five had contributed sixty five more of the coppers, thirteen of the silvers and five small gems to their bulging packs.

Chad patted his pack and said, "We must have a fortune by now."

Bart grinned at his enthusiasm. "Actually we have a little over three golds worth, not counting the gems and the necklace," he corrected.

Holding up his bulging pack, he said, "How can this be worth so little?"

"It's the copper coins," Bart replied. "It takes a lot to make a gold. Of course, the age of the coins could bring more value if we only knew the right person to talk to."

"Do you?" asked Riyan.

Shaking his head, Bart said, "I know a fence where we could get rid of this stuff, but he wouldn't care too much about their age."

"Why would we want to get rid of this stuff?" Riyan asked.

Bart removed one of the coins and held it up. "Anyone who sees this coin is going to wonder where you got it from," he replied. "And in case you didn't already know, Duke Alric has made it law that he gets twenty percent of any treasure recovered in his dukedom. Something like this would be considered recovered treasure I'm afraid."

"You're kidding?" Chad said.

Shaking his head, Bart replied, "No I'm not. In fact, if you're found guilty of finding treasure without turning over his share, it's considered thieving."

"Great!" said Riyan. The plans that had been going through his mind as to what to do with the treasure all of a sudden went up in smoke.

"Don't worry," Bart replied. "A quick trip to Wardean and we'll get this exchanged for regular coins that won't raise as much suspicion."

"How much will the fence take for doing this?" asked Riyan.

"He takes ten percent." Bart looked at both of them and shrugged. "Ten percent, twenty, or take the chance of standing before the Duke's Court on charges of thievery. It's your choice."

Riyan's mood hardly improved, but he could see the wisdom in what Bart said. "Well, ten percent is still better than having one's hand cut off." Which was what the penalty for thieving happened to be.

Chad slaps him on the back and grins. "What price adventure?" he asked.

Then Riyan nodded as a grin spread across his face too. "No point in getting mad," he said. "There's treasure to be found!"

When they were ready to leave the room, they had a choice before them. They could either return out the way they came in and continue searching from there, or they could leave by the entryway on the opposite side. After a second of deliberation, they chose to return the way they entered. That way they wouldn't miss anything or take the chance of becoming turned around.

So back out to the passage where they continued following the passage to the left. A short ways further down they encountered another room on their right holding two biers. Bart was quick to disarm the traps, or triggered them safely as the case warranted. They acquired another twenty seven copper coins and five silver. As they left the room and continued down the passage, Riyan got to thinking that the coins he had in his pack represented more money than he and his mother could expect to make in a year or two with the sheep. He felt better about things when he came to that realization and was better able to enjoy the adventure.

Once back out in the passage, they followed it a little further until it turned to the left. From there it went down a ways past two larger rooms on the right, each of the rooms contained three biers. They were quick to loot the gold and gems within the drawers of the six biers before continuing on. Then they followed the passage until it turned back to the left once more.

After the turn, they found two more two-bier rooms on the right and the opening to the large room with the six biers and three columns they had went through earlier on their left. Once they went through the two-bier rooms, they continued down the passage until it turned once more to the left.

The main passage had formed a square, with the six-bier room that had the three columns running through it, as its center. After they rounded the fourth corner of the square, they came across another set of stairs descending down into darkness.

"What do you say we go up and have lunch before we see what's down there?" suggested Chad. Then in the silence the others heard his stomach give out with a loud growl.

"Good idea," agreed Riyan. "We all could use a bite to eat and some fresh air." They headed back up to the uppermost level and gathered what they would need for lunch. Then they went topside and cleared the mustiness from their lungs with the fresh summer air while they ate.

Chapter 9

Upon their return back into what they've begun to call The Crypt, they once again deposited all of their equipment, except their packs and treasure, on the floor of the passage beneath the entrance. Riyan came up with the bright idea of depositing all the copper coins, save a couple for each, within one of the chests that they had searched earlier here on the top level. His pack had grown quite heavy with the weight of the coins and he didn't really feel like lugging it around. The silver coins, gems and the single gold necklace they distributed evenly among their packs.

Once the copper had been dropped off, they moved to the steps leading down to the second level. Then from the bottom of the steps they turned left and walked over to where the next set of steps descended further down.

Riyan took the lead as he stepped into the opening of the stairs. Just like the previous stair, this one held twenty steps leading from this level down to the next. He quickly descended the twenty steps and at the bottom came out into another passage running left and right. The lantern's light revealed the passage extending into darkness to the left, but to the right it continued a short ways before abruptly turning to the left. "Might be square just like the one above," he commented.

Turning to the right, he led the others as he headed for the corner and followed it around to the left. Not too much further from the turn they came across another entryway to a two-bier room. It was practically identical to the one above only this time, the two chests were sitting on the biers themselves at the foot of the deceased.

Riyan and Chad stayed out in the passage while Bart took the lantern inside and began to examine the chests. The first one had a mark by the keyhole indicating the possibility of a trap.

Over lunch they had been discussing traps and the way chest makers would put a mark to indicate the presence of one. Riyan had thought it rather dumb, seeing as how it only seemed to work to the thief's best inter-est. But Chad had come up with another probable reason.

"Maybe it could be put there to discourage thieves?" he had guessed. "I mean, if a thief knew it was trapped, wouldn't he be more likely to move on to a less life threatening target?"

"Perhaps," Riyan had said. "But I still think it's a pretty stupid idea." He had looked to Bart and added, "It hasn't dissuaded us in any way."

"You got a point there," replied Bart.

But now they stood there and watched as Bart worked on the chests. He managed to get them open in short order and within each they found a total of twelve silver coins. For the first time, the copper coins were not present.

Riyan nodded as they divvied up the coins. "That's more like it," he stated. Since twenty copper coins were the equivalent of a silver, having only silver kept the weight down.

They left the room and Riyan again took the lead as they continued down the passage. The light from the lantern soon revealed two openings coming up ahead. One on the right that was similar in width to the one they just left, and a much wider one to the left. As they drew closer, the lantern's light revealed the opening to the left to be almost three times as wide as any they've come across thus far.

Riyan slowed his steps as he came nearer the two openings. A quick look through the one on the right showed that it was another of the two-bier rooms with chests resting atop the biers. Leaving the two-bier room alone for the time being, he turned his attention to the larger opening on the left.

This room was almost three times as large as the three columned room with six biers they had found above. It was shaped as a diamond, with the entryway where they were standing being one of the diamond's points. As it turned out, there were entryways at each of the four points of the dia-mond.

A single bier rested against the wall of each of the four sides of the dia-mond. Just beyond the head and foot of each of the biers, tall columns stretched upward from the floor all the way to the ceiling.

As Riyan entered the room with the others right behind, the light from the lantern revealed a sword and shield hanging on the wall above each of the biers. Also, in the center of the floor between the four biers, was an opening with stairs leading down.

They gave the stairs a quick look and when nothing other than darkness could be seen, turned their attention to the swords and shields upon the walls. Closer examination revealed that they had survived the passage of time well. Not a speck of rust marred their surfaces and each looked as if there was strength remaining in them.

Each of the shields bore a different coat of arms that was an exact match to the coat of arms depicted on the armor of the deceased soldier lying beneath. One was of a sword pointed downward with a dragon grasping the hilt as its body twined around the blade. The next was a simple red background with but a stripe of green running from the upper left corner to the bottom right. The third coat of arms was that of a two headed grey falcon, one head looking to the right and the other to the left. In the falcon's left claw was grasped a stick with but a single leaf upon the upper end, and in the other claw was a dagger with the blade pointing down.

The fourth coat of arms drew the attention of them all. It was a black field upon which lay a five pointed golden crown surrounded in a nimbus of light. And beneath the crown was the symbol that has been depicted on all the coins.

They took a closer look at the body laid out upon the bier beneath the shield bearing the crown. They saw the helm that the skeletal remains was wearing had a crown of sorts worked into the design. The five points of the crown depicted on the shield were matched by five protruding points spaced evenly around the helm. Gems sparkled as they reflected the lantern's light from where they were embedded in the tips of the spikes.

"He must have been a king," breathed Chad.

"I would have to agree," said Bart.

Riyan nodded too. "But I've never seen his coat of arms anywhere before, nor any of the others."

"Neither have I," Bart admitted. Then he moved closer to the bier until he was almost touching it so he could examine the sword and shield on the wall better. "I don't see how they managed to survive so well all this time."

"Unless they're magical," suggested Riyan.

Bart turned to him and nodded. "That would explain it."

"Uh," began Chad, "I think it might be wise to leave this room alone. It's bad enough we're grave robbers, but to take anything from this room just seems wrong."

"I get that feeling too," agreed Riyan. Riyan gazed at the shield bearing the crown and the sword beside it. How he longed for such things, magical weapons and armor just like in the sagas. For the sword and shield had to be magical to have survived so well for so long. Sighing, he said, "Come on, we still have more of this level to check before we head down the stairs to the next."

The others agreed with him and they returned back to the passage from whence they entered the diamond shaped chamber. Once there, they crossed the passage and entered the two-bier room and began the looting of the rest of this level.

Just as Riyan had predicted, the passage did form a square as it moved around the diamond shaped room. As they went along, they came across seven more of the two-bier rooms and collected another seventy two silver pieces and six small gems. Again, there were no coppers.

As they rounded the final corner of the square, they came across an entryway into a large room with fourteen biers. The dead lying upon them were different than the ones they had come across thus far. Instead of being arrayed in armor with a sword lying upon their chest, these were archers. Each held a quiver of arrows rather than a sword upon their chest. The arrows themselves didn't look all that great, most of them were seriously warped. At the foot of each bier sat a chest.

While Bart worked to get the chests open, Chad commented to Riyan, "You know, this whole place may be some king's final resting place. I heard that in some places, when a king dies he's buried with soldiers, so that in the afterlife he'll be protected."

Riyan nodded agreement. "I've heard that too."

"Got it!" hollered Bart as he moved on to the second chest.

Chad glanced to Riyan and shrugged. Then they walked over to the chest Bart had just disarmed and resumed the looting process. Once all the chests were disarmed and searched, they garnered another twenty silver coins and three gems.

"Today's been rather successful so far," Riyan announced as they were leaving the room.

"Including what we left up on the top level, I'd say we're pushing close to the equivalent of twenty six golds," Bart told them. "And that's not counting what the gems may bring."

As they made their way down the passage to the diamond room and the stairs leading down, Riyan asked his friend Chad, "Do you think this will be enough to help your father?"

"I can't take all of this for myself," he said.

"Don't worry about it," replied Bart. "You need it more than us right now. Use what you have to and get the grinding wheels fixed, then we'll split the rest."

"I appreciate this," Chad told them. "I really do."

"Hey," said Riyan as he placed a hand on his shoulder, "what are friends for?"

Then they turned into the diamond room and made their way over to the head of the stairs. Riyan didn't even hesitate as he stepped upon the top step and began his descent to the next level.

Unlike the two previous flights of steps they took as they descended from one level to the next, this one had forty steps before reaching the bottom. Where the steps ended a passage extended forward for twenty feet before reaching an entryway into another room. For the first time since they've been down here, they came across a door.

The door sat opened and was swung within the hallway towards them. It was a rather sturdy wooden door with reinforced iron bindings. If the door had been shut, it would have taken quite a bit of force to get it open.

"Odd to find a door here," Chad stated.

"Isn't it though?" asked Bart.

Then they passed by the open door and into the room on the other side. Here they were taken aback as they entered a massive room. Thirty biers were spaced in six rows of five with three rows of three columns each dividing the room equally into thirds. One row of five biers, then a row of columns. Two rows of five biers, then another row of columns. Then two more rows of biers, a row of columns, and then one last row of five biers. Upon each of the biers were more of the armored individuals laid out just as all the others they came across had been since they entered The Crypt.

"This could take some time," Bart said as he gauged the length of time it's going to take him to search each of the thirty biers and disarm whatever traps they may have.

"We got time," Chad replied. "It's not like we have anywhere to go."

"Yeah, but you guys aren't the ones having to do all the work," he admonished.

"We'll lug the treasure for you if that will make you feel better," offered Riyan.

Bart nodded and grinned. "It would, now that you mentioned it." He then set his pack down and began removing the coins he's been carrying. Once he transferred them to Riyan and Chad, he stood back up. "Better."

"I bet," said Riyan as he hefted his now much heavier pack.

Bart moved to the first bier and began to inspect it. Chad lit the wick of the second lantern they carried and said to Riyan, "Why don't we explore a little while we're waiting?"

"Sure," agreed Riyan.

On the far side of the room across from the end of the center set of columns, was a pair of double doors. Both stood wide open into the room. When they reached them they found another passage moved directly away from the doors then turned to the right.

"You two be careful," Bart hollered in warning.

"We promise not to touch anything," Chad hollered back. Then he and Riyan passed through the doors and into the passage. They walked down to where it turned to the right and followed it around the corner. Stretching before them was a long passage, longer than what the lantern's light could reveal.

As they began walking down it, Chad said to Riyan, "Just like one of those stories we would tell each other."

Riyan grinned. "Better." Then he held up his arm that was bandaged due to his impatience in opening the drawer. "Even this doesn't dampen my enthusiasm for what we're doing."

Chad glanced at the bandage and asked, "Is it bothering you at all?"

Shaking his head, Riyan replied, "Only a twinge now and then when I flex my arm."

"I was worried about it," he said.

"So was I at first," admitted Riyan. "But since nothing has developed, I don't give it much thought."

Up ahead, they see another door standing open at the end of the hallway. Moving forward, they pass through the entryway and enter another room just like the one they had left Bart in. Thirty biers separated in six rows of five, which in turn are divided by three rows of three columns.

"Bart's going to be busy," grinned Chad.

"Maybe we should give him a larger share of the treasure," suggested Riyan. "After all, he's taking the most risk in disarming the traps."

"That would be alright with me," replied Chad. "So long as I am still able to give my father ample gold to cover the cost of the two new grinding stones."

"Of course," Riyan agreed.

Far to their right, another set of double doors stood open. After a brief inspection of the room, they made their way towards the double doors. Again on the other side of the doors was a passage moving directly away from them before turning sharply to the left.

They passed through the double doors and followed the passage until it turned left. After that they continued to follow it quite a ways to where another door stood open at the end. On the other side was yet another bier filled room.

This room turned out to be larger by far than the two other previous rooms they had discovered on this level. A quick count revealed sixty biers with armored dead lying in neat rows from one wall to the other with only a two foot gap between them. Six massive columns stood in two rows of three down the center of the room.

"Man," breathed Riyan. "I guess this king really felt the need for protection in the afterlife."

"It looks like it," Chad agreed. "It's going to take Bart days to work his way through all these."

"I know," said Riyan. "Feel sorry for him. He'll definitely deserve the dragon's share after this."

They walked between the biers and briefly gave the dead lying upon them a once over. The walls of this room bore the scenes of fighting as they had discovered in that one room up above. Soldiers fighting the bestial, demonic looking creatures. A shiver runs through Riyan as he paused to look at one particular nasty scene where it looked as if a group of creatures were eating the flesh from a fallen soldier.

"Let's get out of here," Chad said as he indicated another set of double doors at the far end of the room. "This place kind of gives me the creeps."

"You know it," agreed Riyan.

Moving out, they made their way through the biers until they reached the double doors. There they discovered a passage moving directly away before turning left.

"How many more of these are there?" Chad asked as they passed into the passage.

"I hope not too many more for Bart's sake," replied Riyan. "They seem to be getting bigger as we go along." Chad chuckled at that.

After turning left, the passage continued to run twice as far as the others on this level before opening up onto a room.

When the light from the lantern hit the room, they could tell that here at last they had found something different. There were no biers within this room. What they saw caused them to come to an abrupt halt.

From the end of the passage, the walls of the room angled outward forty five degrees until ending at the far wall of the room. Just within the room, on either side of the entryway, were large, empty urns. From the soot coating the upper rim of each, Riyan deduced that they must have at one time been filled with oil and had burned.

But this was not what had made them stop, rather the wall across the room from them. It was covered in sigils and writing unfamiliar to them. Two steps led up to a dais that stood beneath the sigils and writing. Lying on the steps was a skeleton dressed in ragged clothes. His upper body was upon the dais with one of his arms outstretched towards the pattern of sigils on the wall.

Riyan moved to approach the figure on the steps but Chad placed a restraining hand before him. "I think we should get Bart in here before we do anything," he advised.

All set to argue, Riyan saw the look in his friend's eye and gave in. "Very well," he said. He glanced once more back to the skeletal figure and just as he turned back to return down the passage, a glint of something caught his eye. Turning back, he looked more closely and saw something golden in the figure's hand.

"Look!" he said as he pointed to it. Again he tried to move forward, and again Chad stopped him.

"Let's go get Bart first," he insisted.

Sighing, Riyan nodded. Hurrying back down the passage, they returned to the room where Bart was working on the biers.

By this time Bart was feeling quite frustrated. He was in the middle of inspecting his fourth bier and so far hadn't found any catches or releases to open secret drawers in any of them. He was beginning to wonder if these even had any.

He meticulously worked over this fourth bier with a growing feeling of annoyance. Finally, he gave up and set the lantern on top of the bier by the deceased warrior's feet. With hands on his hips, he surveyed the twenty six other biers still within the room and shook his head. "I'm not going to waste my time on any more of these," he told himself. Just as he grabbed the lantern and was about to leave the room through the doors Riyan and Chad had, they burst into the room at a run.

"We found something!"

"You've got to come and see!" Chad and Riyan blurted out simultaneously.

Bart could see something had them all excited. Holding up his hand, he said, "Calm down." They came to a stop before him. When they looked like they were both about to speak again, he cut them off by holding his hand up. Then he turned to Riyan. "Riyan, what is it?"

"We found a room unlike any other down here," he replied.

"What do you mean?" Bart asked.

"Come on," urged Chad. "We've got to show you."

Bart nodded. "Okay. I don't think these biers in here are going to yield anything anyway." He followed them out of the room and down the passage. When he got to the next room with thirty biers, he was stunned by so many.

"That's nothing," Chad said. "Wait until you see the big one."

"Big one?" he asked.

Riyan grinned. "Yeah, big one."

Chad and Riyan led him between the biers and left the room through the far door. Chad and Riyan were hurrying Bart along down the passage to the larger room with sixty biers. They wanted to reach the final room at the end and see what Bart had to say about it.

When he followed the other two into the massive room containing rows and rows of biers, with an armored figure laid out upon each, he stopped in awe. He had never seen such a thing. "This is incredible," he said.

"Pretty impressive isn't it?" asked Chad.

All he could do was nod in reply.'

Riyan took the lead and moved between the biers to the door at the other side. Once there, he paused a moment then turned to Bart. "The next room is the one we were talking about," he explained. "I think you should lead from here."

Bart nodded and passed Riyan as he moved into the passage. He turned the corner to the left and followed it down until the end of the passage began to open up onto the room with the sigils and writing.

When he reached where the walls began to widen to form the sides of the room, he stopped. The light from the two lanterns illuminated the entire room well enough for him to make out the room's features. He saw the long dead figure lying on the steps leading up to the dais, then his eyes moved to the sigils and writing upon the wall across from him.

Chad pointed to the figure on the steps and said, "There's something in his hand."

Bart turned his attention to the figure's outstretched hand and saw the glint of something golden. "Stay here," he told the other two as he worked his way towards the steps. This room gave off a feeling of unease that made him be extra careful. There was something about the figure sprawled on the steps that screamed for him to proceed with caution.

He figured what was lying before him had been a man at one time, though it's hard to tell as all that's left were bones and the remnants of his clothes he was wearing when he died. On the steps next to the man sat a pack that was all but worn away by time. As he came to a stop by the man's feet, a foot from the edge of the first step, he looked closely at what was glittering in the man's hand.

It looked like a piece of what had once been a circular torc of some kind. The bones of the man's hand shielded most of it from view, but he figured the width of the piece had to be at least three to four inches.

Why was the man in the position that he was? That was the question that has been nagging at him ever since he saw him. The man had to have arrived here after the place was constructed, otherwise the builders would have removed his body. In Bart's mind that made the figure before him a thief, or some sort of robber.

He also had to have worked alone, for if he had partners, Bart doubted that they would have left the golden item in his hand when they left. So the question remained, what was he doing here?

Then Bart turned his attention to the wall above the dais and the sigils inscribed upon it. The way the man's hand was outstretched led him to believe the wall was in some way the man's destination. Also, the fact that steps led up to it had to mean something as well.

"What do you think?" asked Riyan.

Bart turned back to them and said, "I think he was a thief here to loot the place."

"But if he was," supposed Chad, "why weren't the biers in the above levels touched."

"Good question," Bart replied. Then more to himself than to the others he said quietly, "Yes, why wouldn't he have searched the biers as we did?" He must have been after something, something specific and didn't want to be bothered with what little the biers would have given him.

"Could that wall there hold some sort of secret door," suggested Riyan. "Maybe on the other side is the king's treasure room."

"Possibly," agreed Bart. That would make sense. He turned his gaze back to the wall and examined the sigils and writing. One pattern seemed to stand out more than the others. At the pattern's center was a circle, one of many such designs inscribed in the stone. But something about this one caught his eye.

It was sunken into the wall more than the others!

He looked to the golden item in the man's hand and then back to the circle. **Yes!** It would fit perfectly within the circular depression of that sigil. Turning his head towards where the other two stood at the entrance, he said, "I believe you're right."

Pointing to the golden item in the man's hand, he said, "I think that fits nicely within that sigil there." He then moved his hand and pointed toward the sigil whose circle was indented.

"Do you think it would open up if we placed it in there?" asked Riyan. The tone of his voice held excitement that he almost was unable to restrain.

"Maybe," he said. "But it looks like it's only about a quarter of the circle that would fit in there."

"Check his pack," suggested Chad. "The other pieces could be in there."

Bart nodded and then turned back to the steps. The pack in question was resting on the second step. Bart could reach it if he stood close to the bottom step and stretched his arm forward. He came forward until the toe of his foot was less than an inch from the bottom step and then reached for the pack. He took hold of the pack by one of the straps and very carefully picked it up. He halfway expected something to happen, and when it didn't he was most relieved.

Turning around, he brought the pack over to the others. He then set it on the ground and very carefully started to open it. The cloth of the pack disintegrated under his fingers and revealed what once had been papers within. But time had destroyed the papers beyond all recognition, the barest touch causing them to crumble into dust.

"There aren't any other pieces of the circle here," he said after a moment's search.

"But there has to be!" exclaimed Riyan. "Why would he be here if he didn't have the entire key to the secret door?"

"Could be he didn't know that he only had a part of it," suggested Bart. "Greed can blind you that way. Or he could have thought that just a single piece would have opened it."

"Do you think it could?" Chad asked. "I mean, if he thought this would have opened it, he may have known more about it than we do."

"Worth a shot." Taking the staff that he's been using to trigger traps with, he returned to the steps and stopped several feet away. He placed the end of the staff on the first step and pressed down on it. When nothing happened, he moved the end of the staff to the second step and repeated the process. Again, nothing happened. Then he did it to the dais with the same results.

Turning around, he handed the staff back to Riyan and then began moving to the steps. Taking them one at a time carefully, he climbed to the dais and removed the golden piece of the circle from the dead man's hand.

It was heavy. He paused a moment as he closely inspected the item. On one side were sigils similar in nature to those on the wall. And on the other was what looked for all the world as part of a map. There were mountains and what looked like two lakes. A river flowed from one lake to the other, and a set of miniscule notations were inscribed at a point alongside the smaller lake further from the mountains. Once he was done examining it, he stepped towards the wall.

He brought the piece of the circle near the sigil and quickly realized that the markings on the one side matched perfectly with those surrounding the circular indentation in the wall. He maneuvered the piece of the sigil so that the markings on it lined up perfectly with those on the wall, then set it into the depression. He held his breath, not sure exactly what to expect. But nothing happened.

For a full minute he held it there and nothing changed. The wall remained the same. He had halfway expected the sigils to flare to life and was somewhat relieved when they failed to. Finally, he pulled the quarter circle away from the wall and turned towards the others. "I don't think it's going to work," he said.

"Then what are we to do?" asked Chad.

Beginning to leave the dais, he moved to the steps and replied, "I don't know." He no sooner stepped onto the top step than was struck in the back by something. He cried out from the unexpected attack and the other two rushed forward as he stumbled down the steps.

"My back!" he cried out as the others reached him.

Riyan looked at his back and saw that a two inch dart had pierced his skin several inches to the right of his spine. He grabbed it and pulled it out which elicited another cry from Bart. Then he and Chad helped him to the floor.

When he showed Bart the dart, he said, "Check my back. See if there are any red lines radiating from the wound, or if there is any swelling."

Chad helped Riyan to pull up his tunic to bare his back. When they had it bared, they saw the wound, then glanced at each other worriedly.

"Anything?" he asked.

They saw the hole where the dart had punctured Bart's skin. It was still welling drops of blood but that wasn't the cause of their concern. What was, were the dark red, spidery tendrils that were beginning to spread outward from the wound.

Chapter 10

"I've been poisoned!" he exclaimed when they described what was happening to the skin around the wound.

"What do we do?" Chad cried out anxiously.

"Get me out of here," he said. Then he pointed to the skeleton on the steps. "I think that was what killed him. He and I both triggered the same trap." Then as he tried to get to his feet, his knees buckled under him. "I don't know how much longer I have."

Perspiration had already begun to form on his forehead and when Riyan checked to see if he had a fever, he felt warm. "Take his other arm," he said to Chad. "We're going home."

"But it took us over a day to get here!" exclaimed Chad as he placed one of Bart's arms around his neck.

"Don't you think I know that?" hollered Riyan back at him. He and Chad grabbed their packs as they made ready to return to the surface, Riyan also took his staff.

A sudden clinking sound drew his attention to the floor where the golden item had all of a sudden fallen from Bart's hand. Riyan looked to his friend and saw that he had passed out. Picking up the piece of the golden key, he stuffed it into his pack. With Chad holding one of the lanterns and Riyan his staff, they began heading out. As they hurried down the passage and reached the turn to the right, Riyan cast one last glance back to the room. The glow from the second lantern which they left burning just within the room almost seemed to be beckoning to him. Turning back to the matter at hand, he passed around the corner and the light disappeared from sight.

It took them some doing to get Bart up to the surface. When they reached the uppermost level of The Crypt and were moving past the room where they had stashed the copper coins, Riyan said, "We'll come back for them."

"Hope so," replied Chad.

At the hole leading to the surface, they worked to get Bart up the slope. They found it exceedingly difficult to haul a limp body up a steep incline, but they finally managed it.

Once he was lying on the grass just outside the hole, Chad sat down.

"There's no time to rest!" admonished Riyan.

"My arms are like rubber," he said. In fact, both of them were fatigued by the effort of practically carrying Bart up through the four levels.

Riyan felt the same way. His arms ached and his legs could use a rest, but Bart might die if they dilly dallied. He pulled up Bart's tunic to inspect his back and gasped. The dark red, spidery tendrils had spread. Now they covered a good portion of his back. The area around the puncture wound had turned red and angry looking as well.

He turned to Chad who had also seen the progression of the poison. "We don't have much time," he said with emotion choking him.

Chad nodded. Then he suggested, "Let's make a stretcher. It would make carrying him easier."

"Alright," agreed Riyan. "I'll find another long stick and we'll use it and my staff for the poles. You get our blankets out and discard everything we don't need back down the hole."

"You got it," replied Chad.

Riyan got up from the ground and rushed over to the stream where a copse of trees stood. There he hunted for a long branch that would work. He finally took out his sword and used it to cut one off of a tree. On the way back to where he left Chad and Bart, he trimmed the branches until all he was left with was a long pole.

Chad had their three blankets laid out and ready, Riyan's staff was already in position. Next to the blankets their packs sat ready for them. "I just left the food, coins and gems," he said. "Everything else is down the hole.

"Good." Riyan came and laid the branch on the blankets. Then he and Chad began folding the blankets over the staff and branch to create a stretcher. Once they had it finished, they picked up Bart and placed him upon the stretcher. Each took their pack and slung it across their back, Bart's they placed between his feet on the stretcher.

Then Riyan moved to the end of the poles at Bart's feet while Chad took the ones by his head. They lifted him up and with Riyan leading the way, began the trek back.

All afternoon long they carried Bart as quickly as they could toward Quillim. Despite the threat spreading through Bart's system, they were forced to stop twice to rest. If they hadn't, they risked weakening themselves to the point where they might have dropped the stretcher.

When it finally began to grow dark, they continued on. Once night settled in, they used the moon and stars above to light their way. And still they continued.

"How's he doing?" asked Riyan for the dozenth time.

"Bad," replied Chad. In the gloom of night, the only indication that he was even alive was the groans he gave out with every now and then. "I'm not sure but I think the fever's worsened."

"It shouldn't be too long before we reach my home," he replied.

"Then what are we to do?" asked Chad.

"I'll leave you there with him and I'll head over to Glia's," he explained. Old Glia was an odd sort of woman. She lived alone out in the hills, most people thought she was a witch or something and had very little to do with her. The people of Quillim tolerated her presence for the simple fact that she's the only one in the area who makes potions. Many people owed their lives to the potions she brewed. The one she's most famous for was the one that will purge poison out of your system, which was useful seeing as how the mountain spiders made an appearance every once in awhile. They were very aggressive and poisonous.

Riyan had always liked her, and whenever he moved his flock to graze in the area near her hut, would visit with her. She's the oldest living person in the Quillim area, none knew just how old she was. She has been a fixture in these parts for as long as anyone could remember.

They continued carrying Bart for another hour before Riyan began to recognize the hills they were passing through. "We're almost there," he announced to Chad.

"Thank goodness," gasped Chad. It's all he's been able to do to simply continue to hold the ends of the stretcher. He was sure that if he were to but let go, he'd never be able to pick it back up again. His arms have all but grown numb and his back ached horribly.

Riyan altered their course slightly to maneuver through the hills in a more direct approach to his home. When at last they topped a hill and saw his home in the distance, they breathed a sigh of relief. The light coming through the window seemed to renew their strength as they headed down the hill.

Once they came close he shouted, "Mother!" Practically running forward, he was about to call again when the front door opened.

The smile on her face died quickly when she saw Bart lying on the stretcher. A worried look came over her as she opened the door to let them in. "What happened?" she asked.

"Bart was ..." began Chad.

"... bit by something." Riyan cut Chad off and finished the sentence. Then he flashed a meaningful look to his friend.

Once they had him through the door, she shut it and said, "Let's put him on your bed Riyan."

They carried him through the front room to his and when they were outside the door to his room, they set the stretcher down on the floor. Riyan grabbed Bart's ankles and Chad gripped him under the arms as they lifted him off the stretcher. They carried him through the bedroom door and laid him on the bed.

Riyan's mother appeared a split second later with a bowl of cool water and a towel. She sat on the bed near Bart's head and dipped the towel in the water, then began to dab his forehead. "How long has he been like this?" she asked.

"Since about noon," replied Chad.

Riyan was out in the hallway collecting Bart's pack. He took off his and as he entered the room, had Chad give him his. When Chad removed his pack and handed it to him, the coins within clinked together. Riyan flashed a look to his mother and was relieved to see that she made no indication that she had heard. He took the three packs to his closet and set them down inside, careful to not repeat the clinking sound.

He opened his pack and removed several of the small gems for Glia's potion. Once he had them in his pocket, he closed his pack again and shut the closet door. "I'm going to Glia's to get a potion for him," he told her.

"You better hurry," she said. "I'm not sure how long he's going to last."

Riyan paused a moment to look at his friend. His mother had pulled his tunic up and he could see the spidery tendrils had spread even further. They've already made their way completely around his side and were beginning to creep across his chest. Even his throat showed signs of the tendrils.

Without another word, he raced from the room and was soon outside heading through the hills towards the hut she called home. Old Glia lived a mile or so from where his home sat and it took him some minutes to cross over the hills before her hut came into view.

It was a small dwelling, barely more than one room. He was relieved to see light coming through her window and smoke rising from her chimney. Running towards her door, he hollered, "Glia!" When he reached her door, he knocked loudly while hollering, "Glia, I need your help."

The door opened and he saw her standing there. Dressed in a tattered dress, the same dress he's seen her wear for as long as he's known her. He has at times wondered how it could possible have survived year after year without becoming threadbare and ruined. "Why Riyan," she said with a smile, "what brings you to my door at so late an hour?"

"Bart's been poisoned," he blurted out. "I need one of your potions."

Her smile faded away as she opened the door wider and said, "Come inside."

He moved through the door and entered her hut. It always seemed bigger on the inside than it appeared on the outside.

When she shut the door, she turned to him. "What bit him?" she asked.

Riyan hesitated a moment, not sure how to answer as he didn't want anyone to know what they've been up to.

"Been up to something have you?" she asked.

"What?" he replied. "No, of course not."

She gave him a look as if she didn't believe him. People have said that she had the knack of knowing truth from lies.

"Okay," he said, giving in. "But you can't tell anyone!"

"Who am I to tell?" she asked. "Other than you, no one else ever comes here except when they are in need. Whatever you tell me will stay between us."

"We found an old burial complex out in the hills," he told her. "We were rooting around in it when Bart set off some kind of trap and was struck with a dart."

"Poisoned I take it?" she asked. When he nodded, she moved over to where she concocted her potions. "What happened next?"

He then went into the details of how the dark red spidery tendrils formed and began to spread, Bart's subsequent passing out, and the fever. "My mother doesn't think he has long to live," he finally concluded.

"She's right," Glia replied. "If those tendrils you described are what I think they are, his life will end should their tips meet on his chest or reach his eyes."

"Can you help?" he asked. Pulling forth the gems he said, "I can pay you."

She glanced at the gems in his hand and plucked two from his palm. "These will do nicely, thank you," she said. Then she cleared an area on her table and began gathering the needed ingredients.

Riyan watched as she worked. After producing a large bowl, she began filling it with various powders and liquids. Once she had all the necessary ingredients, she took what looked like a femur of some small animal and mixed the powders and liquids together with it. He moved closer to see what the concoction in the bowl looked like and quickly pulled back when the odor emanating from it hit his nose.

"Ugh!" he exclaimed. "What's in there?"

She grinned at him and said, "A little of this and a touch of that." As soon as the mixture met her approval, she removed the bone and passed her hand over the mixture as she said a word so quietly that Riyan couldn't make it out. The mixture sparkled for a second then turned a slight greenish brown color.

Then she pulled a long necked bottle from off one of her shelves and poured the mixture into it. After sealing the bottle with a cork, she handed it to Riyan. "Just a second," she said as he turned to leave. She moved to the back of her hut for a moment then returned holding a small vial.

"The potion you hold will purge the poison from his system if he is not yet dead," she explained. Then she handed him the small vial. "This will heal most of the damage done to him by the poison. Be sure to return the bottles when you're done."

Taking the vial, Riyan said, "I will and thank you."

"You're welcome Riyan." As he turned to leave, she added, "I hope you get back in time."

"So do I," he replied.

"Come visit when you can." Her words followed him out into the night as he broke into a run back to his home. He prayed that Bart would still be alive when he returned. When his home came into sight he saw Chad standing outside looking in his general direction. The sight of his friend sent a chill down his spine that he might be too late.

"Is he still alive?" he hollered as he ran to the house.

Chad saw him coming and replied, "Yes. But not by much." When Riyan reached him he added, "Your mother doesn't think he'll last long."

He showed his friend the potion and said, "Old Glia said this would save him."

Chad opened the door for him and he raced through to his room. There he saw his mother still on the bed beside Bart. Bart's tunic was off and he could see the spidery tendrils all over his chest now. And the ones that had been on his throat have spread to his upper lip.

Moving quickly to the side of the bed, he uncorked the bottle containing the potion to purge the poison. Putting it to his lips, he glanced to his mother and said, "I hope this works."

"So do we all," she replied. Which kind of surprised him that she would say that. She had never cared much for Bart.

Riyan began to pour the liquid into Bart's mouth slowly. As the potion hit his tongue and began trickling to the back of his throat, he saw Bart's throat contract as he swallowed. Encouraged by the reaction, he poured the liquid a little bit faster.

"Not too much at once," cautioned his mother. "You don't want to make him choke."

Nodding at her wisdom, he backed off and continued to trickle the potion into him little by little. Once the bottle was drained, he set it on the nightstand next to the bed and produced the other vial. When his mother looked questioningly at it, he said, "She said that this would heal whatever damage the poison did to him."

"Better wait and let the other potion work first," she advised.

"Very well," he said.

All three of them watched Bart carefully, none daring to speak as if breaking the silence would work against him somehow. Riyan's mother put her hand to Bart's forehead and whispered, "I think his fever is going down. That's a good sign."

As they watched, the spidery tendrils started to recede. Though they began to disappear, they left a pale pattern of tendril-like markings behind in their wake.

"It's working!" exclaimed Chad. He gave the others a grin at the speed with which the spidery tendrils were disappearing. When all traces save a pale patchwork were gone from his chest, face, and throat, Riyan opened the small vial. He glanced to his mother who nodded for him to go ahead.

Placing the vial to Bart's mouth, he slowly poured its contents between his lips just as he had the other. Once all of it was administered, he stoppered the vial back up and set it on the stand next to the first bottle.

Bart suddenly gave out with a sigh and then settled into a quiet sleep. Riyan looked to his mother who said, "I think he's just asleep now. We'll know better how he's faring in the morning."

Chad clapped Riyan on the back. "We did it," he said. "For awhile there I didn't think he was going to make it."

"Neither did I," admitted Riyan.

"You two look dead to the world," his mother said. "Why don't you get some sleep? Riyan, you take my bed. Chad, you can sleep out in the front room. I'll sit up with him."

"Thank you mother," Riyan said. He gave her a peck on the cheek and nodded for Chad to leave the room with him. They closed his bedroom door and headed out to the front room.

"I don't think we should tell her about what we found," Riyan told Chad. They went to sit down at the table while they talked. "I would hate to think what would happen to that place if Rupert were to find out about it."

Chad nodded. "He would go through there and take everything but the bones of the dead."

"Exactly," agreed Riyan. "And remember what Bart said about how Duke Yoric was supposed to get twenty percent. If no one knows, then perhaps we won't lose that much."

"Okay," he said. "I'll keep quiet."

"In the morning we'll see how Bart is doing," Riyan said, "then we'll figure out what to do with the treasure."

"Alright," Chad agreed. All of a sudden a mighty yawn escaped him.

Riyan grinned at his friend. The trip from The Crypt had exhausted both of them. Getting up, he told Chad he would see him in the morning. Making his way into his mother's room, he took off his shoes and dirty outer garments before collapsing on her bed. Before he even realized it, he was out.

The following morning found Bart awake but weak as a kitten. Riyan had awakened at dawn and tiptoed through the front room so as not to awaken Chad. His snores came from where he slept on the couch.

He opened the door to his room slowly and saw his mother asleep in a chair next to the bed. Pushing the door open, it let out with a creak and

Bart's eyes popped open. Riyan grinned at his friend and closed the door before going over to his side.

"You okay?" he asked.

"Tired," he replied. "I can barely move, but I'm alive."

Riyan gestured to the two bottles he got the night before from Old Glia and said, "Your condition turned around once some of Glia's brew got into you."

"Thanks," he said. "Don't know how you two managed to carry me back here. Last thing I remembered was you checking my back. Then I woke up and saw your mother sitting there. I figured you two had somehow managed to get me back here."

Riyan moved closer to Bart's ear and whispered, "My mother doesn't know anything about where we went. It might be best to keep it that way."

Bart nodded and replied, "I agree."

Just then his mother began to stir. She opened her eyes and saw them talking. "How are you this morning Bart?" she asked.

"Feeling alright," he replied. "But I don't have any strength."

"That's to be expected," she said. Getting up, she placed her hand on his forehead. "You feel normal." Then she turned to her son and said, "I'll fix some breakfast."

"Chad's still out there sleeping," Riyan told her.

"I'll be quiet," she assured him as she headed to the door.

Once she left and had closed the door, Riyan got up and sat in the chair she just vacated. "What are we to do now?" he asked.

"About what?" Bart glanced to him but it seemed difficult for him to keep his eyes open. "Don't worry, I'm not asleep. It's just more comfortable for me."

"It's alright," Riyan told him. "What I meant was, what are we to do about the coins and gems?"

His eyes parted slightly and he turned his head towards his friend. "You and Chad are going to need to make a trip to Wardean," he explained. "There you can find Thyrr and exchange the stuff we collected for regular coins."

"Is he the fence you mentioned?" asked Riyan.

"That's right. You can find his shop on Dulcet Street." He again closed his eyes and for a moment Riyan thought he had fallen asleep. Then his eyes opened again and he grinned.

"What's so funny?" Riyan asked.

"Nothing. Just glad to be alive." He laid there silently for a minute before he asked, "Could you bring me my pack?"

"Why?" inquired Riyan.

"You'll need to have something before Thyrr will talk to you," he explained.

Getting up off the bed, Riyan went over to his closet and retrieved Bart's pack. He brought it over to the bed and set it down next to him.

Bart sat up a little bit more and grabbed his pack. It was evident that he had trouble even with the little effort he was forced to expend in moving the pack closer. The poison had really drained his strength. After digging through the pack, he pulled out one of his darts. Handing it to Riyan he said, "Tell him a friend sent you then show him this."

Riyan took the dart and nodded. "Is he a friend of yours?"

"We've done business with one another before," he replied. Just what that business had been he didn't go into.

Riyan stood up and returned Bart's pack to the closet. He transferred the coins and gems that were in Bart's pack to his. Then he saw the golden piece of the circular key that they found back in The Crypt. He had begun thinking of it as a key, or rather part of a key. For he believed that if they could find all the other pieces and put it back together, they would be able to open the king's treasure room. And his imagination had been working over time ever since on what may be in there. He put the key in Bart's pack and then stuffed it way in the back of his closet.

Just then the door to his room opened and Chad stuck his head in. "How are you doing?" he asked Bart.

"Weak, but alive," Bart replied.

"Shut the door," Riyan told him as he returned to the bed.

After shutting the door, Chad came and sat on the bed with them. "Your mother woke me up," he said.

"About time you were awake anyway," grinned Bart.

Riyan then filled him in on what they were talking about, and the impending trip he and Chad will be taking to Wardean.

"We should leave soon," Chad said. "Maybe right after breakfast."

"We've only got the one horse," explained Riyan.

"I don't think I should try to get one of my father's right now," said Chad. "We'll just have to ride double."

Until his mother called them to breakfast, they talked about what they found at the bottom of The Crypt. Bart had Riyan fetch the piece of the broken key and showed them the map on the other side. "Does this look familiar to either of you?" he asked.

They both shook their heads. "Could be anywhere," offered Chad. "Would need the rest to fully figure out what area it represents."

"Oh well," sighed Bart. Then he had Riyan put it back. "I want to find the other parts."

On his way back from returning the piece of the key to Bart's pack, Riyan nodded and said, "So do I."

"How are we going to find them?" asked Chad.

"I don't know," said Bart. "I'll think about it while you guys go to Wardean."

Then from the other side of the door they heard his mother announce that breakfast was ready. Riyan looked questioningly to Bart to see if he thought he could make it. "Lend me a hand," Bart said as he worked his way to a sitting position on the edge of the bed. With Bart and Riyan on either side, they managed to help him out to the table so he could eat with the rest of them.

Chapter 11

After giving his mother some excuse about needing to run an errand for Bart, Riyan and Chad saddled the horse and were soon underway. Each wore their pack which contained the treasure they took from The Crypt. Bart had suggested they wrap the coins in cloth so they wouldn't jingle and give away their presence.

Before they left Quillim and headed to Wardean, they made a stop at Old Glia's to return the bottles as she had requested. When she learned of their impending journey to Wardean, she asked them if they could pick up a few things for her at the apothecary where she buys some of her ingredients.

Riyan said they would and they waited while she prepared a list. "Just give this to Gyman," she told them as she handed Riyan the list. Then she explained where to find his shop. She also handed him the two small gems that she had taken for the potions which saved Bart's life. "This should cover the cost. You two can split whatever is left over for your trouble."

"Thank you Glia," Riyan said.

She eyed the packs they were wearing and how their bottoms bulged out some. But what thoughts she may have been thinking she kept to herself.

They left her hut and headed cross country toward the road leading south to Wardean. The route they took bypassed Quillim in order to avoid encountering anyone.

On the way to Wardean, Riyan came to the conclusion that what they had taken from The Crypt wouldn't be enough for him to change the mind of Freya's father. He had forgotten to ask his mother how things were going as far as her engagement with Rupert. He hoped that the date for their marriage would be sometime next year. Thoughts such as these haunted him along every mile of the road to Wardean.

Riyan's mother helped Bart from the bed and to the table when it came time for the noon meal. He had slept throughout the morning, having fallen asleep not long after Chad and Riyan left for Wardean.

Now he sat at the table while Riyan's mother filled a bowl with a light stew that was more broth than anything substantial. He looked at it for a second after she placed it before him and then glanced to her.

"Eat it," she said. "It will help you get your strength back."

Knowing better than to argue with a woman when she thinks she's doing something for your own good, he took up his spoon and began slurping broth. He continued to eat the stew for several minutes in silence, neither one doing much in the way of engaging the other in conversation.

Finally, Riyan's mother said, "A stranger arrived in town about the time you, Riyan, and Chad went camping." She paused a moment as she glanced to him. When no response was forthcoming, she continued. "He was asking around about you." She glanced to him again and saw that the spoon was poised just before his mouth, motionless. The look that came over him could only be considered one of dread.

He held that position for a couple seconds before resuming to eat the soup. "Oh?" he asked.

"He claimed that he was your friend," she told him. "He's been wandering around town ever since."

Trying not to appear unnerved by what she was telling him, he asked, "What does this man look like?"

"Oh, he's of average height," she replied. "Dark hair with brown eyes. Seemed to have an air of confidence about him according to what Laerin said."

He continued eating while he assimilated the information. The fact that the man had appeared in town the day after he and Chad went to Wardean couldn't be dismissed as a coincidence. Someone must have seen him while he was there and tracked him back to Quillim.

A worried look came over him as he glanced to Riyan's mother. Anyone near him now was in great danger. "Have you mentioned to anyone that we returned last night?" he asked.

She shook her head negatively. "I haven't been further than the pen outside to feed the sheep," she replied.

"It might be better to not let anyone know that we have returned," he said. "Especially that I am staying here."

She turned a grim look to him. "I knew you were trouble," she said. "Usually Riyan has good judgment when it comes to people, but why he chose to be friends with you I have never figured out."

"If you feel that way about me," he said, a touch of hurt entering his voice, "why are you taking care of me?"

"Because Riyan cares about you," she replied. "I'm doing it for him."

He finished his stew and she began ladling him another bowlful. "I'll leave as soon as I am able," he assured her.

"Oh stop," she stated. "I've never turned away a person in need before and I'm not about to now." When his bowl was again full, she sat back down and continued eating her portion of the stew.

Bart ate quickly and finished the stew. When she offered him a third bowl he turned her down, saying that he was tired and needed rest. He allowed her to assist him back to the room and into bed. He laid there calmly until she left the room and closed the door.

No sooner was the door shut than he swung his legs back over the side of the bed facing the closet. He had to get to his pack. If the man searching for him was a member of a certain group as he feared, then it would only be a matter of time before they tracked him here to Riyan's place.

Riyan's staff was leaning against the wall close to the bed and he was able to get a hold of it. Using it as a crutch, he crossed the short space to the closet. Leaning heavily on the staff, he opened the door and then worked to reach his pack that was hidden in the back.

He stretched in order to reach it and overextended himself. Losing his balance, he fell to the floor of the closet and the staff hit the floor with a clatter. He froze there on the floor, listening for the approaching footsteps of Riyan's mother as she came to see what the noise was. To his relief, no such footsteps developed.

Crawling now, he reached his pack and opened it. He pulled out one of the rolled pieces of leather nestled inside and tried to toss it over onto the bed. It didn't quite make it all the way and landed on the floor next to it. He closed the pack again and worked his way out of the closet, cursing his weakened condition the entire time.

Once the closet door was closed, he managed to return the staff back to its original position propped against the wall. Then he crawled over to where the rolled leather had landed, picked it up and set it on the bed.

After that, he gripped the side of the bed and pulled himself back up onto it.

After he made it up, he had to lay there for several minutes before his limbs would stop trembling. The exertion of going to the closet and back had used up what strength he had left. It took awhile, but when his muscles finally calmed down he untied the thong securing the rolled leather pack. Then he unrolled it and revealed a dozen, four inch darts. Three small vials filled with a dark liquid were secured in line with the darts.

Over the next hour, he worked most carefully to remove each dart, dip it in the liquid, then return it to its place in the leather pack. Once he was finished with applying the liquid to all the darts, he replaced the small vials back in their places. Leaving two of the darts out, he rolled the pack back up and laid it on the bed next to him. He then placed the two darts he left out on top of it.

By the time he was finished, his muscles were again complaining. He laid his head back on the pillow and prayed that they would not find him here. Glancing at the darts lying atop the rolled leather pack, he at least was ready should they come for him.

"I think we're too late to do anything tonight," Riyan announced. They were still on the road and the sun had gone down an hour ago.

"Best if we find an inn and conduct our business in the morning," offered Chad.

"I don't know if we have enough coins for a room." Riyan knew that all he had brought was the treasure on his back. He should have anticipated that they might not reach Wardean before nightfall.

"I have three coppers," Chad told him after checking his pouch.

"Great," moaned Riyan. "Food or a room, and a cheap room at that."

"We always have the gems," suggested Chad. "Perhaps we could trade one for a room?"

"Worth a try."

Two hours later the lights of Wardean appeared out of the dark ahead of them. Riyan sighed with relief, he had been worried about bandits the whole way here. True, Wardean was the seat of the Border Lord. But at night? Well, you just never know.

The walls approached quickly and they were soon passing through the gate. As they passed through, Riyan asked one of the guards about an inn that was nice but not too dear. The guard told them the Silent Shepherd would be suitable and gave them directions.

"Silent Shepherd," mused Riyan with a grin. "I like the name."

Chad gave out with a chuckle and said, "I thought you might."

Following the directions the guard had given them, they soon rode up to a modest two story building. Out front was a sign depicting a shepherd sleeping on a hill while his flock was down below grazing.

Inside they found a middle aged woman coming down the stair from the second floor. When she saw them entering, she came forward and greeted them.

"Welcome to the Silent Shepherd gentlemen," she said with a smile. "How can we be of service to you?"

"My friend and I would like a room for the night," Riyan explained.

"One with two beds if that's possible," interjected Chad.

"Absolutely," she assured him with a smile. She indicated for them to follow her as she led them over to a counter where they were to check in. Once there, she immediately went behind the counter and then turned to face them.

"It will be seven coppers for the night," she said.

Riyan nodded then set his pack on the floor. After a few moments rummaging through its contents, he removed one of the smaller gems. "I'm afraid we're a bit short on coins," he explained. Then he showed her the gem. "Would this be sufficient for a room, dinner, and breakfast in the morning?"

She took the gem and examined it. When she was finished, she turned back to them with a smile and nodded. "It will be acceptable."

Riyan and Chad both sighed with relief. "Thank you," he said.

Removing a key from under the counter, she handed it to Riyan telling them that their room was upstairs, third door on the left.

"Thank you," Chad said.

"I hope you enjoy your stay here," she wished.

"I'm sure we will," Riyan assured here.

Turning from the counter, they headed for the stairs and once on the second floor, found their room. It had two beds as Chad had requested. He immediately went and laid on the one furthest from the door. "This is the life," he said with a satisfied smile.

Riyan set his pack on the floor by the head of his bed and then sat down. "Comfy."

"Let's go downstairs and get something to eat," Chad said as he sat back up. "I'm starved."

"Alright," agreed Riyan. When Chad was heading for the door without his pack, Riyan said, "I don't think we should leave our packs up here unguarded."

"May be right there," nodded Chad. He returned for his then they went down to the common room to see about getting a meal. Both were feeling quite good about everything. Off on their own and independent, what a heady feeling.

Over the course of the day, his strength had gradually returned. For dinner Riyan's mother had cooked a much more substantial meal than the thin stew she fed him for lunch. He had worried that whoever the man was that was in town would make an appearance, but so far nothing.

Riyan's mother had stayed near the house all day, only venturing out to take care of the sheep from time to time. The boy that Riyan had paid to take the sheep out while he had been 'camping' wasn't able to do it today. His father needed him for some chore or another.

Every time she left the house, she looked for any sign that someone was nearby. Even now, sitting at the table, she continued to glance out the windows. Bart felt bad that his presence was causing problems, but there was nothing he could do about it now. He did come to the decision that when Riyan and Chad returned with his share of the coins, that he was going to leave Quillim. It was no longer safe for him here.

Once he finished eating, he thanked her for the meal and returned to bed. He still needed to lean on Riyan's staff to get there, but at least he no longer had to bother her with helping him.

Sometime after the sun went down the sheep outside began stirring. Not like they were alarmed by the presence of a predator or anything, just making noises. Bart didn't think too much about it, for to him the sheep always seemed to be making noise of one kind or another.

He was almost asleep when the bedroom door opened and Riyan's mother poked her head in. The worried look on her face gave him cause for concern. "There's someone out there," she whispered.

His concern flared into full blown alarm at her words. Glancing to the bedroom window, all he could see was blackness. Turning back to her he asked, "Are you sure?" She nodded silently.

"Blow out that candle," he said to her quietly. When she blew it out, the room was plunged into darkness and at the window next to the bed was the moon shrouded silhouette of a man looking in.

"Get to your room and bar the door!" Bart yelled as the man broke the window.

Riyan's mother screamed and fled down the hall.

As Bart rolled off the bed away from the window, he grabbed the leather pack and the two darts lying on top. He hit the floor just as the man was passing through the broken frame.

"Bartholomew Agreani," the man said as he came fully into the room. A glint of light flashed off the weapon the man held in his hand. "The time has come." In the darkness, Bart could see the man move around the bed on his way to where he was laying.

Bart took one of his darts and threw it. The dart flew true and struck the man in the shoulder. Pain caused the man to cry out as he pulled it from his flesh. "Don't make this any harder than it has to be," the man told him.

Then the man cried out again as another dart struck him in the chest. "I'm going to enjoy this," he cried as he came forward and raised his sword.

Bart kicked out and took the man in the leg. It didn't break anything but it did cause him to stumble backwards a step.

"Now ..." the man said then paused a moment. He shook his head as if to clear it before he raised his sword again. "Now ... it's ..." Unable to continue, the man dropped to one knee and the sword fell from his grip.

Bart sat up and scooted back against the wall, all the while keeping an eye on the man before him. Placing his back firmly against the wall, he braced himself and began working his way up to a standing position. By the time he was erect, the man had completely collapsed to the floor. Removing another of the darts from the leather pack, he made his way to the hall.

The silence in the house was absolute. He listened for any indication that another intruder was present, but aside from the normal noise of the sheep, there was only silence.

He worked his way down to the front room and then over to the door leading into Riyan's mother's room. The house was dark. When he reached the door, he tapped upon it. "Kaitlyn," he said softly, "it's Bart."

There wasn't an immediate answer so he knocked one more time. "It's me, Bart. Everything's alright."

Then from the other side he heard the bar being lifted and the door started to open. "He's gone?" she asked once the door was opened a crack.

"No," replied Bart, "but he won't be bothering us again."

"Did you kill him?" she asked.

"Yes."

She opened the door fully. "Are there any others?"

"I haven't seen anyone," he said. "He may have been working alone."

He stepped aside as she passed into the front room. She was but a shadow as she made her way through the house to the room where the man lay.

She picked up the candle again and was about to light it when Bart told her it might not be a good idea. "He could have had someone working with him," he explained. "They do that sometimes."

Placing the unlit candle back on the table, she turned her head back toward him and asked, "Who are 'they'?"

"I'm pretty sure he came from Wardean," he said.

Moving into the hall, she asked, "What do they want with you?"

"I was on the wrong side in a power struggle you might say," he explained. "I and others have been marked for death. I understand there's a reward offered for my demise."

"I see," she said. Entering the room, she glanced over to the shattered window through which the man made his entrance. Bart followed her and had one of his darts clutched in his hand in the event of another attack.

She moved around the bed to where the man lay sprawled out across the floor. In the dark he was nothing but a vague shadow. With her foot she nudged him to see if he would respond. When he didn't, she bent down and turned him over onto his back. After a brief examination she turned towards Bart and said, "He's dead."

Bart didn't answer, just stood there while she gazed up at him. She finally stood up when he failed to answer. "How are we to find out if there's another person out there?"

"I'll go check," he replied. "Stay in your room."

"You can barely walk," she stated.

"I can walk well enough for this," he said. Then with the staff in hand, he left the room and headed for the front door. Once there, he cracked it open slightly and gazed out. No shadows moved in the moonlight. The sheep were behaving normally which was a good sign.

He opened the door and slipped out. For several minutes he did a circuit around the home until he was sure there was no one else out there. Then returning back into the house, he informed Riyan's mother that the man had come alone.

"Is it safe for us to have light now?" she asked.

"Yes, I think so."

She lit the candle on the table, then picked up a second and lit it from the flame of the first. "Here," she said as she offered him the second candle.

"Thanks," he told her as he took the candle. "We better get the man outside and hidden before someone comes looking for him. If they find out that he was killed in this house, you and Riyan will be marked for death as well."

A grim expression came over her as she turned her face towards him. He could tell that her opinion of him was getting worse by the minute. But she nodded and between them, they managed to drag the dead man out of the house and into the hills. She returned to the house for a shovel and then began digging a grave in a copse of trees. Before they put his body into the grave, Bart removed everything from the man's pockets and anything else of value he had including the scabbard for the sword still laying on the bedroom floor.

It was some time before the work was completed and they returned to the house. "I'm sorry I brought this trouble to your door," he said once they were back inside and sitting at the table. Laid out upon the table before him were the items he liberated from the man's pockets.

She didn't respond, just gave him a meaningful look.

"I don't think he would have told anyone what he was doing before he came here," he said. "He wouldn't have wanted to take the chance on anyone else beating him to the reward."

"How much is the reward?" she asked.

"I'm not exactly sure," he admitted. "But I would hazard a guess it's more than a thousand golds."

Her eyes widened at the figure. "That is quite a sum," she said. He only nodded in reply. They sat there while he went through the items laid out before him, but there was nothing that indicated who the man was.

Finally she asked him, "How did you manage to kill him?"

"Poisoned dart," he replied. "When you told me someone was in town looking for me, I prepared some just in case. Turned out to be most fortuitous."

"Yes, it did," she agreed. Then she stood up abruptly. "I'm going to bed."

"Hope you sleep well," he told her.

She paused there a moment before saying, "You too."

He sat there at the table thinking over the ramifications of the man showing up here. Could he have told someone where he was going? And if so, would there be other attacks? Bart wasn't sure. The only thing he did know for certain was that he needed to leave before trouble came calling again.

Chapter 12

In the morning, Chad and Riyan slept late as the rigors of the past few days had definitely taken their toll. When they finally arose, the sun had already been up for a couple hours. Taking their packs with them, they headed downstairs and were soon enjoying a breakfast of chicken and eggs.

Halfway through their meal Riyan flagged down the serving lady. "Yes?" she asked as she approached their table.

"I was wondering if you could direct us to Dulcet Street?" he said.

She pointed out the window. "There it is."

"You mean it runs right in front of here?" he asked.

Nodding her head, the lady replied, "That's right."

"Thank you," Riyan said with a smile. She flashed him a smile too before returning to her work.

Once they finished eating, they located the lady who gave them their room key the night before and made their way over to her. "Excuse me ma'am," Riyan said.

She looked up from making a notation in a book and gave them a friendly smile. "Are you leaving this morning?" she asked.

"Afraid so," he replied. After returning the key to her, he said, "We have business in town before we head out. I was wondering if it would be alright for us to leave our horse in your stable for a couple hours?"

"Sure," she said. "We're not full and I don't think it will be a problem."

"Thank you," Chad said to her.

"You're most welcome," came the reply. "If you ever find yourselves in Wardean again, I hope you choose to stay here."

Riyan grinned and nodded. "We will."

Turning away from her, they made their way out into the street. They looked up one way then down another, both directions were busy and crowded. "Which way?" Chad asked.

Shrugging, Riyan said, "One way's as good as another." So stepping out, they headed down to their left and entered the throng on the streets.

"Pretty crowded here," commented Chad.

"I know," Riyan said just as he was bumped into by a lady going the other way. After traveling down four blocks with no luck, they finally asked directions of a local and were soon to realize they had been going in the wrong direction.

Turning around, they worked their way back through the mass of people on the street. They passed by the Silent Shepherd and after another three blocks, the building they were told by the man contained Thyrr's shop came into view. More than thankful to leave the river of people on the street behind, they stepped up to the door and entered.

Inside they found a typical chandler's shop selling a variety of goods people would find useful. A man was situated behind a counter going over a ledger while a woman was looking through bolts of fabric. The man looked up as they entered and gave them a once over before returning to his ledger.

"That must be Thyrr," stated Chad.

"You think?" asked Riyan. He then moved towards the man who again looked up and noticed them crossing the shop. Closing the ledger, he grinned them a welcome.

"Can I help you gentlemen?" he asked.

Riyan nodded and set his pack on the counter. "Are you Thyrr?" he asked.

"That's right," the man affirmed.

He then opened his pack and said, "A friend sent me." Pulling forth the dart, he laid it on the counter between them.

Thyrr glanced to the lady and said in a hushed tone, "Put that away!"

Riyan quickly returned the dart to his pack.

Nodding over to a table set against the wall at the back of the store, he said, "Have a seat. I'll be with you when I can." He then nodded his head meaningfully towards the lady.

Understanding what he meant, Riyan and Chad moved over to the table and took their seats. The table was out of the direct view of the door, but they could see the area of the store where the lady was looking through the fabric. They waited for what must have been over ten minutes before she finally settled on the cloth she wanted. Once she paid for it and had left the store, Thyrr came over to the table.

"Sorry about that," he said, "can't be too careful you know."

"We understand," replied Riyan.

"What do you have?" he asked.

Opening his pack, Riyan pulled out several of the silver coins and showed them to him. "Our friend said you might be able to take these off our hands for a fair price," he said.

"How is he?" Thyrr asked. "Haven't seen him for some time."

"He's well," Chad said.

"Good, good." Thyrr took one of the coins and closely examined it. "I haven't run across these for some time."

Surprised, Riyan asked, "You've seen them before?"

Thyrr turned his attention back to the friends and nodded. "They turn up from time to time," he replied. "It's been almost thirty years now since the last person found a cache of these. His were mostly copper though."

"Are they worth much?" Chad asked expectantly.

"Oh yes," he replied. "How many do you have?"

"Three hundred and seventy of the silver," Riyan told him. He nodded to Chad who produced the gold chain. "We also have this gold chain and several gems too."

"Must have found the King's Horde," Thyrr joked.

"King's Horde?" asked Chad.

"You two have never heard the story of the King's Horde?" he asked.

They both shook their heads.

"Supposedly there's this horde of treasure buried in the mountains hereabouts that's guarded by an army of the dead," he explained. Both Chad and Riyan glanced at one another at mention of the army of the dead. The corpses lying on the biers in The Crypt could be construed as just that.

"You see, long ago before the people who now live here arrived from the east, there existed a kingdom of men," he explained. "No one knows what happened to them or who they were." He held up the coin. "But these have been found all over the place among ruins of that lost kingdom."

"Really?" asked Riyan. It was all he could do to keep his growing excitement out of his voice.

"Really," Thyrr acknowledged. "Treasure hunters have been trying to locate this horde for hundreds of years but its hiding place has remained secret. No one hardly looks for it anymore." He then glanced at them. "The last major search was sparked thirty years ago when that last cache of these coins I mentioned were found."

Riyan and Chad glanced to each other again. The last thing they wanted was for others to learn of what they found. Two young men from a sleepy town such as Quillim would easily be swept aside by those with more experience, and lethal determination.

"Now, seeing as how you and I have a mutual friend, I'll try to keep the knowledge of where I got them quiet," he explained. "But keep in mind, there will come a time when the fact that you found three hundred and seventy of the King's silver coins will come to light."

He turned his full attention to the two young men and asked, "Did you find the King's Horde?"

Riyan gulped under the intensity of that glare. He shook his head and lied, "No. We found these in an old chest dug out of a hill." Beside him, Chad nodded agreement.

"Hmmm," he stated. Then his gaze turned back to the packs. "Let me see the gems."

He and Chad then removed the gems and laid them out on the table before him. He picked them up one by one and closely examined each in turn. Then he took the gold chain and gave it a once over as well.

"I'll give you fifty golds for the lot," he said. "And that's only because we have a mutual friend."

"Fifty?" asked Riyan, shocked that he would be offered so much.

"Alright then," Thyrr said, "fifty five. But you'll not get one more copper from me."

"Deal!" blurted out Chad before Thyrr came to his senses.

He began going through the packs and stacking the silver coins on the table. "Just have to make sure there are in fact the number of coins here you claimed," he explained.

So they waited while he counted. When he was satisfied that the count matched what they had claimed, he grabbed a box off a nearby shelf and scraped the coins, gems and the golden necklace into it.

Once the box was closed, he took a key out from his pocket and locked it. "I'll be but a second," he told them. He left the locked box containing the coins on the table as he turned around and went through the door into the back of the store. He returned a moment later with a small, bulging sack. After a quick glance around his store to make sure no one had entered while he had been in the back, he emptied the contents of the sack onto the table.

Riyan and Chad's eyes grew wide as they watched the golden sovereigns spilling from the mouth of the sack. Riyan's heart actually skipped a beat and his breath caught in his throat, so intense was the emotion he felt.

"Go ahead and count them," Thyrr said. "And hurry before someone comes in."

With trembling hands Riyan and Chad began stacking the coins into piles of five for easy counting. Twice the trembling of Chad's hands caused a stack of coins to topple before they finally had eleven stacks of five lined up neatly before them.

Never before had either one of them seen such a fortune. They could work all their lives as a shepherd or miller and not see that much wealth at one time. "The …" began Riyan but then had to clear his throat as he could barely speak. "The count is good."

"Excellent," Thyrr said with a grin. When the two lads made no move to put the gold away and just kept staring at it, he added, "You better put that away before someone sees it."

"Yeah," said Riyan as the gold's spell was broken. He and Chad picked up the coins and refilled the sack before Riyan set it inside his pack.

"Nice to have done business with you," Thyrr said. "If you see your friend again, tell him not to be such a stranger."

"We will," Chad assured him.

As he and Riyan got to their feet, Riyan said, "Thank you."

"You're welcome," he replied. He stood there with his hand resting on the chest as the two friends left the table.

Chad led the way as they made their way to the front door and passed through into the street. "Can you believe …" he started to say before Riyan cut him off.

"Let's not talk about it out here," he said. "Too many ears may be listening." Chad glanced around and nodded.

"On to the apothecary and then we can head home," Riyan said.

The directions Glia had given them were pretty straight forward and it took them little time in finding the place. When they opened the door to enter, a strong odor wafted out. Riyan's nose wrinkled as it enveloped them, but he couldn't decide if it was unpleasant or not. Just the strangeness of it put him off.

Dark and gloomy was the best way to describe Gyman's establishment. The few windows the place had were occluded by grime or blocked by objects hanging from the ceiling. Shelves lined the walls holding the most unusual items either of them had ever seen. Roots, leaves, branches; all things botanical were grouped together in an area that took up almost a third of the store. One area had bones of varying sizes from what had to have been all sorts of creatures. The rest of the place contained items ranging from rocks to dust and one wall contained large bottles containing liquids of varying color.

"How may I help you?"

Chad jumped when the voice came from just behind him.

They turned to find a little old man who couldn't have been more than four feet tall. His features were gnarled and his back was bent. Eyes peered keenly at them from beneath bushy eyebrows. His head was devoid of all hair but for a single tuft of white sticking up several inches from the top of his head.

"Are you Gyman?" Ryan asked.

"That I am," he replied. The way he stood there motionless as he stared at them gave them both the creeps.

"A friend of ours asked us to stop by while we were in Wardean," he explained. Reaching into his pack, he pulled out Glia's list. "This is what she wanted."

The old man stared at the list in his hand but made no move to take it. Riyan glanced to Chad just as Gyman asked, "What was the name of your friend?"

"Glia," replied Chad. "She's an old lady that lives near us."

"Ah yes," he stated with an ever so slight nod of his head. He then reached up and took the list from Riyan. "Wait here and don't touch anything," he said. Taking one step away, he paused and then glanced back at them, "Some of the things here don't like to be bothered."

The two young men watched him as he moved away deeper into the store. "What do you suppose he meant by that?" Chad asked quietly.

"I don't know," replied Riyan in a similar hushed voice. Glancing around he wondered what could possibly be in here that wouldn't like to be bothered.

They stood there for almost ten minutes, all the while fearing to move, before Gyman made his appearance. The little, gnarled old man clutched a small package in one of his hands. Riyan removed the two gems that Glia had given them for the items and held them out.

The old man came to a stop and moved his face close to his hand. He took several moments to examine the gems as they lay in his hand before reaching out and taking them. "Here," he said as he handed the package to Riyan. "Tell her I was able to accommodate her wishes."

"We will," Riyan assured him. Putting the package in his pack, he said, "Thank you," then he and Chad turned for the door. As he opened the door and was about to leave, he glanced back inside only to find Gyman was no longer anywhere to be seen. Turning back, he passed through the door and entered the street.

"That was creepy," he commented to Chad as they headed back to the inn to retrieve their horse.

"You could say that again," he replied. "I never saw anyone act like that before."

"Me either. Let's get out of here and go home."

"You got it," agreed Chad.

They had moved down the street when Chad suddenly remembered that Glia had said they could keep the change. But Gyman didn't give them any and neither one desired to enter Gyman's Apothecary again, even if they could have gained a few coins for the effort. So they resumed their trek back to the inn.

Back at the Silent Shepherd, they saddled their horse and were soon on their way home. By the position of the sun, it was likely they weren't going to make it back before dark.

When Bart had awoken earlier this morning, more of his strength had returned. Not nearly to the degree that he had before being struck down in The Crypt, but at least he no longer needed the aid of Riyan's staff to walk around.

He spent the early morning hours lying in bed. At one point he went over to the closet and took the piece of the golden key from out of his pack and carried it back to the bed. There he examined it closely.

The sigils on the one side that had lined up with the sigils inscribed on the wall in the room at the deepest point of The Crypt, made no sense to him. Despite studying them at length, he learned nothing from them.

On the other side, however, the map was very clear. Not a complete map to be sure, he figured it would take combining this section of the circular key with the others to achieve that. What this one did show was a mountain range running along the bottom. Just to the north of the mountain range was a lake that had a river connecting it to another, smaller lake further to the north with markings next to it. After careful examination, he came to the conclusion that the markings next to the smaller lake represented a city or town of some kind.

Knock! Knock!

The sound of someone knocking on the front door echoed through the house. Suddenly alarmed, he leaped from the bed and quickly secreted the piece of the key back within his pack. Removing two of his darts, he moved to the bedroom door and cracked it open.

Peering out, he saw Riyan's mother at the door talking to someone. From his position in the bedroom, he wasn't able to overhear very well what was being said. He was about to leave the room and go out to the front room when Riyan's mother stepped back and allowed Freya to enter.

He was stunned to see Freya. She was literally the last person he expected. Realizing there was no immediate threat, he placed the darts back into the rolled leather pack that held all of his darts. Then he returned to the door and peered out through the crack between the door and the door jamb. Listening carefully, he tried to hear what was being said.

"… didn't know who else to come to," Freya said. By the tone of her voice, she was obviously distraught. "I don't want to marry Rupert, he doesn't even like me."

"Are you so sure?" Kaitlyn asked.

"Yes," replied Freya. "You sort of know about things like that."

Kaitlyn nodded. "I don't know what I can do to help. This is between your family and Rupert's."

"I know," Freya told her. "Every one of my friends thinks he's a great catch. Wealth and a good standing in the community, but I don't care for that. I would rather be some shepherd's wife living in squalor than as Rupert's and live in wealth." Then her eyes widened and she stammered, "I … I didn't mean to imply …"

Kaitlyn smiled. "I understand," she assured her.

"I heard Riyan was out of town and thought this would be a good time to talk with someone who understands." Freya cast her eyes down before saying, "My father has forbidden me to see or talk with Riyan until after the wedding."

"I know, Riyan told me," she replied. "This marriage is going to be hard on you, Riyan too." Placing her hand under Freya's chin, she raised her face until it looked into hers. She could see the tracks the tears were making as they coursed down her cheeks. "Riyan holds no animosity towards you. In fact I do believe that he will still be a stalwart friend of yours until the end of his days."

"I'm glad," Freya said through the emotion constricting her throat. "I wouldn't want to lose him."

"You won't," Kaitlyn assured her. "I'll be here for you too." Putting her arms around the girl, she held Freya as the sobs began wracking her body. With tears in her own eyes, she patted the girl's back and comforted her until the sobbing quieted.

"When will the wedding be?" Riyan's mother asked.

A few more sniffles then Freya raised her head from off Kaitlyn's shoulder. "Fortunately custom is on my side there," she replied. "As the bride, I get to set the date."

"And?" Kaitlyn prompted.

From his position where he's eavesdropping behind the bedroom door, Bart held his breath.

"As you know, custom allows me to set the date anywhere from three months to a year from the day the betrothal is finalized," she explained. "So I set it one year away."

Kaitlyn nodded, "I can understand your willingness to put this off for as long as possible."

"I know," she replied. "But my father is pressuring me to change it for an earlier time. He wants it done and settled." Not to mention the fact that the longer the engagement lasts, the more the bride tells the community how she feels about the marriage. To set it a year away is practically a slap in Rupert's face.

"As do all fathers." A sad smile came to her as her memory went back to the time when her own father urged her to marry Riyan's father. She was dead set against it, as she was sure all brides were who were not allowed to pick their own groom, and so had set the date as far out as possible. As it turned out, her father made a much better match for her than she had ever dreamed could be possible. She had later regretted the shame she had put her husband through during that time.

As Bart closed the door, Freya and Riyan's mother began talking about things that held very little interest for him. He had heard what he wanted. *A year!* Riyan had a year unless her father's urging changed her mind, but with the way she felt about Rupert, that was as unlikely to happen as Bart to grow a second head.

He'll see what Riyan plans to do before he makes any decisions about leaving Quillim and starting a new life elsewhere. For if one of those seeking him has already discovered him here, then more are likely to follow, it's only a matter of time. The last thing he wants to do is bring his troubles into the lives of the friends he made here.

Lying back on the bed, his mind wandered to what Chad and Riyan were doing now.

Chapter 13

"Why didn't you stay on the road?" exclaimed Chad quietly from where he sat on the horse behind Riyan.

"We can lose them in the hills," replied Riyan.

They leaned low in the saddle as they fled through the hills. A short time ago, three bandits accosted them and it was only through great luck that they managed to get away. Now the bandits were hot on their trail. Riyan had turned off the road and begun heading through the hills.

"Are they still back there?" asked Riyan.

Chad glanced back and saw that they had only a couple hundred foot lead on them. "Oh yeah," he replied. "I think they're gaining." Which wasn't too surprising seeing as how Chad and Riyan were riding double and the bandits were not. "We're not going to be able to stay ahead of them."

"I know," Riyan acknowledged. Not too far ahead of them stood the treeline where the forest began. He hoped that if they could make it to the trees before the bandits closed the gap, they might have a better chance of escaping. Chad saw where Riyan was taking them and silently agreed that it was their best shot.

They didn't even consider putting up a fight since all they had for weapons was the sling that Riyan always carried with him and a couple belt knives. At the moment the sling was buried at the bottom of his pack.

The bandits on the other hand were equipped with swords, knives, and one even had a shield secured behind his saddle. Any stand they were to make against such armed men would prove futile.

Keeping low in the saddle, they urged their horse in maintaining as fast a pace as it could. The bandits behind them continued to slowly gain ground until they reached the forest. By that time the gap between them had been reduced to a mere hundred feet.

Riyan maneuvered between the boles of the trees but initially was unsuccessful in putting any more distance between themselves and the bandits. From behind they heard one of the bandits yell, "Give it up! You'll never get away!"

Ignoring him, Riyan continued to push deeper into the forest.

Overhanging limbs started striking them as they raced between the trees, and bushes were beginning to impede their progress. When their forward momentum began to diminish, Riyan started to think this hadn't been such a smart idea. Fortunately though, the bandits behind them were just as hampered in their movement through the forest as they were.

Riyan finally came to the conclusion that escape was going to be impossible. So it was time to get creative. "Get my sling out of my pack," he hollered to Chad. Then he ducked just as a thick branch loomed up in front of him. Behind him, he heard Chad grunt when he wasn't quick enough to avoid the branch.

"I'll try," he said as he rubbed the red spot on his forehead.

As they maneuvered between the trees, Chad untied the top of Riyan's pack and began digging through it until he felt one of the straps of the sling. "Got it," he said just as the horse jumped over a fallen log. Chad hadn't been prepared and was almost thrown from its back. When he felt himself sliding off, he grabbed onto Riyan with a death grip and managed to right himself.

Handing the sling to his friend, he said, "Here."

Riyan reached back and took the sling. "Now, get five of the gold coins out."

"Why?" he asked.

"Just do it!" Riyan insisted. He felt Chad begin to rummage through his pack again. While he dug out the coins, Riyan began scanning the forest ahead of them for what he wanted.

"We better do something quick," said Chad, "they're almost upon us."

Riyan turned his attention from the forest ahead to the bandits behind. What had been over a hundred feet lead, has shrunk further to three quarters of that. "I know," he replied. "Working on it."

He turned back to the forest ahead and finally saw what he was looking for. "There's a clearing up ahead," he told his friend. "Once we're halfway through it, toss the gold coins to the ground. Make sure they land somewhere visible."

"You think they're going to stop for the coins?" he asked.

"With any luck, yes," he replied. "We're almost there, get ready."

Chad looked over his friend's shoulder and saw the clearing approaching. Through the trees it appeared as a beacon of light in the dark forest seeing as how the sunlight was able to breach the canopy of leaves.

Riyan braced himself as the horse leaped across another fallen log and entered the clearing. It wasn't big, just a small area where it looked like wild animals came to graze. The clearing was primarily covered with grass though a few wild bushes sprouted here and there. "Now Chad!" hollered Riyan as they came to a spot slightly more barren than the rest.

Chad tossed the coins so they landed upon and around the barren area a split second before the bandits entered the clearing behind them. Then Riyan and Chad reached the far side. They glanced back and saw that two of the bandits had indeed stopped to pick up the coins while the third continued the chase.

"It didn't work!" hollered Chad.

"It worked well enough," countered Riyan then they were back in among the trees. "Here," said Riyan as he handed the reins to Chad.

"What are you planning on doing?" Chad asked.

"Something stupid I'm sure," was the reply. Riyan saw a thick branch hanging across their path two feet above their heads, it was perfect. Just before they drew close to it, Riyan took his right foot out of the stirrup and placed it on the saddle beneath him.

"You're crazy!" Chad yelled at him when he realized what he was about to do.

Ignoring his friend, Riyan braced himself and then leaped from the back of the horse when they reached the branch. He sailed through the air and grabbed the overhanging branch. The force of his impact scrapped several inches of skin off his forearms before he was able to stop himself.

A quick glance back showed the pursuing bandit drawing his sword as he looked at Riyan hanging from the branch. Swinging up, he got on top of the branch just as the sword struck the wood right where he had been hanging a moment before. As the bandit pulled the blade from the branch, he reached for another one higher up in the tree and pulled himself even further out of the bandit's reach.

He glanced down at the bandit who was still at the bottom of the tree, then off to where Chad was disappearing in the forest. At least he got Chad out of this, now to save himself. Taking his sling out from where he had stuffed it in his shirt, he contemplated what he was going to do. From the direction of the clearing he could hear the other two bandits making their way towards their partner.

The only ammunition he had for the sling were the coins in his pack. Reaching into it, he pulled out one of the copper coins they had found in The Crypt. Placing it in the cup of his sling, he steadied himself against the tree's trunk as best he could. In all the times he spent practicing this sort of thing while watching the sheep, he never once tried it from the top of a tree. If he ever gets out of this and has the time, he may put in some practice.

"Come on down," the bandit said from atop his horse. "You got nowhere to go." Either the bandit didn't realize that Riyan had a sling, or he didn't care, for he made no effort to avoid the attack.

So Riyan got the sling up to speed quickly then released the coin. It flew down and struck the bandit in the face. With a cry, the bandit fell of his horse backwards. Blood flew everywhere and when he stood back up, Riyan could see the coin embedded where his nose once had been.

The man was shrieking in pain as blood poured from the wound. Riyan didn't want to give him a chance to recover so he got another of the coins into the sling's cup and launched it. This one struck the bandit in the side of the head and when he fell to the ground, he didn't get back up.

By this time the other two bandits had arrived. They saw their partner lying on the ground dead. Then they turned their attention up to where Riyan stood in the tree. "We're going to gut you kid!" one of them threatened. Dismounting, they went to the base of the tree and began climbing up.

First one began to climb, then the other. From his position, Riyan was unable to get a good shot at them. They were much too close to the trunk for his shot to be effective. There were too many branches in the way too.

Then from out of the forest behind the men climbing the tree, Riyan saw Chad approaching. In his hand he held a four foot branch, one end was sharp and jagged from where Chad must have broken it off. Unnoticed, he came up behind the bandit closest to the ground and with all his might, stabbed him in the back with the branch.

The years of hauling grain sacks and barrels of flour at the mill paid off. For when the stick struck, it pierced the man's back and went all the way through, exiting from the other side. Blood spurted out of the man's chest as the jagged end of the stick emerged. The man didn't even cry out, the blow must have killed him instantly.

As the man fell from the tree, Chad jumped backwards to avoid the dead man collapsing on him. Then from above he heard the last bandit yell as he leaped from the tree towards him. Backpedaling quickly, Chad got out of the way.

The man landed with sword in hand. Chad could see the hate for him burning in his eyes. Giving out with an inarticulate cry, the man charged with his right hand holding the sword high. He could see the man intended to cleave him in two. Chad kept moving backwards until his heel hit a root and fell to the ground. There was no time to do anything but brace for the sword stroke that would end his life.

But just before the sword fell, the bandit cried out and sank to his knees. His left hand reached behind him as if he was trying to get something. Chad watched quite perplexed until he saw something shiny fly from the tree wherein Riyan stood and strike the bandit.

This time the blow knocked the bandit to the ground and he laid there crying out in pain. Chad could see the man's back was covered in blood and obviously was in a lot of pain. He glanced up to see Riyan hop down out of the tree. Riyan stopped next to the man with the stick through his back and pulled the stick free.

Then he carried it over to where Chad stood over the man writhing on the ground. "Can't let him suffer," Riyan said. Even though the bandit would have most likely killed them, he couldn't leave the man to suffer. So taking the stick in both hands, he held it aloft over his head for the briefest moment before plunging it into the man and silencing his cries.

"You okay?" Riyan asked as he turned to his friend.

"Yeah," nodded Chad. "You?"

"Just a few scrapes," he said.

"What should we do with them?" Chad asked as he gazed at the dead bandits. Then it suddenly hit him. He and Riyan had fought off three vicious bandits and prevailed. "Our first real battle," he announced.

"I guess you could call it that," agreed Riyan. Grinning, he patted Chad on the back. "We make a great team. And as for what to do with them? I say leave 'em for the animals."

"No point in letting their horses and equipment go to waste though," suggested Chad.

"Absolutely not," agreed Riyan. "To the victor go the spoils." So while Chad went to retrieve Riyan's horse from where he left him, Riyan went about gathering the three bandits' horses together. Then he went to one of the bandits by the tree and removed the man's sword belt from around his waist. Strapping it on around his own, he pulled forth the sword and felt every inch the hero.

The sword itself was a rather plain sword, more for utility than anything else. It had a straight blade that would be considered a longsword, with a plain unadorned crossguard and hilt. Still, it was the first sword Riyan ever held and he felt great holding it.

When Chad returned with the horse, he found Riyan swinging the sword back and forth with a grin on his face. Chad of course had to have one for himself, so he went and removed one from another and strapped it around his waist. It definitely took some getting use to, the scabbard kept trying to trip him up and the whole thing weighed quite a bit more than he expected.

"These might come in useful," Riyan finally said after sliding his sword back in the scabbard. He pulled the hand away that he was using to guide the blade as it slid into the scabbard. Blood was welling from a cut he gave himself as the sword was sliding in.

"If we don't kill ourselves with them first," agreed Chad. "We don't know the first thing about using a sword."

"What's there to know?" asked Riyan. "You get close to an enemy and stick 'em."

Chad looked at his friend doubtfully, "I think there's a bit more than that to it."

Riyan grinned and shrugged. "Let's see what they have on them and then head home."

Other than a few copper coins and a single silver, the bandits didn't have much of what you would call treasure on them. Riyan was disappointed. For in the sagas bards always told, whenever the hero killed a bandit or some other foe, the dead usually held a magical item or maybe a map, something. Needless to say, he was a bit put off. He did use one of the bandit's knives to remove the coins from their bodies that he slung at them. That part was a bit ghastly but he didn't want to leave anything behind. They also retrieved the gold coins they had dropped in an attempt to slow the bandits down.

"At least we aren't going to have to ride double anymore," Chad stated.

"Thank goodness," replied Riyan. "No offense but I was getting tired of you hanging onto me."

"Oh and like I enjoyed smelling your wonderful odor for so long?" The two friends stared at each other until they both erupted in laughter. "Let's get out of here," he said.

They mounted, then each took the reins of one of the two remaining horses and tied them to the rear of their saddles. Once the two spare horses were secured, Riyan began leading them out of the forest. Chad suggested they take the back way to Riyan's house so no one in town would see them arriving with the horses. Just their luck they would run into Rupert who would probably take them.

It was a little before dinner when they finally arrived at Riyan's home. Needless to say, when Bart and Riyan's mother saw them arriving with three extra horses and swords at their hip, they knew something must have happened. So while they were putting the horses into the barn, Chad and Riyan explained what happened. They didn't go into detail as to why they had been in Wardean, and they definitely made no mention of the coins or the King's Horde while Riyan's mother was with them.

Then it was Bart and Riyan's mother's turn to tell them of the man who showed up to kill Bart. It was well past dinner before both parties had finished relating their different adventures.

Riyan's mother mentioned that Freya had stopped by but didn't say much more than that. Later that night after Riyan's mother had gone to bed, the three friends stayed up late in the front room. It was at that time when Bart told them of the conversation he overheard Freya and Riyan's mother have.

"So they won't be getting married for a year," he summed up once he was finished.

"That might be enough time," Riyan said as he glanced to Chad.

"Time for what?" asked Bart.

"To find the rest of the key, and open the King's Horde," he stated quietly.

"King's Horde?"

"Yes," replied Chad. "It's ..." He and Riyan then filled Bart in on what they had learned from Thyrr.

Once they were done, Riyan said, "I intend to find the rest of the key and open it. With the treasure inside, Freya's father would have to agree to let his daughter break off the engagement with Rupert in my favor."

"There's but one minor problem," said Bart.

"What?" Riyan asked.

"You don't know where the rest of it is," he explained. "What we have could be the missing fragment from the whole, or it could be one of many scattered in a dozen different places." He paused a moment as he glanced from one to the other. "From what you said Thyrr told you, people have been searching for this place for centuries."

"I know, but we have something they don't," he stated. "We have a part of the key. Plus we've been in The Crypt and seen the seal protecting the King's Horde."

"That's true Bart," added Chad.

He glanced at them both again and could see they were dead set to do this. Sighing, he indicated for them to follow and said, "Come with me a second." Leading them to Riyan's room, he went to the closet and removed the piece of the golden key from his pack. He showed them the map on the one side and the spot he believed indicated a town of some sort. "This is the only place on here that shows something other than geographic representations. It has to mean something."

"Are you saying the rest of the key is there?" asked Riyan.

Bart shrugged. "I don't know," he admitted. "But if we are going to go in search of the rest of the key, it's as good a place as any to start."

"But we still don't know where the place is," said Chad.

"True," nodded Bart.

"There is a large map of the surrounding area in the Magistrate's office," Chad suddenly said. "Maybe we could see if this place is on that map."

"Good idea," agreed Riyan. "We could go down in the morning and take a look."

Chad nodded and then grew silent. After a moment he said, "Somehow I need to figure a way to talk to my mother about the grinding stones and give her the coins they need."

"I could find Eryl in the morning and discover whether your father will be at the mill or not," offered Bart.

"That would be great. Then if he is, I could go pay a visit to my mother." Chad felt better now that he was one step closer to helping his family and hopefully mending the rift that was between himself and his father.

Chad and Bart spent the night at Riyan's place. They crashed in the front room while Riyan took back his bed from Bart. In the morning when they told Riyan's mother that they were heading into town, she asked about the sheep.

"Your friend Davin hasn't been taking them out much," she said. "They really need to graze."

"I know mother," replied Riyan. "But this is more important right now."

She gave him a look saying that she didn't agree but wasn't about to argue the point. He felt guilty. He knew that she counted on him to help with the sheep and he couldn't help but feel that he was letting her down some-how. "I'll take them out later this afternoon, okay?" he said.

"See that you do," she said.

Feeling somewhat better now that she's been mollified, he and the other two left and headed into town. Riyan thought about wearing his sword but decided against it. If he were to be seen wearing a sword around Quillim, it would have raised too many questions he wouldn't want to answer.

The first thing they did was to hunt down Eryl. Finding Chad's brother wasn't too difficult and when asked, he told them that their father would be at the mill until lunchtime. He was working to prepare the wooden frame-work for the two wheels that were coming in later in the week.

"How's mother doing?" asked Chad.

"Fine," replied his brother. "She's sad about all that's going on. I hope things can work out again."

"Me too," Chad assured him. "I'm going home now to talk to her."

"Good luck," Eryl wished him.

"Thanks," Chad replied.

They left Eryl where he was playing with several other youths of similar age and headed directly to Chad's home. Despite what his father said, he still felt that it was his home too.

Making their way through the streets, they kept a lookout for Rupert but he and his three buddies were nowhere to be seen. Before they reached Chad's home, another young man that lived in town saw them passing through and moved to intercept them.

"Bart," the young man said. "There's been a stranger in town asking about you."

"Yeah, I heard," replied Bart. "We just got back."

"He was kind of strange," Egrin replied. Egrin was the son of the local baker. He wasn't as close to Chad and Riyan as he was to Bart, though he's had more dealings with Chad due to the fact his father bought flour from Chad's father.

Bart came to a stop as he talked with Egrin. "You two go on ahead," he said. "I'll catch up."

"Alright," Riyan said as he and Chad continued on towards Chad's home.

It didn't take them long before they arrived. Chad's mother was outside drawing water from their well when she saw them approaching. Leaving the bucket sitting on the ground, she turned towards them and waited for her son to approach.

Chad was filled with uncertainty when he saw here. He wasn't sure just how she was going to react to him after everything that's happened. Coming close, he said the only thing he could, "I'm sorry mother," and then gave her an embrace.

She returned it with feeling and when they broke it off, had tears in her eyes. "Oh Chad," she said, "why did you go against your father's wishes?"

He felt bad. "I was just trying to help," he replied. "I didn't mean to make the situation worse."

"I know," she said.

"How's father?' he asked.

"Not good," she told him. Emotions got the better of her and it took a minute to get them under control. "He hasn't changed his mind about you."

"I realize that," stated Bart. "How much are the two new grinding stones going to set him back?"

"Fifty golds," she replied. "We had twenty saved against adversity and those are already gone. The magistrate was good enough to loan us the rest. He said that it wouldn't do for Quillim not to have an operable mill."

"Fifty?" he asked incredulous. That amounted to a veritable fortune by the standards of those in Quillim. He was surprised that his family had actually managed to squirrel away twenty golds.

She nodded. "I know. I don't know how we'll ever pay him back."

Chad glanced to Riyan who nodded.

Before they left, they had placed all the gold coins they had received from Thyrr into his pack. "I have something for you and father," he said. "To make up for what I did." She looked at him questioningly. Then he opened his pack and showed her the gold inside.

When she looked inside and saw the shining golden coins, she had a sharp intake of breath. "Oh my," she said. "How many are in there?"

"Fifty five," he replied. "We found some gems up in the mountains while we were camping and sold them in Wardean. Me, Riyan and Bart have decided to give you and father what is needed to replace the grinding wheels."

"You can't be serious!" she exclaimed. "Oh Chadric." Tears began to flow unbidden as she sobbed in happiness.

"Will father accept this?" Chad asked. "I know how proud he is about some things."

"I think he will," she said. "But it might be best if I tell him. If you were to be here he might get his back up and no amount of logic would sway him."

"He can stay at my place," offered Riyan.

"That would be best," she said, "at least for now."

So they went inside the house to take the fifty coins out of the pack. When Chad's mother was about to pick up the water bucket to take it back to the house, Riyan beat her to it and carried the bucket inside for her.

Once inside, Chad removed the coins and stacked them on the table. "I hope this makes things better between father and me," he said.

"I'm sure it will," she replied. "But even with this it may take time for things to be as they were."

"I know." Chad gave her a hug before he and Riyan took off for the magistrate's office. "Send Eryl to Riyan's if things change and I can come back."

"I will," she said as fresh tears began to course down her face.

"I love you mother," Chad said after another hug.

"I love you too," she replied.

When at last she was able to release her son, he and Riyan left and headed over to the magistrate's office. Chad was awfully quiet as they made their way back through town. "You okay?" Riyan asked.

"Better," he replied. "If my father forgives me then I will be." He really didn't realize how much he cared about the way his father felt about him until he lost his goodwill. Now he almost felt empty inside and knew that only regaining his father's favor would fill it.

They encountered Bart who was on his way to meet them at Chad's family's home. "Everything go alright?" he asked.

"Won't know that until Eryl comes with word," Riyan replied.

"I'm sure it's going to work out for the best," Bart said reassuringly as they approached the Town Hall where the magistrate's office lies.

When they entered the building, they stopped to see Ceci and asked her if they could see the magistrate.

"I'm sorry Riyan," she replied. "He and Rupert went up to Yarix and won't be back for three days." Yarix was a small town less than a day's ride to the north. It too was a small town of herders and farmers like Quillim.

"Thank you," he said.

Once they were outside, Riyan said under his breath, "Three days!"

"Don't worry Riyan," Bart said. "We're going to get in and see that map before then."

"What do you mean?" he asked. "Ceci isn't about to allow us to go poking around his office while he's out."

"I know," he replied with a grin. "But if you don't want to wait three days, I do have another idea."

Riyan glanced at his friend and asked, "What?"

Chapter 14

Later that night when the town grew quiet, three shadows moved in the dark. They wended their way through the buildings until the Town Hall rose out of the darkness before them. Stopping for only a brief moment in the shadows of a bordering building, Bart made sure no one was around. Then he led Riyan and Chad towards the main door.

"Are you sure this is such a good idea?" asked Riyan.

"No one's around this late at night," replied Bart. "Besides, we'll only be a moment."

"Exactly," Chad interjected. "It's not like we're planning on taking anything."

"Just keep an eye out until I get the door opened," Bart told the other two. Taking out his lockpicks, he pulled out two of the instruments and began working on the lock. This lock was a rather simple one, nothing better had ever been needed in the quiet town of Quillim. It took him but a moment before he felt the lock turn.

"Okay," he whispered and opened the door. Bart moved inside and was quickly followed by Chad and Riyan. He relocked the door once it was shut.

They followed him to the stairs where they made their way up to the third floor in the dark. Moving in the all but absolute darkness of the Town Hall's interior forced them to step carefully. Riyan had thought they should bring a lantern, but Bart had argued against it.

"You aren't really going to need it if you just move slowly enough," he explained. "Also, it might be seen by someone passing by outside." He did however bring along an item for light, something he called a 'tube lantern'. It was little more than a hollowed out piece of wood, six inches long with a diameter of three inches, with the stub of a candle set inside. When the candle was lit, it aimed a beam of light at a specified location rather than illuminating the entire room. He told them this was a little item his father claimed to have thought up.

Riyan recognized it from earlier this afternoon. He had taken the flock out to graze as he promised his mother, Chad and Bart had accompanied him. They also dropped off Old Glia's package for which she was very thankful. While they were out, Bart had found the piece of wood and begun carving out its insides. When they asked what he was doing, he just grinned but wouldn't answer. As it turned out, he had been making the tube lantern.

They followed the stairs up until they reached the third floor landing. Then they headed down the hallway to the end and the Magistrate's Office. None were surprised to find that the door was locked. But it was just as simple as the one below and Bart had it opened in no time. "They don't worry too much about break-ins around here do they?" he asked once the lock was opened.

Chad chuckled, "What would anyone steal?"

"True," Bart replied then opened the door. Several windows spaced along two of the walls allowed light from the moon and stars to filter in. It cast the room in a multitude of shadows.

"Over here," Riyan said as he moved to their right. In the faint light coming in through the windows they saw the outline of a map framed upon the wall.

"Just give me a second," Bart said as he settled to the floor. He set the tube lantern on the floor before him and worked to get the stub of a candle lit. Once the wick caught fire, light came out of the end and created a line of light across the floor.

"That's pretty cool," Chad said.

"I know," Bart replied with a grin. Standing up, he took the tube lantern in hand and showed them how it only illuminated a circular area directly in front of where he pointing it. "My father has all sorts of things like this."

"Never heard of anything like this before," Riyan said as he watched the circle of light move across the wall.

"No, I wouldn't think so," said Bart. "He's pretty protective of his things. Not too many people even know about most of them." As he moved the light to reveal the map, Riyan took the piece of the golden key from out of his pocket.

"Now," murmured Bart, "let's see if we can find out where this place is." He shined the light on the map and saw where Quillim was prominently displayed in the center. The rest of the map radiated out every direction.

The map extended as far north to just above Yarix, and southward a little past Wardean. The mountains to the west filled in the left side of the map while the lands of Duke Yoric filled the right.

"I don't see it," Riyan said.

"No," agreed Bart. "This map doesn't show enough of the land."

"Then how are we to know where this place is?" questioned Chad.

"That's the question," replied Riyan. "How are we going to figure it out without anyone else discovering what we're looking for?" In the back of his mind he remembered Thyrr saying that there would come a time when the coins he bought from them would become known. The last thing Riyan wanted was for them to leave a trail for others to follow.

"Is there another place that would have a map?" asked Chad. "One that might show a wider area?"

"In Wardean there's a cartographer by the name of Bennin that has a variety of maps depicting the known world," explained Bart. "Or so he claims."

"But if we seek his help, then others could find out where we went," Riyan objected. "Once the news of our finding the silver coins gets out, and it will according to Thyrr, then the hunt will be on. We can't afford to leave any trail."

"Maybe Crag Keep?" suggested Bart.

"Crag Keep?" asked Riyan. Crag Keep was one of the keeps under the Border Lord Duke Yoric. It was west of Wardean and sat on the southern end of one of the passes between the lands of Duke Yoric and those of the goblins on the far side.

"Exactly," he replied. "I've heard that in the great hall there is a massive map showing the lands on both sides of the mountain range."

"That might be what we need to look at," agreed Riyan.

"How are we going to gain access to the great hall?" asked Chad. "Do you think they are going to just allow anyone to stroll through there?"

"We'll worry about that when we get there," shrugged Bart. "But I don't think we have many other options open to us if we wish to keep this to ourselves."

"I agree," Riyan said. "We can leave in the morning."

Bart put the end of the tube lantern to his lips and blew the candle out. "Then let's get out of here." He led them out of the Magistrate's Office and made sure the door was once again locked. After that they went down the stairs and to the front door. There, Bart peered out to be sure the area was clear, then they quickly exited the building. Bart took a moment to relock the door before the three friends headed back to Riyan's place.

They spent an hour sitting up in the front room planning what they were going to do the following morning. Most of it was fairly simple, getting supplies together, clothes, that sort of thing. But what gave Riyan concern was what he was going to tell his mother. After all, it was just him and her. There was no one else in whom she could rely upon other than her son. He wasn't sure how she would take the news.

In the morning when he told her they were planning on leaving for an indeterminate amount of time, she just stared at him. "We won't be gone forever," he explained. "Maybe a couple weeks."

Chad jumped in to help by saying, "A month, tops."

"Where are you going?" she asked. She had a tight rein on her emotions and Riyan couldn't tell what her reaction was.

"Bart has some business down south and we are going along," he told her.

Apparently that was the wrong thing to say for her expression darkened and her brows knitted together. She turned her eyes on Bart and asked, "Haven't you brought enough trouble into this house?"

"I assure you," Bart replied, "it is nothing like that."

Turning back to her son, she looked at him. Really looked at him for the first time and a tear came to her eye.

"I'll be okay mother, I promise," he said.

She smiled. It was such a sad smile that it almost broke his heart. "I guess this time comes in every mother's life," she said.

"What?" he asked.

"When her son grows up and becomes a man."

Riyan didn't know how to reply to that other than going over and giving her a hug. "I'll be back before Freya's and Rupert's marriage," he said. "Who knows what may happen between now and then?"

She suddenly gripped his shoulders and pushed him back to arm's length. "You're not going to kill him are you?" she asked as she stared into his eyes. Then she glanced to Bart and Chad.

"No!" all three exclaimed at the same time.

Riyan reached into his pocket and pulled out three of the remaining five gold coins they received from Thyrr. Last night the other two agreed for his mother to have them to tide her over until his return. He held them out to her.

She gasped when she saw them. "Where did you get these?"

"Is that important?" he asked.

Her expression hardened one more time. "Yes, it is. Now, where did you get them?"

Riyan glanced at the other two for help but they weren't able to give him any. "We found some treasure up in the mountains," he explained. "When Bart was poisoned. Chad and I went to Wardean and sold what we found to someone that Bart knew. He gave us enough gold to help Chad's parents with replacing the grinding wheels, and now to help you while I'm gone."

"It might be a good idea to keep all this between us," suggested Chad.

"And if anyone comes around looking for me," Bart added, "you haven't seen me and you don't know where I went."

"I don't like this one bit," she said. Then she gazed into the eyes of her son and took the three golds. "But it would seem your mind is already made up."

"It'll work out for the best," he assured her. He indicated the gold in her hand and said, "With that you can pay someone to come and help with the flock."

She nodded. "Be careful," she said.

And with those words Riyan knew that she had resigned herself to his going. He's not sure why, but it didn't make him feel a whole lot better.

"We should get going before someone comes around," Bart said.

"Give me a minute okay?" he asked his two friends.

"Sure," replied Chad then he and Bart went out to the barn to ready the three horses they'll be taking.

Once they were out, Riyan hugged his mother tightly as a tear welled from his eye. "I love you mother," he said. "I'll be back."

"I love you too," she replied with a catch in her voice.

They held each other for quite awhile, neither one wanting to break away. Finally, he disengaged from her embrace. Giving her a peck on the cheek, he left her sitting in the chair in the front room as he exited through the back door.

"You okay?" Chad asked as he appeared in the barn.

Nodding, Riyan said, "Yeah."

Bart was already in the saddle and came forward with the horse Riyan was to ride. He handed him the reins and waited until he was in the saddle. Once Riyan was mounted, they headed out.

Riyan glanced to the doorway at the back of the house and saw his mother standing there. She waved goodbye silently as he rode away. Before he rode out of sight, he turned and waved a final time, then she was gone.

None of them were very good on horseback, though they all had some experience. They made fairly decent time as they worked their way through the hills around town to the road leading south.

Riyan had the sword belt around his waist that he took from the thieves, Chad wore the other. Bart thought they were both dumb to wear them. "You guys don't even know how to use them."

"So?" Riyan asked. "It feels good to have it on."

Chad grinned to him and said, "It does, doesn't it."

Bart just rolled his eyes heavenward. He refused to take the sword of the man who came to kill him. They left it wrapped up in some old clothes in the back of Riyan's closet.

Once they came to the road running north and south, they were quite a ways south of Quillim. "We should be there in just under two days," he told them.

"Ever been to Crag Keep?" asked Chad.

Shaking his head, Bart replied, "No, though I have talked with people who have."

They rode throughout the day and in the latter part of the afternoon the town of Wardean appeared before them. "On the south side is a road heading almost due west," he explained. "If we take that road, we should reach Crag Keep by noon tomorrow."

After what happened the last time Bart set foot within Wardean, they thought it best to skirt around the walls and head cross country to the westward road. In fact, they found a trail of sorts that branched off a mile north of Wardean that ended up bringing them to the road to Crag Keep.

They didn't travel much further than past where the walls of Wardean disappeared behind them before stopping for the night. The day of riding was beginning to take its toll on their posteriors. They found a decent spot in the hills a short way from the road that was an ideal spot to make camp.

The sadness of leaving home had gradually diminished until it was now nothing more than a thought that flittered across his mind from time to time. The adventure of the road had taken over and all regrets at leaving were gone. Here he was with good friends, a clear sky above, and the prospect of adventure. How in the world could he remain sad?

Later that evening after they finished their dinner and were sitting around the fire talking, Chad asked Bart, "What are you going to do with your share?"

"Of the King's Horde?" he asked.

"That's right," replied Chad.

"Probably pay to have the death mark removed," he said.

"You can do that?" Riyan asked.

"Oh sure," he replied. "Though you need to have enough gold to overcome their sense of vengeance."

"How much do you think you're going to need?" Riyan asked.

"I wouldn't dare to make the attempt with less than ten thousand golds," he explained.

"Ten thousand?" exclaimed Chad. "What did you do?"

Bart smiled a sad smile. "I was on the wrong side of a power struggle." He grew silent and didn't say anything further about it.

"As for me," Chad said, "maybe I'll learn to use this sword and go on adventures."

"Now you're talking!" Riyan agreed with great enthusiasm. "We could fight the forces of evil and maybe save a damsel in distress or two."

"You guys are crazy," Bart said with a grin. "I've talked with people who have had adventures such as you two are in love with, and they say they are nothing like the sagas. They're long rides, stretches of boredom that are interrupted with moments of life threatening ordeals, and half the time the rewards are not worth it."

"I don't care what you say," Riyan asserted, "I'm having the time of my life."

"We'll see," he replied. *No one's trying to kill you yet,* he thought to himself.

It wasn't long after that before they turned in for the night. All through the night, Riyan dreamt of treasures untold.

The following morning they had a quick bite to eat then were back in the saddle. The road they were taking will lead them directly to Crag Keep. It has been devoid of traffic ever since they stopped to camp the night before. Even during the night, not one traveler was heard passing by.

"This place seems pretty deserted," commented Chad.

"You need to realize that Crag Keep is little more than a fortress sitting on this side of the Reilkyn Pass," he explained. "Other than merchants heading to the Marketplace, or soldiers going to the Keep, there's not much else out here."

"What's the Marketplace?" Riyan asked.

"You two don't know anything about nothing do you?" Bart exclaimed. "The Marketplace is where goblins and humans meet in the spring and summer months to trade goods."

"Oh," replied Riyan.

"What do the goblins have to trade?" Chad asked.

Bart turned back and glanced at where Chad was riding behind him. "Why do you want to know?"

"Just curious is all," he explained.

"I'm not really sure," he admitted. "Probably hides. I would think they would be more along the lines of being the buyers than sellers."

"You may be right," agreed Riyan.

They rode another two hours, all the while the mountains grew ever closer. The hills they have been traveling through continuously became steeper until finally merging into the sides of the mountains. A river now flowed beside them on their left as it made its way down from the mountains. It also brought colder air along with it.

The road followed the banks of the river until it came to a wooden bridge that spanned the river. Here the river turned, passed under the bridge, and commenced flowing on their right.

Once past the bridge they rode for another hour before the walls of Crag Keep appeared before them. It was built right into the face of one of the mountains with a high wall enclosing it. A single gate loomed in the middle of the wall with a drawbridge that was currently extended. As they rode closer, they could see where a small tributary broke off from the river and made its way beneath the drawbridge forming a moat of sorts.

A soldier stood just outside the portcullis area and watched them as they approached. When their horses began crossing the drawbridge, the soldier raised his arm. "I'm sorry boys," he said. "No one's allowed inside unless they have business."

When the other two came to a halt, Bart rode forward another foot before he too halted. "That's what we're here on," Bart said without skipping a beat. "Our father will be on his way in the morning with a load of goods to trade at the Marketplace from Wardean. He sent us ahead to see about getting everything arranged for making the trip over the pass."

The guard stared at Bart for a second as if he was trying to determine the validity of what he was saying. Then he turned his gaze to Chad and Riyan who worked hard at maintaining a relaxed demeanor. After coming to a decision, the guard nodded and said, "Very well. You can enter."

"Thank you," said Bart as he got his horse moving again. Then with Riyan and Chad behind him, he entered Crag Keep.

Now that they were inside the walls, they could better see the layout of the keep. Between the walls and the cliffside was a large courtyard. A group of five wagons were huddled together off to one side with a party of merchants moving in and around them.

The keep itself was almost entirely within the mountain. At the other end of the courtyard stood the main entrance, a double door of sturdy construction. Other than the door, there was no other opening in the lower portion of the cliffside. Not until twenty feet above the ground did the first opening appear which had to be a window though it was rather narrow. Other windows gaped from the cliff face for another hundred feet above the first one.

"Pretty impressive," stated Chad.

"Now what are we to do?" asked Riyan. Lowering his voice, he turned to Bart and asked, "Tomorrow morning that guard is going to expect to see a caravan show up with our 'father'."

"Keep your voice down," he said. Then he nodded to a small building on the opposite side of the courtyard from the five wagons. "If what I heard is accurate, that's an inn. We can stay there tonight."

"But how are we to get into the great hall and view the map?" Chad asked in a very quiet voice.

Bart shrugged, "I don't know. Let's get settled in. I'll figure something out after that."

"I hope so," said Riyan as Bart led the way over to the building.

It turned out that his source had been correct for it was indeed an inn, a rather pricey inn in fact. They used most of one of the gold coins they had left for a room for themselves and stall space for their horses.

After settling in their horses, and on the way back to the inn, Riyan stopped to stare at the opening to the keep. Two guards stood watch and he knew they wouldn't allow them to simply walk in and look around. He hoped Bart knew what he was doing, the place looked pretty daunting. Then he followed the other two into the inn for dinner.

Chapter 15

The inn had very little in the way of amenities for its guests. The rooms were quite small, in fact they were forced to share a single room with one small bed. Still, it was better than sleeping outside on the ground.

They had but two choices for dinner. One was the stew that the cook at the inn provided or they could choose the food they brought with them. Forget about entertainment. There was a very small spot where a bard of some kind could have entertained those eating there, but none made an appearance. Riyan commented to the others that he thought it unlikely a bard ever came this way.

Once they finished eating, they stepped outside and tried to figure a way into the keep. The same two guards were still standing there to either side of the entrance. Any attempt at scaling the walls would be immediately seen. The prospect of gaining admittance seemed remote in the extreme.

"We could still ask," Riyan said.

"I don't think that would be such a good idea," countered Bart. "Though if no other opportunity presents itself, we may be left with little choice."

For over an hour they wandered around the courtyard, all the while maintaining an eye on the keep while trying to appear like they weren't. Finally, Bart noticed two men emerge between the two guards as they left the keep. They were dressed like merchants and were making their way over to where the five wagons sat.

Bart watched them cross the courtyard and grew thoughtful. Riyan noticed him following the two men with his eyes and asked, "What?"

"Those two men just came out of the keep," he said. "I wonder what they were doing in there?"

"Good question," Chad said. "Maybe you should go over and ask them."

Bart turned to him and nodded. "I think I will," he said. Before Bart or Chad could say anything he stepped out and hurried over to the caravan's camp.

"What does he think he's doing?" asked Chad. He had been kidding when he suggested that he go talk with them.

"I don't know," replied Riyan. Then he watched as Bart arrived at the wagons and begun talking with the two men. "I hope he doesn't get us into trouble."

They remained where they were in the courtyard until whatever conversation Bart had been having came to an end. Then he turned around and began heading back to the inn. He indicated with a nod of his head that they should meet him there. They met up with him at the inn's entrance where he came to a stop. "So?" asked Riyan.

"Inside the keep is where you acquire your permit to travel across the pass to the Marketplace," he explained.

"You need a permit?" asked Chad.

"So it would seem," replied Bart. He grinned and said, "This is just what we needed."

"They're not going to give us a permit," Riyan stated. "We have no logical reason for going over there."

"We can use the same story you used to get us in here," suggested Chad. "That we are waiting for our father's caravan."

"But we can't prove that," objected Riyan.

"Look," said Bart. "If we can just get past the guards at the entrance, then it doesn't matter if we get a pass or not. All we really need is to look at the map in the great hall."

Chad looked to Riyan and shrugged, "It's worth a try."

"Alright," he agreed. "The worst they could do is not let us in."

Bart gave him a grin and said, "That's the spirit. Let's go."

They left the front of the inn and made their way toward the entrance to the keep. Riyan felt his insides tighten up in nervousness that he prayed wasn't mirrored on his face. As they approached the guards at the entrance, Bart took the lead.

One of the guards stepped forward and held up a hand indicating they were to stop. "Sorry boys, but the keep is off limits," he told them.

"We were going to see about getting passes for our father's wagons before they arrived in the morning," Bart said in complete sincerity.

"Passes?" the guard asked.

"That's right," he replied. "Our father wants to see if the goblins would be willing to purchase some jewelry and trinkets that he recently acquired."

"Usually the passes aren't given until the wagons are actually here," explained the guard.

"I know," continued Bart. "Last year we were here with the wagons and it wasn't a problem. Is Sergeant Akers still issuing the passes?"

"Yes he is," the guard replied. His manner seemed to relax just a little.

"How is his little girl doing?" Bart asked. "Still giving him problems?"

"Oh you know it," the guard said with a grin. "She's not so little anymore. She drives him crazy whenever he's home on leave."

"Is he still in the same room as last year?" Bart asked.

"Yes," the guard said. "Down the hall, fourth door on the right."

"Thanks," Bart said then moved forward to enter the keep. Behind him Chad and Riyan follow and to their astonishment, the guard stepped aside and allowed them to enter.

Once they left the guards behind, they entered a large hall. At present no one was in sight. Riyan tried to ask him about how he knew so much about this Sergeant Akers but Bart waved him silent. "Later," he said.

At the far end of the hall was the corridor the guard had referred to. Another corridor left the hall to their right and two closed doors sat in the wall to their left. "Which way?" asked Chad.

"You got me," replied Bart. "Let's hope we find it before they find us." Moving quickly to the corridor on their right, he soon left the hall behind as he made his way deeper into the keep. Sconces bearing burning torches lined the walls, both in the hall and in the corridors extending from it.

The great hall had to be in a prominent location, it would stand to reason that they would want it to be very accessible to visitors. So Bart moved down the corridor with the other two right behind, all three trying to be as quiet as possible.

The corridor extended for over a hundred feet before ending at a closed door. Other doors had sat along either side of the corridor as they moved along it, some open and some closed. The closed ones they left closed, and paused only a moment to peer through the open ones. They were making sure that there was no one on the other side who might see them pass. Not to mention making sure the door didn't open onto the main hall, though Bart doubted if any of theses doors would do that. They simply were not in what he felt was the right place.

When they reached the door at the end, Bart listened at it for a moment until he was sure it was quiet on the other side. Then he opened the door slowly and peered around. There he found another corridor running perpendicular to the one they were in.

Suddenly, footsteps were heard approaching down the corridor on the other side of the door. Bart closed it quickly and turned to the others. "Someone's coming!" he said. They moved back quickly to the closest door to them and opened it. Fortunately it opened up onto a storage room and they hurried inside. No sooner did they get the door closed than they heard the door at the end of the corridor open. The footsteps began walking towards them down the corridor and they listened as they drew abreast of the door then continued on past. A second or two later they heard another door open and close.

Bart cracked open the door to the storage room and looked out. The corridor was once again empty. "Come on," he said to the other two. Opening the door wider, he left the storage room and made his way back to the door at the end of the corridor.

This time when he peered out into the other corridor, there were no footsteps to be heard and both ways were deserted. Waving for the others to follow, he passed through the doorway and started following the corridor to the left.

The corridor they found themselves in now was fairly similar to the one they just left. Voices could be heard coming from up ahead and Bart had them pause in a small alcove as they listened. A few seconds later they determined that the voices were neither approaching nor moving away. So they returned to the corridor and resumed their progress.

Thirty feet further down stood an open doorway and it was from there that the voices were originating. He motioned for Riyan and Chad to remain where they were as he continued forward to peer into the room. Creeping forward silently, he reached the edge of the open door and very slowly looked around to the other side.

It turned out to be a room where several soldiers were taking their ease before a fireplace. The table they were sitting around had a pitcher of ale and several cups resting on top. One of the men was facing in such a way that the doorway was in his direct line of sight. However, in Bart's opinion, the man appeared rather drunk and may not notice when they moved across the doorway quickly.

Turning back to the others, he waved them forward. When they reached his side he said, "Need to be quick." Once he received nods of understanding, he stepped out and very quickly, passed in front of the doorway. Riyan and Chad followed right behind him.

Bart didn't stop when they reached the other side. Instead, he kept leading them forward as he listened for anything that might indicate they were seen by the men in the room behind them. When nothing materialized, he breathed a sigh of relief and continued down the corridor.

Several other corridors at times branched off, but Bart continued following the corridor they were in. Each time they came to a branching, they would slow down, check for anyone in the other corridor, then proceed when clear. It was the third such branching to the left when they saw what had to be the great hall opening up at the end of the new corridor.

"I think that's it," he said as he turned them down it. When Riyan and Chad entered the corridor, they agreed with him. The corridor extended for about twenty feet before opening up on a large hall with many tables set in three neat rows running from one side to the other. A servant was seen passing through towards one of the exits on the far side.

They waited until the servant had left the great hall before they entered. As they stepped from the corridor, Riyan glanced up at the vaulting ceiling that arched overhead "Wow," he breathed in awe as the sheer size of the room overpowered him. He had never been in such a massive room before, other than what they found in The Crypt that is.

"We don't have time for gawking," Bart admonished them. "Let's find the map and get out of here."

They looked for the map and didn't see it. From what Bart had said it should have been quite large and out in the open. Then Chad turned around and looked at the wall through which they just emerged. "I think I found it," he said.

The other two turned about and saw that most of the wall was painted with a map depicting a large portion of the Kingdom of Byrdlon, of which the lands of Duke Yoric were but a part. It also showed the mountains to the west that separated the goblin lands from theirs and beyond.

"There's Quillim!" exclaimed Chad.

Riyan looked to where he pointed and saw a tiny dot with the name of their town upon it. "It isn't that big," he said.

"No it isn't," said Bart as he backed away from the wall to get a better view. As much as he stared at the map on the piece of the key when he was lying in bed, he had the area depicted upon it memorized. His eyes scanned the map and came to an area that matched what was on the key.

Just on the other side of the mountains from Crag Keep was the larger of the two lakes. It sat a little bit west and north of the Marketplace. From its northern shore a river extended northward to the smaller lake where they figured the rest of the key to be. Or at least some indication of where to look for it.

He frowned slightly when he saw that the area on the shore of the smaller lake showed nothing at all. The map on the key had indicated there was something there, yet here, nothing. "Maybe they don't know about it," he mumbled to himself.

"What?" asked Riyan.

He pointed to the two lakes and said, "That's the area inscribed on the back of the key."

Riyan and Chad both turned their gaze to see it. Riyan was about to pull forth the piece of the key to compare it when Bart stopped him. "Not here," he advised. "I know that is it." He committed the general area of the two lakes to memory, then indicated they should start to leave.

"What are you doing in here?" a voice asked.

Turning around in surprise, they saw a middle aged man in uniform. He was staring at them with a rather unpleasant expression.

"We, uh …" began Riyan then grew silent under the man's stern gaze.

"We were trying to find the room where we were told we could acquire passes for our caravan to travel to the Marketplace in the morning," Bart explained.

"Yeah," added Chad. "We sort of lost our way."

The soldier studied them for a moment then said, "Come this way." He turned around and headed to a corridor that left the room behind him. After two steps he paused and glanced back to make sure they were following. When he saw that they were, he continued.

Riyan glanced to Bart and could see the worry he was feeling mirrored in his friend's face. They followed the soldier as he worked his way through the keep. Along the way they passed several other soldiers moving about on various errands. The soldier finally came to a stop before a door.

"You can get your passes in here," he told them. "Don't let me catch you three wandering around again."

"You won't," Bart assured him. "We promise."

Giving them a nod, the soldier left them standing before the door as he returned back the way they came.

"Let's get out of here," urged Chad.

"Not yet," replied Bart. Taking the handle of the door, he opened it and walked in. They found it to be a rather small room with but a single desk covered in neat stacks of paper sitting before the door. Behind the desk was a soldier who had to be Sergeant Akers.

He looked up when the door opened and asked, "Can I help you?"

Bart nodded and stepped up to the desk. Riyan and Chad followed him in. "We need to procure passes for the wagons our father will be bringing up tomorrow," Bart explained.

"Sorry son," Sergeant Akers said as he leaned back in his chair. "We don't give out passes until we've had a chance to look the goods over. The guards out front should have explained that to you."

"I just thought we could expedite things so father could head on up as soon as he arrived," Bart stated.

"I hate to disappoint you, but the procedure is for your father, who is the master of the caravan, to apply for the passes," the sergeant explained. "When he arrives you tell him to come see me."

Bart put a despondent look on his face and said, "Very well. Sorry to have bothered you."

"That's okay," Sergeant Akers assured him.

Bart turned around and ushered Riyan and Chad out ahead of him. Once out in the corridor, they turned and headed for the exit. They remained silent until they passed the two guards that were standing watch, returned to the inn, and were back in their room.

"Now, why did we have to go talk to that sergeant?" asked Chad. "And how did you know his name in the first place?"

Bart grinned. "When I went over to talk to those merchants before we went in, that's when I found out his name. Once I found out why they were inside the keep, I wormed out the name of the man we were to see. It's always easier to enter a place you aren't supposed to be if it appears you know what's going on and have been there before. Since I was convincing enough to make the guard out front believe that we were here last year, he was more inclined to allow us entry."

"Weren't you taking a risk?" Riyan asked.

Bart shrugged. "I suppose so, but the worst he would have done was denied us entry. We would have been no worse off than we were before."

"Okay, but what about going in and talking to Sergeant Akers?" Chad asked. "That seemed a total waste of time."

Bart grinned and shook his head. "No it wasn't." He put his left hand in the right sleeve of his tunic and pulled out several pieces of paper. He held them up and grinned all the wider.

"You stole those?" asked Riyan.

"Of course," he replied. "How else were we to get passes?" He spread them out on the bed and they went through them. They were all passes allowing the bearer to proceed through the pass to the Marketplace. "Tomorrow morning we tag along with that caravan out there and we're on our way."

Riyan took out the key and laid it on the bed next to the passes. Pointing to a spot just south of the mountains, he said, "We're here." Then he moved his finger to the other side of the mountains. "We cross here and then we're at the Marketplace. From there we skirt around this lake," his finger moved around the southern edge of the lower lake to the other side. "Then we follow the river up to this other lake where hopefully we'll find something that will lead us to the rest of the key."

"I hope you both realize that once we leave the protection of the Marketplace that we'll be in goblin territory," Bart explained to them. "From what I've heard, they don't take kindly to trespassers."

Riyan nodded, "I know. We'll simply have to make sure we avoid them."

Bart laughed. "Easier said than done," he stated.

"I say the risks are worth the rewards," Riyan insisted.

"The risks being our continued existence," Chad clarified.

Riyan glanced from one to the other, "But what existence would we be losing? I already lost the one I love. Bart, you have a death mark on you. And Chad? Do you really want to spend the rest of your life as a miller?"

Chad shook his head, "Hardly."

"Alright," said Riyan with finality. "Either we succeed or we die trying."

"You say that so easily now," Bart said. "How are you going to feel when you are being skinned alive for some goblin's roasting spit?"

Riyan didn't reply. This was the only way he could see for him to get Freya back. He had to take the risk!

Later that evening when Riyan and Chad were getting ready to fall asleep, Bart offered for them to share the bed. He said he didn't mind the floor. They happily agreed and were soon lying side by side on the cramped little bed. Riyan could understand why Bart preferred the floor every time Chad's elbow nailed him in the side. Despite the tight sleeping arrangements, Riyan was soon asleep.

At some point in the night he awoke and saw Bart sitting at the table. A candle burned next to him as he worked on something. Sleepily, Riyan started to ask, "What ..."

Bart turned his head toward him and said, "Go back to sleep Riyan."

Laying his head back on the pillow, Riyan quickly fell back to sleep and slept through the rest of the night.

In the morning when Riyan awoke, he saw Bart lying on the floor in front of the door with his head propped on top of his pack. In the bed next to him, Chad was stirring and he elbowed him to get him up. "It's morning Bart," Riyan hollered over to him.

Bart came awake quickly and asked, "It is?" Looking to the window he saw the light coming through. "Damn!" he exclaimed. Coming to his feet, he grabbed his boots and started to pull them on. "We've got to hurry."

"Why?" Riyan asked as he got out of bed.

"After you two fell asleep, I went and talked with a couple of the guards who are escorting that caravan," he explained. "They said they were pulling out early this morning. If we want to go with them we need to hurry." He again looked to the light coming through the window as he pulled his last boot on. Getting to his feet, he said, "I'll get the horses ready. You two get a move on." With that he opened the door and left.

Riyan elbowed a still sleeping Chad a little harder this time and said, "Wake up!"

Chad mumbled something and promptly fell back to sleep.

Exasperated with his friend, Riyan placed both hands on Chad's back and shoved him off the bed.

Arms and legs went in all directions as he tumbled over the edge and hit the floor. "We don't have much time," Riyan said as Chad sat up on the floor. He tried to hide the smile that was threatening to break out. "The caravan is pulling out early."

"Oh," he said and quickly pulled his boots on and grabbed his pack.

By the time they were ready and left the room, Bart had two of the horses saddled and was almost done with the third. Riyan saw the wagons that had been over to the side of the courtyard were already trundling their way towards the gate leading through the outer wall.

"About time you two showed up," Bart said. When Riyan and Chad reached the horses, he cinched the last buckle then turned to them. "Here," he said and handed each of them one of the passes he appropriated the night before.

"What are we to do with these?" Riyan asked. "They're not even signed."

"They are now," replied Bart. "Quit talking and let's get moving."

Riyan took a moment to open the paper. Sure enough, there at the bottom was a signature. He was about ready to ask Bart how this came to be when the memory of Bart working at the table last night returned to him. It was one thing to try to sneak through the pass, quite another to bear forged documents. He's not entirely sure but the penalty for that would have to be severe.

Getting into the saddle, he and Chad followed Bart as he rode towards the wagons. He made sure that the wagons were on the other side before catching up with them. One of the guards riding at the rear saw them coming and grinned. "Wasn't sure if you were going to make it Bart," the guard said.

Nodding to Riyan and Chad, Bart replied, "They overslept."

The guard laughed.

Another member of the caravan on a horse saw the guard talking with them and slowed down until they had caught up with him. "What's this?" the man asked.

"Just a fellow I shared a fire with last night," the guard replied. "He and his friends are trying to catch up with a caravan that has already reached the Marketplace."

"Hmmm," the man said. "Do you boys have passes?"

Bart held his up as did Riyan and Chad.

The man didn't look entirely pleased with the situation but didn't say anything. Nudging his horse in the sides, he quickened his pace until he returned to where he was before moving back.

"Grumpy," Bart commented to the guard.

"You could say that," he replied with a grin. "I think he's more upset that another caravan beat him there than that you are riding with us. Might be best if you and your friends were to drop back a bit."

"Sure," Bart said. He and the others slowed down until about thirty feet separated them and the rear guard of the caravan.

Up ahead, the canyon that Crag Keep sat in grew narrower. The river coursed its way through the opening over thunderous cataracts as it left the mountains. At the narrowest point, the road went through an area barely wide enough for two wagons side by side.

It was at that point a score of soldiers were stationed to be sure travelers heading across the pass had all the necessary documents. When the caravan drew near, one of the soldiers moved forward and began checking the passes of the guards and the drivers of the wagons. The master of the caravan remained with the soldier until he was satisfied that all was in order and waved the caravan on through.

Riyan's heart beat rapidly when it was their turn to approach the soldier. "Good morning young sirs," the soldier greeted them. "Need to see your passes before you can proceed."

"No problem," Bart said then handed his over to the guard. Riyan and Chad did the same.

Riyan was poised to flee as soon as the soldier discovered the passes were forgeries. But to his amazement, the soldier handed the passes back and waved them on through. He almost couldn't believe they had pulled it off.

Once they were past and had put some distance between them and the soldiers, Riyan asked Bart how he had managed it.

Bart grinned. "Quite easy actually. Last night while you and Chad were sleeping, I left the room and went over to where a couple of the caravan guards were relaxing around a fire. One thing led to another and I was invited to share it with them. It was quite easy to lift their passes off of them and take them back to our room. Then I studied the signature and copied it onto ours. After that it was a simple matter to return the passes to their owners."

"Something your father taught you?" Chad asked.

"Actually no," he replied and offered no further explanation.

Chapter 16

The trip through the pass took the better part of the day. They reached the western side an hour or so before sundown. From the pass to the Market-place, humans were supposedly safe from any goblin attacks. The Market-place was considered neutral ground as both sides desired the continued trade and prosperity the place brought.

As they descended out of the narrowness of the pass, they saw how the hills at the mountain's base were thickly forested. The sparkle of water could be seen far off beyond the hills a little to the left of the pass. It had to be the larger of the two lakes depicted on the back of the key.

After leaving the pass, the road meandered its way through the lower hills until it finally reached a point where the Marketplace became visible. It was a large area with several permanent structures wherein the trading between the two races could take place. Over a dozen wagons sat in a caravansary on the side closest to the pass, testament that other traders were already there. That wasn't too surprising seeing as how trading goes on here shortly after the snows melt in the spring until the first snows come again in the fall.

The Marketplace wasn't enclosed by any sort of wall or fence. Rather, there were totems spaced every twenty feet or so on the goblin side. They seemed to be warning the humans that their presence was not welcomed, nor tolerated.

Riyan wondered how they were going to pass through the line of totems and enter the forest without anyone the wiser. All their lives they have heard of the ferocity of the goblins.

A contingent of Byrdlon soldiers were present down below. Also moving around the Marketplace area were shorter individuals who walked with a loping gait. "Goblins," Bart told the other two.

Riyan's eyes widened when he realized he was seeing goblins for the first time. They seemed to be quite a bit shorter than the average human, being around three to four feet in height. The goblins were wearing clothing similar to what you might find the average person on the streets of Wardean wearing. It surprised Riyan at first, but then he realized that he really didn't know what to expect in regards to them.

The trail continued its winding way through the hills, all the way to the main square of the Market place. The main square was a large area which the buildings bordered on. It has been kept relatively clear as the bulk of the trading goes on in the buildings.

Bart said his goodbyes to the guard with whom he befriended when the wagons headed over to the caravansary. "Maybe we should go there as well and mingle," suggested Chad.

"Probably wouldn't be a bad idea," said Bart. Several of the soldiers were giving them a curious look.

Making their way over, they were soon among the wagons of various merchants who have come to trade. It appeared that whatever trading had been going on has come to a halt now that it was getting close to sunset. The merchants and their guards were returning from the buildings with a line of porters following behind carrying goods.

Riyan found them a location at the edge of the caravansary where they could set up camp. It was near enough to a caravan so they hopefully would be considered a part of it, while at the same time not so close as to cause the people of the caravan concern.

While they set up camp and got a fire going, they looked toward the buildings in an attempt to see a goblin. One of their neighbors noticed what they were doing and told them that at night, the goblins returned to the forest. In the morning they would return at sunrise.

"Would be interesting to get a closer look at one," commented Riyan.

Keeping his voice low so as not to be overheard, Bart replied, "In a little bit you may get your wish."

"How are we to get out of here?" Chad asked in a hushed whisper.

"Later tonight when everyone else is asleep," Bart explained, "we'll slip out."

"Won't the soldiers stop us?" Riyan asked.

"Maybe," he admitted. "But I doubt it. I think they're more here to keep order within the Marketplace than to keep fools from passing through the totems."

At that Riyan glanced over towards where one of the totems stood not ten feet away. The menacing visages carved into the wood seemed to warn of dire consequences should their warning not be heeded.

As night settled in, they prepared for a quick nap before they took off. They left their horses saddled with most of their equipment still secured behind the saddle. They got questioning glances from those around them about that but no one said anything.

They took turns at watch while the others slept. Riyan took the first one, then Chad. It was during Bart's turn that the camp grew quiet as even the latest night owl finally went to sleep. There was at least one guard in every caravan that remained awake to keep watch. Even the caravan beside them had a guard.

When Bart felt that the time was right to make their break, he woke the others. The guard on watch in the caravan next to theirs took note of their preparations to leave. But apparently three fools who planned to pass through the ring of totems weren't enough for him to bother with. When they headed out, he grinned as he nodded and gave them a wave. Riyan waved back.

Bart took the lead as they rode from the Marketplace and passed through the ring of totems. Riyan felt a tremor of foreboding as he passed between them, almost as if the totem's faces were actually staring at him. The feeling of foreboding stayed with him until the Marketplace had disappeared in the trees behind them.

To the west was the closest lake, the larger of the two. From there they would have to follow the river northward until they reached the smaller lake. If the markings on the key were any indication, what they were looking for lies on the western shore of the smaller lake. All they had to do now was to pass through goblin territory without being discovered.

The night was eerily quiet. Nocturnal creatures could be heard throughout the forest as the three companions slowly made their way through the dark forest. Shadows surrounded them as the light from the moon above barely managed to filter its way through the forest's canopy. They dared not travel very fast else they would risk giving away their presence to any goblins that may be in the area.

Bart tried to keep them on a fairly westerly heading, but the forest wasn't like the city. His bump of direction that was infallible within the city, didn't feel quite as reliable out here in the forest now that the sun had gone down.

They rode in single file along what Riyan soon realized was a game trail. Bart was in the lead while Chad brought up the rear. Every once in a while one of their horses would snort or make some other noise and Riyan's heart would almost freeze in panic as his mind imagined goblins rushing out of the forest to attack. But no such attack developed.

It was about a half hour since they left the Marketplace when the smell of wood smoke began to be noticed. Shortly after that, the sound of guttural speech came from down the game trail ahead of them.

Bart signaled for them to stop and had the others come in close. "You two stay here," he said. "I'm going to go ahead on foot and see what's going on."

"Be careful," warned Chad.

"Don't worry," he assured them. "Just stay here and be quiet." Dismounting, he handed his horse's reins to Riyan then disappeared down the trail towards the voices.

Riyan glanced nervously to Chad. "Goblins," he whispered. Chad nodded in reply.

As he left the other two behind, Bart was feeling a bit nervous. The tales of goblins he had heard all his life painted them as a blood thirsty savage race that would sooner eat you than look at you. Any number of the sagas dealing with these creatures always had despicable acts of mayhem and carnage attributed to them. So now that he was approaching what could very well be a war party, he felt decidedly nervous.

Moving forward, he stepped as carefully as he could so as not to make any sound that would give away his presence. The sound of the goblin's voices grew louder as he edged closer. Finally, a light appeared through the trees ahead, just a little to the right of the game trail.

He continued working his way closer until he could see a small encampment of goblins set off the game trail a ways. When he was close enough to make them out, he was shocked to discover that they weren't wearing any clothes. A few of them sported jewelry of one kind or another, but as far as clothes went, nothing. Bart just shook his head.

The goblins were sitting around a roaring fire near the center of the encampment. There were a couple buildings nearby, the architecture was slightly different than what he was used to. They were long and squat with a chimney rising high at either end. Having grown up on the streets of Wardean, he could tell that they were very well crafted.

Turning his attention back to the goblins themselves, he didn't think they were too concerned about the possibility of humans being in the area. They looked rather relaxed as they spoke to one another in their guttural language.

He crouched there among the trees and watched them for several minutes before coming to the conclusion that they were no immediate threat to him and the others. He started to back away. Once he felt he was far enough away not to be heard, he turned and quickened his pace back to Riyan and Chad.

"There's a group of them ahead," he told them upon his return. "Maybe fifteen or twenty." He then briefly described the buildings he saw and the fact that they were naked.

"Naked?" asked Riyan in disbelief.

Bart nodded. "As the day they were born," he affirmed.

Chad shook his head. "You would think they would get cold at night," he said.

"Perhaps," shrugged Bart. "But I think we need to give them a wide berth. Once on the far side of their encampment we should start looking for some place to hole up before dawn."

"Yeah," agreed Riyan. "We don't want to be moving around during the day."

Bart nodded then took the lead as he led them from the game trail and entered the forest. He took it slow and steady, always working to maintain their distance from the goblin encampment.

Some time after they circumvented the encampment and left the voices behind, they came across a small stream flowing in the general direction Bart figured the lake to be. Realizing this would lead them to where they wanted to go, he altered their course to follow the stream.

Despite keeping a constant lookout for a place to hole up, all they encountered as they made their way through the forest were trees. No suitable place of concealment presented itself. Bart finally came to the conclusion that when the sky began to lighten, they would most likely be forced to find a dense copse of trees where they could hide throughout the day.

They followed the stream for another hour before it emptied into the lake. The twinkling of the stars above reflected off the surface of the water, giving it a dazzling appearance. Across the lake on the opposite shore, they saw the unmistakable sight of a goblin settlement. Not a large one to be sure, but a settlement nonetheless.

Before they arrived and saw the goblin settlement, they had thought to go around the southern shore and then follow it north. For the area indicated on the back of the key was on the western side. But if they did they would risk encountering that settlement and the goblins inhabiting it. At least a dozen lights could be seen coming from the buildings over there.

"Perhaps we should head north from here," suggested Chad.

While standing at the water's edge, they gave the route around the eastern shore of the lake a careful look. Unlike the western shore, it was dark and looked deserted. "Around to the east it is," announced Bart.

As they progressed around the lake, Riyan kept glancing to the lights on the distant shore. Almost as if he expected pursuit at any minute. But nothing developed and the longer they followed the shore, the fainter the lights became until they could no longer be seen. The sight of the settlement had seemed strange to him. After all, weren't goblins little better than beasts? Wild and dangerous who's only thought was that of killing any human they came in contact with? A shudder ran through him at the thought that so many could even now be in close proximity to them.

A thought flashed through his mind and made him shudder. If they were caught, it would be the end of them. The goblins would use their claws and teeth to rip their flesh, and they would use their skulls to drink their blood in dark rituals.

He tried to banish such unpleasant thoughts by concentrating on Freya. And how her father was going to welcome him home with open arms once they found the parts of the key and opened the King's Horde. Oh what a glorious day that would be.

"We better find somewhere to hole up soon," Bart suddenly announced.

Snapped out of his reverie, Riyan realized the sky to the east was beginning to lighten behind the peaks of the mountains. He definitely didn't want to risk being out here in the open once it became light. The bloodthirsty goblins would definitely find them and attack and ... *Enough! You've got to stop thinking about such things!* he admonished himself. Turning his attention to the forest, he tried to locate someplace where they could hole up until night returned.

The stars began to fade with the coming of dawn, and still they hadn't located a very good spot to hide in. When it grew too light and they no longer dared to ride so exposed along the shoreline, Bart led them into the forest.

Still no spot presented itself that was very suitable for hiding throughout the day. Finally they decided on an area fifty feet or so from the shore where the trees were slightly thicker than the rest of the forest. It wasn't great, if a goblin should pass by even as close as the shoreline, they would be seen.

"Keep the saddles on," advised Riyan. "We may need a quick getaway."

"If we're discovered," said Bart, "it's unlikely we could ride fast enough to get away."

"Let me have my illusions," Riyan said as he turned to him. "Please."

Bart could see the worry in his eyes and nodded. "As you will. I'll take the first watch while you two get some sleep."

They both agreed to that and after a quick meal of cold rations that were beginning to grow stale, they laid down and tried to go to sleep. Despite the fatigue that he was feeling, it took Riyan some time before sleep came. When it did, it brought nightmares of being chased through the forest by demonic, fire breathing goblins with red eyes the color of hellish flames. He was glad when Chad finally awakened him for his turn at watch.

Throughout the day's watch, the only anxious moment any of them had was during the middle watch. Chad was pacing around the forest doing his best to keep awake when the sound of many goblins moving through the trees came to him. Fearful that they might be heading in their direction, he snuck closer only to find that the group of goblins was gathering branches and dead wood. For what purpose Chad was unable to find out. He was simply happy the goblins weren't approaching any further to their camp. After ten minutes of foraging for wood, they departed back to the east.

Before the sun hit the horizon at the end of the day, they were awake. They talked in hushed voices about what they should do once night set in. They decided to continue following the shoreline northward until they came across the river that flowed from the second lake further to the north. Once they found the mouth of the river, they would have to discover a way of fording to the other side. For the area they wished to find lay on the western side.

"I'm surprised we've made it this far," commented Chad. "This area doesn't seem too densely settled by them."

"Thank goodness," Riyan said nervously. Aside from that one settlement on the southwestern shore of the lake, the forest has been fairly empty of them.

"You're not worried are you?" asked Bart with a grin. When Riyan only glared at him he added. "This is the meat and bones of adventuring."

"I'm having the time of my life," replied Riyan rather unconvincingly. To be honest with himself, he had to admit that this wasn't exactly the glorious expedition that he had anticipated. He also hadn't planned on being scared most of the time either. But the last thing he was going to do was admit that to Bart and Chad.

"Me too," agreed Chad. Only from the way he said it, it sounded like he genuinely meant it.

Once night had settled in enough for the stars to begin filling the sky, they mounted their horses and returned to the shore of the lake. The trees weren't nearly as dense there so it made for an easier ride.

They followed the edge of the lake for several hours almost due north before they reached the point where the shoreline turned back to the west. Another hour of riding brought them to a large river flowing into the lake.

"Think this is the one?" Chad asked.

Bart considered the size of the river and nodded. "It has to be," he stated. "Couldn't imagine another river of comparable size in the area."

"Can we ford here?" Riyan asked. Then he took a better look at the river and saw that it was over a hundred feet wide and moving quickly.

"Can't tell just how deep it is here in the dark," Bart said. "It might be a good idea to follow it north a ways before we attempt to cross."

"Would be shallower," agreed Chad.

So with Bart once more in the lead, they turned northwards and followed the river as it wound its way through the forest. Along the way they came across several smaller tributaries that flowed into it. By the time Riyan figured midnight had come and gone, the river had narrowed to only about fifty feet. It was still a bit too wide to attempt to cross.

When the sky began to lighten several hours later, the river was still around fifty feet across though it didn't look nearly so deep as it had earlier. "Let's find a place to hole up until nightfall again," suggested Bart. They kept a lookout for a thickening of the trees and a short time later came across one that was slightly better than the previous night's.

After they entered the thicket and were settled in, they left their horses in the thicket and worked their way back to the river. They wanted to see if this might be a good place to ford come nightfall.

They stayed within the treeline until the sun's rays were seen hitting the tops of the trees. "Alright," Riyan said. "Let's find a place to cross." Once they made sure that the area was clear of goblins, they moved to the bank of the river.

First thing they did was to fill their water bottles. After that they started moving upriver and searched for a place to ford. They needed to find an area where the river widened. That would indicate the water's level would be lower and thus make the crossing easier.

A half hour after they began hunting for a place to ford they came to a bend in the river. At that point, the river widened to a width of about a hundred feet again. They knew this was the place to ford, not only because the water would be shallower, but because of a road that emerged from the trees on their side of the river and went to the bank of the river. On the other side they saw where it resumed before reentering the forest.

"A road?" asked Riyan.

"Looks like it," said Bart.

"Why would goblins have a road?" he asked.

Bart turned and looked at him like he was an idiot. "Probably for the same reason we have them," he explained. "To get from one place to another."

"But, they're goblins," stated Riyan.

"So?" asked Chad. "They need them too."

Riyan couldn't argue with that logic. It was just so unexpected to discover them to have roads, and well maintained ones if the one they saw in front of them was any indication.

"If there's a road then that means they could be around," Bart said. "We better get back to the horses."

Turning around, they returned to where they left their horses. There they had a meal of rations and settled in until dark. Watches were in the same order as the previous night with Bart taking the first one.

Throughout the day nothing much happened. They slept, took turns at watch, and when the sun began its descent to the horizon, made ready to leave.

When the stars were out and the forest was once again dark, they left the copse of trees and followed the river back to where the road forded the water. As they drew near the road, they slowed to a crawl. Due to their uneasiness about being in this area, every sound of the forest seemed to herald the approach of goblins upon the road. When at last they came to the bend in the river and saw the road in the moonlight, Bart brought them to a sudden halt.

"Wait here," he said as he dismounted.

Chad was about to ask him why they stopped when he waved for him to be quiet.

Moving forward, Bart edged closer to the road. He had heard something and wanted to make sure it was safe before they rode to the ford. Before he made it to the road, he heard the sound of rapidly approaching horses coming down the road on his side of the river. He froze for just a moment before dodging behind the trunk of a nearby tree.

He peered around the trunk and saw half a dozen goblin riders appear riding small ponies. They slowed their ponies to a walk as they came to the bank of the river. While they crossed, Bart got a good look at them. Each had on what looked like leather armor with a shortsword at their hips. Across the back of each rider were small curved bows and a quiver of arrows.

Bart stood there in the shadows as the riders forded the river. It wasn't until they had crossed and disappeared into the forest on the other side did he turn around and head back. When he reached where the other two were waiting for him, he told them of the riders.

"Ponies?" asked Chad. When Bart nodded, he added, "At least our horses would be able to outrun them in an emergency."

"That's true," agreed Riyan.

"Come on," Bart said as he swung up into the saddle. "We better get across before more show up." Leading them forward, he brought them to the edge of the road. There they paused for just a second to listen for any other approaching riders. When they failed to hear any, Bart turned toward the river and headed for the ford.

They took the crossing slowly. The water didn't reach much more than a foot up their horses' legs and wasn't flowing all that rapidly. It was an easy crossing and once on the other side they kept to the road. It was risky to keep to the road, but they felt that if they stayed alert for approaching riders, they would be able to leave the road in time. Besides, they could make much better time on the road than if they slugged their way through the forest.

The road entered the forest a short ways before turning to the right and began following the river northward. They continued to follow the road, all the while very aware that a band of six armed goblins had passed this way just before them. An hour later the road began to turn more westward, leaving the river behind.

They followed the road to the west for a short distance until they were certain it wasn't gong to return to its northerly trek. "We're going to have to leave the road if we wish to continue following the river," Bart announced.

"Nothing for it I guess," Chad said.

As they began to turn and head into the forest, the night erupted in a bright flash of light to the west, followed a split second later by the sound of an explosion.

"What was that?" exclaimed Chad as they looked to the west where a glow blossomed into the night.

"I don't know," replied Riyan. "But I think we best get out of here."

"I'm with you there," agreed Bart.

They kicked their horses into motion just as a cry ripped through the night. "That wasn't a goblin," Riyan said as he came to a stop.

"No," replied Chad, "it wasn't. Sounded more like an old man's."

"He may need our help," Riyan said. All thought of danger to himself vanished when he realized another needed help.

"We don't know that he's even still alive," argued Bart. Just then, a crackling sound followed by another explosion broke the stillness of the forest.

Riyan turned his horse and bolted down the road towards the glow in the distance.

"You're going to get us all killed!" hollered Bart after him. Then to Chad he said, "Every goblin within miles will know something's going on."

"Can't let him face this alone," Chad said as he kicked his horse into motion and raced after his friend.

Bart mumbled a few choice words under his breath before he turned his horse and quickly followed after.

Riyan raced down the road as the glow progressively grew larger. When he came close enough, he discovered the glow to be a fire. The trees were beginning to catch and the fire looked like it was about ready to grow out of control.

Zzzt! Zzzt!

From out of the forest near the growing fires, the sound came to him. He looked to see what it was, but the smoke was obscuring the area quite badly. He turned off the road and moved into the forest as he began working his way around the fire to whoever was there. Behind him, he heard Chad and Bart arrive and begin to follow him into the trees.

Zzzt! Zzzt!

The sound came again, this time he could hear a goblin cry out in pain.

Moving quickly, he finally worked his way around the spreading flames and could see the combatants. A dozen goblins were ringed around two figures as they loosed arrows from their bows.

A circular glow surrounded the two men who were being attacked by the goblins. One was an older man, the other was a youth about Riyan's age. The glow surrounding the two men deflected the goblin's arrows. The older man gripped a gnarled staff in one hand and was dressed in a robe that glowed with sigils of power. Obviously this man was a magic user.

Zzzt! Zzzt!

The man sent two red bolts of energy flying from the hand not gripping the staff into the body of one of the goblins. The goblin was thrown backwards off his feet and hit the ground hard. He didn't get back up.

Riyan assumed the younger man must be the magic user's apprentice. He saw him wave his arms and suddenly two of the goblins were encased in a greenish substance that allowed them no freedom of movement. At the same time, a yellowish light surrounded three more of the attacking goblins. The older magic user had his staff pointed at them and the tip glowed yellow for a brief moment before returning to normal. Riyan watched as the three goblins became immobile and toppled to the side.

Realizing the two humans down below needed his help, he quickly dismounted and pulled his sling from off his belt. Bending over, he picked up four stones just as Chad and Bart came to a stop behind him. The heat from the fire was intensifying as the flames began engulfing more of the forest.

"We can't stay here," Bart urged him. "The fire is growing out of control."

"Then leave," replied Riyan. Turning to the battle, he started working his way closer as he put the first stone in the sling's cup. There was no way he could turn his back on fellow men. The horrors of being captured by goblins that have plagued him since leaving the pass were no fate he could leave anyone to face.

Through the trees and smoke, he kept his eyes on the goblins as he moved into a better position. A crack of a branch beside him announced Chad had joined him. He had his sword out and his face was grim as he nodded to Riyan. "Let's go do this," he said.

He finally reached a point where his stones would be less inhibited by the limbs and trees. Bringing his sling up to a quick spin, he launched the missile towards the nearest goblin. The stone flew true and struck the goblin in the side of the head. The blow knocked it off its feet and to the ground. "Good shot," he heard Chad mumble next to him.

Then another goblin suddenly put his hand to his neck and pulled one of Bart's darts from out of its flesh. The creature glanced around before suddenly dropping to the ground.

The other goblins soon realized the magic users had help and scattered. Those that were trapped by the green goo and lying frozen on the ground were left behind.

"Look out!"

Riyan heard Bart yell as he rushed into the clearing. He was waving his arms and shouting a warning for the magic user and his apprentice to get out of there. Then a tree engulfed in flame that was leaning heavily towards the magic users suddenly gave out with a thunderous crack. Its trunk split and the upper branches fell towards the magic users.

The older of the two saw the fiery hell coming towards them. Moving quickly, he grabbed his apprentice and threw him out of the circular glow surrounding them. The apprentice hit the ground and scrambled away as the tree landed on top of the protective glowing shield in a shower of sparks.

"Master!" the apprentice yelled as he came to a stop and saw his master trapped beneath the burning tree.

Upon striking the circular glow, the trunk of the tree broke in two at the point of impact. The fiery brands the impact sent flying began smoldering in the dry brush of the forest's floor.

"Bart!" yelled Chad as two of the goblins returned with their short swords drawn.

Bart turned and saw them appear at the edge of the clearing as they charged forward with bestial cries. He threw one of his darts and struck a charging goblin in the chest. The goblin took two more strides before he fell to the ground. The other goblin continued its attack.

Drawing his knife, Bart braced for the attack knowing his end was near. Then all of a sudden, Chad bowled into the goblin and knocked him to the ground. They both got back to their feet quickly and faced off against each other.

Bart opened the rolled leather that contained his darts and started to pull out another.

Clang!

The goblin struck out at Chad who brought his sword up to block the blow. When the goblin's short sword struck Chad's, the force of the blow knocked the sword out of his hand. As he watched his sword go flying, Chad tried to backpedal quickly to avoid the goblin's next strike.

The goblin moved incredibly fast as it pressed forward to attack. Chad watched as it came and raised its sword for the blow that most assuredly would end his life. Then all of a sudden, the side of the goblin's head exploded outward from the impact of another of Riyan's stones.

The apprentice had moved as close to his master as he could before the heat from the burning tree grew too great. "Master!" he cried out.

Riyan moved closer to the apprentice and could see his master clearly inside the glowing protective circle for the first time. His master had an arrow through the right leg and another protruded from his side just above his left hip.

"It's not going to hold," the master said weakly to his apprentice. From where Riyan was standing he could tell the man was in a tremendous amount of pain. Blood stained his robes and more kept flowing. The man obviously wasn't going to last much longer.

Reaching into his tunic, the apprentice produced a vial and held it towards his master. The master saw it and shook his head. "The shield which keeps the burning tree from me also prevents the vial from passing through," he said sadly. "Go on." Then for the first time he saw Riyan standing there. "See that he gets out of here," he said as he locked eyes with Riyan.

Not knowing what else to do, he nodded.

"Here," the master said to his apprentice. He tossed his staff through the glowing circle towards him. "Take Wyzkoth," he said. Then he glanced at the glowing circle around him, "Won't last much longer. Remember what I taught you."

"Yes master," replied the lad, "I will."

"Riyan!" Bart hollered, "We can't stay here." He pointed over to where the goblins had been frozen.

Riyan glanced over to them and saw that they were beginning to stir. He went to the apprentice and placed his hand on his shoulder. "We must leave."

The apprentice turned to Riyan with his master's staff in his hand. "I can't leave him," he said in anguish.

"You don't have a choice," replied Riyan.

Then the shield surrounding his master gave out and the burning tree crashed down upon him. They heard him shriek as the fire touched him then there was nothing but the crackle and roar of the flames.

Bart and Chad joined them. "Come on," Bart said. Chad was putting his recovered sword into his scabbard.

The apprentice nodded. Rushing over to the side of the clearing, he grabbed two packs that were lying in the midst of what must have been their camp before the goblins showed up. Then he joined the others as they raced from the growing inferno.

"They'll be after us sure as anything now," stated Bart.

"With any luck they won't know in which direction we fled," offered Chad.

"Let's hope," said Bart.

Back where they left the horses they found that they were no longer there. A quick check in the direction away from the fire turned them up. They mounted quickly and Riyan offered the apprentice to ride with him. Once he was up behind him, they rode quickly away from the raging fire. Pushing onward, they made the best time as they could to put as much distance between themselves and scene of the battle as quickly as possible. Behind him, Riyan could hear the apprentice sobbing at the loss of his master.

Chapter 17

They rode in silence as each listened for the pursuit that they feared would materialize at any moment. What words that did pass between them were hushed and few. Once they had ridden for an hour and still no pursuit presented itself, they began to relax.

All attempts by Riyan to engage their new companion in conversation was met by silence. The apprentice didn't seem really there, he was drawn inward dwelling upon his own misery. Another hour of riding had the fire far behind them. Its glow could still be seen where it raged in the night. Riyan figured the fire wouldn't come their way seeing as how a gentle breeze was blowing from the north. If it had been blowing in from the south he would have been more worried.

"I can't believe he's gone," the apprentice suddenly said.

So shocked by the declaration was Riyan that at first he wasn't exactly sure what was said. He remained quiet as the apprentice continued to speak.

"We came here to gather components for a spell he was working on," he said quietly. "He lost his life for nothing." Bitterness, anger, and sadness could all be heard in his voice.

"What was his name?" asked Riyan. He wanted to keep the apprentice talking so he wouldn't withdraw back into himself again.

"Allar," he replied.

"I'm sure Allar felt the need was worth the risk," he assured him.

"He did," the apprentice stated. Then he quieted for a moment as the sobbing returned for a short time. "He said they had to be harvested this time of year. That to do so at any other would negate their usefulness."

Riyan waited for him to continue but he had lapsed into silence once more. When it didn't look as if the apprentice was going to continue the conversation, he asked, "What's your name?"

"Kevik," he replied. "That's not my true name. Magic users aren't supposed to go by their true name. Kevik was the name my master gave me when he took me on as his apprentice."

"Very well then Kevik," Riyan said. "It might be a good idea for you to travel with us until we can return you back across the mountains."

"Thank you," he replied. "I would appreciate that."

They rode in silence for some time after that. Kevik seemed to have his emotions under control for there were no more outbursts of sobbing. As they rode, the moon overhead continued its arc across the star filled sky.

Then in the early part of the morning, from out of the trees before them, three goblin warriors suddenly appeared. Both sides were startled to see the other. Kevik cried out a word unintelligible to the others and green goo suddenly materialized around the goblins.

"Ride!" yelled Bart and he kicked his horse into motion. As he raced past the goblins, his horse accidentally brushed up against one of the goo coated goblins. His horse stumbled when the goo covering the goblin attached itself to the upper part of his horse's rear left leg. Bart looked back when and saw where the goblin was being dragged along with every step his horse took. The goo was acting like glue as it held the goblin to his horse's leg.

Turning in his saddle, Bart kicked out with his foot in an attempt to dislodge the goblin but only managed to get his foot stuck in the green mess. The goblin was screaming as it struggled to free itself but the goo was too strong, making its attempts futile.

"Riyan!" Bart yelled to his friend who had already disappeared into the trees ahead. "Chad!" He tried to get his horse to move forward, but the added weight in the position it was, made it all but impossible for it to keep going.

Suddenly Riyan and Chad reappeared out of the trees and immediately saw his predicament. "Kevik!" Riyan yelled to the apprentice in the saddle behind him. "What can we do?"

Kevik looked around him and saw the goblin, the horse, and Bart all stuck together. "I can cast a counter spell to dispel it," he explained. "But it will remove it from the others as well."

"Do it!" shouted Bart.

Kevik nodded and with a wave of his hand and two words of magic, the green goo vanished. Immediately the goblin fell free and Bart righted himself back in the saddle.

"Let's go!" Riyan yelled. From the direction they had just fled, he heard the other goblins that were just freed from the goo shouting as they crashed through the brush in pursuit.

They turned their horses away from the sound of the approaching goblins and bolted through the trees. Behind them the goblins shouted in their guttural tongue as they gave chase. Then from just ahead and to the right, other goblins were heard as they begun moving to intercept. In the darkness of the forest they were unable to see exactly where the goblins were, but they couldn't be very far away.

"Find us a way out of this!" Chad yelled to Bart who was now back in the lead.

"What do you think I've been trying to do!" came the reply.

The goblins chased them for what seemed like an hour. Though they never saw their pursuers, they could tell by the continued calls and shouts the goblins made that they weren't increasing their lead.

Light slowly began to brighten the sky and the stars winked out one by one as the coming dawn hid their beauty. In the light of dawn, they were able to catch glimpses of their pursuers from time to time running behind them. It was incredible that they could still be in pursuit and haven't fallen behind by now. The only reason Riyan could come up with was that the sheer size of the horses hampered their movement through the tangled undergrowth of the forest. While the goblins, being smaller in stature, were better able to forge through on foot.

"Stop!" Kevik suddenly yelled.

Riyan failed to heed his warning as he glanced back to him over his shoulder. "We can't!" he yelled. "If we stop they will kill us."

"But you don't understand ..." he began.

"We're not stopping!" Bart yelled from his position at the lead.

Kevik opened his mouth to urge them to stop once more but instead kept silent. He knew it wouldn't do any good. How could he make them understand that it might be worse to continue than to stand and face the goblins.

He had seen the totem that they just passed and understood its significance. The goblins have many totems and his master taught him the meaning of the more common visages they used before setting out. Each of the visages held different meanings for those who understood them. Also, the meanings could convey varying degrees of warning depending upon which visages were combined onto the totem and which position each of them held.

The one that they just passed had been overgrown by the forest and he had caught but a glimpse of it as they rode past. His master had been most emphatic about one certain visage, one that should they come across it, must be avoided at all costs. Kevik wasn't able to see the other visages on the totem due to the brush and the speed of their passing, but he had seen the one at the top very clearly. Goblin totems always have three visages or other representations that give the totem its meaning. The one on top is the primary message the totem is there to convey while the other two give added emphasis as to either the degree in which the top one should be taken, or something else.

The one that he saw simply meant, Death.

Riyan was soon to realize that the sound of pursuit behind them had begun to fade away in the distance. He wasn't sure why, but the goblins were breaking off their pursuit. "Looks like they finally gave up," he said. They began slowing down to an easy walk now, seeing as how there was no longer any immediate danger.

Chad grinned. "Guess they realized they couldn't catch us," he said.

"No," announced Kevik, "that's not the reason they are no longer following us."

"Oh?" asked Chad. "Care to enlighten us?"

"Back when I shouted for us to stop I saw one of their totems," he explained. "You may not realize it, but the totems are like markers, warning signs if you will. The one we passed proclaimed that to proceed beyond it meant death for any that do."

"Death?" asked Bart. Bringing his horse to a stop, he turned around and came back to Riyan and Kevik. "What sort of death?"

"It didn't go into that much detail and I only saw the visage at the top," he replied. "My master warned me about that one. He said that they only used it when extreme danger was present."

Chad glanced around at the forest around them. "It doesn't look all that dangerous," he commented.

"Be that as it may, it warned of danger and I think we should be on our guard," asserted Kevik. "Just because there is no visible danger now, doesn't mean we won't run into what that totem was there to warn us about further in."

At that Riyan and Bart suddenly grew quiet. Riyan glanced at Bart and could see that he was thinking the same thing he was. Perhaps the totem was warning them about where they were heading.

Chad saw their expressions and asked, "What?"

Ignoring his question, Riyan asked Kevik, "Do you know anything about this area?"

He shook his head. "No. My master said he's been here a couple times gathering various spell components. He probably would have known more than I."

"Did he ever mention someplace old in these parts?" Riyan asked. "Say ruins or anything like that?"

Kevik's eyes widened. "Is that why you're here?" Glancing first to Riyan then to the others, he knew that it was. "You're a bunch of treasure hunters."

"I suppose you could call us that," nodded Riyan. "We've been told there is a place around here that may hold great wealth."

Kevik thought about it a second and nodded. "He did mention that there were ruins of a place called Algoth somewhere around here," he said.

"What did he say?" asked Bart.

Kevik noticed that they were keenly interested in what he was about to say. "Nothing much," he replied. "Just that it was old."

"Old?" asked Chad. "That's it?"

"Yes," Kevik said. "He said and I quote, 'There once was a realm here long ago, long before the goblins came. A colleague of mine years ago told me that there were ruins of a place called Algoth on this side of the mountains ...' From there he went into a lecture about various spell components that grew in this region, the best time to harvest them, that sort of stuff. Did you know that the ..."

"Yes, yes, yes," Bart said as he cut him off. "That must be the place we're looking for."

Riyan nodded. "Would stand to reason."

"Then if this Algoth is where we're headed," Chad said, "why would the goblins mark this place as deadly?"

Shrugging, Bart said, "Who knows? Could be they're superstitious about this area. Maybe it's taboo to them?"

"That's not what it said," corrected Kevik. "It proclaimed that to enter here was to die. Period!"

"Alright, calm down," Riyan said. "But you did say that the totem had been overgrown?" When he received a nod from Kevik, he continued. "Then it could be possible that whatever danger there was is no longer present."

"I wouldn't trust to that," Kevik stated.

"What do you two think?" Riyan asked Chad and Bart. "Should we heed the warning of the totem and turn back?"

"Turn back?" asked Chad incredulously. "After all we've done to get this far? You have to be kidding."

"We accepted the possibility of death before we even left the Marketplace," Bart said. "I don't see how this could be any different."

"That's true," agreed Riyan. "We press on then?"

Chad and Bart both nodded their agreement.

Riyan nodded as well. He then turned back to Kevik and said, "If you don't want to accompany us, we'll understand."

"I don't have much of a choice one way or the other," he replied. "The unknown danger ahead with you or take my chance with the goblins behind on my own. Better the unknown than certain death."

"Excellent," Riyan said with a grin. "I was hoping you would say that. Glad to have you with us."

Kevik gave them a halfhearted grin.

Bart turned and resumed leading them northward. With the sun almost ready to crest the horizon to the east, it was easier for him to determine which way was north. He angled slightly more to the east after a bit in order to reach the river flowing south. According to the map on the key fragment, Algoth lay on the western shore of the small lake at the northern end of the river.

As they made their way through the forest, they began to feel relatively safe. Seeing as how this area was warded from goblin incursion by the totem, they rode without fear of being discovered and attacked.

Kevik remained quiet as he rode behind Riyan. He took in his new traveling companions and didn't think much of them. They were all as young as he was, two of them gave the appearance that they may never have done this sort of thing before. The third on the other hand had a definite presence about him. A confidence if you will. He wasn't entirely sure that linking his fate with these three was the wisest course of action for him. But seeing how his alternative was to strike out alone, he had little choice.

"There's the river," Bart said after they had ridden for awhile. Through the trees ahead they could see the sun glinting off the water as it flowed southward.

"How much further to where we want to go do you think?" Chad asked.

"Won't know until we get there," replied Bart. Now that the river was in sight, they began following it upstream. Somewhere ahead is a ruin or something else situated near where the river leaves the small lake.

Kevik at times during the ride would turn inward and remember his master. The things he taught him, the promise of what would have come had his master lived. He had been quite lucky that his master had chosen him to be his apprentice. A magic user of such power and skill was much sought after by those wishing to learn the skills arcane.

He's not really sure why his master had chosen him out of all the others he tested that day. From Kevik's viewpoint, he didn't do all that much better than the others in the tasks that they were set to do. But when Allar had announced that Kevik would be his apprentice, it would be difficult to describe the emotions he felt.

He grinned at the memory of some of the mistakes he made that first month, it's a wonder he's even still alive. All of a sudden he snapped out of his reverie when his eyes passed over another of the totems. "Riyan, stop!" he hollered.

"What?" he asked.

"There's another of the totems," he explained. Pointing toward the river, he directed Riyan's attention to the totem that stood near the edge of the river. It was several feet from the bank on this side and facing the water. "We need to see what the other two visages are. They may give some insight as to why this place is death to those who enter."

"Alright," Riyan said. "Bart!" he hollered up to him. "Kevik wants to stop and examine that totem over there."

When Bart looked over and saw the totem, he nodded.

Riyan rode over to it and Kevik dismounted. Kevik then moved to the other side and looked up at the faces upon the totem.

He pointed to the top one and said, "That one declares that it is death for any who continue past the totem." The visage looked to be a representation of a goblin skull.

The visage just below it was one he recognized as well. "The second one means strength." Just below the skull was carved the semblance of a tree.

"Strength?" asked Chad.

Kevik nodded. "Being in the second position as it is, I believe it's trying to convey how serious the one on top should be taken. Seeing as how it means strength, I think it is saying that death has a strong presence here."

"Death itself?" asked Riyan. "Or could it mean the possibility of death?"

"I don't know," he admitted. "My master just gave me a quick rundown on the most used visages and their meaning."

"What about the third?" Chad asked. The third one was a circle with two wavy lines carved across its center.

He shrugged. "I don't know," he replied. "It doesn't match any of the visages my master told me."

"What is the significance of the third spot?" Bart asked. "If the top one is the overall message and the second one if I understand you right, tells the observer to what degree he needs to heed the first one, then what is the third one's function?"

"It is supposed to give the observer some understanding of what lies ahead," he explained. "Say a totem was placed to warn of a pool of poisoned water. The top one would be the visage representing poison. The second one would state how bad the poison is. And the third would resemble a pool of water. In essence it would say, 'Poison, strong, pool of water.'"

Bart looked back up at the totem before them. "So here we have, 'Death, strong, and a circle with two wavy lines'," he stated.

"Yes, exactly," nodded Kevik.

"Would be nice to know what that third visage could mean," commented Riyan. They stood there for several minutes as they tried to come up with ideas as to what it represented.

That's when Chad happened to glance across the river and noticed a party of a dozen goblin warriors. "We've got company," he said. The others turned towards the far bank of the river.

"They're not crossing," observed Bart.

"No," agreed Riyan. "But it looks like they want to."

The goblins were acting very agitated. One even went so far as to fire an arrow in their direction. But they easily avoided the missile after it peaked at the top of its arc and came at them.

"Maybe it would be a good idea to move further into the trees," suggested Chad. "Out of sight out of mind as it were."

Bart snorted. "We may be out of sight, but I highly doubt if we'll be out of their minds."

"Still, let's get out of here," Riyan said. Moving back to his horse, he mounted and lent a hand to Kevik as he swung up behind him. The other two were mounted by the time Kevik was settled in behind Riyan and Bart took the lead once more as they left the totem by the river. A few minutes later the trees obstructed their view of the river and the totem.

As they rode, each continued to think about what the totem they saw might mean. None of them were very thrilled by its presence, other than the fact it kept the goblins from coming after them.

A short time after they left the totem, Bart noticed an outcropping of stone that seemed to stick up out of the ground ahead. Its presence seemed rather unusual as the rest of the land was relatively even as it moved over the gently rolling hills. It was covered in moss and overgrown with bushes. The only reason he noticed it at all was that it protruded upward more than the lay of the land would warrant.

The course they were taking led them in the direction of the outcropping. As he rode closer, something about the moss covered rock felt odd to him. When he neared it, he realized what it was. Partially hidden beneath the moss were the unmistakable signs of carving. He brought his horse to a halt and dismounted.

"What are you doing?" asked Riyan. Kevik looked around him to where Bart was moving toward the outcropping.

Bart didn't reply, instead he came to the rock and scraped off a section of the moss. He could hear Chad's surprised intake of breath when the section of moss fell away. It had revealed an eye. The eye was on its side and after removing more of the moss, they were able to tell that it was part of a head. Most likely the head of a statue.

The eyes and general features were somewhat eroded away, but the face was definitely that of a human. "Looks like we've reached Algoth," Riyan said as he swung down from his horse."

Bart glanced behind him and saw the others were coming to examine the statue for themselves. The head looked to have been broken off from a larger statue, since after they pushed back some of the bushes the jagged neck was revealed.

Chad moved further down to see if he could find the rest of the statue but only the head was there. "We better be on our guard from here on out," said Chad. Returning to the others he added, "Whatever the totem was warning of is likely to be found within the ruins of Algoth."

"What are you looking for?" Kevik asked. "Why is it so important for you to come here?" The others glanced from one to the other. He could see they didn't want to let him in on what they were up to. "Don't you trust me?" he asked, slightly hurt.

"It's not that we don't trust you," Riyan explained. "It's just that we don't know you well enough. You understand that right?"

Kevik didn't like it but could see the logic in what he was saying. He nodded and said, "Yes."

Riyan gave him a grin and patted him on the shoulder. "Let's go see if we can't find what we're looking for." Returning to his horse, he again helped Kevik up behind him. The staff that his master gave him had been an ever present companion. When riding, he always kept it clutched in his right hand. After they left the head behind and continued on, Riyan asked him if he knew how to use it.

"For the most part," he admitted. "It can paralyze an enemy, that one I know. My master never went into very much detail about it. I'll have to get a king's scroll of identification in order to fully understand what it does."

"What would a king's scroll of identification tell you?" he asked.

"Everything about it," Kevik replied. "But for now I'll have to settle for what my spell of identification can reveal."

"You know how to cast a spell of identification?" Riyan asked hopefully.

"Well, just the basic one," he explained. "As I grow in mastery of the arcane arts, the effects of my spells will become more enhanced."

Riyan grew silent for a moment as he contemplated what he had just heard. He wondered if perhaps Kevik's spell of identification would reveal anything about the fragment of the key. But then he thought that it might be best if he were to purchase one of the scrolls from a scriber like Phyndyr. That way what he learned would remain with just him. He liked Kevik, but he just didn't know if he was one in whom he could trust the secret of what they were doing.

"What other spells can you do?" he inquired.

"Just a couple," he replied. "One of them you already saw. I can restrict the movement of another by encasing them in a green sticky substance." He grinned as he said, "The spell is called, 'Glavir's Miraculous Spell of Binding'. From what I've learned so far, every spell has a fancy name. I just call it my green goo spell." Then he laughed. He was surprised that it burst out of him, he really wasn't expecting it.

"What's so funny," Riyan asked.

"My master would get so mad when I referred to it by 'the green goo spell'," he explained. Then he grew silent as the memory of his loss returned. He had almost been able to put it behind him.

"What else?"

"I can identify objects, inflict damage by sending red bursts of power, and half a dozen cantrips," he told him.

"Must be neat to be able to do such things," he said.

"It is," he admitted. "But it takes a lot of time to learn a new spell. I've been an apprentice now for little over a year and I only know a handful of spells."

"I'm sure that once you've done it longer, you'll be able to learn faster," stated Riyan.

"So my master taught me," he agreed.

They continued making their way through the trees with Bart in the lead. After awhile they came across more evidence of the people who had once lived there. Overgrown sections of walls that once must have stood tall were now little more than shattered remnants of their former glory.

The trees began to thin as they entered an area where the broken remnants of Algoth became more visible. All of it was overgrown and broken. Then all of a sudden a structure appeared through the trees ahead. Rising tall, it was covered in moss and vines. The ground floor and the one above it seemed to be intact, but the jagged outline of the upper walls revealed that it had once stood taller. More structures were visible further behind it.

"Looks like it collapsed," Chad said as they rode towards the building. No doorway was visible so they went around to the right to locate one. When they rounded the corner they saw that the right wall had crumbled and the interior of the building had completely collapsed in on itself. Over the years

dirt had been deposited over the rubble and now trees and bushes grew out of the crumbled remains. One of the trees had grown very large and rose up out of the ruined building to the sky.

Dismounting, they gave the building a once over but found nothing of interest. Moving on, the led their horses over to one of the nearby buildings. This one looked like it may have survived better. It was three stories tall and other than a few cracks coursing through the walls, seemed to be intact.

"This is it!" exclaimed Bart as he rushed forward.

"This is what?" asked Kevik.

When Riyan and Chad saw what had excited Bart, they too realized this was going to be important. For engraved on the front of the double doors that led into the building, was a coat of arms they both had seen before. A sword pointed downward with a dragon grasping the hilt as its body twined around the blade.

Riyan grinned as he looked upon one of the coat of arms they had seen back in the diamond shaped chamber deep within The Crypt.

Chapter 18

"Yes!" Riyan exclaimed in excitement as he ran forward.

Kevik could see that they were getting excited about what was engraved on the doors. "Is this important?" he asked.

"Very," replied Riyan. He ran his hand across the engraving. At one time it must have been brilliantly colored, but now only specks of the color remained. He turned back to Kevik and asked, "Have you ever seen this before?"

Shaking his head, Kevik said, "No. Should I have?"

"I wouldn't think so," Riyan told him.

Bart tried the door on the right but it wouldn't budge. The one on the left was just as immobile. "Going to have to find another way in," he announced as he backed away from the doors. Gazing upward he looked at the windows staring out from the second and third floors.

"Are you going to climb up there?" Chad asked.

"Not unless there's no other way," he replied. Moving out, he began to move around the building hoping to find another way in other than the windows above. As luck would have it, there was another doorway around the back whose door was missing.

The doorway opened up onto a long hallway that looked as if it ran the length of the building. Other doorways sat at intervals along both sides. Light passed through some of those doorways giving the hallway an eerie feeling. Aside from the excitement the three friends were feeling, there was also an undercurrent of trepidation. They haven't forgotten the implied threat of the totems.

Riyan took the lead and was the first to enter with Chad right on his heels. Dirt covered the floor and leaves were scattered from one end to the other. There were even a couple bushes growing in areas illuminated by the sunlight that streamed in from the adjoining rooms.

"Not very promising," Riyan commented.

"It's been open to the elements for a very long time," countered Chad.

"True," nodded Riyan. He worked his way down the hallway and paused when he came to one of the doorways to look into the room. Other than a small animal they startled, the only thing they found was more dirt and debris that had been blown in by the wind. Few of the doorways actually held doors and only one stood shut but yielded quickly to Riyan's boot.

Through another of the doorways they found a short hallway ending at a staircase leading up. The rest of the rooms held nothing of interest. One looked like it had at one time been used as some animal's den, bones and such littered the floor.

Disappointed, Riyan led them up the stairs to the second floor. Again just as the first, they found rooms that held nothing other than dirt, leaves, and a few struggling bushes that were trying to make it in the debris the wind had deposited beneath the windows over the years. Another staircase had been discovered that led up to the third and final floor.

Disappointment was all that the third floor held for them. They did find a few bird's nests built in a couple of the rooms, but they didn't even have eggs. "Nothing," Riyan stated as they finished searching the last room.

Bart went to the window and looked out over the ruins of Algoth. Other buildings similar to the one they were in stretched for a quarter of a mile before the forest once again claimed the land. "This could take awhile," he commented.

The others came to stand next to him. "What are you looking for?" Kevik asked. "If you were to tell me, perhaps I could prove more helpful."

"What we are looking for will most likely be found in the building the lord who use to rule Algoth called his own," Bart explained. He continued gazing out and saw a building larger than the others. Where the rest of the buildings were predominantly one and two stories, with a scattering of three stories here and there, this one was easily five stories tall and twice as wide as the largest building out there. It also held a centralized position among the buildings, sort of like a hub. Pointing, he directed the other's attention to it. "There."

Riyan saw the building and nodded. "That could be it," he agreed.

"We still have several hours of daylight left," Chad commented.

Bart turned towards him and asked, "Your point being?"

"I don't think it wise to linger here after dark," he replied. "Whatever the totems warned of might be more active once the sun goes down."

"Or it might not," countered Bart. "Besides, where are we to go? Maybe the goblins have an inn just the other side of the totems where we could stay." He shook his head. "No, we're stuck here until we decide to leave."

"Your friend is right," Kevik said to Chad. "We have nowhere else to go."

Riyan glanced from one to the other then said, "No sense in lingering here. We should head over there now and find a place to hole up before night comes."

The others agreed with him and they were soon heading out of the room and down the stairs. Once back outside the building, they mounted their horses and rode in the general direction of the central building.

As they made their way through the ruins, they passed many remnants of buildings long fallen to ruin. A few structures had withstood the passage of time well, showing only minor cracking and crumbling. All were overgrown with vines, some even sported bushes and small trees growing out of the cracks in the walls. Over time, they too will add to the erosion of Algoth. On several buildings they passed, they noted the dragon-sword coat of arms that had been on the front doors of the earlier building they searched.

The large centralized building quickly made its appearance above the ruins ahead. Of all the buildings, it had withstood the ravages of time and weather the best. Its walls showed only minor cracks and still looked strong.

Here more than any of the others they've come across, the coat of arms was most prominently displayed. The two large double doors that marked the main entrance each had the coat of arms inscribed upon its surface. Twice as large as any they've yet seen, the coat of arms seemed to project power and prestige.

"If this isn't the place," stated Riyan, "I wouldn't know where else to look."

"You got that right," replied Chad.

They came to a stop before the double doors and dismounted. Nearby grew a tree and it was to its branches that they secured the reins of their horses. They shouldered their packs and approached the doors. Kevik took the two packs he had taken from his and his master's last campsite when they fled the battle and set them on the ground.

Riyan noticed that he was opening them and transferring the contents of one to the other. He took out a large book with what looked like magical writing inscribed upon its cover and placed it in the other pack. Along with the book he removed two potion bottles and several other miscellaneous items. When he finished, the one pack was much lighter yet still contained a few things. That one he secured back onto his horse. Then he turned and saw the others watching him.

"Spell book?" asked Riyan.

"My master's," he explained.

"Really?" Riyan asked. "What's in there?"

"I'm not sure," he said. "He never confided its secrets to me. Besides, it isn't wise to open another's spell book. Such an action often comes with serious repercussions."

Bart nodded. "I believe it."

"There will come a time when I have gained the knowledge and experience to open it safely," explained Kevik. "Until that time, it shall remain closed." He took his master's staff, guess you could call it his now, and moved to join them at the doors.

"Understandable," Chad said.

Riyan and Bart turned back to the doors and approached. Riyan grasped the handle of the door to the right and pushed. To his surprise, it opened. Pushing harder, he worked against centuries, perhaps millennia, of disuse and shoved the door open far enough for him to be able to pass through.

He moved through to the other side and entered a very large hall. The ceiling reached upwards for at least three floors, and on the far side of the hall were two winding staircases that went up to the second floor.

"Wow," Chad said as he entered after Bart. "What a place."

Bart nodded, "It must have been something in its heyday."

"Yeah," agreed Riyan.

Four statues of men were placed in various points around the room. Smaller busts of men were sitting in wall niches along the walls. The walls themselves appeared rather plain, but when Chad inspected them closely, found traces of faded paint. There were also remnants of old couches, chairs and tables which were all but gone.

"Where should we start looking?" asked Chad.

"I hardly think it would be sitting out in the open," replied Bart. "In all probability it will be in a hidden room."

"Hidden room?" exclaimed Chad. "How are we to find that?"

"First order of business is to search every nook and cranny of this place," Bart explained. "What we are looking for are sections of walls wide enough to house a secret room or passage. Once we've located those, then we begin trying to discover which one actually does."

"Your father taught you this?" Riyan asked.

"Not exactly, no," Bart replied. He turned to Riyan and asked, "Do you have any of those coins with you?"

Riyan nodded and after removing his pack and searching it, produced a handful of the copper coins.

Bart took one and held it up so the symbol was facing the others. "Anything with this or the dragon-sword coat of arms on it could indicate something of interest," he stated. "So be on your guard and keep your eyes open."

Kevik looked at the symbol a moment. "Is this what you're after?" he asked.

"You've seen this before?" Riyan asked.

"My master had a coin with this symbol inscribed upon it," he explained. "Never said where he got it though."

"Maybe he got it from here?" suggested Chad.

"Possibly," shrugged Kevik.

"There's still over an hour of daylight left," Bart said to the others. "I suggest we split up in pairs so we can cover more ground." He glanced to Riyan. "I'll take Chad and search the lower two floors while you and Kevik search the ones above." He waited until Riyan nodded before continuing. "Don't open or touch anything. Get me first if you find something of interest."

Riyan and Chad both understood that he was talking about the possibility of traps. "You got it," agreed Riyan.

"Good," he said. "Let's meet back here in the hall a little before sunset."

"See you then," said Riyan. To Kevik he said, "Let's go."

As he and Kevik headed for the stairs, Kevik asked, "Why does he want us to get him before we open anything?"

"There could be traps," Riyan explained. "He has a knack with such things."

Kevik glanced at Bart and nodded in understanding.

They headed to the staircase on the right and started up. It was made of stone, or perhaps marble, so had kept its strength through the years. Once up to the second floor, they quickly found another staircase leading up to the third floor where they were to begin their search.

Beginning with the first room on the third floor they came to, they began their exploration. The room held little of interest, a single window looked out to the west over the ruins. A breeze was felt as it made its way into the building. What furniture once was inside has long since fallen to the ravages of time and the elements.

Riyan sifted through the debris scattered across the floor with the toe of his boot. The only thing he turned up was moldy old leaves and dirt. "Maybe the next one," he said.

"We'll see," Kevik said from where he was looking out the window. "It's quiet."

Riyan came and stood next to him as he too looked out over what was left of Algoth. Nothing stirred but the wind through the trees. Try as he might, Riyan couldn't even find an animal moving anywhere.

Turning to Kevik he said, "We need to search as much as we can before it gets dark."

Kevik glanced at him and nodded. "You're right." He then followed Riyan as he moved away from the window and made for the room's exit.

The rest of the third floor was pretty much the same. Only one room held anything that could be considered of interest. It was a faded mural of knights riding horses across grass covered hills. The sun was shining and the whole scene inspired confidence and majesty.

Riyan noted how on the shield of the man leading the knights was the dragon-sword coat of arms that they have seen on several buildings including the doors to this one. He pointed it out to Kevik. "This must have been the lord of this area."

"Or an ancestor," Kevik offered.

"Could be," he replied.

They then returned to the stair they had discovered earlier that led up to the fourth floor. Once they ascended the stair, they once more began searching all the rooms. These were a bit smaller than the ones on the floor below. It almost seemed like they were administrative offices, which was likely the capacity in which they were used.

Within one office that looked much like all the others, they found the rusted remains of a broken sword lying under a layer of leaves and dirt that had accumulated near the open window. Two inches of jagged metal was still attached to the hilt. A little more searching found the rest of the blade across the room. "Wonder how this came to be?" Kevik asked.

"Can you find out with your identification spell?" Riyan asked.

"Perhaps," he replied. "But keep in mind, my version of the spell is very basic and it won't reveal much."

Riyan held out the two pieces. "Give it a try," he said.

Kevik nodded and took the two halves. "You will need to be quiet as I cast the spell," he explained. "The slightest distraction may break my concentration."

"Alright," agreed Riyan.

Kevik searched the room for a relatively clean spot on the floor before sitting down. He laid the staff on the floor next to him while he placed the two halves of the sword on the floor before him.

He held his hands over the broken pieces of the sword, closed his eyes, and spoke a magical incantation. Riyan watched as the pieces of the sword began to glow an off blue.

In Kevik's mind's eye, a scene began to play:

Hammers struck metal as the blade took form under the skill of master craftsman. Then the scene blurred, and when it clarified ... It felt like a hundred years had passed since its forging. It hung at the waist of a man in armor. Again the scene blurred ... The sword was being wielded in battle, the distinct clang of metal striking metal was heard before a blow took it broadside midway from hilt to tip that broke the blade in two.

When the spell finally ran its course, the blue glow vanished and Kevik opened his eyes.

"Well?" Riyan asked.

Kevik related the vision to him.

"Was that all?" Riyan asked again.

"Yes," replied Kevik. "I told you it wouldn't have given much information." He took hold of his staff and with a hand from Riyan, returned to his feet.

"On the contrary," Riyan told him, "I think it gave some good information."

"Like what?" Kevik asked as they left the room to head to the next.

"For one thing, since we found both pieces of it in this room," explained Riyan, "it would be safe to assume that the battle that broke the blade took place in this building." As they entered the next room and began searching through the debris littering the floor he asked, "Did you see who or what the one wielding the blade was fighting?"

Shaking his head, Kevik said, "No. A more experienced magic user would have been able to learn more from the blade, unfortunately I'm just an apprentice."

"Still, it's useful information," Riyan assured him.

"Thanks," he said.

Riyan was searching through the piles of debris littered about the room when the light suddenly dimmed. He glanced to the window and said, "Uh-oh. The sun just hit the tops of the trees."

Kevik hurried to the window and saw that the shadows had grown long. "We've been here longer than I thought," he said. Turning around, he gazed at Riyan. "It's almost dark."

"Let's go find the others," Riyan said as he ceased rooting through a pile of dead leaves near the window. With Kevik following close behind, Riyan hurried down the two flights of stairs. When he came to the winding staircase that led down to the floor of the large hall, he looked out and saw that Chad and Bart had yet to return. Taking the steps quickly, he descended down to the ground floor.

"Should we go look for them?" asked Kevik.

Shaking his head, Riyan said, "Better not. They'll return shortly."

Kevik nodded and went out to where the horses were tied to the tree while Riyan remained within the hall.

After Kevik left, Riyan realized just how large and empty the hall really was. "Bart! Chad!" he cried. "It's time to go!" When the sound of his cry died out, the only reply was silence. He went to the window and saw the shadows growing longer. "Come on guys," he said under his breath, "we don't want to be here after dark." Glancing around at the lengthening shadows, his nervousness that had been absent while he and Kevik searched the upper floors, returned.

Bart had decided for them to search the second floor first as he didn't really believe they would find anything of note there. And after searching for an hour or so through the rooms up there, he confirmed his suspicions. Nothing.

So he and Chad had returned to the bottom floor and went through things piecemeal. Bart started by searching the statues and the busts in the wall niches for possible secret compartments. Nothing again.

Then he led the way with Chad right behind and started searching through the rooms adjacent to the hall just within the entrance. The first couple of rooms yielded nothing but leaves. One room boasted a rather scraggly bush that had begun growing in one of the piles of leaves and other dead plant material beneath one of the windows.

"Looks like an inside garden," joked Chad when they saw it. His smile quickly disappeared when Bart failed to see the humor in the situation. They checked the bush room thoroughly then went to the next.

"Do you think Riyan understands the gravity of the situation?" Chad asked him.

Bart entered the next room and saw a faded mural on the wall. As he went over to investigate, he asked, "What do you mean?"

"He thinks this is all one big holiday," Chad explains. "I wonder if he realizes the consequences that we face."

Bart glanced back at him. "You mean like us dying?"

Chad nodded. "Yes! Exactly. I don't think that possibility has even registered with him yet."

"You haven't exactly been much help in that respect," Bart said. Turning back to the mural he began running his hand along the wall. "What was it you said? 'What price adventure?' You haven't exactly shown what I'd call the proper appreciation for the gravity of the situation either."

"Well, that's beginning to change," he said. "The run in with the goblins has curbed my enthusiasm for this whole venture somewhat."

"Yeah," replied Bart distractedly. "Near death experiences will do that to you."

"I just hope he calms down a bit before he winds up getting himself, and us, in some real trouble."

"He will I'm sure," Bart said. Not finding anything such as a pressure plate within the mural, he turned back to Chad. "Just as soon as the boredom sets in."

"We'll see," Chad said.

Having given that room a thorough search, they moved on. Once out of the room, they headed down the hallway to the next doorway. Room after room, hallway after hallway, they worked their way through the ground floor. They had found a couple spots that could possibly have hidden a secret room or stash of treasure, but the cursory look Bart gave them turned up nothing.

Somewhat discouraged, they continued the hunt. They found themselves back at the large hall at the entrance and entered the last hallway they had yet been down. The first several rooms they checked turned up nothing, but then they came to one that was slightly different. This time there was a sturdy wooden door set in the left wall at the other end of the room.

"This might be something," Bart said. He crossed the room to the door and tried to open it only to find it locked. He pulled his lockpicks from his pack and set to work on it.

While Bart was working to unlock the door, Chad went to the window and looked out. "The day's almost gone," he observed.

"We'll search here and maybe one more room then return to the hall," he said.

"Sounds good," agreed Chad. He kept looking out the window towards the ruins until he heard Bart say, "Got it." Then he turned and joined him in front of the door as he started to swing it inward.

When the door swung open they found that beyond the door was a short narrow passage extending fifteen feet away from the door. The light coming in through the window in the other room gave just enough illumination for them to see the chest sitting against the far wall.

"Well, well," said Bart. "What do we have here?"

"It looks like a chest," replied Chad.

"Of course it's a ..." he began to say to Chad then stopped when he saw Chad grinning. "Very funny," he said not at all amused, which only gave Chad an even bigger reason to smile.

They entered the short passage and approached the chest. When they were almost to it they heard a creaking noise behind them and saw the door beginning to swing shut.

"The door!" yelled Bart.

Chad saw the door closing and raced back toward it but was too late.

Wham!

The door swung shut with a bang and plunged them into darkness. "Damn!" cursed Bart. It took him a minute to get his tube lantern lit, it being the only source for light they had brought with them.

When he shined the light at the door, he groaned.

"What?" asked Chad.

"Look for yourself," he replied.

Following the beam of light, Chad saw where it illuminated the door. "So?" he asked, not entirely sure what Bart was referring to.

"There's no lock or handle on this side," he explained. Turning to look at Chad he said, "We're locked in here."

Chapter 19

"Where are they?" Riyan asked. It's been a quarter hour since their return to the hall and he was beginning to get worried. Chad and Bart should have returned by now.

"Maybe something happened to them?" suggested Kevik.

"I don't think so," replied Riyan. "We would have heard something, a cry at least."

Riyan stood by the window, anxious now that the sun has all but disappeared. Gazing at the sky, he saw the first star of the evening appear. "We better go look for them," he finally said.

"Let's take a lantern with us," advised Kevik. "It's going to be dark soon."

"Good idea," agreed Riyan. Returning back outside to where the horses were tied, he retrieved his lantern and lit it. He then made his way back into the building and nodded to Kevik. "Alright, let's go find them."

From their experience of searching the upper floors, they knew the building was large and it would take some time to completely search every room. "I hope they don't return while we're gone," Kevik said.

"I hope that they do," replied Riyan. "At least they would be alright." He held the lantern up high as he gazed at the ground. With all the times he and Kevik had crisscrossed the hall, it was hard to determine which way Bart and Chad had gone by the footprints in the dust and dirt. He was quick to realize that this was getting him nowhere and began examining the hallways and rooms to see which way their path led.

There were two places where footprints were clearly visible, one was a hallway and another was a room. He couldn't help but remember the times he had to hunt for Black Face when he wandered off. There were times when the stupid sheep wouldn't make any noise that would help in finding him. Nine times out of ten Black Face would be found contentedly munching the leaves of the berry vines he liked so much.

"Which way?" asked Kevik.

"I'm not sure," replied Riyan. Putting his fingers to his lips, he whistled loudly three times just as he would to call his sheep. After the third whistle, they held still to listen. Silence was all they heard.

"Come on," Riyan said as he entered the hallway. Their trail was clearly visible and they had no trouble in following it. At the first doorway they saw two sets of footprints, one entering the room and another leaving. They followed the trail as it went into the room. Inside they found where Chad and Bart had rooted through the dirt and leaves before leaving. With no other exit and the entirety of the room clearly visible, they stepped back out into the corridor and continued on.

Room after room the path of footprints led them onward in their search. Each room they came to, they made a quick scan to be sure Bart and Chad weren't still there before continuing on. When a room held another exit such as a door or hallway, Riyan would try to determine which way their tracks went. Whichever way they led, he and Kevik would move to follow.

Bart finished checking the door for the third time. There was no handle or keyhole on this side. He even went so far as to wedge his knife in the space between the door and the doorjamb to try and pry it open with the blade. He felt the door move slightly before the locking mechanism stopped it.

"There's no way out," he said as he gave up and turned back toward Chad.

Chad stood there with the tube lantern in hand. He had been holding it to give Bart light with which to work. "Now what?" he asked.

"Wait for Riyan and Kevik to find us," he explained. "Though as big as this place is it could take some time."

"Maybe you could take a look at the chest?" suggested Chad. "Seeing as how we're not going anywhere for awhile."

"Sure," agreed Bart. "Stay just behind me and shine the light on the lock." He took out his lockpicks and selected the two he normally used on locks such as these. "Up a little," he said when Chad had let the light drop down too far. "You need to hold it steady and level. If you hold it at an angle, the candle will burn off center and the wax will melt all the faster."

"Alright," agreed Chad as the light came back to the locking mechanism.

Bart worked on the chest while the light wavered at times in Chad's hand. He found a trap and quickly disarmed it. It was a rather simple trap, a variant on the Prick of Poison where instead of coming out and pricking, this one would actually shoot out.

Once the trap was taken care of, the lock itself was easy. A few moments later, Bart was putting his picks back in the rolled leather carrier. Then while Chad held the light, he opened the lid.

Immediately upon opening, the light from the tube lantern was refracted by the two dozen gems held within. Not only gems but a large pile of coins as well. There were a multitude of bright shiny coppers, with many of the silver mixed in. But what drew their attention were the golden coins. Larger than the silvers, these gold coins were stamped with the same symbol and face as were the copper and silver coins.

Bart picked one up and held it in the light. "This has to be worth quite a bit," he said. Then he gauged its weight as it lay in his palm. "Easily twice the weight of our own gold sovereigns."

"Oh man," Chad said as he came forward.

Also in the chest were three identical bottles, a scabbard with a knife's hilt sticking out, and a three inch long ivory tube. Chad took one of the potion bottles and held it up to the light. He grew excited when he saw there was liquid still inside.

Bart grabbed the scabbard with the knife. When he removed the knife, to his astonishment, he found the blade still serviceable. No trace of rust marred its surface and when he ran the edge along a finger, discovered that it still held an edge. Putting his bloody finger to his lips, he worked to stop the bleeding while he tucked the scabbard with the knife safely held within, into the waistline of his trousers.

The ivory tube, now that was definitely odd. It had writing inscribed upon it and one end looked as if it would pop off. Chad held it in his hand. "What is this?" he asked Bart.

"Not sure," admitted Bart when he moved closer to look at it. "It may hold something though." He then pointed to the end that could come off. "Removing this end might open it."

"Should I?" he asked.

Bart shrugged. "It's up to you."

Chad contemplated whether to open it or not for a moment before handing the tube lantern to Bart. He held the tube vertical and gripped the end. Twisting the end he was pleased to feel it turn in his hand. Emboldened, he twisted and pulled the end completely off.

"Well?" asked Bart when Chad looked into the hollow opening.

"Not sure," he replied. "May be something in here." He cupped his other hand and brought it to the opening to catch whatever might come out as he slowly upended the tube. He slowly tipped the tube on its side until three small granules of white crystal spilled from the end and landed on his palm. He then raised the tube back in an upright position and replaced the end back onto it.

Holding his palm up to the light he asked, "What are these?"

"I've never seen anything like this before," Bart said as he took a closer look.

All of a sudden, it looked as if the crystals turned into liquid and sank into the skin of Chad's palm. No sooner did the liquid disappear than his hand began to grow numb. The numbness started spreading outward from where the liquid had entered his skin.

"Bart!" he cried as he started shaking his hand.

"What's wrong?" Bart asked as he saw Chad shaking his hand and rubbing it on his pant's leg.

"I can't feel my hand!" he cried hysterically.

Bart grabbed the wrist of the affected hand and stilled his thrashing. There were no discolorations or swelling as one would expect from a poison. He poked the palm with his finger. "Did you feel that?"

"No!" exclaimed Chad, fear of what may be happening to him causing him to blurt it out with more feeling than he had intended. "My wrist is growing numb now too," he said in a slightly calmer voice though there was still an undercurrent of fear audible. Chad's eyes grew wide as he saw Bart set the tube lantern on the floor and then remove his belt knife. "What are you going to do?"

"Prick your palm and see if you feel it," he explained.

Chad tried to pull back his hand from the knife's point but Bart had too strong a grip. "Hold still." He brought the tip to Chad's palm and pricked it. "Did you feel that?" he asked.

Shaking his head, Chad said, "No." A small drop of blood welled out from the wound.

Bart began pressing Chad's skin as he worked his way from his palm, past his wrist, and up the arm. By the time Chad said he could feel what he was doing, Bart had made it midway up his forearm.

"I think it's stopped spreading," Chad said. He then tried to flex his fingers but couldn't. Then he concentrated hard as he worked to flex his fingers and only managed a small twitch from his forefinger. With a panicked look, he turned his gaze to Bart. He held up his hand and practically screamed, "I can't move them!"

They had been following the trail left by Bart and Chad for a half hour now, and still hadn't come across them.

"Do you think they might have left the building?" asked Kevik.

Riyan came to a stop as that possibility hadn't even crossed his mind. "Man I hope not," he said. The thought of having to search for them in the dark ruins outside sent a shiver down his spine. "I doubt if they would have gone anywhere."

Lowering his voice Kevik said, "Maybe it was whatever the totem warned us about? Maybe it has already got to them?"

A chill passed through Riyan at his words. "Now don't start talking like that," he told him. "They are here somewhere."

"Then why haven't we found them yet?" replied Kevik.

"I don't know," Riyan said. Then with conviction he said once more, "But they're here!" As he left the hall and proceeded down to another room, the shadows began to have a more ominous feel to them. Scenes of what could have happened to his friends played through his mind, none of which offered him any comfort.

At the entrance to the room, he noted that the trail of footprints they had been following didn't extend past the doorway into the next room. Rather, they entered the room but didn't come out.

It was a fair sized room, similar in nature and size to the ones they had already checked. At the far end of the left wall stood a sturdy door. They did a quick check, found the door to be locked, and reentered the hallway. Then just as he had done a dozen times the last half hour, he blew three sharp whistles.

"Did you hear that?" asked Chad. He was sure he had just heard three whistles, reminiscent of the ones Riyan would use to call his sheep.

"Hear what?" asked Bart.

"I think it was Riyan," he replied. He moved to the door and began banging on it with his good hand. His other hand was still numb and hung at his

0

side. Fortunately, the numbness still hadn't travel any further than midway up his forearm. "Riyan!" he yelled.

Bart came next to him and added his effort in banging on the door.

Riyan was about to walk away from the room when an ominous thumping began to be heard. In the state that he was in, what with beginning to believe that something malign had taken off with his friends, the banging sounded to him like the whisper of heartbeats from those long dead.

"It's coming for us," he said, fear beginning to take hold. His imagination suddenly kicked into high gear which only tightened fear's hold on him.

Kevik drew close to him as he too heard the thumping of the telltale heartbeats. Riyan's fear was contagious and he yelled, "We've got to get out of here!"

Fleeing down the hallway, they ran as fast as they could and didn't stop until they were back in the large hall by the entrance. When they neared the door leading outside, they came to a halt. "I think it's gone," stated Kevik as the heartbeats of the dead could no longer be heard.

Riyan nodded as he worked to quiet his rapidly beating heart. "That was close." He glanced in the direction of the mouth of the hallway from which they had just escaped. The part of the ground floor they have yet to search still lies down that hallway, beyond where they heard the heartbeats of the dead.

Outside, night had fallen with a vengeance. The stars overhead gave an eerie feel to the ruins and his imagination began working overtime once again. When he thought he saw a ghost passing from one building to the next, he quickly turned away from the window.

"It's not real," he told himself. Then he forced himself to look out again and found the ghost was gone.

"You okay?" asked Kevik.

"My imagination is running away with me," he said. Rather unnerved right now, he took a few deep breaths and tried to calm himself. He realized he won't be good for anything if he continued to let his fears control him. Turning towards the hallway, he steeled himself to reenter it again. He must be brave for his friends. Just to reassure himself, he cast a look outside one more time and was relieved when his imagination didn't bring another ghost to haunt him.

"We're going back!" he said with conviction as he glanced to Kevik.

"Alright," Kevik said with less courage than Riyan was displaying.

Riyan took a moment to remove his sling and ready a stone within its cup. Then with lantern in one hand and sling in the other, he crossed the hall and entered the hallway. Behind him he could feel where Kevik was gripping the back of his shirt.

When they drew near to the spot where they heard the heartbeats last time, he paused and listened for a moment. He sighed in relief when the heartbeats could no longer be heard. Maybe it had only been his imagination after all.

Coming to the doorway of the last room they searched, he again saw where the trail of footprints ended. The floor of the hallway extending past the doorway looked as if no one had been on it for ages.

"They entered this room," he said, "then vanished." He again looked at the door he checked the first time, the one that had been locked. Other than the one he and Kevik were standing at, and the window, it's the only other possible way out. He was certain they wouldn't have gone through the window.

Then his gaze settled on the door and he stood there in thought for a moment. "Maybe it wasn't spirits we heard," he said to Kevik. Entering the room, he crossed to the door. "Maybe it was the pounding of fists on this door?" Now that fear no longer held him in its grip, he could come at this with more logic and less emotion.

He came close to the door and whistled three times loudly. No sooner did his third whistle end then banging could be heard coming from the other side. Moving his mouth right next to the door he hollered, "Bart, Chad, are you in there?"

Their response was muffled by the door but he distinctly heard them say, "Yes!"

Riyan grinned and turned to glance at Kevik. "We found them," he said. Then he sobered up and added, "There's no need to tell them we ran away the first time thinking they were ghosts or anything."

Kevik nodded and returned his grin. "No problem there."

Turning his attention back to the door, he tried to open it. "It's locked!" he hollered to those on the other side.

"It's locked he says," Chad says sarcastically to Bart. "Of course it's locked," he yelled through the door. "If it wasn't we wouldn't still be in here."

"Get away," Bart said as he pulled him from the door. "You're not helping any."

Chad gave him a less than pleased look as he came to a stop three feet from the door.

"Riyan!" Bart yelled.

From the other side he could barely hear Riyan reply, "Yes?"

"You have to open the door from your side," he hollered. "Do you understand?" A moment's quiet then he heard, "Yes."

He and Chad stood there for a moment and then heard thudding noises coming from the other side. Bart glanced to Chad and shook his head. "I think he's trying to smash through by running into it."

"Isn't the door a bit strong for that to work?" Chad asked.

"Exactly," Bart replied. He waited until another thump came then hollered. "Riyan!"

"Yes?" the reply came.

"That's not going to work, you'll have to pick the lock," he hollered.

There was another moment of silence then he heard Riyan ask, "With what?"

Bart took a moment to try and think of what Riyan might have that would work. Unfortunately his lockpicks were in here with him. "You'll have to use your knife!"

"Okay," replied Riyan. "How?"

Realizing he was going to have to talk him through it, he got comfortable. This could take awhile.

Ten minutes later, Riyan now had a fair understanding of how locks worked. He had the tip of his knife inserted in the lock and was working more by feel than anything else. From the other side, he heard Bart ask, "Do you feel the grove?"

"Yes," he replied. It took Bart some doing but he had finally gotten it through to him what grove he was talking about.

"Okay," Bart said. "You have to move it along the groove until something stops it."

He very carefully moved the tip of the knife along the grove until the point was stopped by a piece of metal. "I'm there."

"Listen carefully to what I say before you begin," Bart told him. "First of all, you have to push the metal that stopped the tip of your knife upward and slightly to the left. At the same time you have to push inward. If you do it right, the lock will disengage and then you will be able to open the door."

"Alright!" he hollered back. As he began, he heard Kevik say, "Take your time."

He held the knife in both hands as he began doing as Bart had explained to him. He gradually lifted the piece of metal and pushed inward at the same time. Then all of a sudden he felt the piece of metal resting against the blade slip off and move back into its original position.

"It slipped off!" he hollered to Bart.

"That's okay," Bart assured him. "Just keep trying until you have it."

It was on his sixth try when he finally felt the piece of metal click into place. Almost hardly daring to breathe, he nodded for Kevik to try the door. When the handle turned and the door began to swing inward, he about jumped for joy.

"You did it!" Bart exclaimed with a wide grin as he pulled the door the rest of the way open. "Make a thief of you yet."

Chad came out and actually gave him a hug. His left hand was hanging limp and Riyan asked him about it. He explained about the ivory tube and the crystals that caused the effect. "It's beginning to tingle," he said. "I think whatever it did is going away."

"Good," Riyan said happily.

Bart showed him the opened chest at the far end of the room. "Everything it held except for the bulk of the copper is in our packs," he said. Once they were all out of the small room, the door began to swing closed again. They didn't try to stop it.

They showed Riyan and Kevik the potion bottles, the ivory tube, and the knife Bart had taken for his own.

Kevik took one of the bottles in hand and a bluish glow surrounded it. "What's he doing?" Bart asked.

"He's casting a spell that will tell what it is," Riyan explained. "It's one of the few spells he's learned so far."

When the blue glow disappeared, he said, "It's a healing potion."

"That could come in handy," Bart said. Since there were three of them, he gave one to Chad and Riyan to keep in their packs.

Chad handed the ivory tube to Kevik and asked him if he could find out what had affected him. Kevik nodded and the bluish glow enveloped it for a couple seconds before disappearing. "The crystals contained within were used by healers," he explained. "They would use them to deaden an area before cutting into it, so their patient wouldn't feel any pain."

"Never heard of anything like this," stated Bart.

"There are some leaves that do the same thing but not to this degree," Kevik told them. "This could be a derivative of something similar." He then glanced to the new knife Bart had. "Would you like me to do that as well?"

Shrugging, Bart said, "Why not?"

Kevik took the knife and once the spell had run its course handed it back. "It's imbued with magic. There are two properties to the magic, one keeps it sharp and from succumbing to the elements which would ruin it, such as rust."

"What's the other?" Bart asked.

Kevik shrugged, "My spell didn't get that far. Like I was telling Riyan earlier, the spell I am able to do only gives a few general items of information. I do know that it was forged several hundred years before it was put in that chest."

"I thank you for what you could tell me," he said. "Perhaps one day I'll be able to figure out the rest." He undid his belt that secured his other knife around his waist and began sliding the new scabbard onto it. As he was positioning it for an easy draw, he paused and glanced back to Kevik. "It isn't malignant is it?"

Shaking his head, Kevik said, "No. I felt nothing like that."

"Good," he replied. When he had the scabbard on where he wanted it, he buckled the belt back on around his waist. Now he had two knifes, one on either side of him. The new knife he positioned on his left side for an easy draw with his right hand.

"Now," he said as his gaze took in Riyan and Kevik, "did you two find anything?"

Chapter 20

When they returned to the large hall, Bart and Riyan went out and brought the horses in. If there was something going on around here at night, they didn't want their only mode of transportation disappearing by morning.

In one of the front corners of the hall they laid out their bedrolls and made a fire. None of them desired to be out among the ruins in the dark searching for another place to make camp. They closed the front doors and allowed the horses to wander at will within the hall.

Riyan sat eating a bowl of hot stew that Chad had thrown together in their cook pot over the fire. Taking a bite he glanced at the others sitting around the campfire. "In the morning we'll finish searching the rest of this building."

"We came across a couple places large enough to hide a secret room," Bart said. "Once we've completed our search, we should be able to narrow down the possibilities."

"I'll be glad when we find it," Chad said. He glanced to one of the windows and the darkness outside. "Can't wait until this place is just a memory."

"I know what you mean," agreed Riyan.

They turned in shortly after their meal. Chad pulled the last watch while Riyan got the unpleasant slot of just after midnight. You never seem to get a good night's sleep when your rest is interrupted that way.

Kevik, happily enough, had the first watch. The first one was always the best. You usually weren't that tired right away and once you did get to sleep, you remained that way until morning.

The night felt chilling to Kevik despite having ample wood to keep the fire going. He found himself wandering around the hall, at times stopping before the different windows and staring out into the dark. His watch passed without incident.

Riyan took over from Bart sometime after midnight. "Everything okay?" he asked groggily as he made it to his feet. Eyes half closed and rimmed in red, he definitely did not feel like getting up.

"So far," he said. "Things have been quiet." Then he let out with a yawn. "See you in the morning."

"Good night," Riyan said before he went over and put another couple thick branches on the fire. After the branches were in position and had begun to burn, he glanced over to where Bart was laid out on his blanket with head propped on his pack. He was already asleep.

Riyan grinned at his friend, then wrapped his arms around himself as he tried to rid the coldness from his bones. It was supposed to be midsummer, but the temperature here felt more like early fall. Not freezing by any means, just cold enough to sap the warmth from you.

When the heat from the fire finally purged the cold from his body, he started walking about the hall in order to stay awake. He could feel sleep's soft soothing touch as it tried to convince him to return to his blanket.

He went and checked on the horses and found them standing peacefully nearby. Then he went to the window closest to the fire and looked out to the shadowed ruins outside. A shiver ran through him. With only the light from the stars and moon above, the ruins were a maze of shadows and darkness.

Clang!

For the briefest moment he thought he had heard the sound of two swords striking together, such as one would hear during a battle. Obviously it was his imagination again he assured himself.

Clang!

There it went again. He looked around the hall and saw that his companions were still sleeping. The horses too remained as they were, still and quiet. He tried to determine from which direction the sound was originating but couldn't be sure. At one point he was almost ready to go over and wake the others, but then stopped. After all, what could he say? They would just think it was his imagination playing tricks on him.

Riyan returned to the window and gazed out, all traces of sleep by this time having vanished. Nervousness had begun creeping in as visions of the goblin totem, and what it may be there to warn against, ran through his mind.

Clang!

There it went again! This time he was able to tell where it came from. It sounded like it was just outside the main doors. He knew this was not simply his imagination. Looking through the window again, he still saw nothing but darkness outside. No lights, nothing. Just the moon and stars above.

Leaving the window, he moved over to where Bart was sleeping. He hated to disturb him but felt this was rather important. Placing his hand on Bart's shoulder he gave it a slight shake. "Bart," he whispered.

Bart's eyes few open and he quickly sat up. He looked around and when there was no apparent threat, turned his eyes on Riyan. "What is it?"

"I ... I heard something," he told him.

"What?" he asked. "What did you hear?"

"I'm not entirely sure," he explained. "It sounded like swords striking together in battle."

Bart looked at him quizzically as he cocked his head to listen. "I don't hear anything," he said. "It must have been your imagination."

Riyan shook his head. "No, it wasn't. I heard it three times. The last time it sounded like it came from the other side of the doors." They both turned to look at the closed double doors leading out.

He could see in Riyan's eyes that he believed what he was saying. "Was it a solitary sound, or more like a continual battle?"

"Each time it was but a single clang," he answered.

"I wouldn't worry about it too much," Bart said as he laid his head back on his pack. "Probably just the wind blowing something around that's making the noise."

"I don't think so," he argued.

"We've all been a bit jittery since coming here ..." Bart began.

"I'm not jittery!" insisted Riyan. "I want you to come with me to see what's on the other side of the door."

"You're serious aren't you?" asked Bart.

"Yes, I am," he replied.

Bart saw in his eyes that he wasn't likely to get any sleep until they checked the other side of the door. "Alright," he said as he got to his feet. "But if there's nothing there, you'll let me go back to sleep and not bother me again?"

"Yes," Riyan said gratefully. "I promise." So with Bart beside him, they walked to the doors.

Clang!

"There!" exclaimed Riyan. "Did you hear that?" Again the sound came from the other side of the door.

Bart nodded. "Yeah," he said, "I did." Now not so sure it was Riyan's imagination, he strode toward the doors. The doors loomed before them and have now taken on an ominous aspect with the coming of night and the sound coming from the other side.

They both paused when they came to stand before them. Bart glanced to Riyan. "You ready?"

"Yeah," replied Riyan. "Open it."

Bart moved forward the last couple steps and gripped the handle of the door. Then with a final glance to Riyan he pulled it open.

Riyan was braced for anything but what they saw. Nothing. He watched as Bart stepped through the door and looked around before returning inside.

"There's nothing out here," he said.

"Are you sure?" Riyan asked.

"Come see for yourself if you don't believe me." Bart stepped aside to allow Riyan the chance to check.

Riyan stepped through the doorway and into the night. He spent almost a full minute just outside the door looking around. "But there has to be something here that was making the noise," he said. Returning back inside, he glanced to Bart.

"I don't know what it could have been," Bart replied. "But there's nothing out there, just the night." He closed the door. "I'm going back to sleep."

"Sorry," Riyan said as he walked with Bart back to where his blanket was laid out on the floor.

"Don't wake me unless there's something actually happening," he said.

"Alright," replied Riyan. He went back by the fire and spent a few minutes warming himself after the time spent in the cold of outside. It didn't take Bart long before he was once again asleep. Riyan felt bad about waking him, but there must be some explanation as to why he had heard what he did.

It took him some time before the fire warmed him sufficiently. He stared into the fire and watched the flames dancing along the wood. When he was finally warm enough, he put more wood on the fire and then started walking around the hall. The need to sleep began to come to him again, and as long as he stayed in motion, he wouldn't succumb to it.

At one point he reached down to pick up a rock that had somehow made its way into the hall from outside. He was sort of close to one side and he looked over to the windows on the far side across the hall. Figuring he could make it through one of the window frames, he arched his arm back and threw. The stone soared through the air and struck the wall next to the window with a loud **Crack!**

He glanced over to his sleeping comrades and was glad the noise failed to disturb their sleep. Then he walked across the hall and picked up the rock. "I'm going to make it this time," he mumbled to himself.

Aiming for a window gaping in the far wall, he took a few deep breaths to settle himself. When he felt he was ready, he launched the rock towards the window. As it sailed through the air, he braced himself for the impact against the wall. But it flew true and before it reached the window he knew it would make it through the opening.

Smash!

As the rock entered the window space, a loud sound likened to the smashing of glass, split the night. The sound made Riyan jump for there wasn't any glass in any of the windows throughout the ruins. The sound hadn't come from the window the rock sailed through, it had come from the one behind him.

Turning around, he saw a pale ghostly form dressed in armor. It held a sword in his hand and appeared as if he was fighting someone or something that was trying to get in through the window.

Smash! Crash! Bang!

The sound of glass breaking filled the hall as other ghostly forms began to appear before the rest of the windows. In each case, it looked as if they were battling with something that wanted in. The only problem was, it didn't look as if there was anything there at all.

"Bart! Chad!" he yelled. "Get up!"

The horses suddenly reared and bolted to the back of the hall and into one of the hallways.

As he yelled to the others, he raced across the hall to their camp. The horses had disappeared by the time he reached the fire.

Bart sat up and one glance around the hall brought him fully awake.

"We're under attack!" Riyan yelled.

Bam!

The front doors slammed open and more ghost soldiers appeared at the entrance. Swords rose and fell as they attacked whatever was trying to pass through from the outside.

"What's going on?" Chad asked as the four comrades backed into the corner to defend themselves.

"I don't know," replied Riyan. "There was the sound of breaking glass, then this." He and Chad both had their swords out and Bart held his new knife in hand. Though there appeared to be a furious fight going on between the ghosts and unseen adversaries, they didn't seem to take any notice of the four comrades.

More of the ghost soldiers appeared, each bearing the coat of arms depicted on the front of the building, the dragon coiled around the sword. The ghosts at the windows looked to be holding their own but the ones by the door were falling to the blades of unseen enemies.

"Maybe we should get out of here," Kevik said.

"That would be a good idea," agreed Bart. "But how would you suggest we do it? They're fighting at every exit."

"Not at the hallways at the rear of the hall," he said. Indeed, the fighting was contained along the sides and at the entrance.

"Look!" Chad said as he pointed to the winding stairs leading up to the second floor. There at the top was a group of five, ghostly men. They practically ran as they raced down the stairs to join the fray. The one in the lead had to be the lord of Algoth. His shield and armor were emblazoned with the dragon-sword coat of arms. As the lord came to the bottom of the stairs, he began shouting orders to his men.

"Come on," said Bart. "They don't seem to be paying us much attention so let's try to get to the back."

"I'm with you," Riyan said.

As Bart began to wind his way through the fighting, the lord joined the fray. He moved to the fore of his men and began laying into the unseen attackers with great skill. While those around him fell, the lord continued to fight. He was unwilling to give ground.

Around the four companions, the ghosts fought fiercely, but their numbers continued to dwindle. Despite the ferocity of the lord's attack, he began to give ground.

"Watch out!" Kevik yelled from where he was bringing up the rear.

From the side, a magic user appeared on the second floor and began raining death on the unseen attackers. Bolts of flame flew from his outstretched hands and erupted in massive balls of fire by the front entrance. More bolts of energy such as what Kevik's master used flew like a swarm of arrows towards the windows.

For a brief moment, the soldiers defending the building were able to recover ground. But then they began being pressed back once more.

"Where are the horses?" yelled Bart.

"They fled deeper into the building when all this started," explained Riyan.

He and the others reached the far end of the hall just as a large explosion rocked the area near the entrance. Whatever the magic user had done was very powerful. Bart had them pause there as they watched the battle rage.

All of a sudden the defenders begin falling in droves. The magic user that had slowed the advance of the attackers fell from the second floor and landed on the winding stairs. He didn't get back up. The lord still fought at the fore of his men but then was practically dragged from the lines by what must have been his lieutenants.

The four friends watched in awe as the lord was pulled from the battle. His men sacrificed themselves to allow their lord the chance to break away from the battle. Then the lord and the four men with him began moving directly towards the hallway in which Riyan and the others were standing.

"They're heading this way!" exclaimed Chad.

"Down the hallway," Bart said, "quick!"

They turned and fled down the hallway. As they passed rooms situated against the outer wall of the building, they found defenders fighting unknown assailants who appeared to be breaking in through the windows there as well. "What's going on?" Riyan asked.

"Their being slaughtered is what's going on!" replied Bart. Then up ahead there was an opening where another hallway opened up going deeper into the building. "Here!" he cried. "Follow me!" Turning into it, he ran for all he was worth.

The others entered into it after him and Kevik, who was still bringing up the rear, glanced behind them to see whether or not the ghosts were going to follow. When the ghosts appeared, they continued on down the other hallway.

"They're not following," he told the others.

Bart brought them to a halt. "Back!" he yelled. "We've got to follow them!"

"Are you mad?" questioned Chad. "We could get killed."

Bart passed them as he headed back to the previous hallway. "They could be heading to where the key is!" he hollered.

Riyan and Chad glanced at them quickly then turned back to follow Bart.

"What key?" Kevik asked as he too turned and raced after the others.

Bart reached the other hallway and immediately turned to follow the direction the lord and his comrades went. Back the other way he saw where the hallway was filled with battling defenders as they slowed the advance of the attackers.

"Hurry!" he yelled to the others. They had yet to make it back to the hallway down which the lord had fled, and the defending ghosts were falling back quickly.

Riyan reached the junction of hallways and fled down the other one just as the defenders reached the mouth of the hallway he just fled from. Chad and Kevik came to a quick stop as the battling defenders moved backwards and blocked the way.

"Riyan!" Chad shouted as he stood there not five feet from the battling spirits.

"Find another way!" Riyan yelled back to him.

"Come on," Chad said as he turned and raced back down the hallway. Behind them, the battle raged.

Bart kept the lord in sight as he and the others moved quickly deeper into the building. They were traveling down the hallway that ran past the room where he had been trapped with Chad earlier that day.

He raced past the room and continued following the lord. The end of the hallway opened up onto a large kitchen, large enough to feed a thousand men if it had too. Bart was surprised that the lord had come here.

The lord and his men went to the edge of one of the large ovens and appeared to depress three separate bricks in the side of the oven. They paused there for a moment, then seemed to walk into it. When the lord and his men disappeared into the oven, the kitchen was plunged into darkness. The light which the ghosts had been emitting was gone.

"Bart?" hollered Riyan from the hallway.

"In here!" he yelled. He moved back to the hallway and was almost bowled over by Riyan as he emerged into the kitchen.

"Where did they go?" Riyan asked.

"Into the oven," he replied.

"The oven?" he said incredulously.

"That's what it looked like," admitted Bart.

Then down in the hallway the last defending ghost fell. The fallen ghost laid there for a second, then an unseen tremor seemed to roll through the building. When the tremor subsided, all the fallen ghosts simultaneously disappeared and the building was again plunged into darkness.

Bart and Riyan stood there in silence for a few moments before Riyan asked, "Is it over?"

"I think so," Bart said. "We need to get back to the hall where our equipment is."

"Why?" Riyan asked.

He heard Bart chuckle. "In our haste, we forgot our packs. So unless you want to continue to be in the dark, we need to get back there."

"Alright," he said. He then turned around and with his hand laid against the wall of the hallway, began returning to the hall.

After a minute or two, their eyes began acclimating to the darkness. Vague shadows formed from where the moonlight filtered in through the windows in the side rooms.

"Riyan!"

He heard Chad call out from far away. "Here we are Chad!" he hollered back. "Meet us back in the hall. It seems to be over."

"On the way!" Chad replied.

As they came closer to the hall, the light from their fire became a beacon in the dark. The two groups met back at the hall at about the same time. Riyan and Bart arrived first. Just after they arrived they saw a white light, brighter than what a flame would produce, coming from another of the hallways. At first they thought it might be one of the ghosts but then Kevik appeared with a white, glowing sphere that moved and bobbed in the air around him. Then Chad appeared leading their three horses. They had found them in a room where they fled after the initial onslaught of the ghost soldiers.

"What is that?" Bart asked as he saw the glowing sphere.

"Just a simple cantrip I know," replied Kevik. Then the light went out and a second later, it reappeared. "It doesn't last very long though." He let it continue to bob even though the light from the fire was more than sufficient. "This was the first cantrip I learned. Actually it was the very first magical skill I ever mastered."

"It's pretty neat," Chad said. After a few more minutes, the light went out.

The front doors were once again closed and there was no evidence whatsoever of the battle that had raged here a little while ago. "So what happened here?" Bart asked. "Were the ghosts real?"

"I don't know," Kevik replied. "They seemed real. I have heard there are places haunted by spirits. Some ghosts have even been rumored to replay the events leading up to their deaths. Of course that's just conjecture."

"It seemed pretty real though," Chad said. "The sound, the intensity, it all felt as if it was actually happening."

They grew silent as each considered the events, then Kevik said, "I guess we now know why this area is marked as death by the goblins."

Riyan nodded. "If any of them had ever witnessed what we did, I could understand them thinking this place was death."

"Did you feel something when the spirits vanished?" Chad asked Riyan. "We felt a tremor or something like it wash over us."

"Yes, we did too," he replied.

"But you are all not asking the right questions," interrupted Kevik. "Who were they fighting and why? Could whoever or whatever it was have been the reason this civilization fell?"

Bart glanced at him a moment then nodded. "You're right. But I doubt if any of us here will ever know."

"Do you think this happens every night?" Riyan asked. "If our search takes longer, will we have another battle rage through here again?"

"As to that," replied Bart, "I don't expect us to stay here much longer."

"Why do you think that?" Chad asked.

"Because I found what we were looking for."

They all turned and stared at him.

He picked up one of the burning brands from the fire and said, "Come on I'll show you." Standing up, he indicated for the others to follow. When he was certain they were going to follow, he led them to the hallway through which the lord fled the battle. Down its length he walked until he came to the kitchen at its end.

"When I followed the lord here," he explained as he crossed through the kitchen and came to stand next to one of the ovens, "I saw him and his party stop here. Then they pressed this," he reached out and put the tips of his fingers against one of the bricks and pushed. The brick slid in a quarter of an inch. "And here," he said as he pressed a second brick, "and here." Pressing the third and final brick, he watched as the oven began sliding across the floor away from him.

Staying next to the wall, the oven slid back half a foot then came to a stop. Bart brought the burning brand toward the base of the oven and the light revealed an opening. He got down on his knees and peered through it. "There's a stair leading down."

"But why didn't the oven move further?" Chad asked. "There's no way we'll be able to squeeze through that small space."

Bart returned to his feet and said, "I think the mechanism is just old and gave out." He glanced at the others and then nodded to the side of the oven. "Give me a hand and let's see if we can push it out of the way."

The others moved into position then Bart said, "On a count of three. One … Two … Three." At three they shoved with all their might. At first the oven didn't budge, but then very slowly it began sliding across the floor. They kept up the pressure until the opening was wide enough for them to enter.

"An escape route?" asked Riyan.

"Absolutely," replied Bart. "I would also bet that somewhere down there we'll find what we're looking for."

"The key?" asked Kevik. All three turned to look at him. He pointed to Bart and said, "He mentioned it earlier during the battle."

"I did?" asked Bart. Then after a moment's reflection he nodded. "I guess I did."

"What key?" Kevik asked. He looked at the three friends and could see that they were still reluctant to share their secret.

"Part of a key really," Chad finally said and that was all anyone was willing to tell him.

"As you will," he conceded.

"Now," replied Bart. "We are all still rather tired, and after the events of the night it might be hard for us to return to sleep. However, I feel it would be wise to get what rest we can before we descend these steps."

Riyan nodded. "I agree. It's not going anywhere."

They each cast a final look down the secret stairwell before returning to their camp. Once back at the fire, they settled in again to sleep until dawn. Chad, who had pulled the last watch, was forced to remain awake while the others were able to nestle in their blankets. For the rest of the night every little noise made him jump. Not until the sun's first rays of dawn entered the eastern windows did he finally relax.

Chapter 21

Kevik was the first to awaken. He saw Chad over by the fire sitting and watching the flames. When he sat up, Chad glanced over in his direction. He grinned and waved for him to join him.

Getting to his feet, Kevik walked over and sat next to Chad. He held forth his hands to the fire and warmed them. "You guys don't trust me much do you?"

"It's not that," Chad replied. "We simply haven't known you all that long is all. You seem nice enough."

"But only with time will you come to trust me," he concluded.

"Isn't that the way with anyone?" asked Chad.

"I suppose it is," Kevik agreed. He knew he was a trustworthy person, but he could understand why his new companions wouldn't immediately recognize that. He sort of felt the same way about Bart. Something about him put him off even though he's done nothing to warrant it.

"You three came all this way through goblin territory for a key?" he asked.

Chad nodded. "That's right."

"I hope the risk was worth it," Kevik said.

"Oh it will be," Chad assured him. Then he glanced over to where Bart had just sat up. Next to him Riyan was beginning to stir as well. "Good morning," he said to the newly awakened.

"You too," Bart said. Standing and stretching, he came over to the fire. After a minute, Riyan joined them.

"I've been thinking that we should take everything with us when we go down the stairs," Chad said. "It wouldn't do to be stuck somewhere like Bart and I were in that small room yesterday without our equipment."

"I agree," said Bart.

"What about the horses?" Riyan asked. "They can't stay in here, they need grass."

"I would hate to leave them outside where anyone or anything could make off with them," Bart said.

"In that case we need to at least take them out for water and a quick graze before we lock them in here while we're down below," Riyan said. It pained him to have to say that, for he knew it meant prolonging the time before they would be able to explore the secret passage they found the night before. But having been around animals as much as he has, he knew how they would suffer if neglected of food and water.

The others agreed with him. So they took the horses outside and found where a fallen wall had created an area that held water. From the looks of the pool, which was only about seven feet wide, the wall must have fallen years, maybe even decades ago if not longer. Its banks had already formed above the broken masonry as over time, dirt was blown into the water by the wind and subsequently deposited on the edges by the water. After allowing the horses time to drink of the water, they let them graze for an hour before returning to the hall.

While they were out, the ruins gave Riyan a discomforting feeling, especially after the ghosts of the night before. He could tell the others were affected just as he was and none of them were able to relax until they returned to the hall.

Once back within the hall, they made sure to close the front doors. Bart even took two pieces of broken masonry from the remains of the neighboring buildings and placed them before the doors so they wouldn't open while they were gone. As soon as the doors were blocked and they were ready to go, each slung their pack over their shoulder. Along with his pack Kevik took Wyzkoth, the staff his master had given him.

Riyan lit his lantern, then followed Bart into the hallway and down to the kitchen where the secret stairs lay. When they entered the kitchen, the light from the lantern illuminated the oven where it still sat after they had pushed it aside to reveal the hidden steps.

"Ready?" Bart asked. When the others nodded, he stepped onto the top step and began his descent into the darkness below.

The height of the stairwell wasn't all that high and forced them to bend slightly over in order to avoid scraping the tops of their heads on the ceiling. After descending fifteen steps they reached the bottom. A short passage extended forward from the bottom step for about ten feet before reaching a junction.

Another passage crossed over theirs that ran from left to right, while the passage they were in continued on past the junction. The walls of the passages were lined with bricks though the floor was dirt. Sconces were set in the walls every so often where torches could be placed to give the passages light.

"Which way?" asked Bart as he came to a stop at the junction. None of the directions showed anything more than a continuation of the passage past the point where the light from the lantern reached.

"The right maybe?" suggested Riyan.

"Good as any," replied Bart. Turning right, he and the others left the junction behind. They didn't go far before another passage branched off to their right. It was slightly smaller than the one they were in.

"Let's check it out," Chad said.

With Bart still in the lead, the group moved into the branching passage. They followed it for a few feet before the lantern's light revealed a sharp turn to the right. Moving forward, they turned the corner and came to an abrupt halt. The passage ended a short distance ahead where a chest sat against the end of the passage.

"That's suspicious," Bart announced.

"What do you mean?" asked Chad.

"Why in the world would anyone put a chest in such an accessible spot?" he asked.

Kevik glanced to the chest and said, "We are in a hidden area."

"True," admitted Bart. "But this just doesn't seem right."

"Are you going to open it?" Riyan asked.

Bart sighed. "We have to. It could hold what we came here searching for though I find that unlikely in the extreme." He glanced to the others, "You should stay back." While the others remained where the passage turned, he moved forward. His senses were telling him that this wasn't right, but what else could he do.

He took a single, careful step at a time towards the chest. His father had told him of situations like this where chests were placed in catacombs and other places as a lure to the unwary.

Almost his entire concentration was directed to the floor before the chest and where he's placing each foot. He worked his way gradually closer until he felt an ever so slight shift beneath his foot and froze. It was a pressure plate of some kind, he was sure of that. He had a few guesses about what it would do when he removed his foot, but there was nothing he could do about it now.

He brought his other foot, which was still hovering in the air a couple inches off the ground, back down next to the other. Then he slowly crouched down into a squatting position. Beginning to slowly rock back and forth on the balls of his feet, he braced himself. When he finally rocked backwards to the right angle, he leaped with all his strength back towards where the others were standing.

As soon as his feet left the floor, a section of the floor stretching from one side of the passage to the other, and extending from two feet behind the point where his feet had been to just before the chest, opened up.

"Catch him!" Riyan shouted as he raced forward and caught Bart by the arm as he came to land. His leap had cleared the trap opening by a solid foot and he quickly steadied himself.

"Thanks," he said to Riyan.

"What happened?" Kevik asked.

"Sprung a trap," Bart replied. He turned around to face the others and said, "This place could prove quite deadly."

"Yeah," agreed Riyan as he stared at the pit, "I can see that."

"Who's got the rope?" Bart asked.

"I do," replied Chad. He opened up his pack and pulled out the coil of rope. "What do you need if for?"

As Bart took the rope he said, "To see if there are any more traps over there." He nodded over to the two areas of the floor on the far side of the pit, situated to either side of the chest.

The pit as it turned out was fifteen feet deep. When Riyan took the lantern to look into it he found the sides to be sheer all the way down and the bottom looked to be covered in long spiny spikes. The floor that had fallen in was actually hinged to the floor on their side. The gleam of bones among the spikes said this trap had caught the unwary before.

Bart tied the rope to his pack and moved to the edge of the pit. He swung the pack like a pendulum until he had enough momentum then released the rope so the pack would sail over the pit and hit the floor on the right side of the chest. The other end of the rope was firmly held in his hand so he could retrieve his pack after it landed.

When the pack hit the floor next to the chest and nothing happened, he hauled in the rope. Then he did it again, this time having his pack land on the left side of the chest. As soon as the pack hit the left side, the floor tilted towards the pit at a forty five degree angle.

"That's why you never assume it's safe," Bart said as he pulled his pack back in. "First you encounter the pit. If you survive that, and you're foolish to believe the pit was the only trap, you jump across. The thief would then have a fifty-fifty chance of landing on the solid side. If he landed on the other, he would lose his balance when the floor tilted and would plummet down to the spikes below."

"Nasty," said Chad.

"I'm sure that was the intention," he said. Bart didn't untie his pack from the rope when he opened it to get his lockpicks. "Might need it again," he told them.

"You're not planning on opening that chest are you?" asked Kevik.

"Yes I am," he said. He then took the other end of the rope and secured it around his middle. Then he handed the rest of it to Riyan. "Make sure that if I fall you stop me before I hit the bottom."

"I thought it was safe," said Riyan, indicating the floor on the right side.

"The trigger might have rusted over the years," he explained, "or it could be set to only go off when the weight of a man is on it. In case a thief did what I just did with my pack."

"Oh," Riyan said, then he nodded. "I get you."

"Hold on tight but give me enough slack to reach the other side." When he's sure there's enough slack and Riyan gave him the go ahead, he turned back to the pit. Then with a running start, he leaped and cleared the pit opening and landed on the remaining small section of floor next to the chest. Once there he waited a moment to be sure nothing untoward happened.

"Alright," he said to the others, "I think it's safe. Still, don't let go of the rope."

"We won't," Riyan assured him. Chad was there with him holding the rope.

He gave the lock a once over before taking out two of his picks. Pretty sure that there wasn't a trap in the chest itself, he still moved slowly and carefully when he inserted the picks into the lock. After a moment, he felt the tumbler move and the lock was open.

Before he opened the lid, he replaced the picks back in the rolled leather. Then he gripped the lid and very carefully opened it. Inside he could see the glimmer of gold coins. There were a dozen of them lying on the bottom of the chest. They were exactly the same as the others they had found in the chest yesterday.

"Got some more of the gold coins," he said.

Then he collected them and put them in the pouch hanging from his hip. Once he had them all, he closed the lid and jumped back over the pit.

"How many?" asked Riyan.

"A dozen," he replied. He pulled them from his pouch and gave each of them three, including Kevik.

Kevik held up one of the coins from his share and took a really close look at it. When he was done, he saw that the others were staring at him. "What?" he asked.

"Uh, we would appreciate it if you wouldn't tell anyone where we found these," Bart said.

He met Bart's gaze for a moment then asked, "Why?"

"It might arouse certain questions that you will be unable to answer," Riyan said.

"Then maybe you should explain things to me," he suggested.

Riyan and Bart glanced at one another for a moment, then Bart nodded. Riyan turned back to Kevik and asked, "You ever heard of the King's Horde?"

"Sounds familiar," he replied. "What is it?"

"It's a treasure people have been trying to find for centuries," explained Riyan. He then held up one of his coins with the symbol side towards Kevik. "This is the King's insignia, or so we believe."

"Not just us but many others do too," added Bart. "If word got around that you had a coin bearing it, you would be inundated by people wanting to know where you found it."

Kevik glanced at the coin in his hand when Bart finished.

"A stash of copper coins bearing the same markings as these was discovered years ago and sparked a massive surge in treasure hunting," Chad said.

Kevik looked from one to the other then finally settled on Riyan. "You guys are looking for the King's Horde yourself?" he asked. They didn't reply but he could see the truth in their eyes. "And the trail led you here."

Riyan nodded.

"Then the key you expect to find here …?" he asked and trailed off.

"That's right," admitted Riyan. "It will hopefully open the Horde's hiding place."

"Do you know where it is?" he asked.

They grew silent. "We have an idea," Bart finally said.

"Alright," Kevik nodded. "I'm in."

"What do you mean you're in?" asked Chad.

"I mean I'm willing to help you in your search to find the key and open the Horde's lock," he clarified.

"We never ..." Chad said as he began to argue.

"Very well," Riyan said, cutting him off. "A magic user would be most useful in this endeavor I'm sure. Besides," he said as he glanced at Bart and Chad, "he now knows about it."

Chad looked like he was about to argue the point when Bart said, "Fair enough. An equal share." Then he turned to Kevik, "But you have to keep this secret. If word got out ..."

"I understand," he assured them.

A moment of silence hung between them before Riyan cleared his throat. "Maybe we should continue searching for the key?"

Bart nodded and led them back to the main passage. They turned down to the right again and went a short ways before another passage branched off to their left. Ahead of them they could see where the passage they were currently following turned sharply to the right.

"Continue on ahead," Riyan suggested.

Bart nodded and passed by the passage on the left then turned the corner to the right. After the turn, the passage went another ten feet before ending at another passage running left and right.

"Left this time," piped up Chad.

Since one way was as good as another, they turned to the left. The passage continued on for a ways before turning sharply to the left. A little further they came to where a passage branched off to their left and extended past the light of the lantern. Ahead of them the passage went forward several more paces before turning to the right.

"Left again," said Chad.

"Why not?" agreed Riyan.

Turning into the passage branching to the left, they followed it. The passage went straight for a short ways then turned to the right. After another short walk it turned back to the left, went a little further then turned once more to the left. Shortly after that the passage ended at another one moving left and right.

"Try right this time," suggested Riyan.

So Bart led them down to the right and they came to a narrower passage branched off to their left. Bart turned down the new passage, then when it turned to the right, they saw a chest with an open pit before it.

"We've already been here," Bart said.

"This place is a maze," observed Riyan. "How on earth are we ever going to find our way without getting lost?"

They returned back to the main passage and thought about different strategies they could employ. Finally Riyan came up with one they thought would work. They would use the copper coins found in the chest above to mark which way they've already gone. When they came to an intersection, they would put one coin in the passage through which they just approached the intersection, and two coins at the beginning of the passage through which they leave the intersection. That way if they returned to a passage, they would know which way they had come from originally, and which way they had taken when they departed.

So they took a few minutes to go up the stairs and opened the door behind which the chest lay. Riyan stood next to the door to make sure it did not close on them this time. Then the others began filling their packs, including Riyan's, with copper coins. There were easily a couple hundred coins, and they put fifty in each pack. They didn't want to overload themselves. They could always come back for more.

Finished with filling their packs, they returned back to the kitchen and went down the stairs. This time when they returned to the junction just outside the stairs, Riyan placed a single copper coin on the ground at the mouth of the passage with the stairs, indicating that they had come this way. Then when they returned down the passage to the right, he placed two coins at its mouth to indicate this was the way they went.

When they followed the passage back down to the branching leading to the chest and pit, he put two coins on the ground just within the passage saying they've been down there. They continued to retrace their steps until they had gone over the exact same path as they had before.

"Okay," Bart said when they returned to the passage leading to the stairs, "now we can continue."

"This sure seemed complicated," Kevik replied.

"It is," agreed Bart. "But if this place is set up like a labyrinth, then this will help." Bending over, he made an arrow of coins that pointed towards the stairs. "Just in case," he said as he stood back up.

"There's still that one passage off that way," Riyan said as he pointed down the way they went the first time, "that we have yet to explore."

"Okay," Bart said then headed off down the corridor. Starting at the junction with the arrow of coins, they continued down and turned right. Then a short ways further the passage ended at another running left and right. They saw one coin in the one they're exiting and two coins to their left.

Turning left, they followed this passage to where it turned to the right, then continued forward until they came to another passage branching off to their left. Again, a single coin from the way they came. Two coins in the passage to their left, so they continued forward into the passage that had no coins. Thus they were entering uncharted territory. Riyan placed three coins on the ground in the new passage to continue marking the order in which they took the passages.

The passage quickly turned right, then after a short way turned right again. A long passage, the longest single passage they've yet come across, then a turn to the left. Another short passage before they again turned left, then another very long passage ending at a door.

"This must be it," Riyan said. He was about to move forward when Bart stopped him.

"Haven't you learned anything yet?" Bart asked. "Stand back and let me take a look."

Riyan looked sheepish but backed out of his way. He and the others remained ten feet back from the door as Bart moved forward to examine it.

Bart stepped carefully as he approached the door and made it safely all the way to it. Before touching the handle he gave it and the lock a once over. Everything looked normal so he grabbed the handle and tried to pull the door open only to find it locked. Taking out his two picks, he set to work on the lock and felt it click open. Replacing the picks in the rolled leather, he put it back into his pack. Taking the handle, he pulled it open.

Whoosh!

Suddenly the door slammed open and a violent flow of water poured out. It picked him and the others up and carried them down the passage. The water extinguished the lantern and they were plunged into darkness. A bobbing light appeared just as the water washed them into a vertical shaft. They plummeted downward.

Riyan screamed as he knew his end had come. Then all of a sudden, something sticky grabbed hold of him and stopped his fall. He slammed into the side of the shaft but his downward fall had halted. A moment later the torrent of water subsided, then came to a halt.

He was quick to realize that the sticky object happened to be Kevik's arm. He was encased in his own green goo spell and had Chad stuck to him as well. Hanging upside down, he was stuck to the side of the wall. Bart was nowhere to be seen.

"You okay?" Riyan asked Chad.

"Yeah," he replied. "You?"

"A bit rattled but I'll be okay." Riyan then glanced to Kevik and saw his eyes moving. "You alright?"

A muffled reply came out from the goo and he took that as an affirmative.

"Bart!" Riyan cried out. He looked down the shaft but saw only darkness. "Bart!"

"What?" came the reply. Only it came from above not below.

"Man I thought you were a goner!" Riyan yelled up at him.

"Me too," he said. "I managed to catch the lip and somehow held on while the water poured over me. Almost lost my grip a couple times."

"Get us out of here," Chad hollered up to him.

"Hang on," he said. Then they heard him laugh to himself. "I guess you guys are kind of 'stuck' down there." More laughter came as he began lowering the rope.

Riyan watched the rope descend and when it came within reach he and Chad both grabbed hold of it. The only problem was they were still stuck to the goo coating Kevik. "Can you hold all three of us if the goo was gone?" he hollered.

"Maybe," he said. "But there's no way I could pull you up. Someone would have to climb the rope to the top and give me a hand."

"Chad," Riyan said. "How good are you at climbing a rope?"

"About like you," he replied. "Lousy."

"Yeah." Neither one of them ever climbed a rope before. It wasn't likely they'd be able to do it now.

"What are you guys doing down there?" Bart hollered down to them.

Riyan ignored him as a plan came to him. "Kevik, can you dispel the goo then recast it fast?" He could see his head nod slightly. "Alright," he said to Chad, "this is what we're going to do ..."

Bart was waiting impatiently for them to do something but the rope remained slack. "Bart!" he heard Riyan holler. "When you feel tension on the rope, haul Chad up."

"You got it!" he yelled back down. Bracing himself, he waited. Then all of a sudden, the rope jerked as Chad's weight pulled at it. Bart began hauling him up until he appeared at the lip of the pit. From there Chad was able to use his free hand to help haul himself out while Bart continued to pull.

"Thanks man," Chad said when he was fully back in the passage.

"You're welcome," Bart said. He then went to the lip and looked over the edge. It looked as if Riyan and Kevik were further down the shaft than they were before.

"Kevik dispelled the goo," Chad explained. "Then he and Riyan fell past the end of the rope before recasting it again and sticking to the side of the shaft once more."

Bart nodded, "That was a good idea." Then to those still in the shaft, "Here comes the rope." He began lowering the rope. If they had fallen much further the rope wouldn't have been long enough, but as it was, they had a foot to spare.

"You guys get this right," Bart hollered. "We don't have any more slack."

"Don't worry," Riyan hollered back, "you and Chad just work on hauling us up when Kevik dispels the goo."

He and Chad gripped the rope and braced themselves in the passage. "Okay!" Bart hollered. Then all of a sudden, the rope jerked in their hands and they almost lost their grip.

"Damn!" cursed Chad as the weight of Riyan and Kevik pulled on the rope.

"Okay, together," said Bart through clinched teeth. It took great effort to maintain his hold on the rope, and even more to begin hauling it up. Hand over hand, they slowly drew their friends out of the depths.

When they reached about halfway up, Chad grunted, "I'm not going to be able to continue."

"Yes you are!" asserted Bart. "It's not much further."

Chad gritted his teeth and through sheer force of will, kept his protesting muscles moving as Riyan and Kevik drew ever closer to the top.

Finally, the top of Riyan's head appeared over the top and the bobbing orb of Kevik's appeared as it bobbed into view.

"Chad," said Bart with great effort. "I'll hold them. You help them up."

Chad let go of the rope with relief and moved to the edge while Bart held them all by himself. First Riyan, then Kevik came over the lip and onto the passage. When the rope was free again, Bart let go and collapsed to the ground. "Oh my arms," he groaned.

"You okay?" Riyan asked as he came close.

"Just give me a minute," he replied. "I think we need to take a break."

Riyan nodded, "That might not be a bad idea."

The four of them settled against the walls and broke out some rations. It was a bit damp from the dousing of water. Riyan discovered that his lantern must be at the bottom of the pit. Fortunately Chad had a spare attached to his pack and soon light once more filled the passage.

"It would seem we need to have a bit more caution from here on out," Chad said.

"Where did this shaft come from anyway?" Kevik asked. "It wasn't there when we came through the first time."

"Just part of the trap," Bart explained. "I never even heard one like this before. But apparently when the door was opened, the trapdoor opened too. Then the water was to wash the intruder into the shaft and that would be that."

Riyan glanced to Kevik and grinned. "You earned your place with us after such quick thinking," he said. "How did you ever think to use the goo spell in such a way?"

He returned the grin and replied, "My master said that as a magic user, we were at the mercy of the spells we knew. He insisted that I be versatile in applying them, always thinking of different ways in which they could be used. In this case, the picture of how the goblin stuck to the side of your horse back when we first met came to mind and I acted."

"A good thing you did too," Chad praised. "Or it would have been the end of all three of us."

"Just did what I had to," he said. Inside he was beaming though he tried not to show it. His master would have been proud.

Chapter 22

After they finished eating and everyone had rested, Bart explained to the others he planned to go and look at the room where the water came from. He told them to wait on this side of the pit until he returned. Taking the lantern from Chad, he jumped to the other side of the pit and began walking to the room. Behind him, the glow from Kevik's bobbing light appeared.

There was still a trickle of water making its way down the passage from the room. He walked through the door and into the room. It was large, the light from the lantern failed to reach its uppermost reaches. In a couple areas there were steady trickles of water coming from the dark heights of the room. All but one of the trickles made their way down the sides of the room. The other one however fell freely and splashed on the floor.

He inspected the door and the frame. He discovered how once the door was shut, it would create a tight seal with the doorjamb. This would allow the water trickling down to begin filling the room for the next intruder. He admired the work that must have gone into putting this particular trap into effect.

After a quick search to make sure there was no other exit, he left the room and made his way back to the others. He left the door open so the water could escape.

"That was a pretty clever trap," he told the others upon his return. Hopping over the pit, he saw they were ready to continue the exploration.

"Clever enough to almost get us killed," Riyan said.

"I know," replied Bart with a grin. "Impressive."

He set out back the way they had come with the others following along behind. From that point they began the systematic search of what they've begun to call the Labyrinth. They called it that because of the many turns and branching passages.

Every time they would come to a junction, the first thing they checked for was the presence of copper coins. If some were present, they would take the passage that didn't have any as yet. Each time they crossed through the junction, they would add a coin. So if they came to one they already had gone through, there would be two passages marked with coins. One passage would be marked with one coin, which would indicate from which direction they had originally entered the intersection. There would also be a two coin passage indicating the direction they had gone that first time. Then when they took a third way, they would set three coins down, and then four if they happened to pass through a junction where four ways to go were possible.

Their search led them down one passage after another. Truly this place deserved the name, Labyrinth. Finally, they came to a room at the end of one of the smaller, branching passages. It held two chests sitting across from each other at either end of the room.

"Stay out in the hallway," Bart said to the others as he made to enter the room. Carrying the lantern with him, he moved slowly and carefully to the chest on the right.

"Be careful," offered Kevik.

"Don't plan to be otherwise," replied Bart. He worked his way closer to the chest and stopped five feet away. The memory of the last time when the floor opened up was still vivid in his mind.

Taking his pack which was still tied to the rope, he began tossing it onto the floor in front of the chest. When that failed to produce a reaction, he tried the area next to the chest and then finally began hitting the chest itself. Still, nothing happened.

"Maybe this one doesn't have a trap," suggested Chad.

"I wouldn't bet on it," Bart replied.

"We've come across others before that failed to go off," said Riyan. "Maybe it's the same thing here."

"That might be," nodded Bart. He set the lantern on the floor so the light shone brightly upon the face of the key hole, then he took small steps toward the chest. The face of the chest was nondescript, it looked like all the others. He checked near the keyhole for any markings that the chest maker might have put there to indicate a trap was present, but it was clear.

He thought to himself that this chest might actually be safe. After removing his two picks, he knelt down before the lock and began working on it. As he worked, he took his time and finally the lock clicked open. Breathing a sigh of relief, he replaced the picks back in the rolled leather and put it in his shirt before lifting the lid.

Bracing himself, he lifted the lid. Again, nothing happened. Inside he found a small book with red bindings centered in the bottom of the chest. He turned his head to where the others were waiting and said, "There's a book in here."

He reached inside to pick it up. Just as his fingers touched it Kevik asked, "Are there any markings on it?"

That questioned may have saved him from being blinded. He turned his head towards Kevik to reply as he lifted the book from the bottom. He said, "No, there isn't ..." then a spray of liquid shot from the back side of the chest and hit him in the side of the head just behind the ear. When the liquid hit him, he cried out and jumped backwards.

"Bart!" exclaimed Riyan as he came close. The smell of smoldering hair permeated the room. He quickly got his water bottle and began pouring it over the affected area. When the last drop was poured, Bart's hair in that area looked singed. The skin was a bit red underneath and the top of his ear sported a blister, but other than that there was nothing serious.

"If that had hit your face ..." Chad began.

"It would have blinded me," replied Bart. He felt the affected area and then allowed Riyan to inspect it.

"I think you'll survive," Riyan told him. "It doesn't look as if anything permanent was done."

"Thank goodness," he said. He held up the book that was in the chest.

Kevik came closer and took the book. "It doesn't look magical," he stated. He looked it over, gave the front and back careful consideration, but didn't open it.

"Aren't you going to open it?" Bart asked.

"Not yet," he replied. Then suddenly the book began to glow blue, telling the others that he was casting his identification spell. The others waited until the glow faded then looked to him expectantly.

A grin came over him as he stared at the book.

"What?" asked Riyan.

He glanced up at them and said, "There are two spells within this book. Both are new to me."

"Can you use them?" Chad asked.

"Perhaps," he said. "I will need to study them for some time, but first I'm going to copy them into my spell book."

"Not right this second though," Riyan said.

He shook his head. "No. I'll do it when I am not otherwise occupied." Opening his pack, he placed the book inside with the two spell books already there.

"Still one more chest," Bart said as Riyan gave him a hand up. As he turned and began using his pack tied to the rope to test for pits, he overheard Chad asking Riyan, "Why would they put such a thing here?" He meant the little book.

"To encourage thieves to keep pressing their luck," Bart replied for Riyan. He tossed the pack and pulled it back only to toss it yet again. "If you had something of extreme value, say the key we're looking for, you would want to kill off any thief that found their way in here before he got to it. Right?"

"Absolutely," replied Kevik. "Better to lose less valuable items."

"Correct," Bart said as he threw the pack again. "Now, the best thing that could happen is for the thief to die before he even gets to the treasure you're trying to keep hidden. That's what this place is designed for. A thief would hardly continue to trip the various traps you have spent such time in constructing if every time he opened a chest, there was nothing in it. You have to put the carrot before the mule if you want the mule to walk into quicksand." He grinned. "That's a saying my father used to use."

Finished with testing the area with the rope and pack, he tossed it over to the others and began slowly working his way towards the other chest. "That's why it's worthwhile to open each chest we come to."

"But at the same time you risk serious injury and death," argued Riyan.

Bart paused and glanced back to him. He shrugged then said, "Such is the life of a thief." Turning back to the chest he resumed his slow, methodical progress. "Think on this too. If the thief was to find enough of the smaller treasure, he might feel the risk no longer was worth it and leave. After all ..." he paused a moment as he concentrated on the floor before him. Not finding anything, he took another step. "... if someone has the wherewithal to build a complex like this, he surely can afford to lose a few trinkets here and there."

"I think I get what you're trying to say," Riyan said.

"Good," Bart replied. He finally arrived at the side of the chest. "Could you move the lantern closer for me," he said to Chad.

"Sure," Chad said. He then went and picked up the lantern and set it down where Bart indicated. After it was on the floor he returned to where the others were watching.

He knelt down before the chest and was running his fingers lightly along the front. "I don't think so," they heard him mumble to himself. He took out two picks again. Only this time he didn't remove the two he usually did. These were slightly longer with long flat heads.

He placed the head of one into the seam on the right side of the chest between the front and the edge binding, then did the same with the other on the left side of the front. Slowly, he began working the two tools into the seams. When the two heads were completely inserted within the seams, he began prying the front cover. After only a moment of effort, the front side of the chest popped open to reveal a handful of gems glittering inside.

Bart glanced back to the others and grinned. "The top is a fake," he explained. "No matter how much you work at it, there's no way to open it. In fact," he paused while he pointed to the keyhole, "if you were to try to pick the lock, that would trigger the trap."

Reaching in, he removed the gems and handed them to Riyan who put them in his pack. He replaced his tools back with his other picks and slid the rolled leather inside his shirt. Standing up, he indicated the passage leading from the room and said, "Shall we?"

Bart led the way out and they resumed their exploration. After a search down a dead end loop, they turned back and began following another of the main passages, one they hadn't been down before. Not too long after they entered the passage, another smaller one branched off to their right. Thus far, the smaller ones seemed to have yielded treasure of one kind or another.

Turning into it, they followed it down until it turned to the left. There it came to an end ten feet past the turn. The light from the lantern glittered off of a pile of coins and jewels sitting in the middle of the floor at the end of the passage.

"If that isn't a blatant declaration of a trap being present, I don't know what is," Bart said as he glanced at the others.

"Are you going to try and get it?" Riyan asked.

Bart turned back to him and nodded. "We could use the money. Stay here." Turning back to face the treasure, he began using his pack-on-the-rope to test for pitfalls. When none were detected, he set the pack down and slowly moved forward. Everything his father ever said to him screamed that this was trapped. No one ever left treasure lying out in the open like this unless it was being used as a lure.

Whoever built this place has so far used vastly different, ingenious traps for every circumstance. He still couldn't believe that water one. Whoever had devised it certainly deserved a bonus.

He stopped when he was three feet from the pile. Holding up the lantern, he scanned the walls but didn't find anything unusual. The area of the floor around the treasure appeared as it should, which only made him all the more nervous. Something here has to trigger something. It has to!

Crouching down, he ran his hand over the surface of the floor between himself and the treasure. After a minute of careful examination, he found nothing out of the ordinary. He crept forward a little further, close enough for him to actually be able to touch the treasure.

He removed his belt knife, not the new one but the older knife he's had for years and moved its tip towards the edge of the pile.

"Find anything?" Chad suddenly hollered to him.

Chad's question startled him and the knife point accidentally dislodged three of the coins from the pile. He froze as he expected something nasty to develop, but nothing did. Turning back to Chad with an angry expression he said, "Keep quiet!"

With a guilty look upon his face, Chad replied quietly, "Sorry."

Bart took a deep, calming breath then returned his attention back to the pile. The three coins that had fallen lay next to the pile and he picked them up. They were regular gold coins similar to those they had found earlier. He placed them in his belt pouch before moving his knife back towards the pile. It's possible one of the coins or gems could in some way be the trigger. It took a rather special type of triggering mechanism to use an item so small, but he's heard tales of it being done.

He slid the point of the knife carefully beneath a coin. When enough of the blade was beneath it, he lifted the coin very slowly from the pile. Once it was free and nothing happened, he put the coin into his pouch. Then one by one, he repeated the process and put the liberated coins and gems into his belt pouch.

After ten minutes of this, the others realized he was going to take awhile and made themselves comfortable against the wall of the passage where it made the turn.

Bart's back was beginning to ache by the time there were only seven coins and three gems left in the pile. He was amazed he made it this far without anything happening. It was possible though, that whatever trap was here could have become deactivated over time, that does happen.

Moving his knife forward once more he went for the largest of the three remaining gems and slid the knife's point beneath it. Before the tip had even reached halfway beneath the gem, it met resistance. Bart couldn't help himself but grin. There was a trap and it would be triggered by the removal of this gem. Unfortunately the gem happened to be the largest one of the pile and therefore worth a lot of coins.

Two of the remaining coins were positioned beneath the gem, the rest were not. He quickly picked up all the remaining coins and gems but the two that were under the trapped gem. Glancing back at the others he said, "I found the trap."

"Can you disarm it?" asked Riyan.

"I'm not sure," he replied. Then he showed them the sizable gem still there on the floor. "It's attached to that one," he said. "If you were to take the gem up off the floor, it would pull the cord it's attached to and that would set off the trap."

"Can you cut it?" asked Kevik.

"Often traps such as these will go off if it's cut," he explained. "It might be a good idea if you three were to go back and wait out in the main passage until I'm done."

"Just leave it if you think it's too risky," Riyan told him. "It's not worth your life."

He had already thought about that. Unfortunately there's this little matter of a death mark hanging over him and he'll need all the coins he can to get it removed. He seriously needed that gem. Plus he hated to walk away from a challenge.

"I'll be okay," he said. "You just wait out there for me."

"Alright," Riyan said. "If you're sure?" When he received Bart's nod, he and the others left the smaller passage and returned to the main one. Kevik's bobbing sphere appeared to give them light while Bart retained the lantern.

Once they were gone, Bart unrolled the leather pack containing his lockpicks. For this he would need a more specialized tool than the ones he's been using. Another invention of his father's, he removed a three inch tool.

In the middle of the tool was what his father called a vise grip. It was designed for situations such as this. You placed the cord or whatever the triggering mechanism was, provided it was thin and narrow like a string, within the vise grip. Then you tightened the grip until the trigger was held tightly. After that you would be able to cut what you were after from the trigger safely.

The first thing he did was to very carefully move the two coins beneath the gem ever so slightly away from each other. He needed a gap between them wide enough through which to slip the tool. Once he had the space, he got down on his belly and very gently maneuvered the tool beneath the gem between the two coins.

When he felt it was in the correct position, he gradually worked the tool sideways until he felt the triggering cord slip into the vise. Then ever so carefully, he turned the screw at the end of the pick and closed the vise on the cord. He had to be careful for the cord was incredibly old and was likely to break under the slightest pressure.

As soon as the screw was turned as far as it could go, he took out another of the tools. This one was a five inch narrow rod with a blade shielded by a small piece of hardened leather on the end. This was actually the first time he ever had occasion to use this particular instrument. His father had said that when he came up with this one, he ruined many a pick case before he learned to put a cover over the blade.

After removing its cover, he slid the rod under the gem next to the pick holding the cord. Then he began cutting the cord above the pick holding it. Very slowly, one strand of the cord at a time, he sawed through it. When he felt the tool cut the last strand, he braced himself but nothing happened.

He lifted the gem and saw his pick still there holding the cord between its vises. Flipping the gem over, he discovered the cord had been attached to the bottom of the gem by a small metal staple. The holes that the ends of the staple made in the gem would lower its overall value. However, a creative jeweler could set it in a necklace or other ornamental item where the back would be covered by something else. After that, only an expert jeweler would be able to tell.

Quite happy with himself, he pocketed the other two coins that the gem had been resting upon. His knife-pick he replaced back in with the others. That only left the vise-pick. He did not want to leave without it. With the way things were, he may never see another one again. But if he removed it from the cord, it would trigger the trap.

"You okay in there?" Riyan's voice came to him from the passage.

"Yeah," he hollered back. "Be just a minute."

"Alright," came the reply. "Hurry up, Kevik's bobbing light is beginning to drive me crazy."

Bart grinned for he found the constantly bobbing light annoying too. Why anyone would create a spell like that was beyond him. Then he returned to the problem at hand. The vise-pick.

Coming up with an idea, he pulled out the long string he had in the bottom of his pack. Then he secured one end of the string around the screw at the end of the vise pick. After that, he picked up his pack-on-a-rope and the lantern then began walking backwards to the other passage. As he went he played out the string until finally arriving in the main passage with the others.

"What's that for?" Chad asked when he saw the string.

"I'm recovering a tool," he explained. "But it's going to trigger the trap when I do."

"So you got the gem?" Riyan asked.

Bart patted his belt pouch and nodded. "Now all I need to do is get my tool back." He took the end of the string in hand and then began gently pulling on it. The last thing he wanted was for the string attached to the screw to come off or break.

Then suddenly, the strain that had been building on the sting was gone. He could hear the metallic clinking of the tool as it bounced along the floor of the passage.

"Bart!" hollered Riyan. "The ceiling's coming down!"

He looked above him and saw where a stone block, the width of the smaller passage opening, was falling at him. Jumping back out of the way, he quickly pulled the string. The tool bounced along the passage as it headed for the rapidly closing opening. Then just before the stone settled to the floor, the tool emerged from beneath the falling stone.

With a thump, the stone settled against the floor, completely blocking the mouth of the passage. "That was close," commented Kevik.

"I would hate to have been in there when that stone began to fall," observed Chad.

"Me too," agreed Bart. Untying the string from the screw, he put the string back in his pack and the vise-pick in with the others. After that he distributed the coins and gems to the others. He kept the largest gem, the one that the trigger had been attached to, for himself.

"Need a break?" asked Riyan.

Bart shook his head. "No, let's keep going. The sooner we're done with this the better." Taking the lantern, he stepped out and once again they began combing the passages for the key.

They didn't come across anything other than more crisscrossing passages and dead ends. Neither treasure nor rooms, just passages. After awhile they began coming to areas they have already been to, and even with the coins placed on the ground at the junctions, they've begun to get turned around.

Finally they came to the end of a passage with a door. "Man if this isn't it I say we call it a day," Riyan said. The past hour of wandering through passages has left him tired and discouraged.

"I think there is still one more area off that way," Bart said pointing behind them and to the left, "that we haven't been to yet. We passed by a passage with no coins on the way here."

"Okay fine," Riyan replied. "Check here and back there, then we call it a day."

"Agreed," said Bart. In fact, he was becoming rather tired as well. Sighing he said, "Stay here," then went to the door. He went forward to do his pack-on-a-rope trick again. But same as the last dozen times, he failed to find anything. Of course he knew that the one time he didn't do it would be the time he runs afoul of one.

Moving to the door, he grew cautious as he recalled the water behind that previous door he opened that almost killed them. He glanced behind him to tell the others to back away, but they had already done so.

Turning back to the door, he approached and began to notice how there were specks of soot on the door and the surrounding walls. *Fire?* How would there have been a fire here? Unless the trap somehow dealt with fire?

Then he began examining the walls leading away from the door and saw how they too held evidence that fire once raged through here. The specs of soot finally ended twenty feet away from the door.

"What is it?" asked Riyan. They had been watching him closely examining the walls.

"Soot," he replied. Glancing down to them he said, "This whole end of the passage shows signs of there having been a fire here."

"Fire?" asked Chad. "How is that possible?"

"I'm not sure," he replied.

"Better leave the door alone then," suggested Riyan. "No sense in risking it."

But then Bart's suspicious nature kicked in. What if this area had been treated like this in order to convince a thief *not* to try the door? After all the other traps a thief would have come across by this time, he would be getting rather paranoid about a stone passage with soot lining the end. He had almost walked away from it himself.

He turned back to Riyan and said, "I'm going to open the door."

"Are you crazy?" Riyan asked him. "It's not worth it. We can always come back if there is no other way."

But Bart was already moving back to the door as he ignored Riyan. He checked the door again and found it locked. The lock was rather complicated, more complicated in fact than most locks he had come across down here. Despite it's complexity he had it opened in just a few minutes.

After putting the lockpicks away, he took the handle of the door and opened it. The smell of lantern oil hit him a split second before gallons of lantern oil poured through the door and engulfed him.

Kevik was the first to realize what was happening and only his quick reflexes saved Bart from a horrible death. In the blink of an eye, he cast his goo spell and completely encased the lantern where it sat a few feet behind Bart. When the oil hit the lantern, the goo kept it upright and airtight. Otherwise the burning wick in the lantern would have ignited the lantern oil flowing out of the door into a fireball.

A string of expletives erupted from Bart at his own stupidity. The signs were there, he had just misinterpreted them. Now his clothing was soaked with lantern oil, and the fumes were making him cough.

He turned around and saw the others staring at him. They had backed up quite a bit to avoid coming into contact with the oil. "Don't say anything," he said.

Riyan shrugged, "I'm just glad Kevik reacted as fast as he did. I didn't even realize what was happening before he had already reacted."

Kevik grinned. "You have to react fast when you're a magic user. Slow magic users tend not to survive very long."

Bart nodded. "I see that." He glanced to the goo coated lantern, the light coming from the burning wick within cast a green pall to the passage as it made its way through the goo. "I think you can get rid of that now," he told Kevik.

"You sure?" Kevik asked. "Fumes are still present that may be ignited."

Bart glanced to the lantern and could see the flame was dying out from lack of oxygen anyway. "Fine," he said. "Wait until the flame dies out." Bart then heard Riyan groan as Kevik's bobbing sphere appeared to give them light.

"Isn't there some other spell you could use?" Riyan asked.

"Sorry," he replied. "This was the only light spell I've learned. At the time I thought having a light like this would be petty neat."

"Seeing as how you are the only one with a light," Bart said to Kevik, "how about checking out that room." He indicated the room from where the oil poured out. "Don't worry," he added when he saw Kevik grow nervous, "I'll come with you."

"Alright," Kevik agreed and began walking forward. Riyan and Chad accompanied him.

The oil fumes were very strong and they covered their nose and mouths with cloth to avoid breathing the worst of it. Inside the room, they found that it wasn't really all that large, merely five feet square and ten feet high. A small round opening in the ceiling must be where they would pour in the lantern oil after resetting the trap.

"Pretty effective," Bart commented as they left. "Open the door and the oil would be ignited by whatever source of light the thief had on him."

"Unless he had an annoying bobbing light," said Riyan dryly.

Bart chuckled.

By this time the flame in the lantern had died out and Kevik dispelled the goo spell. He picked it up and carried it with him as they quickly left the oil coated passage. When they made it back to the junction of passages, they came to a stop.

"I need to get this washed out," Bart said indicating his oil soaked clothes. "My eyes are beginning to sting from the fumes."

"What about that last area we have yet to check?" Riyan asked.

"Do it tomorrow," he said. "There's no way I can work traps and such as I am now."

"Alright," Riyan said. "Back to the surface." In order to better find the area where they still needed to search, at every junction they came to, he took the coins that had been placed there to mark their passing and formed them into arrows pointing the way back to the unexplored area. That way on their return, they would have only to follow the arrows.

It took them some doing but they finally found the stairs leading back up to the kitchen. "It's still light out!" exclaimed Chad. "I thought we had been down there longer."

They went to a nearby window and looked out. From the position of the sun it looked like they still had a couple more hours of daylight left. Leaving the kitchen behind, they quickly made their way back to the hall where they found their horses safe and sound.

Bart went outside and to the small pool where they watered their horses and began to strip. He was quickly naked and used dirt to work the lantern oil out of his clothes. When the others showed up and saw what he was doing, he said, "Better dirty clothes than ones full of lantern oil."

"But you've fouled the water," complained Kevik. "What are we and the horses supposed to drink now?"

Giving him an irritated look, Bart said, "I'm sure there are other places around here. Go find one."

"Come on," Riyan said and then he and the others took the horses in search of water. As they left Bart behind, they heard a splash as he entered the water and began scrubbing the oil out of his hair and off his skin.

Chapter 23

Later, they were back in the hall after watering the horses and allowing them to graze. Bart's clothes still had a touch of odor from the oil about them but it wasn't nearly as strong. They had decided, or rather Bart had decided, that they should rest before resuming their exploration. "After everything that happened today, I need a break."

"Not to mention the fact that we didn't get all that great a sleep last night either," Chad added.

"You could say that again," Kevik replied. "It took me over an hour to get back to sleep after the ghost battle."

A thoughtful look came over Riyan as he glanced outside. "You know, it might not be a bad idea to find another place to spend the night before it gets dark," he said. "If the battle we witnessed is a nightly occurrence, we'll not get much sleep tonight either."

Bart grinned. "You do have a point."

The others agreed and so it was decided to move to another building that had enough room for them and their horses. They searched the neighboring structures until they came across one that still had all four walls and most of its ceiling. It was a single story structure with a room large enough for their needs.

One wall of the room held windows that looked out towards what Riyan called the 'Command Building' as it held a commanding presence here in the ruins. They made their camp near that wall and put their horses on the far side of the room. There were a few scraggly bushes on that side they could munch on if they needed.

After a short stint of hauling in wood to last them through the night, they soon had a fire going. Seeing as how there was still some light left, Riyan took Chad with him to the edge of the ruins to hunt for a couple rabbits for dinner with his sling.

Chad followed his friend silently for a few minutes until they reached the forest's edge. Then he said, "Adventuring isn't what I had thought it was going to be."

Riyan glanced over his shoulder at his friend. "Oh?"

"I mean, we've narrowly escaped death a couple times now," he explained.

"What did you think it was going to be like?" Riyan asked. "A carefree adventure with no risks?" He glanced to his friend again and grinned. "You can't have one without the other you know."

"I realize that," Chad admitted.

"Remember all those tales we used to tell each other?" When he saw Chad nod, he continued. "This is just like those."

"Yeah, but one of us usually died in those stories," he said.

"Relax," Riyan said reassuringly, "Bart's with us, not to mention we now have a magic user on our side. Kevik seems a rather capable person."

"True," replied Chad. "He's definitely quick with his magic."

"So just relax," Riyan told him as he turned his attention back to the forest. "A tale is a tale, but this is real life. A person is always more careful in real life than in a story." Then from up ahead he saw the bushes move. "Shhh," he said to Chad.

Moving forward, he began to twirl his sling. When the animal poked its head out, they readily recognized it as a kidog. Riyan then rapidly increased the twirl of his sling and released the stone. It flew straight and true, striking the kidog in the side.

With a cry of pain, the kidog lurched back into the bushes in an attempt to flee. The stone didn't immediately kill it, rather it had crushed its left hindquarter. Riyan noticed it dragging its leg as it fled. He was amazed at how fast the kidog moved despite its useless extremity.

"After it!" hollered Riyan and then he and Chad raced into the bushes. They quickly overtook the kidog and came to a halt as it backed up against a tree. It bared its teeth and growled as it set to defend itself.

Chad pulled forth his sword and advanced upon it. "I got this," he said confidently.

"If you say so," replied Riyan. Just to be on the safe side, he placed another stone in his sling.

The kidog snarled and growled with its ears low against its skull as Chad closed the distance. "Be careful," he heard Riyan say behind him. Gripping the sword in both hands, Chad moved to within striking distance. He and the kidog locked eyes for a brief moment before he yelled an inarticulate cry and swung the sword.

The kidog dodged clumsily to the side due to its injured leg but it needn't bothered. Chad's sword struck the tree half a foot above where he had been aiming. The blade sank in deep and lodged in the tree. Then the kidog snarled and leaped at him as he was trying to pull forth the sword from the trunk.

"Watch out!" yelled Riyan at the unexpected attack.

Chad failed to react in time and the kidog's teeth sank into his left forearm. A cry of pain exploded from his throat as he forgot all about the sword and fell to the ground.

Then Riyan was there with his sling. He kept it closed with the rock in it as he began striking the kidog in the back with the stone filled cup.

"Get it off!" Chad yelled as he struggled to free himself. Already, blood was beginning to flow pretty good from where the kidog's teeth were embedded in his flesh. Riyan kept pummeling the kidog with the stone in the sling until it finally let go. The animal backed away and moved off into the bushes.

Once it let go, Riyan immediately removed his shirt and began wrapping it around the wound on Chad's arm. Out of the corner of his eye he kept alert for another attack by the kidog but it had slipped away.

"Is it bad?" asked Chad. His face was a bit pale and Riyan could tell he was fearful of what he might tell him.

"No," he lied. He didn't want to tell his friend that he had seen the white of the bone before he bandaged it up. "Let's get you back to the others so we can fix you up better." He tied it tight to lessen the blood loss, Chad had already lost quite a bit.

"Alright," Chad said. With Riyan's help he made it back to his feet. Then with his good hand he pulled the sword from the tree and somehow managed to return it to his scabbard.

Chad indicated where the kidog had gone and said, "It couldn't have gotten far. We still could use its meat."

"You sure?" questioned Riyan. His friend looked like he was one step away from passing out.

"Yeah," he replied. He placed his good hand against the tree and leaned against it for support.

"I'll take a quick look," Riyan told him. He held his sling ready as he moved into the bushes after the kidog. It had only made it three feet before it had settled down beneath a large bush. Riyan could see its tail sticking out.

He stopped a few feet away and hollered back to Chad, "I found it."

"Good. Kill it and let's get out of here," he said. From the sound of his voice, Riyan could tell that it was more a sense of vengeance than the desire of meat that prompted him wanting Riyan to kill it.

Riyan stared at the tail and saw it move ever so slightly. The kidog wasn't dead. He could see why the town council of Quillim had posted a bounty on this animal. It was one mean critter.

Riyan began twirling his sling and then loosed the missile. It sailed toward the bush and he could hear it hit the kidog but it didn't make a sound. He then removed his sword and walked forward. The tail was no longer moving and when he reached the bush he poked his sword in until he touched the kidog. It didn't move.

Not for a second did he consider the animal dead. He cautiously reached down and grabbed the tail, all the while ready to jump back at the slightest evidence that it wasn't dead.

He began pulling the animal out and when it completely cleared the bush, saw where his stone had smashed its chest area. The animal was definitely dead now. Picking it up, he carried it back to where Chad was waiting then helped his friend back to the others.

When they returned to the building where they were spending the night, Bart and Kevik were quick to realize something was wrong. After all, Chad had Riyan's blood soaked shirt wrapped around his forearm.

"What happened?" Bart asked as he came forward.

"A kidog got hold of him," Riyan replied.

Kevik waved them over to the fire. "Come here and let's have a look at it."

Riyan aided Chad who had grown a little wobbly from loss of blood over to sit next to Kevik.

"Now," said Kevik, "let's see what we have here." While he undid the makeshift bandage from around the wound, he listened to Riyan as he related how this came to happen. When the shirt came free, he saw the damage done by the kidog. "This is bad." Tendons were ripped and his whole forearm was a mass of torn flesh.

"How bad?" asked Chad weakly. His face had grown very pale when he saw his forearm and felt like he was about to pass out.

"Not so bad that we can't fix it," he replied. He motioned to get Riyan's attention. When he had it he asked, "Could you hand me my pack please?"

"Sure," said Riyan then went over to where they were stacked together and brought it over to him.

"Thank you," Kevik said as he took his pack. He set it on the ground before him and pulled out a vial.

Riyan recognized the vial as the one Kevik had tried to give his master when he was beneath the burning tree. "Healing potion?" he asked.

Kevik nodded. "Yes." Then he removed the wax seal from the top of the vial and pulled out the cork. He gave the vial to Chad and said, "Only drink half."

As Chad took the vial and began to drink, Bart asked, "Why only half?"

"My master once told me that if you poured some onto the wound itself, it accelerated the healing process," he explained.

Riyan nodded at the logic and stared at Chad's mauled forearm while he drank the potion. Once Chad consumed half as Kevik had instructed, he handed the vial back to him.

Kevik then took the vial and moved its mouth to an inch above the worst section of the wound. There he began pouring drops of the liquid onto the torn pieces of flesh.

Riyan, Bart, and Chad watched in wonder as the flesh seemed to be moving of its own volition as it moved back into place. Blood began filling the cavity formed by the wound as Kevik continued to drip the potion drop by solitary drop on various sections of the wound.

"What does it feel like?" Riyan asked Chad after the first few drops entered the wounded area.

"It stopped hurting," he told him. "It itches something fierce however."

"Whatever you do," cautioned Kevik, "don't scratch."

"I wasn't planning to," replied Chad.

The blood, now that it had filled the cavities of the wound, began spilling over the edge and dripping down his arm. "Flex your muscles," Kevik advised. "That way the potion will better understand what needs doing." He poured another dozen or so drops of the healing potion onto the wound before the vial was empty. He stoppered it once again and put it back in his pack.

Chad began making a fist with his hand and bending his arm at the elbow.

"I once heard of a man who had a much more severe wound than this on his leg," Kevik continued to say as the wound kept healing over. "He used a healing potion but made the mistake of remaining still. The potion worked fine in repairing his leg and it did save his life."

"But?" asked Bart.

Kevik glanced to him and grinned. "But, the magic of the potion didn't understand the difference between tendon, muscles and regular skin. You see the potion itself knows that it has to heal the body. From what I understand, it takes what's torn or damaged and binds it back together. Of course, it doesn't always discriminate between what it should bind together or leave separate. So when the potion had run its course, it had healed the man alright. But where the wound had been in his leg, was now nothing more than one solid muscle that never worked right again."

"I had never heard that," said Chad as he continued to move and flex his elbow, wrist, and fingers.

"Not too surprising," replied Kevik. "Those who make the potions try to suppress such tales. It hurts their business."

"That's understandable," said Riyan.

"Bart," Kevik said to him, "let me see your water bottle."

Taking it off his belt, he handed it over and said, "Sure."

Kevik opened it and began pouring it over the blood drenched arm. When the first of the water hit his arm, Chad flinched in anticipated pain, but instead only felt a cool sensation.

The water began washing off the blood and soon they could see fresh skin underneath the blood. "It's healed!" exclaimed Chad excitedly. Kevik kept pouring the water until the blood was completely gone. Where a gaping wound had been just minutes before, was now a layer of smooth pink skin.

"How do you feel?" asked Kevik.

"Good," replied Chad. He glanced to Bart and Riyan. "There's no pain."

Kevik pushed his pack toward Chad with his foot. "See how it feels when you pick this up."

Chad reached down with his newly healed arm and picked up the pack. "There's a little pain," he said, "and some stiffness."

"But otherwise it feels okay?" asked Riyan hopefully.

Grinning, Chad said, "I think so." He set the pack down and turned his gaze to Kevik. "I don't know how I can thank you."

"You three saved me," he replied. "It's the least I could do. Now you better get some food and water in you. The potion may have healed your wound, but it took what it needed from you to do so."

"Just stay there and rest," Riyan told his friend. Then he patted him on the shoulder as he went and began to dress the kidog and make a spit to roast it over the fire. Once it was set and the aroma of roasting meat began filling the room, he took his bloody shirt outside and washed it.

Before the sun went down, the kidog was finished. Despite Chad's objections, they gave him most of the meat, while they satisfied themselves with a smaller portion augmented by stale rations.

After they ate, Chad quickly went to sleep since the healing potion had taken much of his energy. He curled up near the fire in his blanket and was out in no time. The others remained awake and talked as the ruins outside grew darker with the setting of the sun.

They were unanimous in deciding to allow Chad to rest through the night instead of pulling a watch. Bart took the first watch, Riyan the second, and Kevik wound up with the third. Riyan was less than happy about the situation, he hated the mid watch. But as Bart explained it, he needed to be rested since he will be the one risking life and limb disarming any traps they may come across. Considering how many they have already come across, it's a fairly safe assumption that there will be more tomorrow. Kevik, he argued, will need to be alert in case he's called upon to cast magic in a hurry as he's done twice before.

Logic. What can you do when you're faced with unwavering logic? Not a dang thing. So Riyan rolled out his blanket near Chad and laid down in an attempt to get what rest he could before Bart woke him. Sleep wouldn't come, the events of the past few days kept running through his mind. Finally he forced his mind to still by concentrating on nothing but his breathing. He listened to his ever inhale and exhale, and when an errant thought tried to intrude, he squelched it. At last, sleep came.

"Riyan," he heard Bart say as he shook his shoulder lightly. Eyes snapping open, he actually groaned with the effort of coming awake.

"It's your turn," Bart said.

"It feels like I just fell asleep," Riyan said. He sat up and looked around. Chad and Kevik were still sleeping and the fire was burning merrily.

"You were out about four hours," replied Bart with a yawn. "It's been quiet."

Riyan got to his feet and went to the window overlooking the Command Building wherein the entrance to the secret underground network of passages lay. "Anything happen over there yet?" he asked Bart.

"Not that I've noticed," he said. Lying down, Bart pulled his pack close to use as a pillow and tried to make himself comfortable.

Riyan turned back to the window and looked out. Overhead the quarter moon was beginning its arc across the sky, a hint of a breeze was blowing in, and the place was unnaturally quiet. He remembered how last night it had been quiet too, just before all hell broke loose. At least they're not going to be in the middle of it again if it should happen tonight.

He continued to gaze out the window for a few more minutes. Then he noticed the fire could use more wood and walked over to put a couple more pieces on the fire. "That's better," he said to himself when the wood began to catch and the fire came back to life. The flames gave a comforting light that pushed back his feelings of unease. Just looking out at the darkened ruins gave him the creeps.

For the next couple of hours he walked around the room they were in, at times stopping to peer out at the ruins through one of the many windows. Now and then, he would return and place more wood on the fire when it began to burn low.

It was during one of the times when he was staring out the window that the horses began to grow restless. He glanced back to where they were huddled together at the far side of the room. His nervousness spiked when he saw all three were awake and acting skittish.

Riyan glanced to the sleeping forms of his comrades. They were still sleeping soundly. Even though the fire wasn't really low enough for more wood, he went over and placed most of their remaining fuel in the flames. He kept an eye on the restless horses as the flames grew higher and higher. When all the shadows were at last banished by the fire, he didn't see anything at the other side of the room except the occasional flash of equine eyes reflecting the fire's light back to him.

Clang!

"Oh no," he said to himself as he heard the clang of metal on metal. It was the same sound he had heard last night before the onslaught of the ghost battle. He immediately moved to the window and looked out over to the Command Building but the night remained quiet.

Clang!

There it went again. His anxiety was definitely peeking as he tried to ascertain where the sound was coming from. At the other end of the room, the horses began to grow even more agitated.

Riyan couldn't take it by himself anymore and he went to awaken Bart. Before he could reach his sleeping friend, the horses began screaming and the smell of blood filled the room.

"Bart! Chad!" he yelled as he looked in horror as two of their horses fell to the floor. Numerous wounds covered their bodies as even more materialized.

Bart was the first one up and saw where Riyan was looking. He turned his attention to the horses just as the last horse fell. Horror filled him as before the final horse hit the ground, something sheared its head off and sent it flying across the room.

Chad and Kevik were up by this time and staring at the carnage. "Run!" Kevik yelled.

They turned and bolted for the door. Chad and Kevik made it through the door first, while Bart dove through the window. "Where do we go?" Kevik hollered.

"There!" yelled Riyan as he fled the building. He was pointing to the Command Building. "It's our only hope." Sprinting, they headed for the building.

"What's happening?" asked Chad. Then he stumbled and fell to the ground. Riyan was quick to his side and helped him to his feet. With an arm around Riyan's neck, he hurried as fast as he could.

"I don't know," Riyan replied.

Clang!

The noise of the swords striking one another followed them to the double doors of the building.

Clang!

Bart reached the doors first and swung one open. "Hurry!" he yelled as he held it open for them. Within the darkness behind Riyan and Chad he could see a barely visible shimmering. "Don't look back!" he hollered as he urged them on.

Kevik flew through the doors first and came to a stop just inside. He turned back just as Riyan and Chad appeared. He cast his bobbing sphere spell to give them light.

Clang!

Bart followed them in and slammed the door shut. He and the others came together as they stared at the doors, afraid of what might be out there.

Smash!

A noise like breaking glass came from behind them. They turned and saw a ghost in armor with a sword, fighting with something that could not be seen at the window.

"Here we go again," moaned Chad.

Smash! Crash! Bang!

Throughout the room, the sounds of shattering glass could be heard as other ghostly forms began appearing and fighting unseen opponents. All around them ghostly forms continued to materialize just as …

Bam!

… the front doors burst open.

"Back!" yelled Bart. "Back to the hallways!"

They turned and fled the hall until they reached the hallways leading further into the building. No sooner do they get there than the lord and his entourage appeared just as they had the night before. Moving to the fore of his men, the lord again fought whatever was attacking them.

"Over here to this hallway," Bart told the others. He led them over to the hallway leading back to the kitchen, the one the lord had escaped through the previous night. He entered the hallway and moved down until reaching one of the hallways branching off. There he paused and motioned for the others to enter the side hallway before him.

He waited there at the junction for a second or two. Then he heard the explosions announcing that the ghost magic user had joined the fray. "It won't be much longer now," he said.

"What do you mean?" asked Kevik.

Still standing in the junction of hallways, he glanced at Kevik and said, "It's just like the night before. If I'm right, then the lord should run past here on his way to the kitchen. Then, shortly after that, the last of the ghosts will fall and it will be over."

Bart turned his attention back down the hallway and saw the ghostly form of the lord entering the hallway. He nodded as he said, "Here he comes." Stepping back into the branching hallway with the others, he has them step back from the junction a dozen feet or more before coming to a stop.

They turned to look back at the junction just as the lord and his men rushed past. "Follow me," Bart said as he moved to reenter the hallway and follow the lord.

Riyan helped Chad as they followed Bart. When they entered the hallway they could see ghosts fighting at the end that opened up on the hall. "They're covering his retreat," commented Chad.

"Exactly," Bart said. "Just as they did the night before." He continued to lead them towards the kitchen. When he arrived there, the lord and his party were just entering the secret stairwell.

"Aren't we going to follow?" asked Kevik when Bart hesitated.

Bart shook his head. "No. All of our equipment, including my lockpicks, is back in the other building." He kept an eye at the ghosts fighting in the hallway. Then, when the last one died, it laid there for a minute before an unseen tremor rolled through the building. When the tremor died, the fallen ghosts vanished.

By the light of the bobbing sphere, they glanced at each other. "Do you think it's safe?" asked Kevik.

"It was last night," replied Riyan. He glanced to Bart and received a nod in agreement.

Bart took the lead and they made their way slowly back down the hallway to the large hall. As long as they kept the pace slow to moderate, Chad was able to keep up on his own. His body still hadn't recovered the strength that had been sapped by the potion.

That had actually been the first potion ever used on him. He never realized how healing potions used the energy, or strength, of the one they healed. In all the stories he heard growing up, the hero drank down a healing potion and was cured. There was never any mention of recovery time to regain strength. But then that wouldn't have been a very exciting point to include in the story.

Back out in the hall, they found the door they came through closed. Again, no sign of any ghosts, nor was there any evidence of ghosts having been there. Just as it had been last night.

"You know," Riyan commented as they headed for the open door, "they may do this every night."

"That occurred to me too," Bart said. "Every night for who knows how long."

They left the Command Building and returned to where they had been spending the night. The smell hit them before they even came close. Death. Bart was the first to enter, and when Kevik followed him in with his bobbing sphere, they saw what was left of their horses.

The fire was still burning. Bart and Riyan both grabbed a burning brand before they crossed over to the horses' remains. "What did this?" asked Chad. They were a gory mess on the floor, almost unrecognizable as the horses had been so horribly mutilated.

Bart and Riyan glanced at each other. Bart shrugged.

"I'm not sure," Riyan replied after a moment. "I heard the clanging of metal on metal again just before the horses were attacked. It was the same as I heard last night before all hell broke loose."

"Now what are we to do?" Kevik asked. Everyone suddenly realized what Kevik already had. Without the horses they'll be forced to walk out of the goblin's territory. A prospect none of them looked forward to.

"We still need to finish our search below," Bart said. "Once that's completed, we'll worry about how to get out of here."

Riyan was still looking at the remains of the horses. He turned to the others. "This could very well be what the totems had warned against," he said. The other three turned to face him as he continued. "I wonder if what happened to the horses happens to anything caught outside in the ruins at night. Maybe the only safe place is in the Command Building the ghosts were defending."

"You may have a point," agreed Bart. "It hit here first, then almost seemed like it followed us there."

"That's true," added Kevik. "It wasn't until after we got there that the ghost warriors appeared and began fighting whatever it was."

They returned to the fire and settled in on their blankets for a little while longer, debating the whys and wherefores of what happened. When they came to the conclusion that they really didn't know what was going on, they decided to return to sleep while Kevik kept watch until the morning. The remains of the horses on the far side of the room didn't bother them nearly as bad as returning to the dark ruins outside.

Kevik threw more fuel on the fire and huddled close to the comforting flames.

Chapter 24

Early the next morning they gathered their things and returned to the Command Building. They agreed that if they were going to still be in the ruins of Algoth come nightfall, they would spend the night in the kitchen where the secret stairs were located. At least that way they should avoid most of what would take place out in the hall.

When they arrived at the kitchen, they deposited most of their equipment there except for their packs. Those they were taking with them when they descended below, just in case they came across any more treasure, which of course they were all counting on.

"I hope we find the key today," announced Chad. He was feeling better as much of his energy had returned. A good breakfast and most of a night's rest had done wonders.

"So do I," replied Riyan.

As soon as Bart had the lantern lit, they made their way down the stairs and resumed the search for the key. Riyan was quite happy that he had the foresight to make arrows out of the marker coins at all the intersections to point the way back. It was now a simple matter to follow them to what they believed was the last area yet to search.

"What do we do if after searching we fail to find anything?" asked Kevik.

The three friends were silent for a few minutes before Bart replied. "In that case, we'll wait until tonight. When the battle manifests again, as I'm convinced it will, then when the lord makes his way down here, we'll follow him. He should lead us to something."

"Good idea," said Riyan. "Let's just hope it doesn't come to that."

They passed through two more junctions as they continued following the path indicated by the arrows. When they reached the junction containing the final arrow, Bart took the lead. The passage through which they went continued for twenty feet before ending at another cross passage. There were no coins positioned at any of these passage openings so they knew they were in unexplored territory. A quick glance down to the left and right revealed both ways extended past the light of the lantern.

He glanced to Riyan who shrugged. "I'd say left," was Riyan's suggestion.

"Left it is," Bart replied. He waited a moment for Riyan to place marker coins in the appropriate spots on the floor to mark their progress. Once Riyan was done, Bart entered the left hand passage.

They followed it down for a ways before coming to another passage branching off to their left. Again, this one had no marker coins. They decided to proceed forward and Riyan marked the way appropriately. Then not too far past the left hand branching, they reached where the passage ended at another 'T' junction. After the marker coins were placed, they turned to follow the right hand passage.

This one continued forwards a good distance before turning to the left, then a short way to another right hand turn. They followed this passage until the lantern's light showed where it turned once again to the left.

Ahhhh!

Before they came to the turn, Kevik screamed as the floor suddenly opened up directly beneath his feet. He must have stepped on a pressure plate and triggered a trap.

Kevik plummeted down and only his fast thinking saved him. Casting his goo spell again, he encased himself in the sticky substance, then started thrashing about in an attempt to make contact with the wall of the shaft. His fall was abruptly halted when his hand touched the wall and the goo adhered to it.

"Kevik!" yelled Riyan.

It was hard to look up, but Kevik was able to see the other three standing at the opening in the floor.

"Make your light if you can!" Bart hollered down to him.

Suddenly his bobbing sphere appeared. "We see you," Riyan said.

Riyan turned to Bart, "You'll have to lower me down on the rope," he said.

"Can't," Bart replied. "I won't be able to haul you both up here on my own." Indicating Chad he added, "With his arm recently healed, he'll be no help."

Riyan stared at him and was about to argue when he realized Bart was right. "What do we do?" he asked.

Bart began uncoiling his rope and went to the edge of the pit. "Kevik!" he hollered as he tied a loop in the end, "I'm going to tie a loop on the end of the rope and then lower the rope down to you." He paused and listened but no reply came.

"If he's covered in that goo stuff of his," Riyan said, "he won't be able to reply."

Lowering the rope down to where the bobbing sphere was, he said, "Here comes the rope. When it's in the right position, cancel your light then make it reappear." He continued to lower the rope rapidly until he saw the bobbing sphere disappear, then a few seconds later, reappear.

Riyan grasped the rope behind him. "Now," Bart hollered, "you'll have to grab hold of the rope so we can pull you up."

Chad stood next to the edge of the pit to watch what happened below. He could barely make out where Kevik was stuck to the wall. All that was readily apparent was the bobbing sphere. Then suddenly, he saw movement as Kevik went for the rope.

Bart and Riyan felt tension begin to drag on the rope for a second before it again went slack.

"He didn't make it," said Chad. He and the others watched in horror as Kevik's body fell until coming to a sudden stop when he hit the bottom. As soon as he hit, the bobbing sphere went out.

"Kevik!" Riyan hollered. They listened for a reply but none was forthcoming.

"Is he dead?" asked Chad.

"Maybe," replied Bart. "My rope isn't long enough to reach him."

"We can't leave him down there," insisted Riyan.

"How do you propose we reach him?" Bart asked. "He's not even conscious."

"There has to be a way," said Chad.

Bart considered it for a minute and tried to recall what his father had told him about situations such as this.

Always keep in mind,' his father had said, *'if a pit is deep enough, they had to have a way for those who dug it to get out. At times it could be depressions carved into the sides of the pit to enable them to climb out, or a passage of some sort leading away at the bottom.'*

'But wouldn't that allow the thief a chance to escape the trap?' Bart had asked.

'If the pit is deep enough,' his father explained, 'the builder wouldn't worry about that as the fall would either kill the thief, or damage him to such an extent that he couldn't get away.'

"There may be a way to reach him," Bart said as he came back to the here and now. "Check the sides of the passage for anything that might be used for handholds."

A quick check revealed there were none. "It's possible there's a way out at the bottom," Bart old them. "We just have to find the other end."

"So we are to just leave him?" Chad asked. "That doesn't seem right."

"What else is there for us to do?" replied Bart. "We can't get to him from here. By the time we managed to get back to the Marketplace to procure a rope, providing of course there are any there to be had, and returned, he'd be dead. His only chance is for us to continue and hopefully find a way to him."

"If he's alive, he does have another healing potion," offered Riyan.

Bart nodded. "So I suggest we stop standing here talking and press onward."

Riyan felt bad about leaving Kevik in the pit, but in the face of Bart's logic, there seemed no other alternative. Leaning over the edge, he stared down into the darkness and hollered, "Kevik! If you can hear me, we are not going to leave you there to die. We'll find a way to you, I promise." The pit remained dark. Had he been conscious, Riyan was sure his bobbing sphere would have been present.

"Here," Bart said to the others as he held out his rope to them. "I suggest we tie ourselves together in the event we trigger another such pitfall." Bart of course took the lead with Chad in the middle. Riyan anchored them at the rear. He knew that if what happened to Kevik happened to Bart, it would be up to him to prevent them all from falling.

Before he set out again, Bart turned to them and said, "Single file from here on out. There could be other traps such as what Kevik ran afoul of." When Riyan and Chad nodded understanding, he began to move away from the pit. Riyan cast a last glance at the opening in the floor before the rope pulled him forward.

Bart stayed on the left side of the passage as he quickly led them forward. All the time the possibility that he could meet the same fate as Kevik was foremost on his mind. He turned the corner to the left, proceeded forward another short distance then followed the passage as it turned left once more. From there it ran forward down a longer stretch until it ended at a room.

When the lantern's light began to illuminate the room, a monstrous apparition appeared before them. The shock of seeing it startled Bart so badly that he actually backpedaled into Chad.

Chad stopped him with a hand against his back and asked, "What's wrong?" He hadn't seen what had scared Bart so badly.

Bart didn't reply, only stared at the darkness within the room. When his nerves settled down, and nothing materialized from out of the darkness, he started forward again. The monstrous apparition turned out to be a statue, one of two that sat prominently in the room.

Both were nearly identical. The statues were of life size demonic creatures. The fact that they were standing upon two foot high pedestals gave them the appearance of looming over Bart and the others. Their faces were bestial with small horns sprouting from their foreheads. A long scaly tail extended outward behind them.

"Look familiar?" asked Riyan as he turned his gaze to the other two.

"Yeah," replied Chad. "From The Crypt."

"Exactly," said Riyan. "Remember the mural we found there? The knights were fighting creatures like these."

"Then perhaps they weren't just an artist's rendition to magnify the glory of the dead," supposed Bart. "They may have actually existed at one time."

"Do you think they still do?" asked Riyan.

Bart shook his head. "No. If they did I'm sure we would have heard about it by now." He gave the two statues a cursory examination, especially the base. It looked as if the bases were solid and didn't hold a hidden compartment, there were no seams.

Another exit led from the room ten feet further down along the same wall they had entered through. "Shall we go?" asked Bart.

Riyan and Chad were transfixed by the creatures. A shudder went through Riyan as he gazed into the eyes of one. They seemed so real. Then the spell was broken as Bart laid a hand on his shoulder. He turned to Bart just as he said, "We shouldn't dawdle here. Kevik could need our help."

Riyan nodded. "Right." Then he and Chad followed Bart from the room.

Once into the passage leaving the room, they followed it in single file just as before. It went straight for a bit, then turned left and continued on for the same distance before turning left again. They continued to follow the passage until it turned back to the right.

The passage then continued forward ten feet before opening up onto a large circular room. Emanating from the room ahead of them was a subtle, yet noxious odor. The light from the lantern revealed the floor was smooth as glass, though its light didn't illuminate far enough to show the other side of the room.

Bart came to a halt at the opening. The sight of the floor sent warning signals running through him.

When Riyan came to stand beside him and saw the floor, he too was leery. "What is it?" he asked.

"I'm not sure," replied Bart. "You have any more of those copper coins?"

"A couple," Riyan told him.

"Hand me one will you?"

"Sure," Riyan said and removed one from his belt pouch. "Here." He handed one of his few remaining coppers to Bart. There weren't that many left, most were still sitting on the floors of converging passages as arrows.

Bart took the coin and tossed it into the room.

Plunk!

When the coin hit the floor, the surface splashed. It was a liquid of some kind. "Give me another," Bart told Riyan. When he had the coin in hand, he knelt down by the edge of the room's floor and very carefully dipped the coin into the liquid.

As soon as the coin hit the surface, he noticed a very faint acrid odor coming from the point of contact. He dipped the coin halfway into the liquid and then pulled it back out. The surface of the coin that had been within the liquid was pitted and scarred.

"Acid," he said.

"Acid?" asked Chad incredulously. "Why would they fill the bottom of a room with acid?"

"That would seem pretty obvious," replied Bart.

"To keep us from continuing?" guessed Riyan.

"Exactly." Standing up, he pitched the ruined coin into the room and they watched as it disappeared beneath the surface. "At least we know we're finally on the right track." Turning back to the other two, he pointed to the pool of acid and added, "They wouldn't have gone to the trouble of creating that, unless there was something of incredible value on the other side."

"Such as the key?" asked Riyan.

Bart nodded. "Exactly."

"And a possible way of reaching Kevik," said Riyan.

"First thing we have to do though, is to get past this pool of acid," Bart told them.

"Any ideas?" Chad asked.

"I think it would be a safe assumption that this would be part of the escape route the lord took when he fled the battle," began Bart. "If so, then there has to be an easy and quick way to get through here in an emergency."

"That would make sense," agreed Riyan.

"But how?" mused Bart.

"A secret way around it?" suggested Chad.

Nodding, Bart said, "Could be. There has to be a secret trigger somewhere that will do something to enable us to continue." He pointed to the edge of the acid pool. "Let's begin here and work our way back."

So they began to check the floors and walls starting at the edge of the room and began working their way back down the passage. It was a slow and painstaking process, but they were left with little choice.

Riyan had the idea that they could wait for the lord to show up and find out where he pressed. But then Bart reminded him that Kevik was still down the shaft and might not have that much time. It would be half a day yet, or longer, before the ghost battle manifested.

They finally worked their way back to the turn in the passage and continued to search for some sort of triggering mechanism as they went. It was when they were about halfway past the turn when Chad triggered the trap.

He had been working on one side of the passage while Riyan and Bart had been doing the other. Somehow his foot must have hit a pressure plate for the floor opened up on him just as it had for Kevik. If it wasn't for the rope that still bound him to the others, he would have been a goner.

When he fell, both Riyan and Bart were caught off guard. Riyan was pulled into the opening and barely stopped himself in time by grabbing onto the edge. Bart had hit the floor and came to a stop at the edge of the pit.

They held their positions for a moment, none daring to breathe for fear of disrupting the delicate balance they held. Bart spoke first when his heart stopped racing so fast. "Is everyone alright?" he asked.

"I'm fine," replied Riyan. He had both arms braced above the pit while the rest of him hung within the pit. Chad's weight was a heavy burden and it was all he could do to keep himself from being dragged down with him.

"Chad!" hollered Bart when he didn't answer. "Are you okay?"

"I think so," he replied. "I would really appreciate it if you could get me out of here!"

Riyan couldn't help but give a halfhearted chuckle at that.

"Riyan, you hold still while I pull him out," Bart told him.

"Not a problem," he assured him.

Bart very gingerly began to maneuver himself into a better position for pulling Chad up. Once he was braced, he hollered down to Chad, "I'm going to pull you up. Don't move!"

"What? Did you think I was going to start swinging down here?" came the reply.

Bart just shook his head as he began pulling in the rope. Foot by foot, he brought Chad closer to the opening. Riyan was keeping an eye on his progress and gave Bart updates from time to time. After a couple minutes of pulling, Riyan said, "He's almost there."

"Just stay where you are," grunted Bart. "Don't do anything until he's up and out."

Riyan nodded and then said to Chad as he came abreast of him, "Have a nice fall?"

"You could say that," Chad replied, though from the expression on his face, it had been anything but pleasant. When Bart finally had him near the opening, he reached up and helped by gripping the edge and pulling himself the rest of the way. Once he was up he gave Bart a hand with Riyan.

"Whew," said Riyan. "Glad we had the rope tied about us."

"Should have had us do it after that very first pit trap we encountered," admitted Bart. "But I just didn't think about it."

"You know, I heard what sounded like a river flowing down there," said Chad.

"A river?" asked Riyan.

"Sounded like it," he said.

Riyan moved to the opening and looked down. "Wonder how far it is?"

"Further than we can get to," Bart said as he returned to his feet. "We still need to find that trigger." Chad and Riyan got to their feet and they resumed their search. From that point on while they were searching, they stepped most cautiously. Fortunately, no further pitfalls opened up.

It took them some time, but they finally ended up back at the room with the two demonic statues. "Somehow I figured we'd end up back here," said Riyan.

"So did I," agreed Bart. He undid himself from the rope. "You two check the walls. I'll go over the statues."

"You already went over them once," Chad told him.

Bart shrugged. "I wasn't looking all that hard and could have missed something. This time, I will take more care and be a bit more thorough." He began at the head of the first statue and very carefully pushed, twisted, and pulled anything that could possibly be used as a trigger. It wasn't until he was checking the area of the statue where the tail left the main body that he came across something interesting.

Just underneath the tail, where the creature's butt would've been had it been alive, he found a small opening. It was barely large enough for a single finger. He inserted his finger into it to the second knuckle before his fingertip encountered resistance. The resistance shifted slightly under pressure but otherwise didn't move.

Excited by the find, he removed his finger then went to the other statue to see if a similar opening was present there as well. Sure enough, when he checked under the tail, he found an exact duplicate of the previous opening. Sticking in his finger, he tried pushing the resistance. But just like the other one, it only shifted a little bit.

"Riyan," he said. "I need your help."

Turning away from the section of wall he had been checking, Riyan asked, "You find something?"

"I think so," replied Bart. "Come here and give me a hand." When Riyan came to his side, he showed him where the opening was. "There's another just like it on the other statue. I think we may need to press them simultaneously."

While Bart moved to the other statue, Riyan commented, "If this is the trigger, it would have thwarted a lone thief." Indeed, the statues were sitting too far apart to allow a single individual to reach both openings at the same time.

Bart reached the other statue and placed his finger in the opening under the tail. Then just as he was about to tell Riyan to press it, Chad started laughing. "What's so funny?" he asked.

Chad was shaking his head as the laughter rolled forth. "You guys have no idea what you're doing looks like." He stood there staring at them and the laughter bubbled up again. Riyan and Bart were both standing next to the statues with their fingers, 'up the butt' as it were, of the demonic creatures.

Bart ignored him and turned his attention to Riyan. He saw Riyan had a big grin on his face too as he came to realize what he must look like. "Riyan!" Bart said loudly and got his attention. "When I count to three, press it."

Riyan nodded.

"One … two … three …" When Bart said three, he and Riyan simultaneously pushed against the resistance. This time, Bart felt it slide back an inch. When nothing in the room changed, he quickly led them back through the passages to the acid room.

That was definitely the trigger they had been searching for. A line of stepping stones had risen out of the pool and led across the center of the room. Just within the room before them, there were two stones sitting side by side. Then another set of two stones past the first set before the line became single stones.

"Not yet," Bart said as he stopped Riyan from stepping on the stones.

"Why?" asked Riyan.

He pointed to the two pairs of stones before them. "Step on the wrong one and something bad could happen," he explained.

"Then which one should we step on?" Chad asked.

The first pair was a foot and a half from the edge of the passage. The next pair was the same distance away from the first. Bart thought about it for a second then said, "You two hold onto my arm while I lean out and put my weight on each of the stones."

Riyan nodded as he and Chad both gripped his arm. Bart placed his left foot two inches from the edge of the acid pool. Then leaning outward, he brought his right foot down on the left stone. He no sooner had begun to put weight on it than the stone receded back into the pool.

Riyan and Chad pulled him back as soon as they saw the stone begin to sink. Then they tried it again with the other one and found it to be secure. Once Bart had his full weight upon the stone, they let go.

"One more time," Bart said as he looked to the next pair of stones.

"There's not enough room there for all three of us at the same time," Riyan said. In fact, the stone barely had enough room for two of them to stand on it at the same time.

Bart nodded. "Riyan, you come and help me then."

Riyan untied the rope from around his middle and gave it to Chad. "Hold onto this," he said.

"Be careful," Chad said as he took the rope.

Bart then gave him a hand as he passed from the mouth of the passage to the stone. Once there, he took Bart's arm and provided the counter weight while he leaned out to check the stones. Again, it was the left hand stone that sank into the acid.

"The rest of the stones should be alright," Bart said. "Just take your time and don't fall in." Then he had Chad hand Riyan the lantern who in turn passed it to him. With the lantern now in hand, Bart began moving from one stone to the next until he crossed the room and reached the passage leading away on the other side.

Once there, he noticed a lever mounted in the wall several feet within the passage. He figured it would reset the stones to beneath the surface of the acid pool. Once Riyan and Chad joined him, he showed them the lever and told them what he thought it would do.

"Are you going to pull it?" Riyan asked.

Shaking his head, Bart said, "No. We may need to return this way for some unforeseen reason. I think it would be best to leave the stepping stones where they are."

"Very well," agreed Riyan.

Before setting off down the passage, they tied themselves in tandem once again just in case of another pitfall trap. Bart took the lead with the lantern in hand.

The passage soon turned to the right. From there it continued straight ahead for fifty feet or so before turning to the left. Bart took it slow and careful as he studied the floor of the passage as they went. After the last turn to the left, the passage continued for some time before coming to an end.

At the end of the passage was a single large door, much larger than any they had thus far encountered. Emblazoned upon the door was the coat of arms that has been so prevalent in the Ruins of Algoth. A sword pointing downward with a dragon grasping the hilt in one claw while it's body twined around the blade.

"This has to be it," said Riyan when the light illuminated the coat of arms.

"Most likely," agreed Bart. He moved forward to the door and after a quick check for traps, tried to open it. To his amazement, it actually swung upon. He had expected it to be locked. This was far too easy. When the door swung open enough for the lantern's light to shine within the room on the other side, they gasped by what they saw.

"The lord's treasure room!" Riyan practically shouted. For when the door opened, the light revealed that the room contained six chests. Two sat against the wall across from them and two each against the walls to their right and left.

Upon a stand in the middle of the floor sat an ornamental wooden boat that looked to have survived the passage of time well. The coat of arms that had been on the door was engraved into the side of the boat and the prow boasted a carving of a dragon's head. The boat was large enough to sit eight men comfortably and looked to be made most sturdily.

Bart had to physically stop Riyan from running into the room in his excitement. "Wait a minute!" he shouted as he grabbed him by the arm. Yanking him out of the room and back into the passage, he said, "You better calm down right now!"

Riyan glared at him for the way he had been treated.

"If you go running around in there," Bart began to explain to him, "you may wind up getting yourself killed." He gazed into Riyan's eyes. "Let me search it first."

Riyan gave him a kind of embarrassed smile. "Sorry," he apologized. "Forgot myself there for a moment."

"You two stay here," he told them. Then he turned back to the doorway and entered the room.

First thing he did was to make a quick circuit around the room to get a good feel for the layout. He also discovered that further down the wall from where the door stood, was a very large depiction of the coat of arms engraved into the wall itself. It went from floor to ceiling and was encrusted with many gems. The lantern's light was refracted in a myriad of color.

Once he made a complete circuit of the room, he returned to Chad and Riyan. "I think it's okay if you come in," he told them. "Just don't touch anything." As they entered the room, he went to the first chest and began inspecting it for traps.

"This is amazing," observed Riyan. Upon entering the room, his eyes naturally went to the gem encrusted coat of arms on the wall. He and Chad stood in front of it and marveled at the gems. They had to be worth a fortune.

"I couldn't take any of those," Chad said indicating the gems. "It wouldn't seem right."

Riyan glanced at his friend and nodded. "I get that feeling too."

After a few more moments admiring the coat of arms, they went over to the boat. What once must have been some of the finest cloth ever made draped the seats inside. There was also a small chest sitting on the forward seat directly behind the dragon's head.

"Bart," Riyan hollered over to him. "There's a small chest in here too."

"Alright, I'll get to it in a minute," came the reply. "This one's open, you two can go through it now." He glanced over to where they were standing by the boat as he held the lid of the chest open. "I think you're going to like this."

"Really?" asked Chad excitedly. He and Riyan crossed the room quickly to the open chest. It was filled with dozens of gems of varying sizes. The majority were small ones, but at least five were pretty big. As they began removing the gems and putting them in their packs, Bart moved on to the next chest.

It took Bart the better part of an hour to disarm and open all six chests. Only one of the traps went off while he was working on it. Fortunately, it was a variation of the Prick of Poison and when it went off, his fingers were nowhere near the lock.

The second chest held coins, hundreds of coins. More than half of them were gold, the rest being silver.

The third chest held jewelry. Fourteen rings, seven necklaces and a smattering of other smaller paraphernalia like broaches and such. Each was worked in precious metal, some even held gems of varying sizes.

The fourth chest held a well crafted longsword that had resisted the ravages of time. The scabbard was plain and nondescript, as was the hilt. Engraved in the nexus of the crossguard was the dragon-sword coat of arms. Attached to the belt along with the longsword's scabbard was another scabbard holding a knife. When Riyan pulled it forth, he could see the dragon-sword coat of arms was engraved in the knife's crossguard as well.

Riyan glanced to Chad questioningly. "Do you mind?" he asked. Chad looked longingly at the sword and knife but nodded for Riyan to have it. "Thank you," he said as he began unbelting the scabbard he was currently wearing and quickly belted the new one with the knife on around his waist.

"Next sword we find I get," Chad stated.

"You got it," agreed Riyan. "And if we don't come across another one, you get to have first pick of something else."

The fifth chest held a piece of cloth. It was a foot and a half long with runes inscribed along its length. From the uniform bulge running from one end to the other, it was easy to see that it held something. Chad reached in and picked it up. The cloth was actually a long, thin, carrying pouch. Inside was something long and firm.

One end of the cloth pouch opened up and he pulled forth a long stick. It looked rather plain with no markings or inscriptions on it. He held it up to Riyan and asked, "Could it be a wand?"

"Perhaps," replied Riyan. "Better leave it alone for now."

Chad nodded and slipped the wand back in its cloth pouch before placing it in his pack.

The sight of the wand made him think of Kevik and what may have happened to him. He hoped he was okay and that they could get to him soon.

Unable to do anything about it now, he returned to the matter at hand. Leaving behind the fifth chest, he and Chad moved to the sixth where Bart was just finishing with picking the lock.

"Done?" asked Riyan as he and Chad came to a stop several feet away.

"Just about," replied Bart. "Give me another minute, this one's kind of tricky."

They waited patiently while he worked and then he announced that he had it. They hurried over just as he was pulling up the lid and all three looked in to see what the final chest held. Riyan was half hoping the rest of the key to the King's Horde would be inside, but he was disappointed.

Inside the chest were two items. One was an intricately carved small box. The other was a folded cloak. Riyan picked up the box and opened it.

Resting within on a soft cushion, were two rings. Unadorned and plain, they didn't seem all that important.

Riyan showed them to Chad. "Could be magic you think?" he asked.

"Perhaps," nodded Chad. "Better keep them in the box until we know more about them."

Riyan agreed with him. He remembered the tale that a bard had told one night he had stayed at the Sterling Sheep. It was about a group of adventurers that had uncovered some lost temple or other. During their exploration, they had come across a ring. Thinking it magical and valuable, one of their members had put it on. Turned out to be cursed, a trap laid by the former occupants of the temple against thieves. The man had died a few days later. Closing the box, Riyan put it in his pack. Then he glanced over to Bart who held the cloak.

"This is fine material," Bart said. "I think I'll keep it if you two don't mind?"

They both shook their heads. If anyone deserved to have what they wanted, it was Bart. After all, he was the one putting his life on the line with every chest and trap.

Bart grinned and said, "Thanks." He folded it into a smaller square then placed it within his pack. After that he went over to the boat and soon had the small box Riyan had found open. Within was a grey powder. He quickly shut the box again and locked it. He didn't want something like what happened to Chad happening to him. After putting the box with the powder in his pack, he began looking around.

"What?" asked Riyan.

"If this was the place where the lord ran when his forces were overrun," he began to explain, "then it would stand to reason that there has to be a way to continue from here."

"You think so?" asked Chad.

Bart turned to him and nodded. "Most definitely." He indicated the open chests around them. "I hardly think this is the lords true treasure room. I would imagine it's here to satisfy thieves who made it this far so they wouldn't continue to search."

"I don't know," argued Riyan. "This all seems rather valuable."

Bart thought about that for a moment then shook his head. "No. Maybe if I wasn't aware the lord had come this way as an escape route I would feel different."

"So what do we do now?" asked Chad.

He glanced around the room with a sigh before replying. "We painstakingly search this room until we find the way the lord went."

Chapter 25

Dark. Pain filled darkness greeted him as he regained consciousness. He tried to move and alleviate the pain but it only increased his agony tenfold when he attempted to move his left leg. *It must be broken,* he thought to himself.

Light suddenly filled the bottom of the shaft as his bobbing sphere blossomed to life. He looked in shock at his left leg. It wasn't the fact that it was broken that was causing him such pain. Rather it was due to the fact that one of the many foot long spikes that were set into the floor had impaled its way through it from one side to the other. When he fell and hit the bottom, his leg must have struck it. The tip of the spike protruded two inches out of his skin.

Kevik did a quick check of the rest of him, and other than a few places that will likely form bruises, he was alright. Except for his leg.

"Riyan! Bart!" he called up to the top of the shaft. When no answer came, he cancelled his bobbing sphere of light to see if the light from their lantern could be seen at the top of the shaft. He grew despondent when all he could see was darkness. Realizing they were no longer there, he recast his bobbing sphere spell and light once more filled the bottom of the shaft.

First order of business was his leg. He didn't think the bone was damaged, it felt like the spike had gone through the muscle. Before he attempted to remove his leg from the spike he looked around the bottom of the shaft to find his pack. There was still one healing potion left that his master had brought with them when they set out from Gilbeth, the town where his master had lived.

His eyes widened when he saw the skeleton lying in the midst of the spikes. Obviously here was another soul who had fallen to the traps of this place. There was not a speck of flesh left upon his bones and what clothes the person had been wearing are all but gone. After his cursory inspection of the skeleton, he returned to the more immediate matter of finding his pack and the healing potion.

He panicked at first when he couldn't see it. Then he realized he was still wearing his pack and that it was underneath him. Shifting around as best he could without causing his leg any more pain than absolutely necessary, he worked the pack out from under him.

When he had it sitting next to him and opened, he was quite relieved to find the vial containing the healing potion to still be intact. He had feared that it might have suffered damage during the fall. Removing it, he placed it on the ground next to him then turned his attention back to his leg.

A pool of blood had collected at the base of the spike. Fortunately, the spike itself was 'plugging the hole' so to speak and kept his blood from flowing more freely. But once he pulled his leg off the spike, he wouldn't have much time before blood loss was going to render him unconscious. He unstoppered the vial and then grabbed his leg.

The anticipation of the pain this was going to bring him almost made him vomit, but he steeled himself. After taking two deep breaths to calm his shaking nerves, he gripped his leg. Then in one fluid motion, he pulled it off the spike.

Pain erupted and a cry escaped his lips as his leg slid upward and came free of the spike. When his leg came free, blood flowed dangerously fast. Dots danced before his eyes and he feared the pain was going to cause him to pass out. He fought unconsciousness and reached for the vial. He brought it to his lips and quickly drank half of it then sat up as he poured the rest of the elixir into the wound. He didn't drip it carefully into the wound as he had with Chad. Instead he upended it and dumped the rest of it out onto the wound. Once the last drop fell, he let go of the vial and laid his head back on the ground, panting.

He could feel the potion beginning to dull the pain as it worked to heal. A warm feeling began to radiate from the site of the injury as the muscles and flesh of his leg started to knit back together. He continued to lie there and fought off the onset of unconsciousness until the warmth began to subside.

There at the bottom of the shaft, he laid there for several more minutes as his body calmed down and the last vestiges of pain faded away. Then he moved to the wall of the shaft and sat against it while he inspected his leg. Pulling his trousers' leg up, he inspected the wound. It had completely healed over and a jagged circle of pink flesh now covered where the spike had exited his leg. He'll bear a scar there for the rest of his life, but at least he'll now have the rest of his life.

If I can get out of here, he thought to himself.

For the first time he really gave the bottom of the shaft a good look. One of the walls held an opening. It looked as if it was a natural fissure that had been artificially widened at some point. Wide enough for a man to pass through, it looked to be his only hope in getting out of here.

His staff was lying on the other side of the pit. He worked his way over to it on his hands and knees, careful to avoid the spikes. When he had it in hand, he used it to help him to his feet. To his surprise, the leg that was injured bore him with strength. Still, he used his staff to support himself anyway as he didn't wish to strain the newly formed muscles.

On the way back across the spiky bottom of the shaft to retrieve his pack, a glimmer caught his attention. He turned his attention towards it and realized it came from the skeleton. There was a ring upon the man's right hand. Intrigued, Kevik moved closer for a closer look.

As he came closer, he reached down and pulled the ring from the skeletal finger. It was made of silver and had a red stone set in the top. There were markings inscribed on the inner side of the band but they were in a language he was unfamiliar with.

He thought about using his identification spell on it, but was just too tired. So he put it in his belt pouch and continued on to get his pack. Once he had it on his back again, he headed to the fissure in the side of the shaft.

At the opening he could see a narrow tunnel extending away from the shaft, past the edge of the bobbing sphere's light. Ducking his head, he entered the opening and began making his way through the narrow tunnel.

It led him for perhaps twenty feet. Along the way, Kevik encountered two sections that bore marks where the tunnel had been widened to allow a man to pass. When he reached the end, it opened out onto a wider passage, actually it was more like a subterranean cave. There were rock formations such as stalactites and stalagmites, and along the side of the cavern to his right, a small flow of water cascaded down. Where it reached the floor of the cavern it formed a pool of water before overflowing into a rivulet that worked its way across the cavern's floor.

The shadows of the cavern were in constant motion due to the bobbing of his sphere. He began to agree with Riyan about how annoying this form of illumination was. First opportunity he has, he's going to learn a normal type of light spell. Now he understood why his master thought it amusing when he chose to learn this particular spell.

The rivulet flowed away from him down the cavern as it meandered from one side to the other. Kevik followed the water as he began working his way through the cavern. He kept his eyes open for any possible way out.

Not long after he began moving through the cavern, he started hearing a noise coming from further ahead. At first he thought what he was hearing came from the rivulet as it flowed through the cavern. But after another minute or so, he began to realize that the noise was coming from something else. He quickened his steps and soon realized the sound was that of an underground river.

The sound continued to grow the further he went. He soon came to where the cavern began tapering off until it became only a narrow passage a couple feet wide. The rivulet which he had been following flowed out of the cavern and through the narrow passage.

He didn't relish the idea of stepping into the rivulet, he knew the water was bitterly cold from when he quenched his thirst earlier. But what choice had he? So bracing himself, he stepped into the cold water. It only went up to his ankles but the water soon began seeping into his shoes. Not for the first time since joining Riyan and his companions did he wish he wore boots.

The water sent a shiver through him as he squeezed his way to the other side of the opening. The narrowness of it lasted for at least ten feet before ending at a ledge overlooking an underground river. Sitting a scant foot above the flowing river, the ledge was slippery from where spray would at times be thrown by the crashing water. The underground river itself wasn't flowing all that fast, it was just the many rocks protruding out of the water that made the water a bit frothy.

The ledge was very uneven, slippery, and barely wide enough to enable him to sit upon it cross-legged. He looked out over the flowing water but couldn't see the far side, the light from his bobbing sphere didn't extend far enough. Then he turned his attention to the river itself. The thought of entering its dark, bitterly cold water made him shiver.

Kevik sank down on the ledge and did his best to avoid the water flowing from the opening behind him into the river. Despite his best efforts, he started to become soaked. Sitting there in the dark, he began to give into hopelessness. He knew that to remain on the ledge would be his death, if not now then when his food ran out and he starved. He leaned back against the cavern wall as he perched on his ledge and rested, knowing full well that at some point, he would have to brave the water if he was going to live.

Bart had begun the search of the treasure room at the dragon-sword coat of arms engraved in the wall. It simply seemed like the most logical place for a hidden door to be. The other walls all had chests lined against them so it was unlikely it would be there.

Now a half hour later, he was still examining the coat of arms. Riyan and Chad haven't been idle during this time. They've been going over the other walls and the floors. They even climbed into the boat and looked in there but failed to find anything.

Bart checked the gems embedded in the coat of arms, as well as every possible nook and cranny it held. He came up with nothing.

"You know," commented Riyan. "If you feel that coat of arms there on the wall has to be the way, wouldn't that mean it isn't?"

"What?" asked Bart.

"Look at it from the point of view of the ones who built this place," he explained. Then he smiled, "I guess everything you've told us about thieves and thwarting them is rubbing off or something. Anyway, to have it there would be a bit obvious don't you think?"

Bart thought about it for a second then shrugged, "Maybe. You could be right."

"Doesn't look as if you're going to find anything there anyway," Chad added.

Again Bart paused and grew still. He began thinking about what Chad and Riyan had said. It actually made a lot of sense. Coming back to the here and now, he glanced at the other two. "Alright." Moving to the doorway, he passed into the passage then turned around as he began reenacting the lord's escape. "Here I am, lord of this place, and I am being pursued by enemies seeking my death or capture. What do I do?"

"You get the heck out of here as fast as possible," replied Chad.

"Exactly!" stated Bart. Moving into the room, he said, "There needs to be something here that can be quickly activated on my way to wherever the secret exit lies."

Getting into the spirit of the reenactment, Riyan jumps from the boat. "If as you say the secret exit is behind the coat of arms, then wouldn't the trigger have to be before the coat of arms? That way it would begin to open before you arrived, thus enabling you to escape that much quicker?"

"Yes," Bart said. Moving further into the room, he turned and headed towards the coat of arms. His path took him to within a foot of the boat resting in the middle of the room. "The boat maybe?" he asked.

"But we already looked it over," said Chad.

"Hmm." Bart turned his attention to the side of the boat facing him. "If our suppositions are accurate, the trigger would have to be here ..." he said then turned to face the wall on the other side of him, "Or there." Pointing to the wall, he paused as his eyes quickly searched its surface.

"Maybe it's on the floor?" suggested Riyan.

Bart shook his head. "No. A trigger for a trap maybe, but not a secret exit. The lord couldn't afford to have his enemies stumbling upon it by accident."

Riyan grinned, "You've got a point."

Moving to the side of the boat, Bart began pushing and pulling its various planks and knotholes. After a thorough search, still nothing.

"That just leaves the wall?" asked Chad.

"Looks that way," he replied.

The wall in question looked the same as all the others. Stones placed in staggered formation, a torch sconce where a torch could be burnt to light the room, and an all but faded tapestry.

His eyes went to the torch sconce. "No," he said to himself, shaking his head. "It couldn't be that easy."

"What?" asked Riyan.

Bart pointed to the torch sconce. "That is the oldest trick in the book," he explained. "A movable torch sconce that will open a secret door."

"You going to try it?" asked Chad. "This place is pretty old, maybe this is where they came up with that ploy."

"I don't think I've seen you even try a torch sconce in all the times you've hunted for secret doors," Riyan added. "Not even when we were down in the Crypt."

"That's because it's never used anymore," he explained.

"So try it," Riyan suggested. "What do you have to lose?"

Shrugging, Bart went to the torch sconce and pulled it down. At first it didn't move then Riyan told him to try harder. So he gripped it with both hands and jumped up a little and came down hard. To his utter surprise, it moved downward several inches. Then a grinding noise could be heard as the wall bearing the coat of arms began rising into the ceiling.

"I'll be damned," he said. "Someone who could afford to build a place like this and all he could come up with was a torch sconce." Smiling to himself, he turned to the others and shrugged. "Let's go."

He grabbed his pack and the lantern before hurrying towards the gradually rising wall. On the other side was a short passage similar to the ones they've traveled along since coming down here. It extended forward ten feet before turning to their right. Around the corner was a flight of steps descending down into darkness.

Bart took the lead again as they went down the steps quickly. Riyan counted and there were a total of forty steps before they ended at a massive underground cavern. The cavern began rather narrow as it moved away from the foot of the stair, but quickly grew wider and taller. Light from the lantern reflected off crystals in the walls which created a dazzling display.

"Nice," commented Riyan.

Chad took out his belt knife and pried a three inch long piece of crystal from the wall. Holding it up, he watched as it refracted the lantern's light. "This is truly unbelievable."

"I take it you two have never seen crystal before?" asked Bart.

Riyan shook his head and Chad said, "No."

They worked their way through the cavern, soon the upper reaches were no longer visible as it rose above the range of the lantern's light. About this time, the cavern began curving toward the right and they came to a stream. Over time the water had formed a channel over four feet deep and five feet across that it now flowed through.

With a running jump, they were able to clear the channel and make it to the other side. The stream exited through the cavern's right wall not far from where they crossed the channel. The sound of it cascading down like a waterfall came from the other side of the opening it flowed through.

They continued down the cavern another hundred feet and found where the stream entered the cavern through the wall on the left side. Shortly after leaving the stream behind, the cavern began to narrow once again. At the far end where the sides of the cavern finally converged again, was a large pile of boulders. It looked like at some time in the past the side of the cavern might have caved in.

At first worried that the cave-in might have blocked their way, they were soon to realize that on the far side of the boulders, the exit was still accessible. It was clearly manmade, nothing of nature could make such even lines.

"We're on the right track," Riyan said.

"Wonder how much further this goes?" asked Chad.

"As far as it does and no further," replied Bart.

"What?" Chad asked, confused by the answer.

"Nothing," Bart said with a grin. "Just something my father use to say to me when I would ask a question like that."

"Oh," replied Chad.

Once past the exit, they were again in a passage carved out of the rock. A bit narrower than what they were use to up above, but serviceable. It wound through the rock until it turned sharply to the right. Around the corner they found the top of another set of stairs leading down. These were narrow and the steps crudely formed.

Bart again took the lead as they began descending the stairs. These went down for quite a ways, and they were forced to step extra carefully as the steps were quite slippery. They hadn't gone down many steps before the sound of flowing water could be heard coming up from the bottom.

"It's a river," Bart stated after the sound grew clearer.

"Maybe it's the same one that I heard when you were hauling me up from the pit trap?" asked Chad.

"Most likely," agreed Riyan.

At the bottom of the steps they encountered a rickety old pier that had been built over the flowing water a very long time ago. The wooden planks were still together but they were not sure how well they would hold up under their weight.

"End of the trail," announced Bart.

Riyan looked at the river in dismay. Then he had an idea. "Could we use the boat that was in the treasure room?"

Bart shook his head. "That thing must have weighed five hundred pounds," he said. "No way would we three be able to carry it down here."

"Then what can we do?" he asked.

"Swim?" asked Chad. "The river's not flowing all that fast."

"You've got to be crazy," Bart exclaimed. "Do you have any idea how cold that water is? Besides, we don't know what to expect further down. There could be a waterfall for all we know."

"I don't think there would be one of those," countered Riyan. "They never would have built a pier here and made this their escape route if there were." He glanced at the pier itself and saw how the planks were still fairly connected. "Maybe we could make a raft out of this."

"Yeah!" agreed Chad. "Float down on top of a few boards."

Riyan glanced at Bart. "What do you think? Worth a try?"

Bart didn't look all that enthused about the prospect of trusting his life to the rickety old pier. "I don't know …" he said.

"Piece of cake," Riyan said. He pointed to a section that was still fairly intact. "All we have to do is separate that section from the rest and off we go."

"Just like that?" asked Bart skeptically.

"Just like that," affirmed Riyan.

"I say we try it," Chad joined in.

Bart glanced from one to the other and could tell their minds were made up. "Very well," he said. He set the lantern down on the landing as they began trying to figure out the best way to do this.

The section they wanted to use was literally a third of the old wooden platform. In order to disengage it from the rest of the dock, they would have to either break it away or pry up a number of the planks connecting it to the rest.

Riyan set his pack on the stone landing. "I'll go out and start separating it," he told the other two. "Bart, you get your rope ready in case we need it to secure some of the planks together."

Bart nodded and began readying the rope.

"Be careful," Chad said to Riyan.

Riyan turned his head towards him and grinned. "Don't worry. I don't plan to be anything else." Turning back, he gauged the planks of the pier before him. They looked sturdy enough to support him. Stepping out, he gingerly placed a foot on the first one.

There were nine planks between where he stood and the far side. Once there, he had to somehow separate the section they wanted from the rest. He lifted his other foot off the stone landing and moved it towards the second plank. When it rested on the second plank, his entire weight was now on the pier. Glancing down, he could see where the water ran beneath the planks beginning with the second one.

"Take it easy," cautioned Bart.

Riyan glanced behind him and saw Bart and Chad standing together watching his progress. Bart had the rope coiled in his hand, waiting. Turning back to the matter at hand, he lifted his foot off the first plank and brought it forward to the third. As soon as he began putting his weight on the third plank, an audible cracking noise could be heard coming from the wood.

"Riyan!" Chad hollered as he heard the noise too.

Riyan lifted his foot off the third plank and held it in the air. He was beginning to think that this may not have been one of his better ideas. The fourth plank was a bit further than he was willing to stretch. Once he put his foot on it, he would be hard pressed in lifting it back off gently should it be unable to hold his weight too.

"I'm coming back," he hollered to the other two.

"Good," Bart said. "I never thought ..."

Before he had the chance to finish his sentence, the second board cracked and gave way beneath him. Riyan fell forward into the boards, smashing through planks three through seven. He hit the river and the coldness of the water took his breath away as the current began dragging him from the pier. When his head cleared the surface, he gasped for air and turned to look in the direction of the lantern's light.

"... the rope!" he heard Bart say as the rope flew through the air towards him. It hit the water several feet upstream from him and he began swimming furiously against the current to reach it. Inch by inch the rope floated towards him until he was able to grab onto it. "He's got it!" he heard Bart say when his weight pulled the tension of the rope tight.

Crack!

"Get back!" Chad yelled.

Riyan looked towards them and saw the section of the pier they wanted to use began breaking away from the rest of it. Wood splintered and more cracking of planks was heard as the current began pulling it away from the landing. It didn't take long for Riyan to realize that the current was bringing it straight toward him.

"Riyan!" Chad hollered when he realized his friend's danger. "Get out of the way!"

But Riyan had other plans. While Bart and Chad were hauling him in, he wound the rope around his left arm as many times as he could. Then, when the pier section came near, he snagged it with his right arm. The current continued dragging it downstream until it was on the other side of him, then came to an abrupt halt. The jolt almost pulled Riyan's arm from its socket, but he refused to let it go.

Chad and Bart had stopped pulling him in when they saw him grab the section of the pier. "Keep going!" he yelled at them. "I've got it."

"Hang on Riyan," Chad yelled.

Then he began feeling the rope once again pulling against his arm as they drew him closer to the landing. Every time they hauled in the rope, pain coursed through his arms. Between the river trying to drag the section of the pier away, and them pulling on the rope, he's surprised that his arms were even still attached. A thought came to him that after this, he'll have a better appreciation of how people feel when they're being stretched on the rack.

It seemed an eternity before they managed to pull him back to the landing. When he came within arm's reach, Chad grabbed his arm while Bart snagged the pier section. Riyan was more than glad to let go and leave it to Bart.

Using the rope he had, Bart tied one end around a large brace that ran beneath the planks. Then once the rope was on and secure, he hauled the pier section as close to the landing as he could.

"Thanks," Riyan said as his teeth chattered. "You have no idea how good it feels to be out of that water."

"I think we'll have a good idea when we ride this down the river," said Bart indicating the pier section. "It's riding right on the water and we're going to get soaked."

"Give me a minute to warm up some before we leave," Riyan told them.

"You bet," Chad said.

Bart continued to hold the rope and kept their 'raft' from floating away. He still wasn't too enthused about trusting this raft with their lives, but was willing to give it a try.

Riyan sat there shivering a solid ten minutes before realizing that only a fire would warm him again. He stood up and came to where Bart still held the rope.

"Ready?" Bart asked.

"No time like the present," he replied.

"Alright. Take off your packs and set them down here in front of me," Bart told them.

When they had done that, he said, "I want you two to come here and grab hold of our raft. I'm going to use the rope to tie the packs together so we won't lose them if things go wrong."

As Chad leaned over towards the raft and grabbed hold, he asked, "What about the lantern?"

"We'll have to hold that," he said. "Can't afford to let any water get in with the oil." Once the other two had a good hold of their raft, he untied the rope from it and threaded the end through their pack straps. Then he tied them together tightly.

"Now, we have to get on," he said. "I think Riyan showed us that this wood isn't going to withstand a whole lot of weight. So we need to board it by crawling on our hands and knees to better distribute the weight." He glanced to Chad. "You first. Once you're out there, grab hold of that." He pointed to a thick wooden piling up from the water to which the pier had originally been attached.

Chad began crawling out upon the boards of the raft and when the water hit him for the first time cried out, "It's cold!"

"Didn't I tell you it was cold?" asked Riyan. Once Chad had made it out and was lying spread out upon the planks to better distribute his weight, he reached out and took hold of the piling.

"Okay Riyan, you're next," Bart said as he grabbed hold of the raft to steady it.

Riyan crawled out onto the boards next to Chad. When he was in position, Bart said, "Here." Turning around, he saw Bart handing him the three packs that were tied together. He took them and placed them near the center of the raft next to him. Then he took the lantern and held it close.

"Chad," Bart said, "hold it steady. I'm coming on." When he let go, the raft began drifting away from the landing despite Chad's best effort.

"Hurry up man," Chad said as he began losing his grip.

Bart quickly scrambled aboard just as the current yanked the raft and pulled Chad's hands off the piling.

Chapter 26

Kevik still sat on the narrow ledge that he's been sitting on now for over an hour. The rivulet that ran through the opening has soaked him pretty good. Though he was already cold with teeth chattering, he still hadn't worked up the courage to enter the frigid water of the river.

How much longer could he afford to sit here? Every minute sapped that much more warmth and energy from his body. If he waited much longer, he won't have the strength to keep his head above the water once he makes his move.

So he sat there cold, miserable, and alone. All the sadness at the loss of his master welled to the surface again. He put his head on his knees as the strong emotions got the best of him, and sobbed.

"Keep it away from the rocks!"

His head jerked up as he looked up the river to where the voice came from. A light could be seen drawing closer.

"Paddle man!" he heard Chad yell. "If it hits the rocks it'll bust up!"

With hope rekindled, he climbed to his feet just as the source of the light came into view. He saw the glow was from a lantern floating along the far side of the water. Three forms moved upon the water and it took him only a split second to recognize his former comrades. They looked to be riding some kind of raft.

"Riyan!" he yelled and began waving his arms.

The person in the center of the raft, who looked to be Bart, turned and saw him there on his precarious ledge. "Kevik!" Bart yelled. The other two turned to see him and his bobbing orb.

"Riyan!" Chad yelled, "The rocks!"

Kevik watched as Riyan turned onto his back and used his feet to keep the current from bashing the raft onto the rocky wall. His feet kicked out at the wall in an attempt to push the raft back into the river. Then Kevik saw Bart take something and begin twirling it over his head.

"Your goo spell!" Bart yelled as the object he had been twirling suddenly sailed towards him.

Kevik saw three packs that were tied together suddenly flying through the air in his direction. He quickly understood Bart's plan and when they came close, covered them in the sticky goo.

Splat!

The goo coated packs struck the wall not two feet downstream from him and stuck. Bart hung onto the rope as the current used the packs attached to the wall as a fulcrum. When the rope grew taut in Bart's hands, their raft was pulled from the far side of the river and began to draw close to the other.

"Riyan, Chad," Bart hollered. "Get to the other side or we're going to hit."

They saw the wall of the channel the river flowed through approaching and moved into position. Just as Riyan had done previously, they moved to the edge approaching the wall and laid on their backs. When the raft was about to hit, they extended their feet to act as shock absorbers. The current swept the raft to the wall but their feet provided enough cushioning to keep it from being smashed apart.

At that point the tension of the rope increased twofold and the rope was almost torn from Bart's hand. He tried to pull the raft closer to Kevik, but the current was too strong. He saw Kevik standing there, his annoying bobbing sphere dancing around him.

"You're going to have to come to us!" he hollered. "I can't hold this much longer."

Kevik realized that if he was to join them he would have to do it himself. So he put the pack across his back and made ready to enter the water. "Hurry!" he heard Bart grunt. With one hand on the rope attached to the packs, and another holding his master's staff, he entered the water.

Immediately, the current began pulling him downriver and he lost his balance. He gripped the rope with his one hand while his other tried to retain hold of the staff. At one point his head went under. When he broke the surface again, he heard Bart yelling, "... the staff!"

"What?" he hollered back but then the water sucked him under once more. Still holding onto the rope and the staff he managed to get his head back above water.

"… go of the staff!" he heard when he broke the surface. Then he realized Bart was trying to say, 'Let go of the staff'. But this was his master's staff, given to him just before he died. How could he willingly let it go?

Then the water sucked him down a third time and it was all he could do to simply get back to the surface. That was when he realized that if he didn't let go, he wouldn't reach the raft. Against the pull of the current, he was going to need both hands on the rope. "Forgive me master," he said as he let go of the staff and gripped the rope with both hands.

As the staff began floating away, he started working his way down the rope to the raft. He could hear Bart grunting as he worked to keep the current from taking the raft. Moving as fast as he could, he finally reached the raft.

"Get on," said Bart. "But be careful, this wood isn't going to hold under your full weight."

Nodding understanding, Kevik placed both hands on the raft and pulled himself up.

Crack!

His left hand broke one of the boards and the river just about sucked him away when his grip on the raft faltered. Panic set in until both hands were once again holding onto the raft. Then he calmed himself by a sheer force of will and began to climb on board once more.

A little slower this time, he inched his way on top until all but his lower legs were still in the water.

"Cancel the spell!" Bart yelled at him.

Mumbling the words, Kevik dispelled the goo holding the packs to the wall. Then he felt the current begin dragging the raft downriver once more. "Thanks," he said to them.

"Later," Bart said as he hauled the packs back onto the raft. "Keep your eyes open for any possible rocks or anything else we may run into.

"Right," Kevik said. He remained where he was and turned onto his back like the others. He scanned for possible danger spots while Chad and Riyan continued working to keep the raft from striking the wall.

For several minutes the current carried them on until something from the opposite side of the river entered the lantern's light and caught his attention. It looked like a wooden dock. "Bart!" he yelled then directed Bart's attention to the dock.

Bart nodded and said, "We need to get to it!" He sat up on the makeshift raft and started twirling the three waterlogged packs over his head.

Crack! Snap!

Beneath him he could feel and hear the planks about to give way. Ignoring the aged wood's warning, he said to Kevik, "Goo spell." Then with a final impetus, he launched the packs toward the approaching dock.

When the packs reached halfway there, Kevik cast his spell. The packs hit the wall with a splat a little upstream of the dock. Then just like before, the river used it as a fulcrum and swung the raft towards the dock's side of the river.

Chad and Riyan scrambled to the other side of the raft and reached it a second before the raft struck the wall. Using their legs, they kept the raft a safe distance away.

"Kevik," Bart said. "You're going to have to help me to pull the raft closer." They were now ten feet downriver of the dock.

Crack!

The wood beneath Bart gave out with another threatening crack as the pressure he was exerting against the raft to prevent the river from taking it was now being focused on the board his feet were braced against. Kevik moved over until he was in position and grabbed the rope. Then between both of them, they slowly brought the raft to the dockside.

"Okay Kevik," Bart said. "Get on the dock. But be careful, it may not hold."

Nodding, Kevik began moving across the raft to the edge of the dock.

Crack!

"And hurry!" Bart saw the board he had his feet braced against begin to come apart. "Just hold for a little bit longer," he said softly to the board. Once Kevik made it onto the dock, he told Riyan to go next.

Riyan grabbed the lantern then worked his way from the raft to the dock. By this time, Kevik had already made it to the stone landing on the other side. Once Riyan was on the dock and began working his way to the landing, it was Chad's turn.

"But it's going to hit against the wall!" Chad hollered to Bart. His feet even now were pressed against the side of the channel as he worked to maintain the foot of space between the raft and the wall.

"I know!" Bart replied. "Just get on the dock."

No sooner did Chad remove his feet and begin moving along the raft to the dockside than the current began banging the side of the raft into the wall. They could hear the wood begin splintering and even before he reached the dock, one of the rear planks broke off and was carried away by the current.

Bart continued holding the rope, the strain on his arms becoming quite bad. Between what he did when Kevik joined them and what he's doing here, his muscles were a knotted mass of pain. Frankly, he's surprised he's been able to hold this for as long as he has.

He watched Chad's progress and when he saw him leave the raft and make the dock, he sighed with relief.

Crack!

A large chunk of the raft behind him splintered off after striking the wall hard. He glanced back and saw that there was only one more plank behind him. The loss of that section of the raft slightly eased the pressure being exerted on his arms.

Then out of the corner of his eye, he saw Riyan moving across the wooden dock towards the rope in an attempt to help him. "Riyan, stop!" he yelled. The last thing he wanted was for the situation to worsen by Riyan breaking through the aged wood and falling into the river.

Riyan paused as he turned to Bart. Then a loud cracking was heard and Riyan's left foot suddenly broke through. Chad was quick to his side and lent him a hand back onto the stone landing. The three of them turned their gaze to where Bart sat upon the raft. His feet were braced against the wood and he was holding the rope for all he was worth.

Bart lifted a foot from where it was braced against the raft and felt the raft subtly shift under him. He moved the foot closer to the end of the raft, then did the same with the other. Only two more planks separated him from the edge of the raft. One by one, he worked his way to the edge.

Crack! Snap!

All of a sudden the raft disintegrated and he was in the water. He held onto the rope as the current dragged him under. His pack across his back didn't help matters but he wasn't about to let that go, it held his lockpicks. Death would take him before he willingly gave them up.

So holding onto the rope with one hand, he used his other to bring him back to the surface. "Grab my hand!" he heard Riyan holler to him when his head broke through. Looking up, he saw Riyan at the edge of the dock, reaching out his hand.

He tried to grab the hand but the current pulled him under once more. When he finally made it back to the surface, Riyan's hand was still outstretched. Again he tried to reach it, and this time Riyan managed to grab his hand and began pulling him to the dock.

Once he had both hands holding onto the dock, he handed the rope to Riyan. "Thanks," he said.

"Don't thank me until you're safely on the landing," Riyan said. He then took hold of the back of Bart's pack and helped him up.

Crack!

The wood beneath them was beginning to give way. "Move!" they heard Chad yell. Realizing they didn't have much time, Riyan and Bart scrambled for the landing.

Snap! Crack!

The dock disintegrated under them. Riyan was the first to make the landing and just as Bart reached it, the dock completely collapsed into the river. Bart cried out as he lost his grip and felt his feet entering the river.

Kevik dove for him and grabbed his arm before the current could drag him away. Then with Chad and Riyan's help, he pulled Bart onto the landing.

He laid there a moment panting, barely having the strength to move. Riyan came and knelt down by his side. "Guess what?" he asked.

"What?" Bart replied. His heart had finally quit racing and his muscles began to quiet their protesting.

Riyan pointed behind him to the far side of the landing and grinned. "Another passage."

"Let me have some rest first," Bart told him.

"No problem there," he said. "We need to dry out anyway before we all catch our death." Getting up, he had Chad help him in tearing apart the remnants of the pier. Little of it remained though, most of it was now on its way down the river. At least there was enough left that they could build a fire.

Kevik came and sat by Bart while the other two worked at collecting the wood. "Thank you for taking the time to rescue me," he said.

"That's alright," Bart replied. "Couldn't very well leave you there all alone." He saw a bit of sadness in Kevik's eyes and said, "Sorry about your staff."

Kevik shrugged. "I'm sure Allar would have understood," he said.

A pile of wood was beginning to grow in the middle of the landing as Riyan and Chad continued tearing chunks and pieces from the remaining sections of planks and the pilings. When they figured they had enough, Riyan stacked the smaller, driest bits in a loose pile. Then he put one of the smaller pieces in the flame of the lantern until it began to burn. Once it had caught and didn't look like it was going to go out, he placed it beneath the stack. It took him three separate attempts before the pile of wood began to burn on its own.

Slowly at first they added more wood to the flames until they had a roaring fire going on the landing. By this time some of Bart's energy had returned and he sat up and scooted closer to get warm. The four comrades sat in the fire's warm glow as they stripped down to their small clothes and began drying their things out.

"Our food's ruined," announced Chad. He pulled a rather nasty looking mess from out of his pack that had once been dried bread and other rations, including half a loaf of stale bread. The only thing that had survived was a few strips of dried beef. He went to the edge of the water and washed away the moist rations that had adhered to the meat. After that he distributed them evenly among the four of them.

"Anyone else have anything?" Bart asked. Two more strips of beef were discovered in Riyan's pack. Other than that, nothing was salvageable.

"Once we get out of here food won't be that much of a problem," Riyan said as he patted his sling.

"But getting out of here will," Chad said. Then he pointed over to the mouth of the passage. "What do we do if that passage doesn't lead anywhere?"

"Get back in the water and swim," replied Bart matter-of-factly.

None of them relished that possibility. They didn't even have the pier this time to turn into a makeshift raft, the bulk of it has already disappeared downstream. What was left was barely enough to keep their fire going.

"Anyone look into it yet?" Bart asked indicating the passage.

"Just peeked in through the entrance," Riyan said. "It continued further than what the lantern's light revealed."

Bart nodded. Then he asked Kevik what happened to him after he fell down the shaft. For the next hour they heard his tale and in turn told of what they had gone through and what they found. They showed him the various items they took from the treasure room. He was especially interested in the wand.

"Do you know what it does?" asked Riyan.

"No," he admitted. "And I'm not about ready to find out either." He glanced to the others before continuing. "I'm about used up, magically speaking. I've done more magic since I've met you than I did the month prior to our meeting."

"Hopefully you won't be called on to do any more for awhile," Bart said.

"That would be good," he replied. "I need a break."

When half of their wood supply had been consumed, they banked the fire and put their semi dried clothes back on. Then they made ready to explore the passage. "Think the key could be down here?" Riyan asked Bart.

Shrugging, he said, "Maybe."

Bart took the lead. Swinging his mostly dry pack onto his back, he picked up the lantern and moved to the passage. His muscles still felt the effects of what he had put them through, but a least they no longer constantly complained. They just gave off with a dull ache now and then, along with a feeling of tiredness.

He entered the passage and found that it was constructed similar to the ones above. It extended forward easily forty feet before turning to the right. Then another ten feet before they came to the top of a stairway leading down.

Bart followed the steps down with the others right behind. At the bottom, the steps ended at another passage which extended for a short ways before ending at a plain room. It was twice as wide as it was long. No ornamentation, no engravings, nothing. Simply bare rock. The only thing in the room was a plain, four foot marble pedestal situated in the center of the room. When they came close to it, they saw that the top of the pedestal bore the insignia that was engraved on all the coins.

"Well isn't this just lovely," Riyan commented. "Someone beat us to it."

"Damn!" exclaimed Chad.

"Looks like they took it with them when they fled here," observed Bart. "Which would make sense."

"But where would they have taken it?" Riyan asked him.

Bart shrugged. He glanced around the room another time then began moving around the pedestal.

"You think there could be a secret compartment?" Riyan asked hopefully.

"I doubt it," he replied. "This has all the look of where it would have rested." He had almost completed his circuit of the pedestal when the floor opened up beneath him. "Damn!" he cried out as he reached out. His left hand grasped hold of the opening's edge and the sudden halt of his fall knocked the lantern from out of his other hand. Just as he brought his right hand up to join his left in hanging on, the lantern smashed against the bottom of the shaft.

The others were right there a second later and helped him back up out of the pit. They looked down at the bottom a good thirty feet below where their sole lantern lay busted. The base of the lantern had ruptured when it hit and burning oil covered most of the ground down there.

"Now what?" Chad asked. Then he groaned as Kevik's bobbing sphere appeared and began bobbing about.

"It's better than the dark," Riyan said.

"Not by much," replied Chad.

Bart stared down at the flames. He sighed and was about to turn away when something caught his eye. At first he wasn't exactly sure what it was, only that something was other than it should be. Then he finally figured it out. One side of the pit at the bottom near the flames was darker than the others. It could be a passage.

"Well, well, well," he said with a grin.

"What?" asked Riyan as he and the others came to see what he was talking about.

Bart directed their gaze to the bottom of the shaft. "Look there to the right, "he said. "I think that's a passage."

"A passage?" asked Chad. "Isn't that sort of a dumb place for one?"

Bart shook his head. "Actually I think it's a pretty ingenious place for one," he countered. "If the lantern hadn't dropped, we never would have suspected it was there." Then he turned to Riyan. "And what would we have done then?"

"Left thinking that the key was gone?" he guessed.

"Precisely!" he exclaimed. "I would bet every bit of treasure we have found so far that the key lies somewhere down that passage."

"But how are we to get down there?" asked Kevik. "It's pretty far."

"Simple," explained Bart. "If you're up for one more of your goo spells you could use it to adhere the end of the rope up here while we climb down." He looked to Kevik until he nodded that he could. "Excellent. How long does it last?"

"Up to an hour," he said, "if I don't dispel it first."

"That should give us enough time," he said. Then he began preparing his rope. "You three may wish to leave your packs up here," he told them. "Make it easier for you to shinny down the rope."

They began taking off their packs and setting them by the base of the pedestal. When Kevik had his off, he turned to find Bart ready with the rope. He had placed its end at the edge of the pit directly over the opening of the passage below. The end of the rope rested a foot from the edge. "Just cast it there," Bart told him as he pointed to the end of the rope.

Kevik nodded and cast his spell. A green globule appeared atop the rope and quickly adhered it to the stone. By the time the goo finished settling, some of it had oozed over the edge of the pit.

Bart tugged the rope hard but the goo wouldn't release it. "Good enough," he said. "I'll go down first. Once I'm there I'll holler up and then you follow one at a time." The others nodded. He then went to the edge of the pit and began lowering himself over the edge. Before he disappeared out of sight, he pointed to where the green goo oozed over the side, "Be careful of that. You get stuck and you may have to stay there until we're done." Then he began descending the rope quickly.

The smoke in the shaft was annoying but not overwhelming as the lantern oil burned below. He had to make sure that when he landed at the bottom that he didn't settle onto a burning patch. Foot by foot he continued his descent. When he neared the bottom, he could feel the heat from the flames.

Glancing down, he saw the opening just below him and the pool of burning oil on the floor before it. He came up with an idea. Moving to the side of the opening, he worked his way down a little further. Then just before he reached the floor, he kicked against the wall with his feet. Angling slightly over towards the opening, he swung outward and then came back into the mouth of the passage. Once past the pool of burning oil, he came to land a good foot from the edge of the flames.

He moved back as far as he could and stuck his head out of the passage. "I'm down," he hollered back up to the others.

At the top of the shaft, the others looked at each other. "Who's next?" Chad asked.

When no one else volunteered, Riyan said, "I'll go. Then you Kevik." When Kevik nodded, Riyan moved to the edge of the pit and grabbed the rope. Edging ever so gently over the side, he made sure to avoid coming in contact with the green goo. Then he began entering the pit. He had a few heart stopping moments before he reached the passage opening. Once there, Bart grabbed hold of him and helped him in avoiding the flames.

Next came Kevik and then Chad. Once they were all down, Kevik's bobbing sphere appeared among them. "Stay close," Bart told him as he took the lead. The passage extended straight away from the pit for over a hundred feet before coming to a room very similar to the one with the pedestal. Only this time there wasn't a pedestal. Instead there were three doors set in the far wall about three feet apart.

When Riyan saw the doors he asked, "I take it only one door will open to where we want to go?"

"That's the way I would figure it," replied Bart. "The other two I'm sure will be trapped in some way."

"Joy," groaned Chad.

To Riyan and Chad, Bart said, "You two wait out in the passage."

"What about me?" asked Kevik.

"I need your light so you're staying with me," he explained.

Kevik did not like the sound of that. "Very well," he replied with little enthusiasm.

With Kevik's light bouncing about, Bart moved to the doors and began an examination of each. He fervently hoped that they would give him some indication which one would be safe to open. But, after ten minutes of fruitless searching, he came up with nothing.

"Guess we'll just have to open them and hope for the best," he said.

"Do you think that's wise?" asked Kevik.

"Not in the least," Bart replied. "Which one should we open first?"

Kevik looked at him in shock. "You want me to pick?"

"Sure," Bart said with a grin. "I can't tell which one so your guess is as good as any."

He glanced over to Riyan and Chad but they were no help. Turning back to Bart he said, "The one on the left?"

"Left it is," said Bart. He then moved to the left door and grabbed the handle. Turning it ever so slowly, he braced himself to dart backward if things went bad. When nothing happened, he slowly pulled the door open.

As the door opened, they began to hear a grinding noise coming from the other side. He glanced to the others questioningly then pulled the door all the way open. The door opened onto a wall of stone that was beginning to sink into the ground.

"Could be opening the way to the key," suggested Riyan.

Bart didn't think so but kept his opinion to himself. Then all of a sudden, drops of water appeared at the top of the door. Then the drops became drips that steadily increased in volume and speed.

"Oh my god!" Bart yelled as he shut the door quickly. "It's opening up a conduit for the river to enter." He then motioned for Riyan and Chad to come forward. "You two hold this door," he said. "If you don't, we'll all drown."

They came and put their shoulders against it as Bart turned to the other two doors. He didn't think it would be the middle one as it was in close proximity to the water trap. So he tried the door on the right. It was locked. He placed his pack on the ground and quickly removed his picks. That's when he noticed water beginning to pool on the floor. He glanced to the door Riyan and Chad were holding and saw a steady stream of water seeping in through the cracks all around the door.

"Can you hold it?" he asked. Riyan nodded but he could see that he and Chad were under great strain in holding the door closed. Returning to the locked door, he quickly removed his two picks and set to work on the lock. In a matter of seconds he had it opened.

He replaced his picks in the rolled leather and put the rolled leather back in his pack. Then he pulled the door quickly open. On the other side was another long passage extending away.

"Kevik, come with me," he said. Then to Riyan and Chad he added, "I'll be back." Riyan only nodded. With Kevik following along behind, he practically flew down the passage as he knew time was rapidly running out.

The passage went for over a hundred feet before ending abruptly at a sigil inscribed wall. He was quick to recognize it as identical in nature to what they had found at the bottom of The Crypt. The only difference was that in the middle of the sigils were four separate, indented spaces. Each of the indented spaces was curved and sank three inches into the wall with a two inch space separating it from its neighbors. Looking at the spaces together, they appeared to form a circle.

"What is that?" Kevik asked.

Bart turned to looked at him. "It's what we came here for." He examined the spaces more closely. Upon the stone within the backs of the spaces were engravings. When he had Kevik come closer so his bobbing sphere could illuminate them better, he discovered that the engravings were of the four coats of arms that they had seen at the bottom of the crypt. The dragon-sword, the two headed falcon, the one with the stripe running from the upper left corner diagonally to the bottom right, and the five pointed crown that they believed belonged to the king himself.

In his mind's eye, he pictured the key that they had in their possession. He had studied it enough while lying in Riyan's bed recovering from the poison. It looked as if their part of the key would fit snugly into any one of the spaces. But would just one work? His mind raced over the problem, he knew he didn't have much time.

"Bart …" Kevik began but Bart waved him quiet. He had to concentrate.

There were four spaces which could only mean there were four segments of the key. If that supposition was correct, and one of the segments lay beyond this wall, then why have four spaces here in this wall? Obviously you couldn't use the key segment lying beyond the wall to open the wall; it had to mean something else.

"Bart …" Kevik said again, this time with a little more urgency.

"Not now!" Bart said sternly back at him.

The segments of the key had to be magical in nature, of that he was positive. What if the sigils inscribed upon the wall were set to recognize the various keys? Maybe by placing one in its correct space upon the wall, that would cause a secret door to open? It was worth a shot. Then he remembered that their segment was sitting way back above the shaft where Riyan and the others had left their packs.

Turning around, he started to tell Kevik to follow when his foot splashed in water. There was over an inch of water on the floor. He glanced up to Kevik who said, "That's what I was trying to tell you."

"Come on!" Bart yelled. "We haven't much time." Racing down the passage, they splashed through the water until they returned to the room where Riyan and Chad were holding the door against the water.

"Tell me you have it!" Riyan hollered when Bart and Kevik entered the room. Water was flowing steadily through the cracks in the door and it looked like the door was beginning to bow in from the pressure on the other side.

"Almost," he replied. "I need the key we found." He and Kevik started to race back down the passage to the shaft when Riyan hollered for him to stop.

"It's not up there," Riyan said. "It's in my belt pouch."

Bart looked and saw that his belt pouch was bulging pretty good. He had thought it was the many coins they had found. "Thank goodness," he said and moved to get it.

"What's going on?" asked Chad.

"I'll tell you when we get out of here," he replied. Undoing the string holding the pouch closed, he reached in and pulled forth the key. Light from the bobbing sphere reflected off its shiny surface. He saw Kevik's eyebrows arch when he saw it. "Back we go," he told him, then they raced back down the passage to the wall.

When he reached the wall, he started to put the key segment into one of the spaces then stopped. What if he put it in the wrong one? Which one was the right one? Then he glanced to the key segment and saw the sigils. Perhaps they would align with those crisscrossing the wall before him?

Testing that theory, he moved it closer to the wall and placed it before each of the spaces to see which would line up with the sigils best. As it turned out, the space with the five pointed crown was a perfect match. Hoping he was understanding this right, he inserted the key into the wall.

As soon as he inserted the key all the way to the back of the space, the sigils surrounding it flared. Then the wall to his right began rising into the ceiling. "Yes!" he yelled. Once the wall was up far enough, he ducked under and passed through to the other side.

It was a bare and nondescript room, with but a single pedestal rising out of the middle of the floor. His eyes lit up as he saw lying there before him on the pedestal, which was an exact duplicate of the one they found in the room above, another segment of the key. Grinning, he moved forward and picked it up. After what he just did to open this place, it was quite unlikely there would be a trap here.

Once he held the segment in hand, he quickly put it in his pack and left the room. The water covering the floor was several inches deep now and it was time to leave. He went to the four recesses and used his knife to pry out the first segment. Once it was out, the wall began sliding back down to hide the hidden room.

"Let's get out of here," he said to Kevik and then broke into a run back to where they had left Riyan and Chad.

Back at the room, they were still holding the door with all their might, but it continued to gradually bow outward. The water flowing from the cracks around the door was no longer a trickle but more like a steady stream.

Bart and Kevik ran back into the room. "Got it!" Bart yelled triumphantly. "Now let's get out of here."

Riyan and Chad glanced to each other and simultaneously let go of the door. No sooner had they let it loose than the water on the other side broke through. The water burst through the door with such power, that it knocked the door from its hinges and slammed it into Riyan and Chad.

When the door hit them they went down with a cry as a veritable torrent of water shot through the opening. It was as if the entire river had been diverted to flow through the doorway.

"Riyan!" Bart yelled as he saw them go down. The water pushed him back as it rapidly began filling the room and the passages of this level. "Kevik, help me!"

Riyan broke the surface but there was no sign of Chad.

Bart immediately dove under the water and groped with his hands until he found Chad. He then pulled him upwards and Chad gave out with a groan as he broke through to the surface.

Kevik appeared beside him and together they managed to keep Chad above water. "Are you two okay?" Bart asked.

Riyan nodded but Chad looked like he was in some serious pain.

"We have to make it to the shaft!" Bart yelled over the roar of the water. Already the water level was chest high and rising. "Help Chad."

Riyan came forward and together with Kevik, began helping Chad into and then down the long passage to the shaft that led up to the pedestal room on the next level. "Keep going!" yelled Bart when Kevik paused to look back to him. He could see Bart had hold of the door that broke off and was pushing it along the surface of the water after them. There was no time to wonder what he was going to do with it as the water was now up to their chins with only another foot of space before reaching the ceiling. Urging Chad onward, they drew ever closer to the shaft.

Bart was finding it increasingly difficult to continue moving the door down the passage. The water was now so high that he didn't have proper leverage on the floor and was beginning to lag behind. He was afraid that he might not make it in time.

Ahead of him he could see that Riyan had already reached the shaft and that Kevik and Chad were right behind him. With but inches separating the water and the ceiling, it was all he could do to continue moving forward and breathe. Finally he gave up trying to push along the floor and simply began swimming.

He kicked and paddled as he pushed the door along until he felt the door being pulled from the other side. The last few feet to the shaft he was completely submerged under the water as the water had finally completely filled the passage.

When he broke the surface, he found himself in the shaft and the water was shooting them up to the top quickly. He grabbed his rope that was still secured by the goo spell. "Kevik!" he hollered. "Get rid of the goo." He looked up and saw the opening coming fast. Just before they reached the top, he hollered, "Try to grab your packs. The room up there will fill with water too as it's beneath the level of the river."

Then the water shot them out and they were literally thrown into the air before coming to land. Bart couldn't tell if they managed to get their packs or not as he was concerned with maintaining contact with the door. But in the churning water he lost his hold and couldn't locate it as the water continued to fountain out of the shaft with incredible pressure.

The water was a churning torrent that threw them one way then another. When he realized they would be lucky to make it out with their lives, he hollered, "Get to the stairs!" Looking around, he saw that Kevik and Chad were already entering the passage leading to the stairwell. Of Riyan there was no sign.

He knew he had to get out of there, the room was already practically filled with water and completely would be in a matter of seconds. Swimming for the passage, he almost made it when he was bumped into by Riyan coming up from beneath the water.

"Where did you go?" he asked.

"Got the packs," Riyan replied with a grin. Then together they swam for the stairs.

The water quickly filled the room and pushed them along the stairwell. It took them almost to the top before the rising water subsided. Kevik and Chad were the first to climb out of the water and onto the stairs with Bart right behind. Riyan brought up the rear, dragging their three packs with him. He saw the rope coiled around Bart's arm.

They made it to the top of the stairs then collapsed.

Chapter 27

Riyan was quick to get the fire they left banked on the landing restored to life. The others came from the steps and embraced its warmth. Chad wasn't doing too good, there was pain coming from his back. When the door struck him, it had injured his back in some way, maybe even broken something. He was fortunate that the blow didn't paralyze him.

After Kevik and Bart helped him to the fire, Bart dug one of the potions they had found earlier out of his pack and gave it to him. "Here," he said as he handed it to him.

Chad could barely reach out to take it as the movement of his muscles aggravated his injury and flared the already unbearable pain to such an extent that dots formed before his eyes. Kevik had to help him open the bottle before he could drink it. Then he put it to his lips and drank it down. As soon as the elixir within the bottle passed through his throat, the pain began subsiding.

Bart could see the pain in his eyes beginning to ease, along with the stiffness in the rest of his body.

"Man that feels better," Chad said after a few minutes. In the area of his back where the pain had flared the worst, he began to notice a warming sensation that continued to intensify until just before it became uncomfortable. Not an unpleasant sensation, it was more a reassuring one as Chad new the injury was being repaired by the potion.

"I was worried about you for awhile there," admitted Riyan.

Chad gave him a grin, "So was I."

Then they saw the glitter of gold as Bart removed the two segments of the key and showed them to the others. He went on to tell them what he saw down below, how he had opened the door, and finally the finding of the second segment.

"So does this mean there are two more somewhere?" asked Kevik.

"It looks that way," he replied. Then he glanced to Riyan. "It may take some time before we can discover where to find the other two segments."

Riyan nodded. "I figured that as soon as I saw the second segment."

Bart held the two pieces close together and then turned them so the map on the back was visible. "They go together," he told the others. Indeed, they could see how the edge of the map of the original one matched the edge of the second. If you were to put them together there would be one continuous map.

"Are there any indications of where the other segments may be?" Chad asked. Since markings on the first one had led them to the Ruins of Algoth where the second segment was located, he hoped there would be something similar on the second segment that would lead them to a third.

Bart brought the second segment closer to the light of the fire and examined it closely but couldn't make out any such markings. He finally looked up at the others and shook his head. "No, nothing."

"Too bad," Chad said.

The fire crackled in the silence as the four comrades sat on the ledge next to the flowing river. Bart was fiddling with the two segments and brought them together so the edges touched, he was wondering if they would fuse together or something. To his disappointment, nothing happened when they touched. Shrugging, he handed the two segments to Chad so he and the others could examine them. Then he stood up and stretched.

Riyan glanced at him and saw Bart begin moving to the passage leading back to the flooded stairwell and tunnels. "Where are you going?" he asked.

Bart paused and said, "I want to see if I can find that door."

"What do you want that for anyway?" Kevik asked.

Turning to gaze towards him, Bart said, "It would give us something to hold onto when we went down the river."

Kevik nodded his head in understanding. "Do you need some help?" he asked.

"Maybe your light would be helpful," he replied.

"Alright," Kevik said then got to his feet and joined him. His bobbing sphere appeared and they began walking down the passage together.

When they reached the top of the stairs, the light from the sphere revealed that the water flooding the lower area came to within ten feet of the top of the stairs. The door was nowhere in sight.

"I was hoping it wouldn't come to this," Bart sighed as he shed his pack. He set it down against the wall and began uncoiling his rope.

"What do you plan to do?" Kevik asked.

With the rope now uncoiled, Bart tied it around his waist as he turned back to Kevik. "I'm going after it," he explained. "I would appreciate it if you could hold onto the end of the rope for me."

"Sure," he said. "I can do that." He picked up the other end of the rope and stood ready.

"Once I go under, start counting," Bart told him. "If you get to two hundred before I return, start pulling me back."

"Are you sure you can hold your breath that long?" Kevik asked.

Bart nodded. "Two hundred and no more understand?"

"I understand."

Tuning back to the stairs, Bart began moving down them to the water's edge. When his foot entered the water, it sent a shiver of cold through him. He tried to disregard the coldness as he moved further into the water. Once he reached the place where it was up to his neck, he glanced back to Kevik and saw that he was ready. He then took several deep breaths in succession before diving under the surface.

"One ... two ... three ...," Kevik began counting.

Bart soon left the glow from Kevik's bobbing sphere behind as he swam down into the darkness below. He knew that the door would be pressed against the ceiling somewhere, its buoyancy would see to that. So as he swam he periodically ran his hand along the stone ceiling in search of the wood.

He's pretty sure that the door would still be in the room at the top of the shaft. That's where he had lost track of it. Somehow he's got to get it into the passage leading to the stairwell before his air ran out.

Deeper he went into the darkness until he felt the ceiling all of a sudden rise higher telling him he had entered the room. From there he began checking the room's ceiling. By this time, the effort to keep from breathing was growing increasingly harder. He knew he didn't have much time left so quickly searched for the door.

After a few moments his hand hit something. It was the door. The water held it pressed tightly to the ceiling. He then moved to the other side and began working it to the opening of the passage leading to the stairwell.

It was hard going but he moved it several feet before he felt a tug on the rope as Kevik began reeling him back in. He let go of the door and quickly swam back along the rope's path until his head broke through the surface.

The air that had been trapped inside burst out as his lungs began drawing fresh air into them. He started coughing as droplets of water were sucked down with his first inhalation.

"Did you find it?"

He looked up to see Riyan and Chad standing next to Kevik. Nodding, he coughed a couple more times then said, "Yes I did. It's in the room at the other end of the passage. Give me a minute to catch my breath and I'll try again."

Then he glanced to Chad. "How's your back?"

"Good as new," he replied then did a few bends and twists to emphasize the point.

"Don't overdue it," cautioned Bart.

"I won't," Chad assured him. He looked tired, the magic of the potion again having used energy from his body in its healing.

Bart rested a few minutes then returned to the water. It took him another two times before he was able to bring the door out of the room and up the stairwell. When he broke the surface with the door in hand, the other three cheered.

Riyan and Kevik grabbed the door and brought it out to the landing where they set it down next to the fire. When Chad returned with Bart, Riyan asked, "What do you plan to do with it?"

"Quite simple really," he explained. "We set our packs in the center of the door then wind the rope in and around them to create four loops large enough to hold each of us. One loop will extend over each of the four sides of the door so we won't be knocked together if things get rough. Then Kevik casts his goo spell so that it will coat all the packs and bind the rope to the door." He could see that the others were beginning to understand his plan.

"After that it's fairly straightforward," he continued. "We put the door with packs and rope already secured by the goo into the water. Then we get into the water, place ourselves within the loops, and ride the river out of here."

"What if it doesn't go anywhere?" asked Chad.

Bart turned a grim smile towards him. "Then our adventure comes to an end." He glanced around at the others and said, "If anyone here has a better plan, now would be the time to mention it." When the others remained silent, he nodded. "Very well then. Shall we get it ready?"

They took their four packs and placed them in the center of the door just as Bart had said. They weren't willing to risk the two segments of the key by keeping them in the packs, so Bart and Riyan each put one of the segments in their belt pouches for safekeeping.

Once the packs were in position on the door, Bart took his rope and looped it around so it crisscrossed through the packs several times. When he was done, a loop extended past the edge of the door on all four sides. Then he said to Kevik, "Your turn."

Nodding, Kevik cast his goo spell. The green globule appeared on top of the packs and quickly oozed its way down to the door beneath. When its movement finally stopped, Bart had each of them grip a different loop. Then with all of them straining hard, they pulled and jerked the loops. Bart grinned to himself when after all they tried to do, not one loop came undone from the goo coating.

"So we have about an hour?" he asked Kevik about the goo.

"Something like that," he replied. "I've never actually timed it before, but that's what I was told by my master."

Bart nodded. "Good enough for me. If after an hour we're still in the water, we'll try to find someplace to land and redo it." Taking his loop in hand he and the others lifted the makeshift door-raft and carried it to the water's edge.

"Let me get in first," suggested Riyan. "That way I can steady it while the rest of you take your position." Riyan let go of his loop and quickly slipped over the side of the landing. Once he was in the water and had a secure hold on the landing's edge, he indicated for them to put the raft in the water.

Moving it to the edge, they slid it into the water. Riyan immediately ducked under the surface and came up within the loop closest to the landing. Then he again gripped the landing's edge. "Alright," he said, "now the rest of you one at a time."

Bart was the first one to enter the water and took his position in another loop. Then he helped Riyan hold the raft against the current while first Kevik, then Chad, entered the water and took their position.

Chad, being the last to enter, had to work his way around the edge of the raft before he came to the last loop. Once he was within the loop, Bart and Riyan let go. The current immediately pulled them away from the landing and swept them downstream quickly.

The underground river turned to the right and the raft drifted to the outside of the curve. Chad happened to be on that side and when the current moved them too close to the wall, he used his feet to kick them back towards the middle.

Above the raft were three bobbing spheres. Riyan had requested Kevik to supply more light so they could better keep an eye on what was coming ahead. They didn't have paddles or oars so would need some warning if they should all of a sudden need to change their position on the river to avoid an obstacle.

As the river finished its curve, it began moving along a straighter channel. Not too far past the curve, Kevik noticed another landing on the inside bank of the river. "Another landing!" he hollered when he saw it.

"It might be the way out!" cried Bart.

They used their arms and legs in an attempt to gain the other side of the river but the current was too strong. Bart suggested they dismantle their raft and use the ropes and packs like they had done before. But they were moving far too quickly away from the landing for them to have it ready in time to use, so they decided against it. All they could do was float in the water, secure in their loops, while the landing disappeared behind them.

Floating along as they were was fairly comfortable actually. If they could ignore the coldness of the water it really wasn't all that bad. They had the rope loops to keep them from sinking, while the door itself gave them something to hold onto.

Several minutes after the landing disappeared behind them, the current of the river felt as if it was picking up. Then from further ahead came the unmistakable sound of rapids. "This could get interesting," commented Riyan.

"No matter what happens," Bart said, "don't let go of your loop."

"Wasn't planning on it," Chad told him.

The surface of the water that had been so placid thus far began rocking them back and forth. They hung on as the river's speed increased and they saw the approach of the rapids. Their little makeshift raft was soon being thrown about as the water crashed over the rocks. They would be plunged down one watery furrow, before a swell would raise them high only to be slammed back down again. Once when the wave slammed them down, they were jarred fiercely when the door landed on a rock that was protruding out of the water.

"We're stuck," hollered Kevin fearfully as they teetered there upon the tip of the stone.

"Rock it back and forth!" yelled Bart. Water kept crashing into them but failed to dislodge their raft. They shifted their weight from one side to the next as they attempted to dislodge their raft from the rock. Riyan and Chad were in good position to use their feet against the sides of the rock for leverage. Then suddenly, they were free and again being tossed by the water.

Their raft would turn round about as the water kept thrashing them. First Riyan's side of the raft would be facing downstream, then it would be Kevik's turn. Back and forth and roundabout they went as the water continued to crash over the rocks. They each kept a look ahead of them as best they could to avoid dangers.

"A rock!" said Bart.

Just ahead of them a large rock thrust its way out of the water, the river was crashing fiercely upon its side. Riyan was in perfect position to be rammed into it. He pointed to the left and yelled, "That way!" Using their feet and arms they worked the raft so that it only grazed the side of the rock. Riyan kicked out at it to keep his body from being crushed between it and the edge of the door.

"How much more of this is there?" yelled Chad.

From Bart's position he could see ahead of them for as far as the spheres illuminated. "Still a ways," he replied. Then he saw where the river was about to go down a series of shallow falls. "Hold on!" he yelled.

Riyan looked over his shoulder and saw what was coming. "Oh my god," he said then braced himself as the raft went over the first drop. It was only five feet, but when he hit, Riyan felt like he had fallen a hundred. Then the raft slammed painfully into his chest and pushed him even further under the water.

The blow to his chest seemed to stun his lungs for when he broke the surface, he couldn't get a breath. Then his lungs eased up and after few anxious moments, could start drawing breaths again.

"Here comes another one!" Kevik yelled as they headed for the lip of the next fall.

Riyan panicked at the thought of another blow like the last one. But then he realized the raft had turned and he wouldn't be directly beneath it when it hit this time. He gripped the loop holding him to the raft tightly as they went over the edge.

This one was a three tiered fall and by the time they reached the bottom, they were all bruised and battered. Kevik thought he may have broken his leg. At this point the river calmed down and began flowing normally once more.

"Everyone alright?" Riyan asked.

"No," replied Kevik through gritted teeth. "My leg hit a rock during those last rapids. I think it may be broken."

Riyan turned to Chad and Bart. "We need to get him out of the water and look at it," he told them. They nodded and began searching for a place where they could make landfall. A few minutes later, an area came into view that looked like it would do. The walls of the channel the water flowed through began to widen and a shelf of sorts appeared on their right. It was at least six inches higher than the surface of the water and wide enough for them to rest upon.

They paddled as best they could towards it. Kevik of course was dead weight due to his injury. When they drew close to the shelf, they found that the river was shallower here and they could touch the bottom. When they're next to the edge, Bart and Riyan helped Kevik out of his loop and up onto the shelf. Chad took charge of the raft and made sure it didn't float away.

Setting Kevik on the shelf, Bart placed his hands on the suspected broken leg. He moved them gently up and down as he sought the break. After several minutes he looked to Kevik and said, "I don't think it's broken."

"You sure?" he asked.

Bart nodded. "The bone feels fine," he explained. "You probably just bruised it."

"That's a relief," he said.

They decided to take a break there on the shelf to give them some time out of the water before continuing. Bart and Riyan helped Chad in pulling the raft up onto the shelf. Once it was out of the water and resting on the ground, Kevik canceled his goo spell so Riyan could give him some of his healing potion. Not all of it, just enough to ease the pain.

Propping themselves against the back wall of the shelf, they rested for a short time. While Riyan was resting he noticed how the shelf ran along the river past where the light from the spheres extended. "Wonder if we could walk the rest of the way?" he asked.

"Rest of the way to where?" asked Kevik.

"I don't know," he admitted. "Maybe this comes out at the lake or something."

Bart nodded, "Could definitely give it a try. If it doesn't, we could always come back here to the raft."

"I just wish we had a regular lantern or torch," said Chad.

Riyan glanced at the bobbing spheres which have begun to grate on everyone's nerves. "Me too," he agreed.

After resting for a little longer to give the potion ample time to work on Kevik, they returned to their feet. They each took their pack and Bart coiled the rope before placing it in his. Then they began making their way along the shelf. The shelf continued to follow the river and at times would grow quite narrow as to be almost nonexistent. Other times it widened sufficiently so all four could walk abreast if they wished.

They had followed the shelf for twenty minutes before it ended at a rock formation that jutted out from the wall. In order to continue they would have to enter the river and work their way around the obstruction to the other side. Which after a quick confab they decided to do.

Riyan went first with Chad following right behind. Bart brought up the rear as they entered the water and edged out to move around the outcrop. Riyan maintained his balance against the current by holding on as best he could to the cracks and crevices in the face of the outcrop.

The worst part was when he began moving around the end of the outcrop. He almost lost his footing as the current was at its strongest there. But he managed to work his way around to the other side.

"The shelf continues on," he hollered back to the others when he could see it.

"Good news," he heard Bart reply.

One by one they made their way around the point of the outcrop. Riyan had remained out at the point to assist the others. It didn't take long before they were once again back on the shelf and continuing on.

The underground channel they were walking through was quiet except for the occasional lapping of water against the sides. None of them felt much like talking, exhaustion resulting from all they've recently gone through had sapped their desire for conversation. And it was in this quiet that the warbling of a bird was suddenly heard.

Riyan came to a stop and asked, "Did you hear that?"

Again the warbling echoed down the channel. "It's a bird!" exclaimed Kevik.

"That means the way out can't be too far away," Bart said. "Can you tell where it's coming from."

They paused for a moment as each listened to the bird's call. "It's coming from up ahead," Chad finally said.

"Then what are we waiting for?" Kevik said. "I for one am anxious to get out of here."

Bart sighed. "So am I."

With the possibility of escaping this underground world and returning to the outside before them, they hurried forward with renewed energy. Shortly, they began to smell flowers and other vegetation and then they were out. The river left the mouth of an underground cave and then worked its way down among the hills to the small lake off in the distance.

It was still night, the moon overhead shining bright. "Were we down there all day?" asked Chad.

"It would seem so," replied Bart.

"No wonder I'm so tired," yawned Riyan.

"But now is not the time to rest," Bart told the others. "We still need to get out of goblin territory."

"Are we finished in Algoth then?" asked Chad.

"We found what we came for," replied Bart. "Now it's time to go."

They couldn't help but to turn their gaze southeastward towards the mountains that marked the boundary between goblin lands and that of humans. Hidden in the night, their mighty peaks were but a pale shadowy whisper against the backdrop of stars.

Riyan finally broke the quiet by saying, "It's not getting any closer with us just standing here." And with that they headed out.

Lights could be seen on the far side of the small lake where the underground river finally ended, indicating another of the goblin villages. Riyan, Chad, and Kevik began to move off through the hills when Bart suddenly stopped and grew thoughtful. Riyan was quick to notice his friend not following and came to a stop as well.

"What is it?" he asked. Chad and Kevik came to a stop and returned back to the other two.

"I was thinking that if we were to take a boat from yonder village," he explained as he pointed off to the distant lights, "then we could reach the Marketplace all the quicker."

"Seems a bit risky to me," argued Chad.

Bart turned to him and said, "So is hoofing it on foot across goblin infested lands. They know we're here somewhere," Then he sniffed and added, "From the smell of it the fire is still burning and it's between us and the mountains."

The air did still smell of smoke. "They have ponies too," Riyan said in support of Bart's suggestion. "On horses we could outrun them, but not on foot."

"And don't forget," chimed in Kevik, "even when the goblins were on foot the only reason they didn't catch us was that we passed the totem and entered Algoth."

Chad could see they were in support of Bart's plan. "Very well," he agreed.

Bart nodded. "Okay. Let's get down to the water's edge and then Chad and Kevik, you two wait on the shore while Riyan and I go steal us a boat."

"Me?" asked Riyan. He was nervous about entering into a goblin village. Visions of his death rolled through his mind.

"Yes you," Bart said. "I need someone to watch my back and you're the only one not weakened by recent injury."

Riyan swallowed and nodded. "Alright," he said. His voice revealed the nervousness that he was feeling.

Chapter 28

Once they reached the lakeshore, Riyan and Bart had removed their packs and left them there with Chad and Kevik to await their return. Bart did put his lockpicks within his shirt. Riyan eyed him questioningly about that.

"My picks go where I go," was the only answer he gave before they headed out.

Now, they stood behind the bole of a large tree at the edge of the goblin village. The buildings were similar in size and design to the ones Bart had seen in the settlement they had come across on their way to Algoth. The whole place looked peaceful with only a small portion of the windows having light.

"Looks like almost everyone is asleep," Riyan whispered.

Bart nodded. Then he pointed further into the village toward the shore of the lake. There they saw a dock to which a dozen or so boats were moored in the moonlight. "Come on," he said, "and be silent."

Riyan followed as Bart moved quickly to the side of the nearest building. Its windows were dark and was situated closest to the water's edge. Then after a brief pause to be sure they remained undetected, they repeated their dash to the next building. From building to building they repeated their mad dash as they drew ever closer to the dock and the boats secured there.

Suddenly, Bart placed an arm across Riyan's chest and pressed him to the side of the building. A split second later, two goblin men emerged from the side of the building and began making their way toward the dock.

They were talking to themselves in their guttural language. One held a large net and the other two small boxes. From the looks of them Riyan guessed they were fishermen heading out for an early morning catch.

Bart and Riyan remained motionless against the building as the two goblins reached the dock and began removing the mooring lines from one of the boats. Other sounds began coming to them as the village started to stir and they could see where lights appeared in more of the windows. The village was waking up.

"We can't stay here!" Riyan whispered earnestly in fear.

"Quiet!" replied Bart.

The two fishermen had finished releasing the mooring lines and were beginning to head out.

"Come on," Bart said. Moving out quickly, he practically ran in the dark towards the dock. Riyan followed.

All around them they could hear goblins speaking to one another within their homes. Terror at being caught almost immobilized Riyan but he somehow kept going. They hit the dock and Bart immediately went all the way down to the small, four-seater moored at the end of the dock. "Hurry Riyan," he whispered back to him as he reached the boat and started untying the lines.

Riyan quickly raced down the end of the dock and made his way into the boat. He glanced back to the village and could see goblins moving about, fortunately none were heading their way at the moment.

Then the rope that had moored the boat to the dock was tossed inside followed quickly by Bart. Riyan held one of the oars in his hand that had been lying in the bottom and handed the other to Bart. Working together, they began paddling the boat quickly out onto the lake.

Riyan kept glancing back to the village, but so far none of the goblins had yet discovered the theft. He sighed in relief and his fear began subsiding as the distance between them and the dock grew.

To the east, the sky was just beginning to lighten with the coming of dawn. They needed to find Kevik and Chad quickly before it grew light enough for the goblins to see them out upon the lake.

They rowed for another quarter hour as they searched the shoreline for the other two. The fishermen they had seen earlier must have gone to a different location to fish as they didn't encounter them.

Finally, they saw the pair on the shoreline waving to them. They paddled harder and when they reached the shore, ran the prow of the boat up onto the beach. "I started thinking something had happened to you," Chad said as he threw the packs into the boat.

"We need to hurry," Riyan said to them. Gesturing back to the village he added, "They're beginning to awaken."

With the packs now in the bottom of the boat, Kevik hopped in and then Chad pushed them off the shore. As Chad jumped in, Riyan and Bart used the oars to turn the boat around and headed towards the mouth of the river leading to the larger lake by the Marketplace.

The sky continued to lighten as they rowed across the lake. The mountaintops of the range separating the two lands became more distinct and the darkness around the four comrades in the boat began to diminish. Also visible was a dark plume of smoke rising some distance away between them and the mountains. Obviously the fire still continued to rage.

"Look!" said Kevik and they turned to see several other boats now out on the water. Goblins were seen throwing nets out over the water as they gathered in the fish.

"Doesn't look like they're searching for the missing boat," Riyan observed.

"No it doesn't," replied Bart. "It may not ever occur to them that it was stolen by humans. After all, how often do humans make it this far?"

"I hope you're right," said Chad.

They continued rowing hard until the mouth of the river appeared ahead of them. As the bow of the boat entered the river, Riyan glanced back one last time to see if any pursuit had developed. He was greatly relieved to see that none had.

While the sky continued lightening, they rowed. They kept on the lookout for a place to hole up through the day as they didn't dare risk being on the river during the daylight hours. When the sky lightened to the extent that they dared not proceed any further, they beached the boat and carried it inland to hide among the trees.

The boat was fairly heavy but they managed to lift it and carry it into the trees so as not to leave a tell-tale drag mark on the shore. They carried it a hundred feet into the forest before setting it back to the ground. Exhausted and hungry, they settled down to wait for the coming of night when they would return to the river and make their way to the large lake before morning dawned once more.

"Riyan," Bart said. "Why don't you use your sling and find us something to eat?"

"I really don't want raw meat," Riyan said. "I'd rather go hungry another day."

"With the smoke in the air from the fire downstream, I doubt if anyone is going to notice if we have a fire," Bart argued.

Riyan knew they were all hungry, with naught but a few strips of meat a day or so ago to sustain them. "Very well," he said, and took his sling. Picking up a couple stones he soon disappeared into the trees.

By the time he returned with two rabbits, the others had a fire going. They built it close to the side of the boat in order to hide it in the event a goblin passed by. But given the relative wildness of the surrounding trees and bush, it's unlikely goblins have traveled through this area recently.

The meal of roast rabbit was one of the best meals Riyan had ever had in his life. His mother always said hunger was the best seasoning, and she was right. Once the meal was over, they turned in. Riyan took the first watch as the others began resting. He kept an ever vigilant eye out for possible incursions near their camp by goblins, but what was on his mind mostly was the fire.

Smoke rose high into the sky before the upper air currents began pushing it eastward. What little breeze there was blew towards the fire, so hopefully it would keep it moving away from them. But, whether it does or not made no difference come morning for they planned to ride the river south, directly into the flames. Riyan wished they didn't have to come near the fire, but being on foot such as they would have to be in order to circumvent it, would take them far too long to reach another pass. And every extra day on this side of the mountains increased their chance of being spotted.

Throughout the day as the others took their turns at watch, they too couldn't help but watch the smoke rising. One shift at watch led to the next until darkness came again and they deemed the time was right to go. Bart went to scout the area by the river and once he made sure it was clear, returned to help bring the boat back to the water.

The mood in the boat was somber as it began floating down the river. Each kept his thoughts to himself as the river brought them ever closer to the forest fire.

It didn't take long before smoke began having more of a presence in the air. The further they went the thicker it became. Then from up ahead they saw the glow of the fire coming up ahead of them.

Sections of the forest were burning off a ways from the river on both sides. Smoldering areas adjacent to the river grew more frequent and in the moonlight they could see the burnt, smoking husks that had at one time been tall, stately trees.

Ash started to rain down on them as it settled back to earth and the heat from the fires began to be felt as well. Then all of a sudden, the boat came to a jarring stop as it ran aground. They were knocked off their seats from the unexpected impact.

"What happened?" asked Riyan as he got himself off the bottom of the boat.

"We ran into something," replied Bart.

As it turned out, they had run aground at the spot where they had forded the river on their way in. They could make out the roads moving from the river on both sides. "Everyone out," Bart said. "We have to pull the boat across the ford to deeper water."

They climbed out and positioned themselves around the boat. Then altogether they pulled it across the ford to the deeper water on the other side. When the boat once again floated freely, they hopped back in and continued on.

Smoke thickened, ash rained down on them constantly, and the temperature was beginning to climb. Some of the pieces of ash coming down were still glowing red, even full blown embers began dropping out of the sky. Riyan wondered about that until a tree next to the river suddenly popped.

Embers flew in all directions and they saw that the interior of the tree was glowing red. Even though the fire had already swept through this area, some of the trees were still smoldering on the inside.

"Kevik." Bart broke the silence as he said, "We need some light."

"But they'll see us!" argued Chad.

"We'll announce our presence," Riyan warned.

"Look, the smoke has all but obscured the moon's light," he explained. "We can't see where we're going. Besides, if there are any goblins in the area they'll either be going to the fire to fight it, or moving away from it in flight."

"Very well," replied Kevik. Then his bobbing orb appeared and began dancing above the boat.

"Thank you," said Bart. Kevik just nodded in reply.

Around them they could now better see the destruction left by the fire. Trees broken and smoldering, the ground a charred mess, and the ash raining down looked deceptively like snowflakes. Further along they began seeing small animals, or rather what was left of them, that had sought refuge by the fire. Some lay dead looking for all the world as if they were asleep, these must have died from the smoke. While others had their fur singed off and in some cases were still smoking, there was no doubt that the fire had gotten to those.

"Oh man," Chad said.

Riyan turned his gaze from the dead animals and glanced to Chad. He saw that he was looking ahead of them in fear. Riyan turned his gaze downriver and saw the fire arcing to the sky. To either side of the river the forest burned. The river looked like it was going to pass through the fires of hell, which wasn't that far from the truth.

When Bart turned and saw the inferno they were approaching, he immediately grabbed an oar and said, "Riyan, help me bring us to the shore."

Riyan grabbed the other oar and began paddling. The boat turned and began to angle towards the riverbank. "Are we going the rest of the way on foot?" he asked.

"No," Bart replied. "I was thinking we could soak our clothes and fill the bottom with water."

"That won't do any good," countered Kevik. "Not with what we're about to go through."

"What would you suggest then?" Bart asked. He again glanced to the inferno that began a little over a mile away.

"Turn the boat over," he said. When the others looked at him, he explained. "Turn the boat over and use it as a cover." Reaching down, he grabbed the edge of the seat. "We can hold onto the seats to keep our heads out of the water. Then we allow the river to carry us through."

Chad nodded. "That might work better than just soaking our clothes."

Bart grinned. "I like it too. Let's do it." Paddling hard, he and Riyan soon had the boat grounded on the riverbank.

They stepped out of the boat and put their packs on. Then they all moved to one side of the boat and as one, lifted the edge until it tipped over. Riyan and Bart then each took the oars and carried them as all four of them dragged the boat back into the water.

When they had it out far enough that they could duck under the surface of the water and get inside, Bart and Kevik went first while Riyan and Chad held the boat steady. "I hope we survive this," commented Chad.

"We will," Riyan assured him. "This idea of Kevik's is pretty good." A knocking came to them from the inside of the boat telling them Bart and Kevik were set. The two friends then ducked under the water and came up under the overturned boat.

"Grab on," Bart said as they broke the surface. Inside they found the bobbing sphere doing its annoying dance.

Riyan laid the oar he brought with him on top of the upside down seat and then grabbed on. The water wasn't so deep that their feet couldn't touch, so they began walking the boat out to deeper water. It didn't take long before they were floating free and the current was taking them towards the inferno.

"You can get rid of the light now," Chad said. A second later the orb disappeared.

Beneath the boat it was dark as they continued to float blind down the river. Then the water around them began to glow as they drew ever closer to the fire. Soon, the glow coming through the water was bright enough to allow them to see each other vaguely.

"We're within the fire," stated Chad. Indeed, the water was growing warm as the fire consuming the nearby trees heated it. The air within the boat grew warmer by the minute as well. Then falling debris began to patter against the topside like rain on a tin roof.

"We never would have made it through the fire if we were still sitting exposed in the boat out there," Riyan said.

"It doesn't look like it," Kevik said.

Suddenly from the other side of the bottom of the boat, they heard pounding. It wasn't the sound of debris falling, rather it sounded like the rhythmic banging a panicked person would do.

"Someone's out there!" Riyan exclaimed. Fear of goblins again surged within him. Then he saw the light coming through the water near him become occluded as the lower half of a body was seen right next to the boat. It was unmistakably that of a goblin.

"We can't leave it out there to burn," Chad said. From the intensity of the glow coming through the water, it was clear the temperature from the flames had to be pretty hot.

Then it grew quiet as the pounding ceased. Riyan watched the shadow of the body as it began to sag into the river. The need to help someone in danger somehow overcame his fear. He reached under the side of the boat and grabbed hold of it. When he pulled it beneath the boat with them, they discovered it was a young male goblin. One side of its face was scarred pretty badly with burns, and it lay unconscious in Riyan's grasp. The skin of the goblin was tougher than that of a human, to Riyan it felt akin to that of a reptile.

"Keep its head above water," Bart said as he moved over to assist Riyan. Together they managed to hold onto the goblin lad as they continued down the river.

"Is it alive?" asked Kevik.

"Yes," replied Riyan. He gazed at the face of the goblin youth and wondered just how old it was. It couldn't be too young as its size was approximately two thirds that of an adult.

"What are we going to do with it?" asked Kevik.

Bart turned to him and said, "Once we're safely past the fire and near the goblin settlement on the shore of the larger lake, we'll drop it off."

Riyan nodded, "They'll find him and take care of him." He and Bart continued holding on to the goblin youth as they drifted further into the inferno burning on the other side of the boat. The glow in the water by this time had intensified from an off orange to a brighter white. Curious, Riyan touched the top of the boat and drew his hand back quickly.

"Hot?" asked Bart with a grin.

"Very," he replied. "What do we do if the bottom of the boat catches fire?"

"If we're lucky we'll never find out," said Chad.

They continued floating for some time as they worked their way through the burning inferno. The temperature within the boat continued to rise. Already it was approaching an uncomfortable range. The goblin youth, other than a few grunts now and then, remained still and quiet.

Wham!

They were startled as something slammed into the bottom of the boat. It didn't inhibit their progress any, but it did scare them pretty good. "A falling limb perhaps?" guessed Kevik.

"Would think so," replied Riyan. "If it had been a tree the boat would have shattered or been pressed to the bottom of the river."

Still they floated on. From time to time their feet would touch the river bottom. When that happened they would try to move the boat back to the center of the river where the water was deeper. In some cases it was due to the fact that the river widened and thus the water level had dropped. During those times they feared running into another fording area where the depth of the river had diminished. They didn't relish the idea of having to leave the protection of the boat in order to carry it across. For the water outside the boat still glowed from the light of the fire, though it was no longer the white hot light. The reddish glow gave them hope that they had passed through the worst of it.

Riyan didn't worry too much about the eventuality of having to carry the boat over a ford. After all, rivers tended to grow in size the further they went, not diminish. It was during one of those times when they couldn't touch the bottom that he began to notice a red glow coming from the bottom of the boat above his head.

"The boat's on fire!" he yelled in a panic.

"What do we do?" Chad asked.

Riyan started splashing water on the glow in an attempt to inhibit the burning process. Some of the water hit the face of the goblin youth and it started to stir.

Bart stuck his hand under the side of the boat and moved it to the outside surface. When his hand broke the water, the air felt hot, but not lethally so. "Move us to the side of the river," he told the others. "We may be able to put it out."

Kicking hard, they worked their way to one side until they could feel the river bottom under their feet once again. "Hold it here," he said. "I'm going to go check it out." Without waiting for the others to reply, Bart ducked under the water and moved out from under the boat.

He stayed underneath the water as he looked up to see how bad the fire around them was. The banks of the river couldn't be seen, but the glow of fire was all around him. He took but a moment to gauge the best location to break the surface. Once he made his decision, he kicked off the bottom of the riverbed and shot up fast. Waving his arms wildly, he splashed about to create a protective cover of water as he broke the surface. When he opened his eyes, he was amazed at what he saw.

The woods on either side were dark, the forest fire was a good mile behind them. What had been making the water glow and burning the bottom of the boat was a large clump of burning branches that was lying along the upturned bottom of the boat. He moved to the burning branches and removed his pack. Then using the water soaked pack, he began hitting the branches with it and knocking them off into the water. It took him a minute or so before the last branch was off the boat and floating down with the current.

Bart ducked back under the water and came up inside the boat. "We're past the fire," he told them. Then he explained about the branches and how they had left the forest fire behind them.

Riyan chuckled. "All this time we thought we were still in the fire, and instead were fooled by a bunch of burning branches." The others broke into laughter at that. Not so much at what he said but due to the relief each felt at having survived to reach the far side of the fire.

"Now let's move over to the bank and flip the boat upright again," Bart said. He and the others left the warm, stale air inside the overturned boat and were soon once again in the cool, smoke filled air of the forest.

When Riyan ducked under the water with the goblin youth, it woke completely. Thrashing about, it almost broke free of Riyan's grasp but he managed to keep hold of it until they broke the surface on the other side of the boat.

"Hold him still," Kevik said as he moved behind Riyan and opened his pack. He had seen the burns on the goblin youth's face and wanted to help him.

While Riyan held onto the youth, he removed the last of the healing potions and returned to Riyan's side. The goblin's eyes were opened wide in fear as he saw Kevik move the bottle towards him.

The goblin youth thrashed about intensely as he fought to free himself of Riyan's grip. "Hold him steady," Kevik said.

Bart realized what he was trying to do and moved to help Riyan in holding the youth still. Chad stayed where he was and kept hold of the boat to prevent the current from taking it away.

With Bart's help, the youth was soon being held tightly and Kevik moved the mouth of the bottle to its lips. "Just a bit to help with your burns," he said soothingly to the goblin. When the goblin wasn't being cooperative in opening its mouth, Kevik said to Bart, "See if you can get its lips open.

Bart moved a hand to the goblin's mouth and spread its lips apart. He tilted the goblin's head back as Kevik poured a small portion of the potion onto the goblin's teeth. It may not be perfect but at least some of it will get into its system. After that he moved the bottle to the burn covering the right half of the youth's face. The goblin's eyes widened as the bottle came closer. And then before the first drop left the bottle, the youth relaxed in Riyan's grip.

Believing the youth was no longer going to struggle, Riyan relaxed his grip as well. As soon as the first drop fell onto the burned area of its face, it lashed out with a frantic struggle to free itself. Caught unawares, Riyan couldn't hold him.

"Get him!" yelled Bart as the youth twisted out of his grip. Then it was free and made a dash for the trees. Before anyone could catch it, it was gone.

They stood there but a moment before Chad, who was standing by the boat said, "Let's get out of here before he brings others!"

That broke the spell of the moment and the other three rushed to help him in righting the boat in the water. Once it was again floating right side up, they tossed their packs into the bottom and climbed aboard. Bart and Riyan quickly began using the oars to move down the river.

Riyan glanced back to the trees where the goblin lad had disappeared until they had moved too far away to see it. He couldn't help but be amazed by the fact that he had actually touched and held an actual goblin. Surprised by the fact he hoped it would be okay, he returned his attention to his paddling and sent them quickly down the river.

Behind them, the glow from the fire was still quite visible and they were more than happy to leave it behind them. In no time at all they came to where the river flowed into the larger lake. "The Marketplace shouldn't be too much further," commented Riyan.

"We should be able to make it before dawn," Chad agreed.

Once out onto the lake, they used the silhouettes of the mountains as a guide and paddled for them. It took them an hour to cross the lake before the shore where they needed to disembark appeared before them. Off to their right the lights from the goblin village they saw the first time they passed this way were visible. From this distance it was hard to tell but it did look like there was movement among their buildings. At least the area where they were about to land looked quiet and deserted.

The dirt and rocks of the shore ground beneath the boat's bottom as it ran aground. When they were out of the boat Riyan asked if they should hide it.

"No," replied Chad, "it's a goblin boat in goblin territory. Who's going to care?"

Riyan grinned. "Guess you have a point there." He tossed the oar into the bottom of the boat and then grabbed his pack. Once they were ready, they left the boat behind and entered the trees. Somewhere at the base of the mountains ahead of them lay the Marketplace and the pass leading home.

Chapter 29

The forest was quiet as they made their way from the lake. They knew the general direction the Marketplace lay from the last time and headed that way. Bart stayed some distance ahead of the others so he could better determine if there were goblins about. Riyan, Chad, and Kevik followed along behind and made sure they didn't lose him.

They made their way through the trees for over an hour before Bart came to a stop. The others stopped once they realized he had and waited. He stood there motionless for several seconds before ducking down low.

"Get down," whispered Riyan as he scrunched down near the base of a nearby tree. The other two followed suit. It wasn't long before the sound of several goblins making their way through the underbrush from the direction of the Marketplace came to them. The path the goblins were taking would lead them close to where they crouched in hiding.

Riyan held his breath as they approached. He could hear their guttural language being spoken as they passed by, and even caught a glimpse of their silhouettes in the moonlight. The smoke here wasn't so thick as to obscure them and he could tell there were at least five.

The goblins, completely oblivious to where they were hiding just yards away, continued on by. Not until their voices could no longer be heard did Riyan see Bart return to his feet. Riyan waved to him saying they were okay and for him to continue. Bart waved back and then resumed moving towards the Marketplace.

It took them another three hours before they were able to see the light of a solitary campfire at the Marketplace. At this point Bart waited while the other three joined him, then they moved forward as a group. Bart still took the lead but the others stayed close behind him.

Every few minutes Bart would pause to listen for any sound out of the ordinary, then would continue. Time and again he would pause, listen, and then continue on. When the buildings of the Marketplace could be seen through the trees, he started to edge around them to where the mountain began its rise.

During a brief pause, Bart explained what he intended for them to do. "If we move around the Marketplace and come at the pass on the far side," he explained quietly, "we'll attract less attention."

"Wonder if the soldiers stationed here would come to our aid if the goblins were to attack us?" asked Riyan.

"Only if we were on the other side of the totems," replied Bart. "This side is goblin territory. We need to get past the totems to be safe."

"Then let's do it," urged Riyan.

Bart nodded and they resumed their progress. As they made their way around the edge of the Marketplace, they began to notice that the place had a deserted look to it. The area where many caravans had been camped before was now empty. It looked like there were no merchants here to trade with the goblins.

"Could be due to the encroaching fire," suggested Kevik. "They may wait until the threat is passed before returning."

"Sounds plausible," agreed Chad. "Should make it easier for us to get through."

Fifteen minutes later, they reached where they had to begin angling to the pass. Riyan felt extreme relief when they passed through the line of totems. They were safely on the human side again. But then Bart brought them to a halt as he pointed to the mouth of the pass.

Even though the Marketplace was deserted, there was still a contingent of soldiers stationed there. Half a dozen were standing around the solitary campfire they had initially seen a short time go. The soldiers were no more than a few dozen yards from the mouth of the pass. Any attempt to enter the pass would surely be discovered.

"What does it matter if they see us or not?" asked Kevik.

"We have no business being here," replied Bart. "If it became known that we had spent time in goblin territory, there would arise certain questions which we would be reluctant to answer."

Kevik turned to him. "You mean about the key and what you three are trying to do?"

"That's right," he said. "The less others know about what we do, the less someone else can beat us to it."

"But they can't do anything without the keys we carry," he argued.

"True. But if it became common knowledge that we carried them," Bart explained, "our lives wouldn't be worth spit. Everyone would be after them."

In the darkness, they worked to come up with a plan to draw the soldiers away from the pass. Most of the ideas, including Chad's which was to set the forest on fire, weren't very practical. Then Bart came up with an idea that might just work. The others offered their opinions and together, they worked it out.

Half an hour later they had it all set. They returned to their place among the trees near the pass, everyone that was but Riyan. He was in position at one of two small trees that were bent over and held in place with ropes. In Riyan's hand was the knife he had found in the treasure room, the one with the dragon-sword coat of arms depicted on the crossguard.

When he had allowed enough time to pass and figured the others to be in position, he cut the rope of the first tree. The tree snapped up and threw a score of hand sized rocks toward the far side of the Marketplace. The rocks struck the side of the canyon less than a hundred feet from the six soldiers at the campsite. Bart had aimed it perfectly.

By the time Riyan had rejoined the others, three of the soldiers had gone to investigate the noise. As soon as Bart saw Riyan return, and that the three soldiers investigating the noise were in the proper position, he said, "Now Kevik."

Kevik nodded and dispelled the green goo that had been holding the other rope of the second tree. When the goo disappeared, the tree straightened up rapidly and launched about forty small pebbles outward that were nestled in a piece of bark wedged between two of its branches. The pebbles rained down on the three soldiers who were investigating the first volley of rocks.

Cries of alarm rang out as they were struck by the missiles. The remaining three at the campsite immediately rushed to their aid. "Now!" whispered Bart and they ran for the entrance to the pass.

Not until they were some distance past the campfire did they finally slow down. They looked back to see if the soldiers were showing any indication that they had seen their passing, but the mouth of the pass remained empty.

"We made it!" whispered Chad excitedly.

"Yes we did," replied Riyan with a grin.

Bart glanced back at the jubilant pair and said, "Best if we don't cele-brate just yet. Once we're past Crag Keep, then we can relax."

That sobered them up quickly. They had forgotten about the checkpoint at the other end where their forged passes had been examined on the way in. Somehow they would have to get past them too.

Moving quickly, they continued through the pass. Several hours later it began to lighten with the coming of the dawn. An hour after that, a solitary rider was heard approaching from the Crag Keep side of the pass. With nowhere to hide, they simply continued on.

The rider turned out to be a soldier, possibly one from Crag Keep. He was quick to notice them there in the pass and slowed as he approached. "What are you boys doing here?" he asked.

"Came here to see goblins," Bart explained to him. "But the soldiers at the other end wouldn't let us through. Told us to leave."

The soldier got that look people get when they hear something dumb. "Why in the world would you boys want to see a goblin?" he asked. "Mean and vicious they are."

Bart shrugged. "Just did. Still want to."

"The Marketplace isn't a safe place for those with no business there," the soldier told them. "They were right to send you away." He then looked at each in turn and said, "You continue on to Crag Keep, and once there, keep going."

"Yes sir," replied a humbled Bart.

The soldier gave them another stern gaze then continued on his way. They could hear him talking about the idiots of the world as he left them behind.

"That was smart thinking," Kevik said.

"A good lie is worth its weight in gold," he said. "Been thinking about what to tell someone in just such a circumstance ever since we entered the pass."

Kevik nodded. "How much further to this Crag Keep?"

"On foot? Probably reach it sometime tomorrow," he replied.

They continued towards the Keep at a quick walk. They were worried about the soldier they had encountered. When he reached the soldiers at the Marketplace, they may put two and two together and come up with the four of them.

By the time it grew dark, no one had appeared from the Marketplace's side of the pass. Despite the exhaustion they were all feeling, Bart pushed them onward. "It will be easier to make it by Crag Keep in the dark than it will in broad daylight," he argued. So onward they went.

Most of the night went by before they saw the campfire of those watching the Crag Keep end of the pass. Bart had the others remain back as he moved forward to take a look around. He kept to the shadows as he approached. Once he could see the men around the campfire he came to a stop.

There were three of them standing near the fire, one had a horn slung at his side. They were talking among themselves, completely oblivious to the fact that there was someone in the darkness watching them.

Bart gauged the situation, then quietly took off his pack and set it on the ground. He knelt down and removed his darts from his pack.

"What's he doing?" whispered Riyan as they watched Bart. They couldn't tell what he was doing, just that he was doing something with his pack.

"I don't know," replied Chad.

Bart glanced back to them. He heard them whispering to one another and hoped they would have the good sense to keep it down. Once he had the tips of three of his darts coated from liquid contained within one of his vials, he took them in hand and stood up.

He then moved a little closer to the three men. When he was in position, he took a dart and threw it. Before it struck the first soldier, the second was already on its way. The first dart struck one of the guards in the shoulder causing him to cry out. Before the other two realized what was happening, they too were struck.

Riyan saw Bart throw the darts and immediately raced to him. He kept an eye on the soldiers while he rushed to Bart's side and saw the one with the horn raise it to his lips. But the note never came as the man swooned and collapsed to the ground. The other two soldiers fell shortly afterward. "You killed them!" he yelled accusingly to Bart.

"Shhh!" Bart said. "Keep it down." He began moving towards the three fallen soldiers. "They're not dead, just unconscious and will wake in a couple hours."

"Are you sure?" Riyan asked.

"Yes. Now let me retrieve my darts then we can get out of here." He moved to the guards and when he noticed the other three were planning on joining him, he said, "Stay out of the light." Riyan nodded as he, Chad, and Kevik came to a stop.

Bart went among the three soldiers and quickly pulled his darts out from where they struck. True, each of the soldiers would have a tell-tale wound, but it couldn't be helped. Once he had recovered his darts, he returned to his pack and replaced them in with the others. He glanced to the walls of Crag Keep and was relieved to find no indication that the men there had noticed anything.

Finished, he stood up and said, "Let's make time." Then he moved out and they practically ran as they made their way past the walls of Crag Keep. They kept far enough away so as not to be observed by the guards walking atop the walls and didn't stop until the sun was cresting the horizon. At that time they found an out of the way place to make camp.

They didn't keep a watch that night. Everyone was so exhausted from the almost two whole days without sleep, plus that final run from Crag Keep, that they practically passed out immediately when their blankets were rolled out and they laid down. They slept the day through and didn't awaken again until almost nightfall.

Two days later found them in the small town of Averin where the river that flowed out of the pass past Crag Keep intersected the north-south highway running on the eastern side of the mountains. They were eating a meal in their room as they required privacy for what they were discussing: Where to find the remaining two segments of the key.

Riyan was explaining to the others his idea. "This idea started to develop as we were riding the river that last time in your makeshift door-raft," he said to Bart. "When we were each in our loops. The four, separate loops."

"I got to thinking about how it was similar to that wall you found with the four spaces," he explained. "You know, where you put the first segment of the key in to open the door of the room hiding the second?"

Bart nodded. "Yes, I remember."

"It wasn't until we were past Crag Keep that it came back to me," he said. "You said that each of the recesses bore one of the coats of arms we found in The Crypt." Again, Bart nodded. "So I began thinking that there may be something significant about the four coats of arms. Four coats of arms, four segments."

"You mean like each segment is associated with a different coat of arms?" asked Bart.

"Something like that," replied Riyan. "Didn't you put the first one in the space with the king's coat of arm?"

"Yes I did," affirmed Bart. "The sigils on the key segment aligned perfectly to the sigils that were on the wall."

"And the second key segment was found in Algoth, whose lord's coat of arms was the dragon-sword."

"So let me get this straight," Kevik said. "Are you thinking that each of the other two segments are to be found in places associated with the other two coats of arms? Kind of like each of them had a hand in hiding one of the segments?"

"Yes," Riyan said. "We need to find out all we can about them. Where they were seen, who they were associated with, those sorts of things."

"But how are we to find those things out?" Bart asked. "Without arousing suspicion that is?"

"We have to find somewhere that holds records of coats of arms," Riyan replied.

"Only the Warriors Guild has a complete record of past and current coats of arms," explained Kevik. "My master once mentioned he had to gain permission from the Guildmaster in Gilbeth to research their archives for one. I doubt if they would allow us access."

Riyan glanced calculatingly at Chad for a moment then said, "They might to guild members."

"Probably," replied Chad. "But who do we know that …" Then he saw Riyan grin. "You don't mean …?"

Riyan nodded. "You and I could join the Warriors Guild."

"How?" he asked.

"As I understand such things," Bart interjected, "there are usually two ways in which you can join one of the guilds. Either have a member advance your petition, usually due to the fact that you are a son, or some kind of relative in such case. Or buy your way in, though the buying option could get pretty pricey."

Riyan reached into his pack sitting on the floor nearby and pulled out a handful of gems. "I think we've got that covered." Then he turned to Chad. "What do you say? Would beat the heck out of being a miller?"

Chad nodded. "You're on. I say we do it."

Bart looked to Kevik. "What do you say? Are you in too?"

Riyan and Chad turned their attention to Kevik. "We'd like to have you." Chad nodded agreement.

Kevik nodded. "I'm in."

"Fantastic," said Riyan. "I propose that we each swear an oath, that we keep secret all things concerning our search for the King's Horde. That from this point on, we are brothers bound in common purpose." He glanced to the others. Then they all said at the same time, "I so swear."

978-0-595-42825-0
0-595-42825-8

Printed in the United States
72399LV00004B/120